BRIEF CHRONICLE OF ANOTHER STUPID HEARTBREAK

Also by Adi Alsaid

Let's Get Lost
Never Always Sometimes
North of Happy

BRIEF CHRONICLE OF ANOTHER STUPID HEARTBREAK

ADI ALSAID

ink
yard
press

ink
yard
press

Recycling programs
for this product may
not exist in your area.

ISBN-13: 978-1-335-01255-5

Brief Chronicle of Another Stupid Heartbreak

This is a work of fiction. Names, characters, places and incidents are either the product of the author's imagination or are used fictitiously, and any resemblance to actual persons, living or dead, business establishments, events or locales is entirely coincidental.

This edition published by arrangement with Harlequin Books S.A.

For questions and comments about the quality of this book, please contact us at CustomerService@Harlequin.com.

® and TM are trademarks of Harlequin Enterprises Limited or its corporate affiliates. Trademarks indicated with ® are registered in the United States Patent and Trademark Office, the Canadian Intellectual Property Office and in other countries.

InkyardPress.com

Printed in U.S.A.

For my teen readers who are wading through the murky swamp

1

TANGLED UP

I would have called bullshit on the whole thing from the beginning if I didn't see both Iris and Cal get the same look in
their eyes. Constantly. When Iris hums to herself as they walk
hand in hand, when Cal insists on doing the dishes at her parents' house, when she underlines whole paragraphs in novels
then simply has to voice her appreciation for what she's just
read, and how he'll stop whatever he's doing to listen, even
if he clearly has no idea what she's talking about.

One eighteen-year-old gets that look, you start feeling sorry
for them. Two of them give that look to each other and no matter what kind of cynic you are, you start thinking only teenagers really understand love. How insane it's supposed to be.

Leo was running late again.

My stupid, beautiful ex-boyfriend—who'd spent the entirety of our relationship arriving on time—had not even
texted to give me a heads-up. I was waiting for him at Madison Square Park, and even out of the sun it was uncomfortably hot and made worse by the smell of garbage. Every
person that entered my periphery was potentially Leo, so my

heart quickened with excitement and then fell into disappointment as soon as I realized it wasn't him. He wasn't hurrying
to come. He was happy he'd left me. He wasn't going to give
me a chance to talk him back into our love.

I heard the snap of a soda can opening and turned to see
my new bench mate.

Skinny white boy, thick-framed hipster glasses, cute enough
to make me forget about Leo and the long stretch of summer ahead without him. He took a sip from his Coke and
then looked at me. Right away, I knew he wouldn't be just
one more face in the nameless masses you see every day in a
big city. He had a face that I knew would stay with me, that
would pop into my mind months later and for no apparent
reason other than the persistent question of what might have
been. He smiled at me, and I forgot about what time it was
and the fact that Leo was probably blowing me off for the
second time this week.

Okay, maybe I didn't entirely forget. It was in the back of
my mind, like it had been for the three weeks since summer
had started and Leo had thrown away what we had. You can't
have love in your life for nearly a year, tangled up in a single
person, then transition into its absence without feeling the
loss. An attractive face helps, but cures nothing.

A French couple stopped in front of our bench, looking
over a map of Manhattan. They were speaking loudly and gesturing wildly, their words a blur of vowels and those throat-
tickling soft French r's. I looked to my right again and my
eyes met his. He raised his eyebrows and smiled at me, gesturing at the couple, whose argument was getting more heated.
I tried to smile back, but couldn't guarantee that what I did
qualified. It was an awkward facial muscle contortion at best.

"Do you understand what they're saying?" he asked, in a stage whisper.

"What?" I said, because conversations with strangers are hard.

He gestured at the French couple. "Do you understand any of that?"

"No, sorry."

"I wonder what they're arguing about." He looked at them wistfully, and I wished I could get a glimpse inside his head.

"I imagine they're lost," I said, eyes more on him than on the couple.

"Where do you think they're going? All the tourist spots are on that map. The city's a grid, and it's pretty easy to get around."

"Maybe they're arguing about which way the map should be held. I hear in France they hold their maps diagonally." The boy laughed; a laugh like rising bread, warm and doughy. "I don't know what that means. Sorry," I said, assuming he'd laughed out of politeness. "Maybe they're looking for some-thing super specific that's not on the map."

"Don't apologize. That was funny," he said calmly, lean-ing forward with his forearms resting on his knees, looking at me intently. He took another baby sip from his Coke. "I'm irrationally intrigued by them. What could they possibly be looking for?"

"I don't know. Treasure? The spot where John Lennon once picked his nose in a photograph? Tourists are weird."

The boy laughed, then leaned back into the bench. He turned and took in the sights of the park, which gave me a little time to admire his face for a bit. *Take that, Leo,* I thought. *I'm staring at a cute boy and I don't feel guilty about it.*

I scanned the morning crowd at the park, still hoping to

catch sight of Leo despite my previous thought. The sun shone through the leaves, casting dancing shadows at Bench Boy's feet. As usual, I kept my ear out for some eavesdropping opportunities, which I'd been trying to use as writing inspiration. Nothing else had worked since Leo left me. I could only hear the French couple trying to make sense of their map.

"There is a legitimate chance that they're using this lost tourist act as a cover so that they can talk about us," Bench Boy said.

"Define *legitimate*."

"You don't think that it's possible?" We turned to look at each other at the same moment. How is it that mere eye contact with an attractive stranger can do all sorts of things to your insides?

I looked ahead so as to not give myself away. "I mean it's possible, but what would they be saying about us?"

Immediately, the boy put on a thick, completely unconvincing French accent. "Oh my God, Celine! Ze people here are unbelievably attractive! Just look at zat boy on ze bench. Mon dieu, he's so attractive I want to stab my eyeballs out and serve zem at a restaurant like escargot!"

I raised my eyebrows at him, unable to contain a chuckle and only slightly worried that I was sitting next to one of those creepy people that can hide their grossness just long enough to get close to you. "I didn't know it was possible to offend French people so quickly, but I think you just did."

He leaned toward me, not smiling, though his eyes betrayed a twinkle of amusement. "No, you have to be her. What's she saying?"

I'm not sure what it was that kept me on that bench. Maybe it was a hope that Leo would still show, or maybe it was nice to have this moment without him. I looked away from the boy and studied the woman in the couple. She was holding the map with one hand, her perfectly manicured fingernails painted royal blue. Her blond hair spilled over her shoulders as she scrunched her mouth to one side of her face and continued studying the map.

"I swear to God, François," I said, in my own terrible French accent, causing the boy to smile adorably. "You make zat threat everywhere we go. One of zees days I'm going to really pluck out your eyeballs myself and feed zem to ze locals."

"Zey should be so lucky," the boy replied with a laugh.

We watched the couple for a second, and in the silence Leo slipped into my thoughts again. I started thinking about how it had felt to see him for the first time every day. The instant swell of joy that his mere presence provided. How I couldn't resist smiling. I thought about how that was just the beginning of the delights Leo brought to my days: his thoughtfulness, his sense of humor, the way his lips on the back of my neck made it seem as if I had a pleasure button which only he knew about and was willing to press repeatedly. I hadn't had that in three weeks, nor, it seemed, would I have it again.

"Should we go up to them and pretend to be French too?" Bench Boy asked, leaning in slightly.

"Absolutely. Just give me a second to transform into an entirely different person with acting skills and the confidence to make a fool out of myself in front of others."

"Is there a way for me to compliment you on the confidence you had to already pretend to be French with me, without implying that you made a fool out of yourself?"

"Well, not when you put it that way, man."

The boy laughed and raised the Coke can to his lips, but before he could take a sip he chuckled again and put the can down.

"I hope I haven't discouraged you from any future fake accent work in public. It would be a great loss to the world if you never said 'feed zem to ze locals' again."

"Hell no. That's my catchphrase, and I'm not going to let a stranger ruin it for me."

"Oh good," the boy said. "Just wondering here, in what other situations does your catchphrase come in handy?"

"If you criticize my catchphrase one more time," I said, going back into the terrible French accent and raising my voice, "I will feed you to ze locals!"

The boy laughed again, a deep-bellied, full-bodied laugh that made me want to actually adopt a catchphrase and see how often I could slip it into conversations throughout my day.

He looked like he was about to say something, but then the French couple had another burst of arguing, both of them pointing furiously at the map.

Bench Boy stood up and walked over to them. There he goes, I thought, never to be seen again. He offered a quiet French "pardon" followed by "Can I help you?" while pointing at the map. He stood with them for a couple of minutes, using mostly hand gestures and mumbling as the couple continued to argue in rapid French. They departed with softly muttered thank-yous and smiles, then, amazingly, fatefully, he sat back down next to me.

"That was nice of you," I said.

"God, that was surprisingly easy," he said, beaming. "Invigorating." He brought the can of soda up to his lips but stopped, as if a thought had occurred to him that shouldn't be interrupted by mere thirst. "I think I'm going to start doing that more often."

"Help tourists find treasure? Practice that terrible French accent?"

He chuckled, which was nice of him, because that was an-

other stupid joke. "No. Just…helping people. That felt good."
I had no idea what to say to that, so I kept quiet and felt the
acute strangeness of myself for a little bit. "I get that urge to
help more often than I act on it. I feel like everyone does.
But I've just decided, right now, sitting here on this bench
with you, I'm going to act on it more often. Help people."

"Um, okay," I said, kind of desperate to turn to my phone
and write down what he was saying word for word into my
notes app.

"Sorry if that's weird. I'm in a weird mood. It's been a
weird hour."

"I dunno, we just pretended to be a French couple serving
your eyeballs as if they were snails," I said. "Nothing weird
about that."

He smiled and took a sip of his Coke. "Imagine you've
spent the last two years on an undefeated two-person paintball team. The excitement of win after win, of kicking so
much ass that it basically feels like you've been beating life itself. Every day you experience that thrill. Until now. I think
we're going to lose."

I bit my lip, stealing another glance at his face.

"Weird."

"Très weird," he replied with another wry smile. I thought
maybe we'd go back into our repartee, which had eased some
of the sorrow I'd felt sitting on my own, but he looked away,
lost in his thoughts.

I looked at the time on my phone. Leo was never going to
come. I wouldn't get that shot of joy from seeing him. I was
keenly aware of the boy sitting there next to me, but I was also
aware of the chatter of the park, the constant din of traffic, a
basketball bouncing nearby. On the grass to my left, a squir-
rel was hanging around the base of a tree. I was most aware,

however, of the pain that still sat squarely in my gut. Of how I wanted to leave it behind and at the same time drown in it. Of how I hated Leo and missed him dearly in tiny moments of the day, and how the two feelings did not exist separately, but were intertwined, tangled up like sweat-soaked bedsheets.

The boy leaned back and groaned, turning his head up to the beautifully blue, stupidly hot sky, keeping his eyes closed to it, as if refusing to take note of the weather. "It's such a bizarre thing we do," he said, not looking at me.

"What is? Help French tourists?"

"Love," he said, just like that, as if strangers went around talking about these things all the time.

A few moments passed by. The boy opened his eyes, took another sip of his Coke before getting up to chuck it in a nearby trash bin. The clunk the can made as it went in told me it was almost full, as if he hadn't been able to stomach any of the soda. He came back, wiped his glasses on the hem of his shirt, squinting at me because the sun was in his face. Then he said sorry, and thanks, and left me on the bench. Alone.

Later, I met my friend Pete at our favorite bookstore, The Strand, before our shift at a nearby chain movie theater. "You should probably stop trying to meet up with him," Pete said, thumbing through a graphic novel. Pete doesn't say much, but when he does you can pretty much always count on honesty, rarely on tact. I guess I appreciate honesty more than tact, because almost as soon as Pete and I met at the theater two summers ago, I latched on to him and haven't let go since.

"I wish he came while that boy and I were talking," I said. "I wanted to make him jealous. It's crazy, I know. But the heart and its wants and all that." I picked up a hardcover, read the first line, put it back down. "I can't believe he didn't show."

"Suspend your disbelief, Lu. That's the fourth time by my count."

I sighed. Pete was probably sick of hearing about Leo. That made sense to me. I was sick of thinking about him. I picked up a couple of new arrivals, flipped through them absently, nothing catching my eye. I ran my fingers over the covers, looking around at the other shoppers.

"Pete?"

"Yeah?"

"Why do you think Leo left me?"

Pete stopped reading for a second. He brushed his black hair out of his eyes, closing the pages of the book around his finger to keep his place. He looked at me with those intense green eyes of his. I feel like Pete could force people to do his bidding with a single look. "We know why he left you," he said in his faint Irish brogue. "He didn't love you as much as you loved him." He turned his attention back to the graphic novel. "I'm gonna finish reading. I'll see you at work."

I sighed and made my way downstairs. Starla, our favorite bookseller, was at the help desk and waved hello. She's tattooed and in her thirties, and never treated us in that eye-rolling "damn teenagers" way that so many adults adopt as their general attitude toward people our age. I waved back, wanting to go talk to her, in no real rush to get to work. But she was busy with a customer, so I just ambled around the bottom floor trying to eavesdrop on people.

Work-space drama; the half conversations of people on cell phones; high school gossip. It'd turned into a compulsion after everything had happened with me and Leo and all my own words dried up.

I used to write my column once a week, and I posted almost daily on my personal blog, wrote in a journal, jotted down novel ideas, the occasional poem, and—more than I cared to admit—little entries into my phone's note function in which I either came up with how to cure all the world's ills or jotted down ideas for animated TV shows.

Since the breakup, I hadn't been able to write anything which my editor, Hafsah, wasn't loving, to say the least. I'd been a columnist for *Misnomer,* one of the most highly trafficked online teen magazines, for a year now. The day Hafsah called me to say I'd been hired as the love and dating columnist was probably the happiest day of my life. I'd always suffered from this idea that I wasn't a writer unless I had readers. And suddenly the world called and said, "Okay, we're on board. You are, in fact, this thing you've always felt yourself to be."

Now, instead of writing, I eavesdropped. I hadn't sent Hafsah anything since the breakup, which was three weeks ago, and even through her emails I could feel her intense eyes narrowing with impatience, her neatly manicured nails tap-tap-tapping on her desk.

I don't know why I turned to eavesdropping. Sometimes I felt like I was chronicling life, or the city, the connections between people. Sometimes I felt like I was addicted to stories, and I was giving normal people a chance to get theirs out there, even if it was just a fraction of them, even if it was just a snippet in a notebook that would never make it into the world at large.

That was probably bullshit. All that was happening was that I had writer's block and I was stealing other people's words. Or I was just nosy.

I scanned the crowd for potential subjects. A middle-aged dude bugging the employee at customer service for books with yellow covers. Two women scanning the self-help aisle talking about auras. A bunch of people on their own, eyes on the shelves, giving nothing away.

Then, I spotted her. Full-bodied Latina, pretty, two perfect mascara streaks running down her cheeks to her pinup-model-red lips. She was on the phone, near Thrillers, W–Z. If it weren't for the tears, she might have looked older, but the kind of sadness on her face resonated with me. Teenage heartbreak. Scurrying to the aisle behind hers, I picked out a random novel, trying to keep my eyes on her through the space I'd made on the shelf, straining to hear her over the hum of the store.

"I don't know what I'm going to do, okay?" she said, wiping the back of her hand across her cheek. I reached into my bag, grabbed the notebook I always kept on me for just this occasion, scrawled her question onto the page, thinking about how it would go on my blog later, the story I could shape from it. The girl clutched at the fabric of her dress as if it were responsible for her tears. "No. No. I don't know how to tell him, that's what I'm saying." She brought a finger up to her mouth, nibbled at the nail, chipped with long-faded red polish. "Yeah, I know I have to."

I held my breath, wanting her to say more, needing it.

"I have to go. Yeah. He's here." She gave a sniffle, another back-of-the-hand swipe across her cheeks, a smudge of mascara by her temple. "Okay, bye."

Then I watched her hang up the phone and slip it into the pocket of her dress. She sighed, made a few more attempts to clean up her appearance, her eyes locked ahead. I didn't want to look away from her, wanted to soak her in, write all of her, because she looked the way I felt. Then I watched her walk down the aisle and across the store toward the entrance to meet the boy I'd talked to on the bench.

2
THINGS HAVE CHANGED

Bench Boy and Crying Girl left the store together, and I rushed after them, almost knocking down a display of new arrivals on my way out the door. The sidewalk was crowded and a fire truck was wailing loudly on its way down Broadway; for a moment, I looked left and right, worried they had disappeared into the ether.

But life is not a spy movie: they were only a few feet away, heading in the opposite direction of the movie theater where my shift was starting in ten minutes. I probably shouldn't have cared enough to follow them, should have shrugged and sighed a brief lament to myself that I'd miss out on hearing their conversation, then gone on to work. Instead, I immediately followed behind.

The thing with eavesdropping is that it's rarely interesting, and if this was the only thing I could write about now, I sure as hell wanted to follow the one good lead I'd come across.

I texted Pete, asking him to cover for me if I was late for my shift, then I opened my notebook and got a little closer to the couple, ears cocked, ready to eavesdrop to my little heart's content. I was only a few steps behind, confident that New York's crowded sidewalks would shroud me in anonymity. Even if they turned around, I'd be just another one of the millions of people who stormed up and down the streets every day.

They crossed Thirteenth Street, expertly maneuvering around an onslaught of oncoming fellow pedestrians. A woman in a green T-shirt wearing big headphones passed by, and a few steps behind me I could hear a girl on her cell phone, saying "literally" way too often. There was a constant whir of tires on pavement, of footsteps on the sidewalk, the chatter of millions.

Bench Boy and Crying Girl weren't talking to each other. His hands were shoved in his pockets, she was picking at the hem of her dress. They walked slowly, and I waited in anticipation for their conversation to begin. I thought about what the boy had told me on the bench, about being on an undefeated two-person paintball team. It had sounded a little nonsensical and perplexing at the time, but now, with their body language and the space in between them, I thought I understood a little more.

"Look, Cal," the girl finally said, just loud enough for me to make it out over the honking taxis making their way down Broadway. But she seemed to run out of steam. Her hands dropped to her sides, clutched at her hemline again.

"What, Iris?"

"I don't know," Iris said.

"I think you do," Cal responded, his voice like cracked glass.

She wiped at her eyes again, took a deep breath. I readied my pen. "I've been thinking and…I don't think I can do long distance. Four years only touching in the summers? Four years of wondering where I am if I don't text you back right away? Four years of our lives growing in different directions?"

The words nearly froze me. Leo had said almost the exact same thing to me. After months of lobbing L-bombs at each other, months of ever-increasing intimacy, sometimes in waves and leaps (like the first entire day we'd spent in each other's company, all twenty-four hours, on the subway and eating pizza and watching a movie, sleeping, talking), and sometimes in inches (one handhold at a time, one little confession at a time)—after months of enjoying each other's company, making plans to continue doing just that, Leo looked into my eyes and told me he didn't think our love could survive four years apart.

My hands shook as I tried to write the scene down in my notebook while keeping pace with them.

"Love," Cal said. The word left him like a whimper. "We have love. What else matters?"

The girl was crying again. I caught the shimmer of light reflecting off her wet cheeks. A honk from a cab driver drowned out something she said, and I got a little closer, almost at their heels. They were moving forward at such a glacial pace that I had to actively think about walking so that I wouldn't run into them. "We're eighteen. Of course we're going to think it can last forever. But it's not that easy."

"That's not true, Iris. I've never once said it will be."

"That's how you talk about us though. Like we're the greatest romance of our time or something. Like we can overcome all these things that everyone else fails at, like we're somehow different." We reached Union Square, and they waited at the stoplight to cross the street. Traffic was sparse and they easily could have crossed, but they weren't paying enough attention to notice.

"You used to talk like that too," Cal said.

I was almost torn apart by that line. I could hear all the

heartbreak that I felt for Leo in Cal's voice. But Iris shrugged it off easily. "Yes, but things have changed, Cal. You have to adapt to the world, to life."

"So now I'm being punished for being a romantic?"

Iris groaned, raising her hands in frustration. Someone pushed past me and then in between them, calling us idiots under his breath as he crossed the street. Cal and Iris didn't notice that either.

I was probably late for work by now, but I couldn't pull myself away. I kept listening, kept writing it all down.

"I'm not punishing you. I'm just saying that there's a difference between our relationship in theory and what happens when we're faced with reality. You want to stay in the city. I want to go to California. I *am* going to California."

"So we'll do long distance," Cal exclaimed. "I thought that was the plan."

I'd said the same thing to Leo three weeks ago, only more tearfully. I could imagine exactly how the rest of the breakup would go, based on my own experience. The shock of the words spoken. The immediate quiet afterward. The person who'd been dumped scampering away.

Usually, in these eavesdropped conversations, I was rooting for drama, for the stuff that makes good stories. But I felt myself dreading what would come next, how they would follow the same steps Leo and I took.

"No," Iris said simply. The light turned green, a throng of people surrounded us, little bumps and shoves to the three of us, everyone as unaware of the fight as Cal and Iris were of them.

The scene unfolded exactly how I didn't want it to. Cal pulling out his phone, in my opinion to keep himself from crying. Then silence, which was probably only meant for the two of them but somehow pulled me into it, so that the sounds of the city fell away as if they'd been physically removed from the world. Iris glanced at Cal, fraught with worry, as if she knew she'd broken him.

Then Cal shoved his hands in his pockets and turned around brusquely. As he stormed off, his shoulder bumped mine, and he mumbled a "sorry" as he sped past me, no recognition in his eyes.

Iris turned around too, watching him go. She didn't immediately call out for him, just watched, tears welling in her eyes. I realized the light was still green and I was the only one standing next to them, which was a total amateur spy move. As much as I wanted to stick around, whatever part of my brain that experienced social awkwardness was buzzing like crazy, so I crossed over toward Union Square. I wrote down everything that happened, the look on Cal's face when he was fleeing the scene, Iris's silence. For the first time in weeks I felt moved to write my own words. But I didn't have a grasp on them, so the only thing I could write down was this gut-wrenching déjà vu moment of the event that had caused my writer's block to begin with.

I wondered how many teens go through the same thing every summer, how many times that conversation is repeated with every end of another school year. I wondered how many survive, not just as a couple in the long term, but the conversation itself. How many people can maneuver through its hidden land mines and invisible walls and crawl out the other end intact?

When I reached the park, I turned back around so I could make my way to work. At the street corner where we'd stood, something caught my eye. On the ground near where Cal had been standing. It was a wallet, cheap and plastic, the design looked like one of those airplane safety cards they put on the back of the seat. I leaned down to pick it up, a little amazed that it hadn't been spotted by anyone else yet, though I guess it did look a little bit like spilled trash.

Even before I opened it, I knew it was his.

"Pete?"

"Yes?"

"Do you think they broke up?"

"Jesus, Lu. Is this going to be the driving question of your life from now on?"

"Would you rather I go back to 'why did Leo leave me?'"

We were sitting at the box office, each logged in to adjacent computers. It was our favorite spot to work because it faced the street and provided the best opportunities for people watching. But at that moment I couldn't care less. I was fumbling with Cal's wallet, studying its contents. One school ID (some prep school in Brooklyn), one well-worn Metro card, a receipt for dinner at an Indian restaurant dated almost two years earlier. A sticky note curling at the edges, neat block letters on it: "I like you. Quite a bit."

And, most important, a half-filled-out raffle ticket from a YMCA. On it, in smooshed, scrawled handwriting, was Iris's full name, address, phone number, and email.

"Debatable," Pete said with a sigh. "What game are we going to play today? How about What Would You Do with That Weirdo? Count the Moles? I Would Bone That Person?"

"You never want to bone anyone," I said, turning the raffle ticket over in my hands. Pete leaned back in his chair, eyes focused on the people passing by the theater. It was the usual array of Lower East Siders that might be wandering around on a weekday morning: some young professionals heading out for an early lunch, the NYU students that stuck around for the summer, the smattering of unclassifiables that are at every New York City street corner, their entire lives a mystery. I kept looking for Cal and Iris to walk past the window, somehow longing to rewatch their breakup happen in real time, even if it felt like watching my own breakup.

"We could play I Would Cuddle That Person," Pete offered. "Dibs on Alice."

"You can't call dibs on Alice. We share Alice." Alice was this adorable old lady who came in without fail once a week to watch a movie. She got a box of Milk Duds, and snuck in a flask of what we were pretty sure was straight-up whiskey. "But I'm not ready to change the subject yet. I want to talk about the couple. I want to know if they're still together."

Pete gave me a little side-eye. "Clearly they broke up."

"You don't know that," I said, though I have no idea what made me so defiant. They had almost certainly broken up.

He turned his attention to a couple of guys in their twenties who'd approached his window. I looked down at my phone. Every day, dozens of times, I'd check that screen, hoping to see Leo's name in it, hoping he was going to offer some sort of apology, or beg for a reconciliation, or even just check in and say hi. Just like that, no capitalization or punctuation or anything. The minimal amount of care one can show electronically, that's all I wanted. Just:

LEO
hi.

He hadn't even apologized for missing our meeting that morning. Next to my phone was my notebook, open to the day's writing, Iris and Cal's fight. Without their names in there and a few other details, it could have been about me and Leo, the only thing I would have written about us since breaking up.

I pictured how my night would go after work: my little brother, Jase, playing video games on the couch, his shouts ringing out through our little apartment. Mom would be cooking some sort of Italian food. I'd sit with my laptop on my knees, typing up what I'd eavesdropped, failing to come up with anything of my own. I'd watch for Leo's name to pop up on my notifications. I'd stumble about on the internet, reaching for something that would make me feel okay.

I read the last few lines I'd written in the notebook. Iris's "no." Cal's departure.

Pete slid the customers their change, then looked over at me. I could see something in his eyes. Pity or concern or frustration, who the hell knows? "What's on your mind, Lu?"

I put Cal's things back in his wallet. "I need to know..." I trailed off.

A guy appeared at my window. In his forties, velvet tracksuit, mustard stain on the shirt beneath. He was looking over my head at where the showtimes were displayed. I smiled like I was supposed to, then gestured to Pete to add the guy to our running tally of tracksuits we'd seen since we started working (543 so far). He bought one ticket for the matinee of *Shit Blowing Up* or something like that.

Pete was still studying me, those clever eyes of his boring into me and reading all my thoughts. "I should probably return the wallet," I said, pointing lamely at it. "Her address is in here. I could take it to her."

Pete's kind of like my wise, old uncle. He asks poignant questions, and delivers poignant answers. He's like Bilbo Baggins. Wait, is Bilbo Baggins the wise, old uncle? Like, he has a beard which he strokes before saying wise, old things? I haven't read those books, but I picture him as having a great beard.

Sadly, Pete has zero facial hair. He's also freakishly adverse to hand gestures, so even if he had a long white beard, he probably wouldn't be the type to stroke it.

I waited for him to unload his speech, all insight and logic and moustache stroking. Honesty and tactlessness.

"Yeah," he said, after a long pause. "That'd be nice of you."

On Becoming Uncrushed

By Lu Charles
September 5

For the first time in my life, I have wriggled out from beneath the weight of a crush unscathed. More than that: I have escaped triumphant. I'm sure someone smarter than me has already waxed poetic on our dubious word choice for the act of becoming romantically interested in someone, so I'll skip the diatribe.

The important part is this: I'm out. Relationships, dating, kissing, those are real things that exist in our world. I can confirm. That door has been pushed open, and I've been allowed inside. I know I've been writing about all the aforementioned things with an air of authority for a few months now, but you guys haven't been coming to me for advice, right? God, I hope you haven't been coming to me for advice. I've mostly relied on the testimony and wisdom of others. No longer.

"How?" is the big question, of course. Aside from "Why are we here?" and "Why is the Midwest always covered in mayo?" Truth be told, I'm not quite sure how it happened. My memories of the transformation are shrouded in mystery, still. I'd run you through the course of events but I just tried that and immediately deleted them because they were trite and uninteresting.

All my previous crushes have ended in disappointment. Not quite rejection, because I never pushed myself to try and get to the next step. Disappointment in myself, mostly. Occasionally in the other person, who proved themselves not to be worthy of my interest. Often, these crushes ended in disappointment in the way love refused to enter my life (regardless of what I did to make it feel welcome). I've had the thought that maybe love is not for me, not at this stage of my life anyway. Maybe I was just meant to chronicle what others experienced, examine life as others lived it. Not the ideal fate, but there have been worse.

It's weird to be on this side of things now. Through a three-week span of escalations, I now find myself seeing someone regularly. Kissing someone regularly. We text each other throughout the night without the eternal question of whether or not something will happen hanging over the conversation.

I don't mean to gloat, readers. I mean to marvel. I have been granted a thing I've wished for. Not the only thing I've wished for, and not the only thing worth wishing for. But a thing that brings me joy. A thing for the first time. That's something.

Who knows for how long I'll be granted this joy, for how long I've left unrequited crushes behind. I'm stepping into new territory, territory I'm not entirely sure I'm good at yet.

I wasn't quite good at crushes either, I think. I enjoyed the way they cast their spells on me and then moved on, like passing thunderstorms, or gross smells wafting by. But if the point of a crush is to lead to a relationship (or a kiss or sex or whatever), then I failed them the way they failed me.

Until now. So for those of you who have been allowed through the door and into this room: let me know what I can do to be better at this new, scary, wonderful thing. And for those still unsure that real people actually kiss and stuff, I will do my best to describe my experiences. We're on this journey together.

3

WHERE WE'D GONE WRONG

By the time I got home that night, there was an email from Hafsah waiting in my inbox.

My mom was on the phone speaking in Tagalog, probably with my grandma, who we call Lola. Jase was on the couch, playing video games like I knew he would be, barking insults into his headset. It sounded like explosions were going off in every corner of the apartment. I figured I'd go into my room and blast some music and try to force some writing.

But as soon as I tried to cross the living room, my mom yelled for me to eat some leftovers. I could still smell the basil in the air. Mom only ever cooks Italian food. Every night. We're not Italian, we're Filipino. But I guess the heart wants what it wants, even if it's spaghetti Bolognese five nights a week.

I sat down next to Jase on the couch with a plate of reheated pasta, watching him murder perfectly nice-seeming animated dudes with guns. My notebook was by my side, but I knew any attempts to pick it up would bring a tirade from my mother about how she wouldn't let her child starve under her watch, so I put the pen down and finished my food.

"How was your day, Jase?"

"Awesome," he answered, before calling his friend a "cheese dick," which I seriously hope is not a real thing.

"You just did this all day, didn't you?"

"I love summer." He smashed on his controller then shouted some more incomprehensible curse words, prompting my mom to yell at him about watching his language.

"Aren't you old enough to start working?" I asked between forkfuls of pasta. "You should really start getting a résumé together. You're almost fourteen. I think child labor laws are about to get reformed. It can only help the economy. Plus you're the only male in the house. Isn't the patriarchy teaching you to be ashamed of not being a breadwinner like Mom and I are?"

Jase gave me a puzzled look, then turned back to murdering people virtually. "My sister is so weird," he mumbled into the mic.

I slurped up some more spaghetti and continued to take in the cacophony of my apartment. Mom was complaining again about Dad traveling so much and not hosting us every other weekend like he was supposed to, the pub down the street was having a busy night, the voices carrying through our window and somehow making themselves heard over video game explosions. For some reason it made me feel lonely, hearing people out there, carefree, laughing together.

As soon as I was done eating I went to my room and lay on my bed with my laptop and my notebook nearby, my crappy little fan blowing and ruffling the sheets of paper. I could see the first line from Hafsah's email in the preview: **Look, Lu, I'm sorry but if we don't have...**

I clicked over to Facebook. Cal's wallet was next to me, and on a whim I typed his name into the search bar. There were about a dozen results, most of them locked accounts with profile pics that looked nothing like him or were too vague to make out.

The sticky note and the receipt that were in the wallet were laid out next to my notebook, as if they were evidence of something I understood. I read the address on the raffle ticket, and though I felt like a creep doing it, I typed it into Google.

Iris lived on the Upper West Side, near Morningside Heights. A nice building with a golden awning, balconies rich with plants and wicker patio furniture. I'd already made up my mind about going the next day, since I didn't have to be at work until the afternoon shift. I had no specific plan, per se, but I figured worst-case scenario I could give the wallet to the doorman.

I clicked over to Tumblr, scrolled through mindlessly for a while, doing my best to avoid Hafsah's email.

When I'd had my fill of that, I started transcribing Cal and Iris's breakup. Not breakup; fight. After rereading it a few times, I had to agree with Pete that it seemed pretty obvious they had split. But something in me fought against that conclusion.

Finally, I could no longer ignore the nagging presence of Hafsah's email.

Look, Lu, I'm sorry but if we don't have something from you soon, we'll have to terminate your contract. I hate to get all ultimatum on you, but the longer you go without a column, the more your readers forget about you and the less it matters when another column comes out. It's been a few weeks already, and I'm worried that if you don't send something in soon, we'll lose all the momentum we've built up for you. People forget easily these days. I'm guessing things were a little crazy with the end of school, and I don't want you to lose your scholarship, so I'll give you until the end of the month. Any longer than that and I'll have pressure to fill your space with another regular contributor.

Hope all is well,

Hafsah

I looked back to my notebook, flipped through the pages of hastily scrawled handwriting trying to capture others' words. My job at the magazine was tied to a scholarship for young women working in journalism, and without it, I wouldn't be able to afford going to NYU in the fall. So, poor timing there, writer's block.

I reread Cal and Iris's fight, wishing I had the same play-by-play from when Leo and I had broken up, though I wasn't sure what good that would do. Maybe I could use their story to figure out where exactly Leo and I had gone wrong. Maybe reading about their heartbreak could mend my heartbreak. Maybe there was a cure for my writer's block in them, somehow. After all, when I was walking behind them, I'd felt the urge to write for the first time in weeks.

I relived their breakup, and mine. I opened up a Word document on my computer, my fingers resting idly on the keyboard for a few minutes before I added my column's usual header. I gave it a title: **On Heartbreak**.

Then I shut my computer and went to sleep.

The next morning, Mom was at work, Jase was back in front of his screen, and I was on my way out the door to return Cal's wallet to Iris.

There are very few reasons why I would subject myself to the New York City subway on a summer day. The suffocating heat turning each platform into a sauna, everyone's sweat glands working overdrive. It brought out the worst in men, leering at any girl in a sundress or shorts, as if we didn't equally deserve to contribute to the sauna by freely sweating into the atmosphere without being stared at for it.

That day, though, the stops zoomed past without me noticing. A wallet should not have been reason enough, but I was inexplicably driven to return it.

I got off the train and walked the six blocks to Iris's building in a daze. Part of me knew that whatever I was doing was not entirely reasonable, I should have been working on a column, I should have just called the number on the raffle ticket and have them come pick it up. But most of me didn't really care. I felt like I was on a mission, even if I didn't yet know what that mission was.

Before I knew it, I was in front of the address written on the ticket. I looked up as best I could at the tenth floor, almost hoping to see Iris in the window, but there was nothing to be seen except the city reflected in the glass.

I texted Pete.

LU
I'm outside Crying Girl's building.

PETE
Returning the wallet?

LU
In theory.

PETE
Um...what could possibly be theoretical about it?

I didn't respond. I wasn't even sure what I had meant by that.

I wasn't sure what my plan here was either. The easy answer was to just go buzz her apartment and return the wallet. But that's not what I did. I took a lap around the block, holding the wallet in my hands, going through its contents, imagining Iris in her room feeling post-breakup blues. I pictured Cal on the bench where we met, thinking up paintball metaphors that only slightly made sense and wanting to help strange French couples. I pictured myself sitting right there with him, waiting on Leo, both of us feeling the same thing in different ways.

When I finally hit the buzzer, I was met with silence. I sighed with relief, then noticed that there was someone behind me. A girl with a skateboard tucked under her arm was crossing from the elevator to the entrance. She had comically large and bright pads on her knees and elbows, and a matching neon green helmet, her long curly hair unfurling in uncontainable waves from beneath. A green backpack hung over her shoulder.

"Hi," she said, her voice as bright as her skating accoutrements. "Are you new here?"

"Um," I said, because conversations with people were hard. Even if they were young, adorable people who knew how to be friendly. "I'm, uh…looking for a friend. Iris?"

"Iris Castillo? She's awesome. She babysits me sometimes. Lets me eat whatever I want and then we sing Broadway hits." She shifted her skateboard and looked over her shoulder. "Don't tell my mom I said that."

I chuckled. "Yeah, I won't. I just came by to give Iris this wallet. I don't think she's home though." I looked over at the intercom to show I'd tried.

"I can get it to her if you want. I live down the hall from her."

"Um," I said, this time because I didn't want to part with the wallet. It felt too soon, like the coincidence of Iris and Cal and me and Leo and the wallet falling into my hands was too meaningful to easily let go of, especially without seeing one of them again.

"My name is Grace, if you wanna text her and check that I live here or something," she said with a smile. I was a little intimidated by the fact that she was better at conversations than me. Grace smiled again, then dropped her skateboard and started rummaging through her backpack.

At the same time, I held out the wallet for her. But she was busy jingling things around, and before she noticed me offering it, I pulled back my hand. I tried to access that part of me that I use when I'm interviewing people.

I'm not sure what happens during those situations. The strange shell I present to the world falls away in favor of my true self, which is a lot like my everyday self, but more comfortable with who I am. Like when I interviewed with Hafsah for the *Misnomer* job, or that time I approached half the sophomore class at my school to ask them about masturbation habits. For a column, not just my own curiosities, of course. People I couldn't ask to borrow pens from, I was suddenly inquiring about their most intimate, private moments.

In those scenarios, I kind of felt the way I did with Leo. Things were easy. Like those mornings when we would meet up before school. He'd greet me with a coffee, slip his fingers between mine, kiss me on the cheek. We'd walk to school together, and for blocks, for months, I didn't have to actively think of what to say. I didn't have to juggle the thoughts at the surface of my brain and those lurking beneath. I could make my dumb jokes without hesitation, without that damn thought that came before I otherwise opened my mouth, the thought that said don't do it, the thought that said you are not valuable to others. I was fully present, fully myself, and Leo loved me for it.

"You know what, I think I can maybe meet up with her later," I said, stepping away from the door.

"Cool," Grace responded, still searching. "See ya!"

"Bye," I said, and turned away, my cheeks starting to flush. I turned down the street and back toward the subway, the wallet still in my hand.

4

THE ATTEMPT TO UNDERSTAND

I shoveled another scoop of overbuttered popcorn into a bucket, unsuccessfully offered the customer the chance to upgrade to a mega-large, and took their money. I was stuck at concessions, which was a strict no-phone zone. That meant I was cut off from the wider world, stuck in this sixteen-theater microcosm of the city, with no idea what was happening outside my scope of vision. It was crazy to me that humans used to live like that, completely separate from the rest of the planet, knowing only what was in front of them. Not that my phone could really tell me much about the things I kept churning over in my mind: Iris and Cal, whether or not they'd broken up, why the hell I hadn't returned the wallet, Leo's back while he slept.

In front of me, lines formed for the latest summer block-buster. Brad the manager was tearing tickets up front, two kids were killing time by playing one of the three barely functioning arcade games in the lobby. Popcorn spills and lost napkins were starting to pile up, the way they always did when it started getting busy.

"Hey, Lu."

Pulled away from my thoughts, I looked up at my next customer and was greeted by Leo's stupid, beautiful face. Dark eyes highlighted by lashes that looked Photoshopped, unblemished brown skin that was a shade darker than mine and so soft I always wanted to just press myself against his cheek. Behind him, his friends Miguel and Karl were trying to hide their snickering, giving each other looks and then smacking each other on the shoulder.

"I didn't know you'd be working today," Leo said, running a hand through his hair, which he was wearing down, instead of in the samurai-esque topknot he usually sported. "Sorry I bailed yesterday. I thought it'd be a little weird."

You know how sometimes your thoughts fill up so quickly that your mind might as well be blank for all the noise it's causing? I stared at the boy I had loved and wondered if he was suffering at all. I didn't say anything. This boy used to do everything for me, once upon a time. He'd offer to write essays for me so that I could get an extra hour of sleep, watch movies I knew he had no interest in seeing, just for me. He even walked forty blocks once to see me because his Metro-Card was empty.

It must have been October, judging from the length I remembered his hair being, and the layers of clothes he'd been wearing. He'd arrived at my door ruddy-cheeked and slightly sweaty, a cup of tea in hand. "Don't you have a huge math test tomorrow?"

"It's a regular-sized test," he'd said, his smile lighting up the hallway.

"I meant the degree of difficulty."

"It was harder not to come here."

"Eww but also aww." I'd let him in, accepting the kind of deep kiss that now made me angry to remember.

"Also, I studied while walking. Did you know they made calculus podcasts?"

"You did not listen to a calculus podcast," I'd said. "You were probably rehearsing for the play."

"I don't *just* sing, Lu, Jesus. I have other interests." We'd made it to my room by then, flopped onto the bed to lay next to each other, my head finding its resting spot on his chest. I'd craned my neck to look at him, judging his last statement. "Fine, I was singing. But, still, I contain multitudes."

I snapped out of the memory to realize I'd been staring at Leo.

"I guess this isn't much better," Leo said with a grimace, which made Miguel and Karl burst out laughing.

I looked past Leo and his jackass friends to my still-long line. I wished Pete were around to rescue me from this, but his shift had finished an hour ago and he was waiting for me at The Strand. I could feel myself start to blush. Rage-blushing, I think it was.

"Um," Leo said, starting to shift uncomfortably. This was the first time we'd seen each other since he broke up with me. This wasn't exactly how I was picturing it, with my co-workers around and the next person in line looking exasperated at any motion that wasn't strictly in my job description.

"We're gonna do the friends combo." He pushed a couple of twenties across the counter. I stared at the money, wishing it was something else. Maybe one of the bills had a love letter written on the back, or an apology. He was a theater geek after all; this could all be some elaborate, dramatic ploy. More chuckles from the jackasses. Leo bit his bottom lip, then looked back at his friends and told them to shut up. He turned toward me but didn't meet my eyes at all, his cheeks reddening. Shame-blushing, I guessed.

I started filling tubs of popcorn, my hands shaking enough that half the kernels spilled onto the floor. The other day at Madison Square Park, I'd had this whole speech prepared for him. I was going to try to convince him that we shouldn't break up, not for something as easily overcome as distance. I'd gone over the words in my head about a thousand times during all those hours when I couldn't sleep because of him, tinkered with their arrangement, wanting every damn sentence to punch him right in the heart so that I could then nurse him back to health. Now though, none of those words came to mind.

I slammed two tubs of popcorn on the counter and tried to ask him what he wanted to drink. But my voice was about to do that whole squeak-when-you're-about-to-cry thing, so I just picked up a couple of large cups and raised my eyebrows at him.

How I wanted those cups to be bottomless. How I wish I could just fill them up with his choice of orange soda for an hour straight until my shift was over, watch the bubbles fizz incessantly so I wouldn't have to face him in this state.

"So…" he said, with a long pause, as if he was trying to decide whether or not he should follow it up with anything or if he just let the words speak for themselves. Relationships don't end in periods, they end in ellipses, stretching the end out as if they don't know it's arrived. "What'd you want to talk to me about the other day?"

I slid the sodas over to him and punched in the order into my register. I thought about Cal's words to me on the bench. *What a weird thing we do*, he'd said. *Love.*

I grabbed Leo's change but just held it in my hand for a moment, looking up at him. "What do you think, Leo?" I managed to say. Instead of meeting my eyes, he looked down at the floor and shrugged. We'd been in love so recently, and now here I was trying to decide whether I should place the bills and coins on the counter to show him how hurt I was or if I should reach out and drop it into his hand for the pleasure of brushing his fingertips with mine.

The last time we'd held hands and meant it we were out on his fire escape, watching the neighbors. It hadn't been the dead of summer yet, the night warm but comfortable. Leo had just come up with a new song to add to the ongoing R & B album of our relationship. This one was titled "Fire Escape Boners" which I promise was a much sweeter song than what it sounds like. He had such a lovely singing voice, and he could come up with song lyrics that fit my sense of humor and made me swoon at the same time.

Nine months we'd dated. If I got to live until I was eighty, our relationship would only take up 0.9% of my lifetime. I tried to tell myself that 0.9% of my lifetime couldn't possibly have this much of an effect on me. It was meaningless. That's how long I spent in karate classes when I was eight, and I sure as hell didn't know any karate now, nor miss its presence in my life. I watched him open his mouth stupidly with no response. He brushed his hair back again.

"My movie's starting," he said, calling his friends over to help him with the snacks. They muttered hellos as if we hadn't noticed each other yet, then scurried away. "Sorry," Leo said.

Again, instead of saying all those words I'd prepared just for Leo the other day, I thought of Cal's, *We have love. Isn't that enough?*

He finally met my gaze and I looked into his eyes, eyes that

I'd looked into most days for the last nine months, eyes that, on more than one occasion, had been the first thing I'd seen in the morning. I wished our time together had endowed me with the ability to know what he was thinking, to identify exactly the amount of love he had for me. But I had no clue, and didn't want to guess.

Then Leo turned and left, a trail of spilled popcorn in his wake.

As soon as I got off work, I grabbed my bag from the employee room and bolted down the street toward The Strand. I found Pete hanging out at the customer service desk with Starla, the two of them leaning over a crossword puzzle. The store was quiet, only a handful of people wandering about half an hour before closing. Indie rock was playing quietly on overhead speakers, and the soft, warm lighting made it feel like we were in a movie.

Starla spotted me first, and she smiled as I approached. "What's up, babycakes?" She did that whole antiquated-term-of-affection thing that usually only sweet, elderly ladies can pull off unironically.

"Oh you know, just my angst," I sighed and plopped my forehead onto the desk.

"Uh-oh," Pete said. "Shift not go so well? Are you disillusioned by the masses swallowing up Hollywood franchises again?"

I kept my head down on the wooden surface, turning so that I could see them, my cheek smooshed and making my words come out garbled. "I mean, yeah, that doesn't help. But..." A groan escaped me. "Leo showed up."

"Is that the ex?" Starla asked in an unsubtle aside to Pete.

"The very one. Let me guess, he didn't try to serenade you back into his arms?"

"Not quite." I stood up, feeling like no amount of sighing could ever help the queasiness in my stomach. "More like he showed up to swallow Hollywood franchises."

"That's a weird way to put it," Pete said. Then he snapped his fingers and grabbed the pen from Starla to write into the crossword. "*Swallow!* Seventeen-down." They high-fived, Starla's many bracelets jingling with the impact. "So, did you confront him?" Pete went on. "Unload the speech that's been building up inside of you lo these many days?"

"Again, no. More like stared into his stupidly pretty eyes and silently begged him to still love me."

"Yeesh," Starla said, eyebrows angled in concern. "Running into exes is never fun. It's just so easy to tell that at least one party involved is holding back some pain, some longing. It lingers there like a fart, making normal conversation impossible."

"Especially when you're the one who farted," Pete chipped in.

"Thanks, Pete, that's helpful."

"Sorry." He chewed on the back of the pen, looked up from the crossword. "Of all the movie theaters in all the world, why'd the dick have to walk into yours?"

"'I didn't know you'd be working today,'" I said, dropping my voice and making it sound as dumb as possible in imitation of Leo. It's not what he sounded like at all. Again, the jerk's voice was beautiful. But I was angry that he hadn't let me convince him to still be an us, hadn't bothered to show up to our meeting but had waltzed into my theater as if he didn't know I'd be there, angry that he wasn't still singing R & B songs with me. I groaned and looked around the shop, trying to find comfort in one of my favorite places, the quiet beauty of colorful, nearly endless stacks of books. All of them chock-full of love and heartache, couples killing themselves because they couldn't be together, couples traveling into hell to find each other, couples climbing over and fighting through and barreling past obstacles to be together. How had that not prepared me for a precollege breakup?

"You alright, girly?" Starla asked me.

"What percentage of these books do you think are about love, in some way?" I asked, ignoring her question and turning my back toward them so I could look out at the whole store. "Or at least have a romantic element in them?"

"Shiiiiiit," Starla said, stretching out the vowel. "If you leave out nonfiction and all the reference books, I'd guess 90 percent."

"That's so crazy," I said. "Why? Why this one thing? Life's much more than just love."

An old, balding white guy picked up a thick paperback from the classics table, turning it over to read the back cover. A black woman and her two tween daughters roamed the children's section, one girl holding her mom's hand, the other rushing ahead and gathering a pile of books.

I turned back to Starla and Pete, who had stopped doing their crossword puzzle and were looking out at the store too. "Because," Starla said, "love's the pinnacle of the human experience, yet it's still a mystery to us. The joys and the pains alike, not to mention the awkward mumblings of seeing an ex for the first time since your breakup. It's the best thing that happens to us—"

"Love's the worst thing that happened to me," I interrupted.

"—but we don't really know why," Starla continued, acknowledging me with a chuckle and a couple of reassuring shoulder pats. "All that art, it's just...the attempt to under-stand it."

"You should know more than anyone," Pete added, the words half-mumbled because of the pen in his mouth. Starla reached over and grabbed the pen from him.

"Gross, dude, that's my pen."

"Me? Why would I understand it?"

"Don't you write about it professionally? Love, specifically."

"Well, yeah. But I've never claimed to be a love expert. I'm wading through the murky shitswamp that is love, and bringing my readers along for the ride."

"Wow, was that your pitch?"

"My love-hate relationship with love is part of my relatable charm. I'm not doling out advice, I'm chronicling what it's like to be a teen maneuvering through this..." I waved my hand and gestured at all these stupid books about love, then at myself for added emphasis.

They went back to their crossword puzzle and I looked out at the store a little longer, thinking about what Starla had said. I spotted the aisle where I first eavesdropped on Iris, wondered how she would deal with her first run-in with Cal after their breakup.

"You're going to be okay," Starla reassured me, offering a light forearm touch, her bracelets cold on my wrist.

"Yeah," I said. "That's what the books and movies keep telling me."

I took my time walking home, not really in a hurry to deal with my mom, or with another failed attempt at sleep. I tried eavesdropping a few times on people around me, even paus-ing near a few bars with patios and pretending to text so that I could listen in, but I couldn't seem to focus.

I climbed up the five short steps of my stoop, unlocked the

front door that led into the mail vestibule, then the inside door that led to the stairway. We'd been living in this apartment since my parents got divorced and my dad moved to New Jersey, but for some reason I'd never really noticed how many stains were on the gray carpet, how the paint along the walls was peeling so much that it looked like it was trying to escape the building. Every apartment I passed by was replete with noise, TVs blasting, music thumping, feet stomping. It was like I was suddenly attuned to something about the city that I'd never really focused on before.

When I unlocked my apartment door, Mom immediately pushed her chair away from the kitchen table. "Oh thank God," she said. "I was so tired." She walked over to the kitchen, setting a mostly empty red-wine glass by the sink. "Hope your day was good. Eggplant parm in the fridge, you can heat it in the microwave for a minute and a half. Good night." She planted a kiss on my forehead, which made me just want to fall into her arms.

I wrapped her into a hug, and she let out a soft "oh" in surprise, then held me tighter, probably thinking all sorts of mom thoughts. I wondered for a moment if I should tell her about Leo. I wanted to, felt the urge rising in my chest, though it was too easily suppressed. After Leo and I broke up, my mom had asked me if I was okay, and I managed to shrug and say a weak, "Yeah." After a few repetitions of this, she didn't bring it up again.

I don't know when Mom and I settled into the kind of relationship where love was not discussed, but it had happened too long ago for me to do anything about it now. I remember when my parents got divorced, I was old enough to see some sort of heartbreak in her, to sense her sorrow past my own.

But I was thirteen and didn't know how to ask her about it, and the topic hadn't been broached since.

"G'night," I said, letting go of her and turning away, hoping she wouldn't call attention to my hug. "Please make pancit one day. Or lumpia. Literally anything not covered in tomato sauce."

"Very funny," she called down the hall. "Don't be loud, you'll wake your brother."

A record-breaking day for sighs, no doubt. I made myself a plate, threw it into the microwave, checked my email. Hafsah's warning still sat there. I read it again, wondered what I would do if I lost the job, lost my scholarship. I grabbed the book I was reading and set it on the kitchen table along with a glass of water, but struggled to read even a page.

Too many thoughts raged through my head, all of them uncomfortable to linger on. Bad furniture, that's what my thoughts were.

I ate as much of my dinner as I could stomach, then went into my room and fell on top of the sheets, wanting to cry but not exactly knowing what had changed from yesterday to today. I'd known Leo was unlikely to change his mind even with a speech, and all I'd done that day was muttered a sentence and handed him his change. *What a weird thing we do to ourselves*, I thought.

Then I sat up with a start. Inspiration poked at me for the first time in months, jabbing its persistent finger into the small of my back. I reached for my phone on the nightstand and clicked to reply to Hafsah's email.

Sorry, H. Been struggling with some heartbreak-induced writer's block. Fitting, right? But I have an idea. Are you free for coffee tomorrow?

5

PANIC VINAIGRETTE

Explaining dreams to someone when you don't really remember the details is one of the worst things a person can do, so I'll spare you. What you should know though, is that when I woke up I was happy. Overwhelmingly happy for just an instant, until I realized that I was happy because I'd dreamed about Leo. We'd been sitting on that bench in Union Square Park where I met Cal, but instead of Leo bailing on me, he'd shown up and taken my hand without a word. I was back within that comfort, within the joy of sitting next to someone you love and just feeling your hand in theirs. He started singing one of our R & B songs for me, then leaned in and kissed me.

I lay in bed, the feeling of being loved lingering even though it had come from a fictionalized version of a person who no longer loved me. I checked my phone and saw that Hafsah had emailed, saying we could meet at noon in Midtown. The desire to fall back asleep and into the dream made my bed a little more comfortable than it usually was, and the relief from Hafsah's email made me want to sink as deep into my mattress as possible. I snoozed my first alarm, not ready to start the day or to think about what it meant to be so happy after a dream like that. It's bizarre how dreams can just bleed into the day after they're done, like they're something tangible, like they're clothes you wear until you go to bed again. I was just about to doze back off when my backup alarm rang out. I groaned into my pillow and pulled myself out of bed. Cal's wallet was still on my nightstand, and I picked it up and rummaged through it for the millionth time before deciding it was best kept out of sight and chucking it into my drawer.

In the living room, Jase was back on the couch with his video games. Mom was at work. I got myself a bowl of cereal and watched Jase kill a few more people, trying to clear my head of the dream. "Don't you have any social interactions planned today?"

"What are you talking about? I'm playing with literally all my friends right now."

"What if you read a book today? Just, like, a page."

"This game actually has a really good storyline." Jase paused his game for a second to take a bite of leftover eggplant parmesan. There were four pieces piled onto the plate, and that's not even counting however many he had devoured before I'd woken up. He used to be such a sweet, small kid. So small. I could pick him up and even physically intimidate him when I needed to. But now he was eating as much in one meal as I was in a week, and his limbs looked like a magician pulling a colored handkerchief out of his sleeve. They just kept going and going.

"What about some community service hours? Volunteer work? Meditation? Any plans to do those today?"

"Prolly not."

"Your generation will be the end of us all," I said, getting up to go shower.

I still had plenty of time, so I decided to save myself the subway fare from Chinatown and walk to Midtown. I wanted to corral my thoughts, so that I could make a good pitch to Hafsah. But my thoughts were un-corral-able, and altogether too painfully focused on Leo. I ended up just eavesdropping the whole way there. Nothing meaningful really. I wasn't within earshot of anyone long enough to get a full conversation. Just lines, words I plucked out of the air.

The restaurant I was meeting Hafsah at was obviously a business-lunch meet up. It was empty at 11:45 when I got in, and at exactly noon the line snaked out the door, all thirty-, forty-, and fiftysomethings in business attire. There was a staggering number of blazers.

I felt weird as hell sitting there, obviously out of place. Well, not that exactly. But like everyone else thought I was out of place. I'd been meeting with Hafsah at places like this for over a year now.

I'd checked into the front desk of the building she worked in and saw the looks the security guards gave me, their eyebrows raised, the contemptuous stares of middle-aged white dudes wondering what I was doing in the elevator with them. In their eyes, I was lost. I'd wandered in accidentally.

But here of all places, I was not lost.

I'd found *Misnomer*'s call for writers online in a Tumblr post, shared hundreds of times before I'd even laid eyes on it. I was probably supposed to be doing homework at the time, but of course had gotten sucked into the black hole of the internet.

The post said the site was looking for "fresh teen voices" in a handful of categories, which immediately filled me with hope that they were looking for exactly me, while also making me question whether my voice was fresh or even typically teenage or what category I was suited for. I'd seen "love" on the list, but had assumed I could do humor or current events or lifestyle, whatever that one meant. They'd asked for a cover letter and a portfolio of writing samples, so I'd spent the next few hours shirking my academic responsibilities in order to go through everything I'd ever written. After overcoming nausea from reading the garbage I'd written over the years, I managed to find a handful of blog entries, essays, and stories that I felt strongly enough about to submit.

A week later I had an email from Hafsah, the managing editor, telling me that since I lived in New York, I should come in for an interview, ready to discuss ideas. I filled three pages in my notebook with pitches on what I could write for her.

That first time in the *Misnomer* offices, I'd felt out of place, sure. Up until I sat down in front of Hafsah's desk. There were many ways I could describe Hafsah, but above all else, she's a badass. At twenty-nine she was the managing editor for a magazine, had a publishing deal for two books of essays, had her work featured in the *New York Times*, the *Atlantic*, and the *Wall Street Journal*, as well as having been interviewed a handful of times on TV for her insight into a number of social issues. I'd researched all of this before coming in for my interview, and I was in the presence of the woman whom I aspired to be someday.

"What do you want to write about, Lu?" she'd asked, right off the bat.

I thought for a second. "Is it a bad interview answer to say 'anything'?"

"Not necessarily." She'd turned to some papers in front of her, presumably my printed writing samples, but they could have easily been, like, hidden Harry Potter manuscripts or classified Pentagon papers or something. She's was *that* cool. "How often do you write?"

"Most days."

"Do you schedule time to do it, or wait for inspiration?"

"At least a half hour before bed. And usually during math classes, as a stimulant. Except on days when I need a break."

She'd smiled. "How do you feel about love?"

"Um."

"I'm sure you saw that one of the positions we're looking to fill is a regular romance and relationship columnist. Not a Dear Abby thing, per se, more like a Carrie Bradshaw thing."

I tilted my head. "The quarterback?"

"As in *Sex and the City*?"

I snapped my fingers. "Right. I knew that." I noticed that the usual discomfort that came after I said something stupid didn't rage in my thoughts. My comment dissipated in my memory. It was a wonderful thing, being unbothered.

Hafsah flipped through the pages in front of her, leaning her chin in her cupped hand for a moment before looking back up at me.

"How would you feel about writing about love?"

"I mean, writing is writing. I'm not too…experienced, or whatever. But I'd be happy to do it."

"Well, (a), that doesn't matter. I just love your voice, and some of these blog posts are exactly what we're looking for. Those two weeks when you had a crush on the kid in chess club led to some compelling, funny reading. And, (b), being in a relationship isn't the sole experience of teen love. God knows it wasn't for me. We're not looking for a relationship advice person, that's too passé. We want someone to muse about love and dating, the absence and longing of both."

"That," I said, "I can write about."

Hafsah smiled again, and I almost felt like my life as a writer-with-an-audience was already beginning. "You've got these insights that I think could resonate with readers. Even now I'm looking forward to reading more from you."

It didn't sound like I was interviewing for a job anymore, which almost prompted me to run a victory lap in her office. I didn't, which is probably why I got the job.

I knew what I had to offer the world, and it was my writing. And ever since I'd started at *Misnomer*, regardless of how I moved within the world, I'd felt more a part of it than ever before. So they could raise their eyebrows all they wanted.

At the fancy restaurant I didn't/did belong in, I sipped on seltzer water until Hafsah arrived, smiling at the hostess and pointing me out as she strode past the line of people waiting for a table.

"Have you been here long?" Hafsah asked as she sat down. She pushed her menu aside and looked around for a waiter, one arm raised slightly, two fingers stretched just enough to catch someone's attention, but not enough that someone might think her desperate for it.

"No, I just got here."

We chatted small stuff for a while, mostly her asking me how it felt to be done with school. To be honest it still just felt like any other summer. A stupidly heartbroken one, but whatever. I wasn't thinking about starting college in the fall yet.

When our food arrived, Hafsah went into business mode. "Alright, what's your pitch?" She unraveled her silverware from its little cloth napkin sleeping bag and started poking away at her pasta. I had a great-looking ahi tuna salad with soy vinaigrette in front of me, but now that it was time for me to tell her my idea, I couldn't bring myself to casually eat while unloading the speech I had been going over in my mind all morning.

It took some stammering and a few expectant looks from Hafsah before I could actually start speaking intelligently. "So, the other day, I eavesdropped on this couple," I said, fidgeting with my fork, my glass of water, my phone, the tablecloth, my tuna, anything within reach. "They were talking about how the girl was leaving to go to college, and the guy was staying here, and the conversation turned to…"

Hafsah waited for me to finish.

"A breakup, I guess. You know, classic summer before college stuff."

"Just like you, huh?"

"Slaying me with the casualness there, H."

"Sorry," she said, offering a forced grimace before turning to her pasta again, probably not wanting to let the afternoon flitter away unproductively. "So, you're thinking a piece about precollege breakups?"

I toyed with my fork for a little while, rubbing some wasabi across the side of a piece of seared tuna. "A series. I was thinking I could profile specific couples. Starting with those two."

"How would you find them again? Didn't you just overhear them?"

"I, uh, have the boy's wallet. It's a weird, long story where I promise I am in no way implicated for any legal wrongdoing. But I have a way to get in touch with them. I could interview them, fresh from their recent heartbreak. And then I could do a whole series of other couples going through the same thing. I could write about it from so many different angles, right? It'd be interesting. Couples who are staying together long-distance, couples who decided to change plans to be together, couples who…didn't."

Hafsah chewed thoughtfully on her pasta, eyeing me. I tried not to squirm. I wasn't uncomfortable in her presence. She was in no way a mean person. It was just intense to be under the scrutiny of someone you admired, someone you knew was damn good at life.

"Are you going to write yourself into the pieces?" she said, finally, wiping at the corner of her mouth with a napkin.

"Um, I hadn't really thought about that," I said, because those words were easier to say than, *Sure, but thinking about my failed relationship is crippling me and I'd rather think about anything else.*

"It would help make it more relatable. Be transparent about what led you to this interest. The readers would love that." She shrugged, maybe because she saw the panic on my face. "Just a thought. But, yeah, I like it. We'll see how the first one turns out before committing to a series. Monday work for you?"

"Oh." I finally managed to take a bite of tuna, buying myself time while chewing. I looked around the restaurant at all the business people going about their days, having conversations about performance, sales, accounting, or... I guess I don't really know what those people talked about over business lunches. I couldn't fathom sitting down to actually write a reflection on Iris and Cal, and definitely not one on myself. But I couldn't risk getting my column dropped. Partly because it would completely unravel the external validation crucial to my (admittedly dwindling) mental health. Mostly, though, if I lost the scholarship that was tied to my job, I wouldn't be able to go to school at all.

"Lu?" Hafsah said. "Can I see a draft by Monday?"

"Yeah, sure." I took another bite of my salad, which was

probably delicious but kind of tasted like a dusty slab of clay at that point. "Wait, what day is it today?"

"Thursday."

I heroically resisted throwing up. "Yeah, sure. Monday. Cool, cool. All weekend. And then some! Ha!"

Understandably, Hafsah looked at me as if I'd just turned into one of those homeless dudes who doesn't really carry a sign or has any sort of clear goal he's trying to accomplish, but rather spends his time yelling out random strings of nonsense words. Luckily, Hafsah knows that I'm much better at stringing words together on paper. "If the couple's slow to get back for an interview, let me know and we'll push it back, but I'd really prefer to see something by Monday."

"Monday," I said again, nodding my head vigorously to reassure my editor that I was totally normal and capable of writing and not a babbling maniac. "Cool."

"Great," Hafsah said. She set her fork and knife neatly across the plate, done with her food and ready to move on to whatever super important badass thing she was doing next. She got a waiter's attention again and set down her corporate card to pay for the bill. I told her I was fine on my own and so she took off, saying she was looking forward to reading what I came up with.

Now I was free to enjoy my panic salad and try to come up with a way to introduce myself to Cal and Iris without coming off as a stalker. Although I'd already kinda met Cal, and now I had his wallet, so I was definitely going to come across as at least a little stalkerish. Which meant they'd have to be really naive about the ways of the world to let me anywhere near them again. Which meant I wouldn't have anything to send Hafsah on Monday. Which meant bye-bye to college and my ability to ever write again.

6

OFF THE RECORD

I spent the rest of that day just kind of staring at the computer and making low guttural sounds. Then on Friday I decided I should probably at least try to find a way to talk to the lovebirds. Cal's name hadn't worked on Facebook, but I realized I had Iris's full name from the raffle ticket, and when I typed it in she came up right away. Her privacy settings weren't superintense either, so I opened up a private message.

Then I stared at it for a long time and made some more guttural sounds. When that didn't seem to cause words to appear on my screen, I texted Pete.

LU
Help, I need to human.

PETE
Why? You have the day off. Be a slug. Slugs have good lives.

LU
Are slugs good at making introductions with strangers on whom they've eavesdropped?

PETE
No conclusive evidence either way on that one.

I told him about my pitch to Hafsah, which I knew would really get him on board with the whole helping me thing. Pete's the biggest fan of my writing, and he takes every opportunity he can to encourage me to do more of it. Which was great at the moment because of the whole sucking-at-writing-since-Leo-dumped-me thing. Just say you found the wallet and want to return it, Pete wrote, oversimplifyingly.

Shut up, that's a word.

LU
And how do I approach the whole we're-strangers-but-I-want-to-interview-you-and-your-very-recently-ex-boyfriend thing?

PETE
...Journalistically?

LU
Shut up, that's not a word.

PETE
You're a journalist, Lu. A writer mostly, but technically a journalist. Just tell them what the situation is. It's really not that weird. Worst thing they can say is no.

LU
And then I get fired and lose my scholarship and

don't go to college and die in vain, another wasted
human life lost into the folds of history.

I slouched deeper into the couch and let loose a few more
guttural sounds. Weird how an audible expression of discomfort helped ease the discomfort itself, even if just for a
second. It probably increased Jase's discomfort, since he was
sitting right next to me, and no amount of video games can
distract from your older sister low-key imitating a walrus half
the morning.

Finally, feeling on the verge of an existential crisis if I didn't
even attempt to hang on to my columnist job, and only after
many, many drafts, I sent Iris Castillo, aka Crying Girl, aka
Bench Boy's version of Leo, a message: Hi! This is going to
sound weird, but I found someone named Cal's wallet the other
day. His name didn't lead to anything on Facebook, but there
was a raffle ticket with your name in there, which is how I found
you. Lemme know if I should get in touch with him or where we
should meet to give you the wallet or whatever you want to do.

Hitting Send felt like the onset of a mild panic attack.

Thankfully I only have normal teen levels of angst-xiety,
and my uncomfortable morning was made calm when Iris
responded fifteen minutes later. OMG! That's so nice of you.
Can you come to the address on the raffle ticket? I'll pass it
along. I'm free any time before three.

I trekked back uptown to Iris's apartment building. This
time, when I got out of the subway I looked around for some
coffee to prepare for the conversation I was about to have.
It's a weird compulsion, getting coffee in advance of a potentially nerve-racking situation. Maybe it was comforting to
have something in my hands, or the constant motion of sip-

ping was somehow soothing. Very often, it ended up being a terrible mistake that made me need to use the bathroom right in the middle of the nerve-racking situation, but I somehow still thought of it as a security blanket.

The night Leo and I broke up, I stormed out of his apartment and went straight to our favorite Vietnamese restaurant to get an iced coffee. We'd had pho there about once a week since we started dating, but even the suddenly painful experience of being in there—the bitter taste of what had once been a happy place now marred by the end of the relationship—wasn't a match for my craving of sweet, stomach-gurgling coffee. I'd sat on the curb, holding the coffee close to me in the early summer heat, wishing its comforts could extend deeper than my taste buds.

On the Upper West Side, I picked up a dollar cup of hot coffee from a bagel cart and walked to Iris's building, the whole time tinkering with how I would ask if I could write about her and Cal. I'd done it a bunch of times already for other articles I'd written, approached someone for permission, or for an interview. For some reason this one felt different. I couldn't put my finger on why, though if I had to guess I'd probably say that my finger would have landed somewhere in or around the awkwardness of eavesdropping on someone's breakup and then introducing yourself.

I checked the time to make sure I wasn't late or freakishly early, then texted her so she would come down. A moment later, as I stepped around the corner, someone coming the other way plowed into me, splashing scalding coffee all over the front of my shirt. I bellowed in pain and looked up to face my attacker, which is when I saw Grace chasing after her skateboard down the street.

"Owwww," I said.

"I'm sorry!" Grace cried. "You were just there suddenly."

I pinched the front of my shirt and pulled it away from my body, so that it wouldn't melt into my skin. "It's okay," I said, recovering from the shock. "I spill things too."

I looked around lamely for a napkin or something to sop up the mess and saw Iris emerging from her building a few doors down. She stood there for a bit before noticing us, and gave one of those looks you give people you're about to meet but have never seen before except for little profile pictures online. You tilt your head and squint your eyes and try to reconcile how they appear in person with the digital version of themselves you've seen before. Then she broke out into an earnest, charming smile and waved as she came toward us. I doubt I'd smiled at anyone since my breakup with Leo.

"Lu?" she asked, sticking her hands into the pockets of her dress. Noticing Grace, she frowned for a moment and said hi to her too, then started piecing together what had happened.

"Let's go upstairs," Iris said, looking at my shirt, which was basically just one big coffee stain. "We'll get napkins or something. Grace, are you okay?" Grace, probably happy to take this as absolution for causing the coffee spill, nodded, hopped on her skateboard, and rolled away, weaving around a couple slow-walking down the sidewalk.

Before I could protest, Iris turned back toward her apartment, gesturing for me to follow along. Her building had a nice elevator with a mirror wall and shiny chrome panels, which we stood in awkwardly for the ten-floor journey upstairs. We passed through an elegant, spacious hallway, the kind you see in hotels, but with fewer rooms. Iris opened the door inside and jetted away, saying she was going to get one of those magical detergent pens. I stood in the entrance to her place, wondering just what the hell I was doing. *Returning the wallet, confessing the eavesdropping, asking for permission to interview her, keeping your job*, the practical side of my brain said. *Figuring out how someone else wades through the insanities of heartbreak*, some other side of my brain retorted. To keep those two sides of my brain from arguing, a third chimed in and said, *Isn't that artisanal rug hanging on the wall over there pretty? It looks Oaxacan!*

Shut up, we don't know what Oaxacan rugs look like! The other two parts of my brain shouted in unison.

Iris came speed-walking back, the pen in her hand. "I'm sorry this happened. The universe really chose to reward your good deed by being a prick, huh?"

"Totally," I said. I uncapped the pen and started dabbing uselessly at the damp coffee stain, which easily covered half of my shirt. There was a quiet moment, thick with the awkwardness of our unfamiliarity.

"Damn, that's not doing much, is it?" Iris said, pouting.

"It's okay. This happens to me about forty times a week."

"Oof."

"Yeah, I'm a lost cause. Like this shirt." I shrugged and capped the pen, giving it back to her.

"I'm sorry you have to walk around like that all day. Do you live nearby?"

"Not really, I live in Chinatown. But it's okay. I don't have any street cred or anything, so it's fine if people judge me on the R train."

Iris laughed, harder than she had to. She even did that thing only '50s starlets do where they cover their mouths with their hands, as if laughter could be contained, or even should be for the sake of propriety. On the way over to her place, I'd imagined her looking as heartbroken as I'd felt, but looking at her now, and over her shoulder at the living room behind her, I saw no evidence that she'd taken her breakup harshly.

There were no blankets crumpled on the couch, Netflix wasn't paused on the TV. Iris even looked like she'd managed to shower at some point in the past few days, which was more than I could say for myself post-breakup.

"Well, I guess I should thank you for coming all this way. Especially since it came at such a high cost." She gestured to my shirt.

"It's really okay," I said, reaching into my bag to grab Cal's wallet. "I found out this shirt is from one of those evil places that uses sweatshops, so I've been meaning to, like, donate it and buy something more humane, or burn it in protest. I don't know which is the most ethical option. Anyway, spilling coffee on it was probably just my guilt lashing out."

Iris snapped her fingers. "Oh! I know what I'll do." She turned and walked away again, leaving me holding the wallet out to no one. I hoped there wasn't anyone else in the apartment that might appear and ask me who I was. "I've got a bunch of shirts here," Iris called out from what I assumed was her room. "You can borrow one."

"You don't have to do that! It's almost dry." I picked at the shirt, which was clinging to my ribs. "Kind of."

Iris came back, holding a baby blue V-neck. "Please, I insist. I've got like three of the same one. It's the least I can do for you coming out of your way to return my stupid boyfriend's wallet."

I froze, my jaw succumbing to gravity and clichés. *I'm sorry, did you just say 'ex-boyfriend'? Because if so you were super quiet on the* ex *part,* I thought, but didn't say, because I can still sometimes human. "Oh, he's your boyfriend?"

"Yeah. He sucks at hanging on to his belongings. I swear he can't go to a movie theater without leaving his cell phone under the seat with the day-old popcorn. The amount of times we've had to go back and..." She trailed off. "Sorry, I'm rambling. Anyway." She stepped forward and held her hand out, offering the T-shirt. "Thanks again. This really means so much."

Gingerly, I reached out and grabbed it, leaving Cal's wallet in her open palm instead. "Yeah, it's no problem," I said, almost a whisper.

There could have been a different outcome.

Iris said "boyfriend," not "ex-boyfriend," so there existed a world, a universe, some parallel dimension where two people like me and Leo could love each other the way we did and not be split up by the circumstances of our collegiate plans. I'd entered that universe somehow, and now I knew why I'd hung on to that wallet.

I'd unknowingly pitched Hafsah gold. It wasn't just a decent idea, an exploration of the murky ground of post-senior-year relationships, it was an actual blueprint. These two had lived through the same fight I'd had with Leo and survived. I wanted to know how. I wanted to share that how with others and help them avoid this stupid feeling I was in the midst of. Hell, maybe I could somehow be saved too.

"The bathroom is just here on the left." Iris stepped aside and pointed at a door. "I was gonna make a pot of coffee. You want some? Your shirt made me crave it." She smiled, humor in her eyes.

I nodded yes, then went into the bathroom to change. I was glad to get the wet shirt off me, and happy that Iris had offered coffee, not just for the comfort, but for the opportunity to linger there and work up the guts to bring up my ulterior motive.

When I walked out of the bathroom, I found Iris sitting on a stool at the kitchen counter looking at her phone. The smell of coffee was strong, the machine burbling loudly. Iris looked up at me and smiled again, flipping her phone face-down on the granite counter.

That was probably the moment that I'd been waiting for, to come clean about eavesdropping. I opened my mouth, then realized how hard it is to say the words, *hey, so, the other day I was spying on you.* Instead, I again opted for words that were easier to say, "So, you and Cal, huh? How long's that been going on for?"

She answered politely at first, but I kept prying, my journalistic instinct kicking in (and kicking aside my subnormal social skills). She was clearly in the mood to talk too, running me through a brief history of their relationship. They'd met online, on Tumblr. They'd started off liking/reblogging each other's posts, many of them little love notes to New York City. After enough of this casual e-flirting, Iris had sent him a private message. "I felt like we'd been looking at each other across a room all night, and I couldn't take the eye-dancing anymore without saying hi. So, I just sent a 'hi' with a little emoticon smiley face." They kept flirting online for a while after that, and a couple of months later they went on their first date. This was almost two years ago. Since then, it seemed like it was all roses and puppy love. No mention of fighting in the streets outside The Strand.

"What are you guys doing for college?" I asked, dipping my toes farther into ulterior-motive territory. Iris's expression didn't give anything away, but she didn't answer immediately either. "I'm just asking because… Okay, this is weird, but have you heard of *Misnomer*?"

She nodded. "Yeah, but I've never really gone on it."

"Well, I actually have this column on it that's all about love and relationships and stuff." I looked down at my lap, fiddling with my hands. "My newest piece is gonna be about couples who are facing the summer before college and the decision to go long-distance, or break up, or go to the same school or whatever. It's so funny that you're in that situation too!"

Iris raised her eyebrows, graciously passing over my stupid comment. "Wow, you have your own column?"

"It's not that big of a deal. I don't think a lot of people read it."

"Still. What's it like interviewing people about their love lives?"

"You can find out, if you let me interview you."

She laughed, then flipped her hair over and ran her hand through the curls, fluffing them out. There was something enchanting about the action, something that spoke of a comfort within her own body that I just didn't have. "Damn, girl, that was smooth," she said. She pushed away from the counter and took our empty mugs to the sink. "I don't know if I'm into that though. He and I had kind of a touchy talk about the topic the other day, and I'd rather not delve into it, especially in front of a stranger." The faucet turned on, and she rinsed the mugs and put them away in the dishwasher. "No offense."

She flashed a smile that I easily recognized as the desire to stop the conversation, but I wasn't quite ready to face the turmoil of my thoughts if I walked away from here without the article that would bust me out of my writer's block. "This is going to sound like I'm prying, but it's just an excuse to say a phrase I've been dying to say since I became a quote-unquote journalist. Off the record, what was the touchy talk about?" Another polite smile, eyes averted. She bided her time by turning on the dishwasher. "I'm only asking because, well…" I trailed off, surprised I was ready to broach the subject with anyone but Pete. "I got dumped recently. My boyfriend and I had planned to stay together after graduation, then he… I dunno. Changed his mind, I guess."

Iris looked at me for a moment, long enough for me to really think about what a weirdo I was. Here I was standing in this Upper West Side kitchen—with its granite countertops, decorative Mexican plates, and a freakin' dishwasher, the light coming in through the big windows that didn't just show the neighboring building but had an actual view   in front of a girl whose nonbreakup I'd witnessed and now wanted to take advantage of for my own personal reasons. And I was revealing my own broken heart to her. Within an hour of meeting her.

"I don't know," Iris said. "This seems...personal."

"Personal is what my column is all about."

"Yeah, but, I don't know you."

"Okay, what do you want to know?"

"Why us? For all you know we're boring as hell."

"Fair question," I said. I couldn't admit the fact that I'd eavesdropped on their conversation, heard lines coming out of her mouth that Leo had spat at me. "For one, I'll admit, it's convenience." I threw out my most casual shrug. "I'm standing in your kitchen and you just told me you're going through the exact thing I want to write about. I also like the coincidence of it all. I found your boyfriend's wallet on the ground and it just so happens you fit the profile for my column. That's kinda cool, right?" Iris considered this for a moment, then conceded my point with a nod. "Most of all, though, I'm just curious. My relationship failed where yours went right. I wanna know how you did it."

The dishwasher started to whir. Iris looked down at it as if she was thankful for its interruption. "I don't know what to say. We talked through it." She fluffed her hair out again and looked at me, maybe hoping I would change the subject. Unfortunately for her, my journalistic instinct was still on, and I knew that if I didn't say anything for a bit she'd feel the need to fill the silence. She turned her back to me and grabbed a dishrag that was folded by the sink, running it across the counter as if there was anything there to clean. "I don't talk easily about personal stuff. You can?"

Of course, I'd talked about the breakup with Pete already. And a little bit with my cousin Cindy when she texted a couple of nights after. But there's something about breakups and certain kinds of sadness that makes you want to return to the subject again and again, no matter how emotionally draining it can be. I guess that's what heartbreak does to you. It makes you long to feel drained.

"To a fault," I chuckled. "I work at a movie theater, and the other day during the thirty-second interaction I had with a customer buying a ticket, I managed to tell them not only that I'd recently been dumped, but that I was planning on a really great speech to win my ex back."

Iris cringed, which was the most appropriate reaction she could have had. "Did the speech work?"

"I've tried to deliver it three times now. He's bailed on me every time."

The dishwasher whirred again. Iris folded the dishrag back up. She looked me in the eyes like she was really trying to look inside. Probably assessing whether I was on some nerfarious mission to tickle them or rearrange their furniture or something, which is a good assessment to attempt on strangers inside your home. "I'll tell you what," Iris said, adding a warm smile. "You and I can chat some other time. You can return the shirt, and maybe by then I'll feel more like opening up. We'll talk about boys and breakups and all that." Then she led me toward the door, her hand touching my shoulder briefly to lead me out of the kitchen. "Off the record."

On Being Super Annoying and Happy

By Lu Charles
September 27

Readers, I have to confess something. This weekend, I made out at Starbucks. Excessively, and unapologetically. I was responsible for propagating the image the world has of the uncontrollable, sex-crazed, inconsiderate teen. And it felt great.

We've all been on the witnessing side of this interaction, and it doesn't feel great. That gross, wet lip smacking, the cringe-inducing prolonged eye contact, the not-at-all-inconspicuous butt grabs. It's uncomfortable for everyone but the people involved in the make-out, oblivious to anything but their little world of two.

For those who haven't shamelessly made out in a public place, I'd like to present a case on its behalf.

Imagine, if you will, a seventeen-year-old girl who's been conditioned by art and media to crave companionship, and who's been coaxed by her hormones and/or society to crave touch. Imagine (or perhaps I should say, recall) the lonely days and nights without companionship or touch. She spends her time thinking about love and why so many are so obsessed with it, to the point where she actually gets paid to do the pondering (how meta).

Then comes a boy. Sweet brown skin, a commandingly sexy stage presence when he's in school plays, the ability to make every moment feel special. He laughs at the girl's jokes and reaches for her hand often, every now and then bringing their clasped hands to his mouth and kissing her fingers, telling her he's lucky he has her in his life. Kisses the way poetry describes kissing.

Now the girl and the boy are at a coffee shop, and they peck each other on the lips just to remind each other that this lovely thing exists in their lives. And it's not like the outside world just falls away. They don't forget about the people in the coffee shop trying to work on their computers or read their books or grumble to each other about their days. They just see each other more than anything else. The pecks escalate.

Should we fault the couple that is so enamored with each other? Why not dive into the joy? The world isn't exactly considerate of its behavior toward them, it does nothing to avoid annoying teens, and in fact annoys them quite often. So why not make out at the Starbucks? Why not take on the sneers and frowns the world so often casts in their direction anyway? They're momentarily protected by this force field of lips and tongues and flesh. What looks like PDA feels like refuge.

So, yes, for those who have been wondering in the comments, I am still in this wacky world of experiencing a relationship rather than philosophizing about them. It's going well, I think, even if I have become a little more annoying. I'm in a safe haven of smooching, and your dirty looks will not bring me down.

7

CARTOONISHLY THWARTED

"Pete, save me."

Someone else would have had the decency to at least offer a weary sigh before continuing on. Pete didn't so much as inhale semiheavily into the phone. "You don't need saving. You've still got a good idea for a column. It just won't be about those two."

"Will you let me mope for a second?"

"No. It even sounds like this Iris girl is interested in being your friend. You have nothing to mope about."

I groaned, really doubling down on my effort just to show Pete how normal people were supposed to act. "I'm going down into the subway. I'll meet you at The Strand in twenty minutes? Three hours? I don't know how long it takes to get back from the Upper West Side."

"Okay." Pete hung up, and I reentered the sweaty underworld of New York. Good, the underworld. A fitting place for me and my doomed writing career and love life. Of course Iris and Cal hadn't broken up. They were hip romantics with a true understanding of love. It was only me who sucked at these things, me who didn't deserve the entirely unlikely but still wholly possible scenario of love extending beyond high school and into college.

It was pretty empty at the station, just one white dude with a backpack and headphones on. Great idea, White Dude in His Twenties. I pulled my headphones out of my bag and put on a thought-suppressing podcast.

About thirty-five minutes later I was standing in front of Pete by the biographies.

"Dude, who reads biographies?"

"No book shaming," he murmured. "People are interesting. There's some comfort in knowing that lives continue on as stories."

I rolled my eyes and picked up an entirely too-heavy tome of President Martin Van Buren. Although I guess if a book were written about my life, I'd be okay with it leaning heavy. "Anyway. You rudely interrupted my attempt to bitch about my article going to hell."

"You have an article. Just find someone else."

"Like who? I don't know anyone else in this situation."

"Look within yourself."

"I don't know the answer. Just tell me."

"I was talking about you and Leo."

I narrowed my eyes at him. "I can't wait to read the part in your biography where you got murdered in The Strand by your best friend."

Pete thumbed through the book he was reading. I nudged him to lift the cover so I could see it, but also to make sure he wouldn't get too engrossed. He eyed me over the brim. "Have you met Diane and Rachel? They're Colleen's friends, dating and just graduated. I could put you in touch."

I reshelved the Van Buren biography and ran my fingers along the book spines in front of me. It's such a cliché thing to do, but I can never resist it. "But I want to write about Cal and Iris."

"They said no. You can either complain about not having a subject, or you can complain about having one. You can't do both."

"Watch me!" I yelled, maybe a little too loudly. A few customers gave me a mean look. They had a definitive tourist vibe to them and I felt like I was giving them the authentic New York experience of rudeness or whatever, so I didn't apologize.

"For the record," Pete said, putting his book down, "I think it'd be really good for you to interview Leo. That is, if I believed he'd take the time to show up for an interview. Which he wouldn't. Because he's a selfish prick."

"There is no record, so your comment has disappeared into the ether," I mumbled. We wandered around the aisles a while longer, the way we usually did, absentmindedly looking at covers and reading back cover copy, occasionally diving into the first few pages of a novel. The store wasn't too busy, so we hung out with Starla at the registers and played one of our people-watching games: How Hard Would It Be to Get That Person to Murder You? Starla was really good at that game, always able to come up with a scenario in which even the most mild-mannered customers might murder her. Maybe it was because an extra decade or so on the planet had the tendency to lessen your faith in people, or maybe because she'd read more spy novels than all suburban middle-aged dads combined.

I also tried eavesdropping on people every chance I got, but didn't get anything too interesting. That's usually the case with eavesdropping. You get the minutiae of everyday life without the context, the lulls without any highlights. I could have eavesdropped for years without coming across another couple like Cal and Iris.

In the lulls, my thoughts went to Leo. Pete had called him a selfish prick, but that was just Pete taking my side, being protective. Leo had never once been selfish in our relationship. It was a new side to him that the breakup had dug up, and even in my stewing, I felt that it wasn't the real Leo.

Pete had always liked Leo while we were dating. He'd even come with me to Leo's plays at school and joined me when the cast and crew went out for burgers, so that I wouldn't be the only quiet nontheater person. I think they'd gone to watch a movie once without me, maybe?

After about an hour or so at the bookstore, my mom called me and told me dinner was almost ready so I should get my ass over to help her grate three pounds of parmesan cheese or something like that. I wasn't really listening. Before I left, I looked at Pete. "Alright, fine."

"Fine, what?"

"Fine, give me the info for Colleen's friends."

"Wise decision," he said, unable to contain a smirk.

"Your mom's a wise decision," I said, gathering my bag and heading out the door. "I have to write a draft by Monday, so can you put them in touch with me tonight?"

He and Starla both chuckled. "See you tomorrow," Pete called out.

I spent the next day mired in abject boredom on my couch, still unable to write. The one exciting thing of note was that Pete got me in touch with his sister Colleen's friends, and they'd agreed to meet up with me after Pete's shift was over. I thought a lot about Iris and Cal, but I was itchy to get to writing, and Pete was right. It was better to move on and actually write something than get bogged down with one couple.

I was still going to get to dive into the topic, pry into someone's life, pick this thing apart and try to discover if it was knowable, if I could understand where Leo and I failed and how. Sure, I was still thinking about Leo nonstop, and I couldn't exactly shake off my interest in Cal and Iris, but at least there were other things going on in my mind. At least I'd be writing.

I'd already told my mom that I had a dinner meeting for the magazine, so at around seven I left home and walked to the theater to meet up with Pete since he'd met Diane and Rachel before and could make things marginally less awkward. We were going to Mamoun's, which had this incredible hot sauce I just had to slather on everything. Unfortunately, this turned me into a sweating, sniffling mess that would surely cancel out any of Pete's efforts to make me seem normal.

They were already waiting for us when we got there, having claimed a table on the tiny patio overlooking St. Marks. They were both black and wore glasses, though Rachel's were thick-framed and square while Diane's were the little circular John Lennon kind. I liked them right away, if only for their choice of table. It wasn't super muggy out, and when the weather is nice in New York, choosing to sit inside is a crime of unparalleled moral depravity. Kind of.

Pete made the introductions, and then he and Diane went to put our order in at the counter. Rachel and I stayed outside, where there was plenty of noise coming from the street— groups of college students deciding where they should eat, a promoter at the nearby comedy club chatting loudly with the bouncer, faint thumping music from one of the bars.

"Have you ever been here before?" Rachel asked.

"Yeah, all the time," I said. "I work nearby, so sometimes I come here for lunch. Also, I've been trying to sneak into the kitchen for about three years in order to steal their hot sauce recipe, but I always get cartoonishly thwarted."

"'Cartoonishly' the way Wile E. Coyote would get thwarted, or like the villain in an episode of Scooby-Doo? There's an important distinction."

"Oh, definitely on the Wile E. Coyote side. Kind of Wile E. meets Tom from *Tom and Jerry*. There's always a stick of dynamite involved."

Rachel laughed, playing with her braided hair. "What would you do with the recipe if you got it? Make millions?"

I pretended to think about it for a while. "Make a swimming pool full of it. I'm not in it for the money, just the love of the sauce. I want to be surrounded by it at all times."

"Oof, I'm not about that. Hot sauce is meant for mouths, absolutely nowhere else."

"Good point," I said, relaxing. You find someone you can joke with right away, it's funny how quickly other anxieties just seem to disappear. Pete and Diane came out then, holding a stack of napkins and a bottle each of hot sauce and tahini.

We ate first, Pete doing most of the talking to catch up with Diane and Rachel. When we finished eating, the table was overrun with crumpled, sweat-and-hot-sauce-stained napkins. "Oh my God, it hurts so good," I said. I tilted my water glass to get an ice cube to ease the heat.

"You weren't kidding about your love for that sauce," Rachel said.

"It's not a healthy relationship, but I can't seem to leave it."

Diane pushed herself away from the table, hand on her stomach. "So, what'd you want to talk to us about? Pete said it's some kind of writing thing, but he didn't really give us details."

I crunched through the ice cube, swirling the bits around my mouth to calm my tingling taste buds. It would have been wise to go easy on the sauce, maybe, but when I'm at Mamoun's wisdom is not my forte. I filled Rachel and Diane in on the magazine and what kind of stuff I liked to write, and then I told them my idea for the new series. I didn't want to bring up Cal and Iris or my breakup, but Pete, as usual, had zero tact.

"Lu here is heartbroken and looking for answers," he said, giving me a condescending arm tap.

"That's not why I'm doing this."

He rolled his eyes. "Sure, the parallels are totally unrelated."

I threw a napkin at him, which he calmly caught and placed back on the table. "Well, what do you wanna know from us?" Diane asked. "Shoot."

I took in a deep breath and opened up my notebook. "How long have you guys been dating?"

Our interview went on for about an hour. Pete ended up leaving us alone, and we felt bad hogging a table at Mamoun's so we just started walking and ended up at Washington Square Park.

Diane and Rachel were really cool and obviously in love. They'd struggled with what to do in the fall when they went to separate schools upstate, whether or not it was silly to believe they could stay together beyond high school. All the same things Leo and I had talked about. But after weeks of it, they decided there were many reasons to stay together.

They ticked off all the boxes that I would have needed for a column. Profiling them would have been exactly what I needed, an exploration of how love can overcome obstacles.

They were in no way less than Cal and Iris. They were inherently interesting, so in love that it made me scroll through pictures of myself with Leo on social media later that night, torturing myself just for the slight pleasure that reliving the love could provide.

But there was something that just wasn't clicking for me. No matter how many details I wrote down, the little lines of dialogue that were better than eavesdropping because they weren't stolen away but given with full permission, nothing sparked. When I said goodbye to Diane and Rachel and went back home, I looked at my notebook and felt completely underwhelmed. I even tried to push through and force myself to write an article. Two sentences is what I managed to type out, and one of those was: **I don't know what to write someone help me.**

I spent the whole night in front of my computer, my notebook splayed open in front of me, begging the words to come, begging my heart to open itself up and transcribe itself, to capture life in the beautiful way only words can. Saturday turned to Sunday. Nothing came.

8
AS BASIC AS EATING

Pete and I were stationed at the box office the next day and I was trying to write in my notebook in between customers. "This is great. I work so much better under pressure."

"Totally," Pete said, tapping at the keyboard. "The Diane and Rachel column coming along?"

"No, couldn't get a single word out. But I have a backup plan!"

"Oh yeah? Who's that?"

"This supersweet couple from Montauk. Joel and Clementine. They tried to erase each other from their memories but their love is too strong and they've just found themselves back in each other's arms."

"That's the plot for *Eternal Sunshine of the Spotless Mind*."

"Are you saying that I'm not allowed to interview fictional characters?" I scoffed. "Don't be such a patriarchal tool, trying to control my behavior. I thought you were better than that."

Pete leaned back in his slightly comfortable office chair, brushing the hair away from his eyes. The afternoon sun shone in the ticket booth, reflecting off a handful of shiny surfaces. We each had a large soda next to us, beads of condensation dripping down the sides. I don't actually like soda, but it was free at work and the act of sipping on something sweet made work at least momentarily easier. "I'm waiting on you to tell me about a backup plan."

"My neighbors, Elizabeth and Mr. Darcy."

"Pride and Prejudice."

"Okay, fine, real couple now. They had a really amazing time in Paris together, but violent circumstances led them to split up despite their very strong feelings for each other. Years later, they ran into each other at Rick's Café in Morocco and he helped save her from—"

Pete interrupted with a sigh, shifting in his chair so that it squeaked as he moved. "Are you done?"

I slammed my forehead down on my depressingly empty notebook. "Not even close."

Behind us, the door to the rest of the theater opened. I couldn't quite muster the energy to lift my head up, so I was hoping it wasn't our manager Brad. "Lu, you can sit up straight, or I can put you on cleanup crew. Which do you want?"

"I want a muse, Brad."

Brad looked over at Pete. "What's she talking about?"

"Probably not worth explaining," Pete said, then turned his attention to some customers.

"Have you ever been in love, Brad?" I said at the same time, turning to look at him. He was holding one of his beloved clipboards, wearing a short-sleeve mustard-yellow button-down with a brown tie. Brad looked like he'd be really at home working at an office in Kansas, but he was alright. He wasn't a dick, and only occasionally made dad jokes that made me want to quit my job in a rage.

"Um."

"What about in high school? Did you date anyone in high school? What happened when you graduated and you had to decide what to do? Did you ever step onto that particular romantic minefield, and if so, how did you survive it?"

Brad stared blankly at me for a moment and then sat down at the computer on my left. He started scribbling down something on his clipboard. Sure that he was going to ignore my tirade, I opened up my notebook, waited for my musings on love to come pouring out of me the way they had been for the last year at *Misnomer*. "I married my high school girlfriend," Brad said.

Now I sat up straight. "You did? What happened when you went to college? Did you guys have, like, a tumultuous on-again, off-again thing throughout the four years, your love for each other tenuously surviving distance and the changes of early adulthood? Would you wake up in the middle of the night terrified that your love would pull so taut that it would snap, sending you each hurtling in opposite directions?"

A silence took hold of the box office. I'm not quite sure why. The poignancy of my soliloquy, probably. Pete was looking over at me, biting his lip thoughtfully. Brad had stopped scribbling. There was even a customer at my window, frozen by how deep I'd delved into the fragile condition of teenage love.

"I didn't go to college," Brad said, shattering the silence. He calmly resumed his vaguely managerial duties. "My wife takes night classes, and sometimes we fight about money and how many kids we want to have, but other than that our love has not been 'pulled so taut it could snap.'" He used air quotes for the last part, then pointed at my window. "You have a customer."

As the day progressed, Pete and I tried to think of anyone

we knew from our respective schools who I could write about, with healthy interludes of Pete suggesting I write about myself, and then me trying my hardest to shoot knives at him with my eyeballs. We scoured our phone contacts and social media friends, asked all of our coworkers. We got a lot of looks, but no stories. I found myself going back to Iris's Facebook, doing a wee bit of stalking, maybe even hoping that she'd suddenly change her mind and message me. I thought about it some more and would love the attention, as well as the chance to be portrayed in your wonderful prose and unique insight!

It was almost six o'clock and I still had nothing. Hafsah would no doubt check her email first thing in the morning, and if she didn't see anything from me I'm sure she'd be unapologetic and ruthless and fire my ass before I'd even woken up.

It's hard to describe what having prolonged writer's block feels like. Like missing a part of yourself, I guess. But not really. It's like you've suddenly forgotten how to do something as basic as eating. Long after mom had said good-night and my apartment had fallen quiet, long after even the city itself seemed to have gone silent, I sat in the dark, sweating despite the open window, bathed in the glow of my computer screen, time ticking away. I had nothing.

I rested my fingers on the keys, as if I could fool myself into repeating the motions I'd successfully performed in the past. Then I clicked back to Tumblr, scrolled through my feed. Usually that helped stimulate my brain; reading through other people's posts, the pictures they chose to share, those little glimpses of personality visible online. It was almost like eavesdropping. Part of me thought that maybe I could find someone posting about their relationship in a way that would spark my creative juices. For a while I searched through hashtags that I thought could lead me to pertinent posts: #relationshiptroubles, #precollegiatebreakups #inarelationshipwhichrecentlysurvivedorwasdestroyedbythe-prospectofeachpersongoingtocollegeinadifferentplaceand-wethoughtwecoulddoitbutturnsoutwearentevengonnatry.

But I was kidding myself. It was almost midnight, and even if I found someone interesting, the chances of them accepting an interview and responding to my questions in time were not great, and that wasn't even accounting for the time it would take me to write a full column. Then I stumbled onto Leo's blog. I still hadn't found the courage to unfollow him, and I got stuck scrolling through his stupid thoughts and selfies. Sweat made my tank top cling to my lower back, and that simultaneously gross and annoying sensation was exactly what it felt like to read Leo's blog.

He hadn't posted much recently, just a few vague entries that I'd already pored over dozens of times, trying to suss out just how hurt he was post-breakup. Which meant that almost immediately I was seeing pictures of us still together. My face buried in the crook of his perfect neck, his eyes looking straight at the camera, a smile to them, like he knew the hair falling across his face was absurdly sexy. The caption read: **The cover to our future R & B album.**

Just to further torture myself, I found the post from late September where he'd reblogged my *Misnomer* column and written: **Me. She's writing about making out with me. I'm dating a talented beast of a writer.**

For some reason, I thought of a moment that occurred a few months ago. It was after winter break, and my latest column had just gone up. We were sitting in homeroom, which was the place where Leo, with one seemingly innocuous shoulder-tap, had initially confessed to reading my column. Our friendship had blossomed because we talked about my column, talked about love all the time, the subject's intimacy naturally bringing us closer together. After we started dating, I asked Leo if I could keep writing about us, and his eyes had lit up. "Lu, that's all I've ever wanted."

But on that particular day, Leo had come into homeroom, sat down next to me, offering a school-chaste kiss on the cheek like he usually did, and never brought up my column. After months of it never slipping his mind, months of compliments and intimate, funny conversations—nothing. I'd felt bad that day, a queasy feeling in my stomach like something had changed between us without my knowing why. Then he'd been sweet to me in one way or another after school, and I hadn't brought it up ever, letting go of this lovely little thing we used to do without questioning why.

When I'd made myself feel sufficiently awful, I finally closed out of Tumblr.

I was screwed. I had nothing. My eyelids were starting to sag with sleep. I bit down on my forearm and yelled into my own skin, trying to unleash all my frustrations while not waking up my mom. Then, accepting my fate, I opened up an email to Hafsah. While I was trying to decide on a strategy (Confident yet humble request for more time? Or pity-inducing groveling to not get fired?), my phone buzzed on the nightstand. I stood from my desk to go check on it, figuring it was Pete asking how the writing was going. Getting up felt good, bringing fresh air to the sweaty creases of skin.

It wasn't Pete though. It was Iris. She'd messaged me on Facebook asking if I wanted to meet up some time that week and return her shirt. She'd also sent me a friend request.

Which, what else, led me down a rabbit hole of trying to find out everything about her and Cal.

I still couldn't see Cal's profile, but I could now see every time he'd posted on her wall, I could see their shared pictures, all the times they'd been tagged at the same location. It seemed like Cal had a job at a coffee shop near Washington Square Park, which Iris went to visit all the time, sneaking pictures of Cal in his apron and posting the photos to Facebook. Her captions, which was where so many relationships become unbearable to the outside world, managed to avoid being of the suck-it-I'm-in-love variety, which only made me want to keep diving into their relationship. For example: Cal adorably mock-scowling behind the counter, his glasses slightly crooked. **Look at this ugly hipster in his little apron.**

Spare the judgments, but I went deep into their online lives that night. I just couldn't stop. It was like looking at the alternate-reality version of me and Leo. Iris had way better style than me, and both Leo and I were Pinoy and had darker skin, but other than that, we were like the same people. Oh, and the in-a-relationship bit too. Also, Cal wore glasses.

Before I knew it, it was 3:00 a.m. and I hadn't even emailed Hafsah yet. The time that I could have used to at least force a crappy article about myself and Leo had withered away. I threw my phone across the room onto my bed, chastising it for making me fall into the wormhole that was Cal and Iris's relationship.

I got up to get a glass of cold water and clear my mind for a bit, but Iris and Cal followed me to the kitchen, whispering sweet nothings to each other. I stood by the sad excuse for an air conditioner and put my forehead against the living room window, looking out at the quiet, tiny portion of the city visible from my apartment. I love New York at night, the thought of so many people simultaneously asleep. One of the greatest cities on earth so calm that you can walk in the middle of the street and nothing will hit you but the glow of a streetlight. I pictured Iris and Cal walking down my street hand in hand, laughing into each other's necks. A memory of me and Leo doing just that popped up too. How he would kiss my forehead as we walked, reach for my hand, hold me close.

Back at my desk, one leg curled beneath me, my eyes continuously flitted toward the corner of my computer screen, mockingly displaying the time. I clicked over to my disgracefully empty Word document and typed in a title. **On (Not) Breaking Up the Summer before College.**

"This is fine," I said to myself. "I'll just write a general intro to the topic and ask people to write in with their stories. A profile can wait until later. I'll just type something up and I'll send it to Hafsah." I cracked my fingers, set them back in the subtle, familiar grooves they'd formed in my keyboard after all my writing. Because I know how to write. I totally do it all the time. "Hafsah will be cool with it. She won't tell me that this isn't the article I pitched her, or that I'm being lazy, or that I will never write for *Misnomer* again."

My fingers wouldn't strike the keys at all. I found myself looking back over my shoulder to my bed, craving to have my phone back in my hands, wanting to delve even deeper into Iris's and Cal's lives. "No," I said again, this time actually out loud, forcing myself to focus. It didn't have to be good, just a first draft, something that I could present to Hafsah.

The seconds ticked by loudly, as if there was a grandfather clock nearby. Which made no sense because there wasn't any sort of clock in my room or my apartment or probably even in my building. I feel like I would have known earlier if there was a grandfather clock in my building.

"Ahhhh," I whisper-yelled, smacking my hands up and down on my laptop because they refused to produce words. Another over-the-shoulder glance at my bed, the comforter wrinkled from my few hours splayed on it, diving into an internet hole. My phone had landed right in the middle of the bed, faceup, the screen reflecting the glow from my computer in a way that made it look like I had a notification. Maybe another one from Iris? Maybe she'd gotten up in the middle of the night, awakened by a premonition that I was suffering. Maybe she'd been stirred by a cosmic sense that she could commit a good deed, with minimal effort.

I shut my computer and slid into bed, grabbing my phone as I slipped between the sheets. They were still warm from my wasted hours curled up in bed, so I kicked them away, muttering a complaint about the lingering heat. Sleep was so desperate to take hold of me, I could feel it coaxing my muscles into inactivity, begging my brain to let it take over. I unlocked my phone anyway, stepping sure-footed back into the wormhole.

9

SOAK UP EVERY OUNCE

I woke up to the sound of my mom knocking on my door. "Lucinda! I'm not letting you leave for work before you have breakfast. Wake up."

I moaned in response, because it was the only verbalization my brain could handle at the moment. My hand automatically felt around for my phone, which I found tucked under my pillow, battery nearly drained. "Lu! Wake up or I'll call your boss and tell him the reason you're late is that you still get treated like a petulant child who won't eat her breakfast. Wouldn't that be embarrassing?"

"I'm not hungry," I said, clearly not loudly enough because she kept banging on the door. I unlocked my phone and suddenly all of last night came rushing back to me, as if I'd been drunk or something. The failure to email Hafsah, the borderline obsessive perusal of Iris's Facebook. Then I saw that I'd responded to Iris's message. I sent it out at 3:05 a.m., which would either make Iris think I was way cooler than I really am, or give her the exact right idea of what I was like. At least the message itself wasn't too ridiculous. Sure thang!

I get off work at five every day this week. Does tomorrow (er, today, I guess? Monday) work for you?

Iris had responded about an hour ago, blissfully ignoring my use of "thang." Sure! But can't come too far downtown. Columbus Circle at 6 okay with you?

My lips spread into a smile, right as my mom pushed the door open. She was wearing her hair in a ponytail, and she had a T-shirt on that looked suspiciously like mine. We're basically the exact same size, and even though I wouldn't advertise it too often, she has a pretty spot-on sense of style. Our clothes ended up in each other's closets all the time. She crossed her arms and raised her eyebrows at me.

"Mom, I'm not going to starve to death if I skip one meal."

"CPS disagrees." She stood in the doorway, one hand on her hip in that way that meant she wasn't going to cave. Although she never really caves, so the hand-on–the-hip thing wasn't necessary at all to drive home the point.

"Look at you, you're wide-awake. Might as well eat something. Come on, I made waffles."

"I'll be right out."

"I don't believe you."

"Go bug Jase for a while."

"Don't be rude, I'm your mother and I get to bug any one of my children that I want. Plus, I don't need to bug Jase, he eats all the food out of the fridge and then some." She gave me a wide-eyed look, as if she'd really proved some point. "Get up, or I'm grabbing my phone and putting pictures of you like this up on Facebook. I know how to do that now."

"Mom..."

"And, Lu, you're really sweaty. That picture would get so many yeses."

"They're called 'likes,'" I said, throwing my legs over the

edge of the bed and sitting up. Waking up was best done in stages. Mom hung around until I stood up. I went to the bathroom we all share and stared in the mirror for a while, not looking at my own reflection or anything, just staring at a spot and waiting for my brain to wake up.

After a few minutes, I went to the living room and sat on the couch eating waffles with Jase, who was shoving them into his mouth two at a time, swallowing like an alligator does, just one or two seconds of chewing before he tilted his head back and let them slide down his throat.

I watched him play video games, trying and failing to follow the action on the screen. I expected to get bored with watching, like I usually do after about six seconds, but instead I noticed how other voices were coming through the TV, other kids talking into headsets in faraway places like Seoul and Long Island. They were all yelling at each other, trading insults, occasionally cracking those dumb thirteen-year-old-boy jokes that no one else in the world thinks are funny. But Jase did, and his laughter made it possible for me to avoid checking my email for a bit. I didn't want to see Hafsah's name in my inbox.

"Dad called," Jase said, after a while. "He's back from London, so he wants us to come over this weekend."

"'Kay. We'll go Friday when I get off work." God, Friday. By then I might be on my way to losing my scholarship. How the hell would I explain that to my parents?

Maybe I could cash in on divorce fallout? I'd never really lashed out, since my parents splitting up had not been traumatic. Or maybe it had. I wasn't a psychiatrist, who was I to exculpate my broken home as a reason for my struggles with love, and therefore my writer's block, and ultimately my loss of scholarship. None of this was my fault.

"Mom," I said, looking back over the couch at her sitting at the kitchen table, reading a newspaper. "Not bringing this up for any reason in particular, but is there a statute of limitations on how long I can use a traumatic childhood event as an excuse for doing something...um...you wouldn't approve of?"

"Lu, what did you do?" she asked, not looking up from the newspaper.

"Nice try, but I'm not going to incriminate myself. I just want to establish a standard, in case in some hypothetical future I need to use it in my defense."

"Then the statute of limitations is thirty-six seconds." She flipped the page and eyed me for a moment. "What traumatic childhood event are you talking about?"

Now's your chance, I thought to myself. Claim the divorce was the root cause of everything. The fact that my parents had never established a familial culture of speaking about the hardships of love, and had not provided an example of love upon which I could model my relationships, leading to my loss of scholarship and collegiate career.

"Lu, that look you're getting is no good. It means you're scheming."

"I'm not scheming. I'm rationalizing future scheming."

Mom turned the page again with dramatic flair. "Eat your waffles, Lulu Bear."

I looked at the time, wondering if maybe I could still send Hafsah an article by the end of the day. But the hours ticked away without inspiration striking.

Twenty minutes before I clocked out, Pete asked me if I wanted to go watch a movie, since we hadn't taken advantage of our employee benefits in a while.

"Um," I said, because admitting that I had done exactly

as he'd predicted and become obsessed with Iris and Cal was hard. "I actually have plans."

"Your body language tells me I'm not going to like it if you elaborate."

"I'm meeting up with Iris."

Pete tightened his lips and nodded slowly. Then he reached over and grabbed the closest thing to him, which was a stack of napkins someone had left at the counter by my register. He picked them up, examined them, looked around the empty lobby, then tossed them at my chest. "Why?"

"Dude, what the hell?" I leaned down to pick up the scattered napkins.

"You know why I did that."

"Your ability to pick up on social cues is really diminishing. Does 'what the hell' not enter into your lexicon?" He put his hands on the glass and lowered his head, shaking it from side to side. "Get your greasy fingers off the counter," I added. "I just cleaned that. You know how Brad gets about smudges."

Pete pinched the bridge of his nose, which is totally not a thing a normal teenager does, further proving my whole notion that Pete is some wise, old uncle type. Sans facial hair. "Look. I get what's going on. But I'm worried you don't."

"What is the big deal?" I slammed the napkins I'd picked up down in front of him. "I'm giving her back a shirt she lent me. And sure, I'm still hanging on to the hope that I can write about her and Bench Boy. I don't see what's wrong with that. My deadline was today and I couldn't write anything about Diane and Rachel. If Iris changes her mind, I might be able to ask Hafsah for an extension."

"You don't understand how your fixation on this couple is a misguided hope that your relationship with Leo can be salvaged. You don't get that you're just avoiding writing or even thinking about your own broken heart. Glad to be proven right." He stood up straight as Brad walked by, and pretended to wipe the counter he'd dirtied. Brad eyed us like he suspected we weren't fully doing our jobs, then continued to go check on… I don't actually know all of Brad's duties, to be honest. Pete smiled, which is his secret weapon. It's totally disarming. My mom once offered him food and he said no with a smile and she was totally cool with it. It was bizarre.

"I'm gonna go clock out," I said to Pete. "I'll see you tomorrow."

"I wish you a very fulfilling T-shirt returning interview," Pete said.

Since I had an hour to kill, I walked uptown to Columbus Circle. I texted Jase to make sure he was still alive in the non-virtual world, then texted my mom that I'd be home late, which turned into a whole thing about how I had to learn to be more appreciative of my family and start making an effort to love her and never grow up, or something along those lines.

When I got to Columbus Circle, I looked around for a while, somewhat tired from the walk, but excited about the meeting. I was even hoping I was early so I could get some eavesdropping in before Iris showed up. It wasn't a part of the city I went to very often, but the crowd was pretty great. Tourists heading to Central Park, the upper edges of the Midtown office crowd, a group of dudes practicing their juggling routines right by a group of protesters and then the people protesting the protesters. It was prime eavesdropping territory.

But Iris was already there, sitting at the steps of the fountain. She was wearing another sundress, that same bright red pinup-girl lipstick she had on the first time I saw her at The Strand. I walked over to her, ready to cheerfully greet her when I realized she was crying. Bawling, almost. To the point where several people were doing double takes as they walked by. A black woman in a pantsuit stopped for a moment, maybe considering saying something.

It was really tempting to just turn around and escape the whole scene. I could remember the looks people gave me the night Leo dumped me, when I was sitting on the curb in front of that Vietnamese restaurant. The pity and confusion, the occasional smirk and amusement. Yes, sometimes people mired in sorrow and misery want to receive compassion and care. But sometimes public sorrow is still sorrow you don't want anyone intruding in on.

I thought about just going to the park for a while, people watching, finding shade beneath a tree and reading. I could text Pete to come join me. He was leaving for school in Rhode Island soon, and it'd be nice to squeeze as much enjoyment out of our remaining time together before that happened. Then I shifted and felt the crumple of napkins in my pocket. I'd meant to throw them out at work. The black woman in the pantsuit saw me pull the napkins out of my pocket and she gave me a little head nod, like she was telling me to do the right thing. The universe and its damn signals.

"Hey, you okay?" I asked, approaching with the napkins out. "Sorry, that was a stupid question."

Iris looked up at me, squinting in the sun, or maybe at my stupidity. Smeared mascara streaked down her cheeks. It seemed to take her a moment to place me. Then she cracked a smile through her tears and grabbed the napkins. "Sorry I'm…" She gestured at her face.

"Oh no, totally okay. Fine. People cry. I cry all the time." I sat next to her, wondering whether she wanted a hand on her shoulder or me to go away or, like, a cup of tea or something. We sat quietly for a while, Iris dabbing at her cheeks with my wadded-up movie napkins while I fiddled with her T-shirt in my bag.

"I'm sorry in advance if I talk about the weather," I said.

Iris chuckled. "What?"

"It's just that I'm one of those people that starts making comments about the weather when they feel a little awkward. Which I do right now. Not because of you crying, necessarily. It's not you at all. It's more my inability to handle social situations far outside my normal comfort level. Which this kind of is. So if I start talking about how it's as sweaty as a lower back after walking around with a backpack on all day, that's why." I snapped my fingers a couple of times and bit my lip. "Damn it, I did it. I warned you."

Iris laughed. "Thanks."

"Thanks? For the rant?"

"For trying to make me feel better. I've been doing such a good job holding it in all day. Then I sat here and saw some stupid guy wearing a T-shirt with the California flag on it and I just..." She crumpled a tear-soaked napkin in her fist and scrunched her mouth to the side. "Lost it."

I looked across the street toward the park. Guys in pedicabs were offering rides to the severely disinterested sunset picnic crowd. A group of middle-schoolers stood in a circle, kicking a soccer ball back and forth at each other. On the other side of the circle, people streamed in and out of the office buildings, a whole swarm of them entering the Whole Foods. "Do you want to talk about it?" I fiddled with my bag's cloth strap, running my fingernail across the little bumps. "Off the record?"

Iris seemed to consider it for a while. The tears had stopped flowing, and she'd rubbed away all the makeup streaks. Fully composed, she scooted back so she could lean against the step behind us. "I'm okay. It's just that… Well, Cal and I are…" She took a deep breath. "We're gonna split up."

I put on what I believed was an appropriately sympathetic face, angling my eyebrows just right. The sun was reflecting off the Columbus Circle shopping mall, making us both squint. "Wait. Did you just say 'gonna'? As in, future tense?"

Iris sighed, and then she ran her hand through her hair and fluffed it out, flipping her curls over to her other shoulder. "It's weird and complicated. But yeah, future tense."

"I know I'm the one being the supportive listener here, and I'm totally open to letting you decide whatever you want to talk about and nothing more than that, but I'm gonna really need you to elaborate on that."

Cal had texted Iris the day after their breakup, saying he wanted to meet up and talk. Unlike some people, Iris had agreed *and* shown up, willing to hear out the person she still loved.

"Then he asked me what day it was, and what day I was planning on leaving for California. Both of which he knew the answer to, which tipped me off that he was thinking something weird. He gets these out-there ideas and you can just tell by looking at him that his mind is whirring."

"I love it and hate it when they do that. The whole world is a possibility when they get that look, the most romantic sentiment you can imagine is on the tip of their tongues, but also your worst nightmare."

"Exactly!" Iris said. She laughed and wiped at the corner of her eye. "I thought he was just going to rehash the argument we'd had during our breakup about long distance not being all that bad."

I nodded, and was about to say how I knew all about that

argument, but managed to shut my idiot mouth up. "So, what did he say?"

"He said that we had eight weeks before I left, and why the hell would we waste those being heartbroken?" Iris crumpled the napkin I'd given her, then tossed it in her lap, shaking her head. "Then he went on this superlong speech about how I was right, how there was a point in time when we thought we were in the greatest romance of our lives, but we were teenagers fooling ourselves. That love is more complicated than how it feels at first." Iris stopped as some taxis got into a honking match with each other. Someone on the street yelled at them to shut up and drive. "Then that smart-ass shrugged his shoulders and said our love always had an expiration date, whether it was the end of high school, our death, or something in between. But he believed the time hadn't arrived yet."

Iris grabbed a new napkin from the stack in my hand, twisting it into a rope. That little piece of paper was so tightly wound I'm sure it could have supported something of real heft. Like two people drifting apart from each other. "So much for me not feeling comfortable opening up, right?"

I laughed. "So, did he have, like, a pitch, or what?"

"He said we should wait. That we could still break up, but on August 4 when I go to California. He said we should do exactly what every song and book and movie relentlessly tells us to—soak up every ounce of love that we still have between us. He said we shouldn't take what we have for granted, at least while we can."

"Damn. So you said yes." Iris was teasing me with this stuff. A column could have written itself in the time it took for her to tell me this story. Writing about love wasn't the only way my words come pouring out of me. But there are certain topics that I don't *choose* whether I'm going to write about them or not. This was one of them, and not writing about Iris and Cal was starting to hurt me, at least spiritually.

"Of course I said yes." Iris sighed. "I hadn't been happy about breaking up, it was just a mature move I was trying to make. My love for Cal hadn't gone anywhere, it was still sitting right there alongside the heartache." Another burst of car honks, which I guess were there with us the whole time and I just noticed them occasionally. The air had cooled ever so slightly, so that sitting outside with Iris felt surprisingly comfortable. "I hadn't even had time to really process the heartache, you know. And here he was spouting poetry at me and the promise that I could have more joy, which is what I really wanted. The worst part is that now I can really feel it coming. Now I know it's there waiting for me."

She looked at me briefly, as if I was the embodiment of that future heartache.

"Yeah," I said. "It does that."

10
BACK TO COLUMBUS CIRCLE

It was not yet twilight, but that Manhattan-specific presunset brought on by the shadows of buildings, that canopy of steel and glass. Iris adjusted herself, crossing her legs in front of her. I mimicked her position, my heart quietly pounding with excitement. Glancing inside my bag, I noticed my notebook resting on top of Iris's shirt. God, I wanted to pull it out and write down all that she was telling me. My thoughts were swirling with questions and ruminations, *words*, those magnificent bastards. They were on the verge of returning, I could feel it.

"Sorry about talking for so long," Iris said. "You didn't sign up to be my therapist. I shouldn't have unloaded on you like that."

"It's okay, I love hearing about other people's lives. Remember?"

Iris gave me a tight-lipped smile, then looked away.

Subtle, Lu.

We both looked around us at the New Yorkers continuing

on with their lives. Suits, briefcases, retail polo shirts, bike messengers with their tattoo-and-gauged-earring uniforms, the worn clothes of homeless people, the glamour of the rich, the more appealing glamour of those who fashioned stylish outfits from less, women in hijabs, tourists in socks and sandals. People watching in New York always leads to clichéd reflections about the lives of strangers, and surprise, surprise, at this point I had a particularly hackneyed thought about their love lives, a superficial curiosity to know the state of their romantic relationships, a fleeting desire to know more about them.

I glanced at Iris, wondering what I would have said if Leo had come up with a proposal like Cal's. "I should probably give you your shirt back." I reached in and pulled it out, smoothing out the wrinkles.

"Thanks." She set it on her lap.

"You okay?"

"Yeah, thanks. Just imagining how many people's social media accounts I ended up on."

"Oh, you're definitely on mine."

Iris laughed. "Great, good to know. You probably don't have a lot of followers though, right?"

"Nah, just a couple hundred thousand. Most of them people you admire."

"Cool, cool." She chuckled. "So, this is a totally normal way to hang out with someone for the first time."

"Technically it's our second hangout, which I think is a perfectly acceptable time to break down in tears. Life is short, right? Kiss on the first date, weep on the second. That's a saying."

"Absolutely." Iris smiled at me, looked across the street at the park. "So, your turn to cry, then?"

"Sure, just show me a viral video of a human being decent to another human and I'll instantly turn into a slobbering mess of tears and feelings."

A few quiet moments passed, and I started to wonder if I could try for an interview again, though I didn't want to press it so soon. "So, Lu. Tell me about yourself. You return wallets. You write things. You cry at people being nice to each other online. What else?"

"I think that's the whole list. Oh, I also won a spelling bee in fifth grade, but didn't accept the prize for political reasons."

"Wow. What were those?"

"It was a Halloween-themed spelling bee and the prize was a bunch of peanut-butter cups."

"So?"

"So, screw peanut butter."

Iris did the thing that everyone does when I say something to the effect of "peanut butter is a scourge upon this earth." She dropped her jaw and widened her eyes as if I'd just attempted to kill her mother. I nodded confidently to show I wasn't going to retract my statement.

After a few moments Iris ruffled her hair. "I guess it's good that you revealed yourself to be a sociopath now instead of later." She chuckled. "What about that writing gig you have? How long have you been doing it?"

I told her that it'd been about a year, then explained that I hadn't really set out to write about relationships until Hafsah pointed out that her favorite part of my writing was my musings on teenage love.

My phone buzzed in my pocket, probably my mom wondering when I was coming home. Just for the comfort of it, I grabbed my notebook from out of my bag. I opened it up and flipped through the few pages I'd filled out since my breakup. Eavesdropped snippets of dialogue, an ill-fated attempt at a poem about heartbreak and Leo's eyes, some crappy doodles. "So, have you thought about me maybe interviewing you? With this new info I'm even more interested in writing about you."

Iris took a deep breath. "No, not really. I've been bummed out all day so hadn't thought about it much, sorry."

"No worries."

I thought about what I could say to convince her, but the only thing going through my mind was just a video loop of me reaching my hand out hungrily and saying, "Give it to me!" That probably wouldn't sway her. I stretched my legs out, my eyes following a gorgeous Latino man walking his dog and grooving out to some music on his headphones.

"I guess I don't really know why you're interested in us," Iris said. "I'm sure there's plenty of other people in our position. Couldn't you just write about yourself?"

I watched as a group of tourists scampered across the road, trying to avoid getting hit by angry cabbies yelling out their windows. She'd shifted positions again, now sitting at the edge of the step, her arms down at her sides, elbows locked.

"The thing is, I haven't really been able to write since my breakup. Nothing comes out. But..." I paused so I wouldn't accidentally mention my initial eavesdropping. "Since we met the other night, I've had the specific urge to write about you. I don't understand why or how, but I don't really understand much about inspiration anyway. I'm sorry if that sounds creepy."

"No, it's not creepy. It's just I don't think we're that interesting."

She bit her bottom lip, avoiding eye contact with me. In her body language, I could see my article fading away before my eyes. I could picture too all of the repercussions unfurling like flowers shedding themselves of their petals. The emails that would flow in, one after the other. Hafsah terminating my contract, the foundation informing me that I no longer qualified for my scholarship, NYU asking for the first payment of the semester.

"'We are brought up in ethic to believe that others, any others, all others are by definition more interesting than ourselves,'" I said, quoting Joan Didion. "I think that's how it goes anyway. Maybe you're underestimating yourself."

Iris flicked away something that had landed on her dress, then kept brushing the same spot over and over again. "I mean, that's a nice sentiment, but whether or not we're interesting isn't really my main objection."

"What is?"

"I just don't want to dwell. You saw me a second ago, weeping in public."

"Yeah, the video's getting a ton of views already," I said, trying to win her over with some levity.

"I've got the summer left with Cal, after which I'll be consumed by heartbreak for a bit. I don't want to sully these next few weeks by overthinking our relationship, our decision to break up." Her voice nearly broke on the last sentence, and I wondered if I was being a bit of an asshole. I could have told her about the scholarship at that point, tried to convince her a little longer. But then I saw the sadness threatening to break through again and I just couldn't do it.

I could see her wanting to flee from the conversation the same way I want to flee…well…most conversations. Maybe changing the topic was a selfless thing to do then, or maybe just the obvious right thing to do. "Alright," I said. "You guys definitely are interesting enough to write about. Especially now that you have this new arrangement. But I did once write a whole column about the love lives of potatoes, so maybe I'm not the best judge of what's interesting."

Iris visibly relaxed, a throaty laugh emanating from deep within her lungs. Relief. "Really? And they ran it?"

"Hell no. I compared those little bumpy wart things they have to STDs. My editor thought it was a joke."

A breeze blew past, the first satisfying one of the day. "God, that felt good," Iris said, just as I was thinking it. She closed her eyes to the cool air, and for a moment I could see what a great match she and Cal made. The way he acted with me on the bench, of course he'd end up with a girl that closed her eyes to the breeze. It was either obvious hipster inclinations, or me reading a bit too much into two people I didn't know at all. "You wanna take a walk somewhere?" Iris asked.

Out of habit, I reached into my pocket to check my phone. As I'd suspected, my mom had texted. But I could read the tone of her message, which was still merely inquisitive, and not yet laced with passive-aggressiveness, and she was still a few texts away from full-on aggression. There was also a message from Pete, telling me that he was going to be at the Barnes and Noble at Union Square if I wanted to hang out.

"Sure," I said, putting my phone away. "I've got some time before my mom freaks out about my absence." I stood up, brushing my butt off.

We headed into the park, where the early evening athletes were out in hordes. Joggers stretched against light posts, and cyclists weaved around pedestrians, calling out "on your left" as they passed by. One of those peanut carts was parked at the entrance, the honey-roasted smell wafting over to us. All around the park, people were having the kind of day that made me realize I didn't come to Central Park often enough. Picnics and Frisbees and canoodling on blankets, sneaking sips from wineglasses.

"This is nice," I said, because neither one of us had said anything in a while.

"Yeah. I'm gonna miss this place when I'm gone."

"What made you pick California for college?"

"Mostly the school. I'm going to Pepperdine, and just seeing the pictures of the campus I knew I had to go. It's right on the water, which just fills me with this overwhelming sense of inner peace. They also have a decent international business program, which is what I told my parents the choice was about. But it's been my dream for a couple of years. I can't believe I get to finally go soon."

"Do you not like living in New York?"

We turned off West Drive down one of the smaller jogging paths. Iris crossed her arms in front of her chest as she walked. "It's not that. I love the city. But I don't want to spend my whole life here. I want to try a change of pace for a while. Something calmer. I don't want to just live in one place and not know what other cities have to offer."

"I have no idea what people want with calm lives," I said, stepping out of the way of a couple jogging in matching spandex. "I love chilling every now and then, yeah. But a calm life freaks me out. Too much time alone with my thoughts is literally the most terrifying thing I can imagine. Like, if you were a filmmaker, and wanted to scare the hell out of me, make a ninety-minute movie where it's nothing but a blank screen."

"Really? I love sitting with just my thoughts for a while." We turned within view of The Pond, which was glinting in the sun. I reached into my bag and grabbed my scratched-up pair of five-dollar sunglasses. "It's a bit of a trip, sure," Iris went on, "but in kind of an incredible way. I can time travel into memories or fantasies, I can picture a million different parallel universes, keep myself entertained for hours with nothing but a bunch of tiny bursts of electricity happening in my brain."

"God, that sounds like the worst."

Iris laughed, a full throaty sound, immensely pleasing because it wasn't one of those polite chuckles which is the usual response people give to my jokes. "I mean, aside from the abject horror of consciousness, it's pretty amazing."

We wandered through the park as the sun slowly set, as if it had a choice on when to give way to night. Iris talked a little more about California, and how she was legitimately excited about studying international business and trying to learn Mandarin. I was curious about how Cal felt when she talked like this around him, since I remembered what it felt like when Leo got psyched about going upstate for school, even when we were still planning on staying together. But I was having fun just shooting the shit with her and so I tried to forget about anything that had to do with her relationship.

We exited the park at Sixtieth Street, walking past that monument of a dude on a horse. "What'd be your ideal job, then?" I asked Iris. "International business sounds worldly and stuff, but I don't actually know how the real world works and what kind of job you'd end up in."

"To be honest, I don't really know either. I'm kind of picturing a job that pays me to travel the world. I know it would be a lot more corporate than that, but I'll let future Iris worry about that part. For now I think I'm allowed to dream of a more idealized version of the job market."

"Dude, I'm pretty sure you're not allowed to say 'job market' until you're twenty-five."

Another throaty laugh from her. "Don't *you* have a job?"

"Two, technically. But that's totally different than *discussing* the job market. Hang on to your youthful innocence, new friend. The world will rip it away soon enough."

"You're a bit of a cynic, aren't you?"

"Depends on the subject. I totally believe in aliens, ghosts, and that the world is slightly more good than bad. But I've got serious side-eye toward the Illuminati, karma, and anyone who's not a fan of cilantro."

"You talked shit about being alone with your thoughts, but you've clearly spent some time mulling this over."

"Exactly! And look at the disastrous nonsense that comes from it."

She reached over and gave me a light smack on the arm. We went on like that for about an hour, making our way vaguely downtown. We snaked our way around Times Square, because no matter how much love one had for New York, it never quite extended to those few hellish blocks.

My mom did call about half a dozen times, but I managed to get permission to call this a free night out on the town. They happen rarely with Mom, who still has memories of New York in the crime-ridden eighties when she moved here. But I'd been feeding her a steady stream of statistics and some guilt-tripping tirades about how if she doesn't let me have some freedom I'll overcompensate as soon as I move out and she'll only ever see me during major holidays or familial crises.

When we hit Union Square I realized I'd forgotten to text Pete back, so I sent him a quick, apologetic message then put my phone away, leading Iris quickly past the Barnes and Noble. It was dark by then, and in the distance we could hear thunder rolling in, the occasional flash of lightning visible between buildings.

Iris didn't seem too worried about oncoming rain, and that kind of confidence about your possessions' impermeability is really contagious. There's a certain momentum to walking through Manhattan with someone.

"I'm hungry," Iris said, when we were deep into NYU territory. "You know anything good around here that's not insanely expensive?"

"Oh sure. Are you a souvlaki girl like myself, or are you more into hot dogs?"

"Definitely souvlaki, but I'm feeling something a little more special today." She stopped walking when we were in front of the Comedy Cellar, nearly colliding with a group of college-looking bros on their way to a nearby bar. I cringed, waiting for them to turn around and say something gross. Thankfully, they spared us. "What about this place?"

Coincidentally, she was pointing at Mamoun's. "Ah, it's fantastic. But I just ate there the other night."

"Don't like repeats?"

"I would eat at Mamoun's every day of my life. But I went half-insane on the hot sauce and I think my digestive system probably needs a break."

"Respect," Iris said. She looked around a little longer, then pulled out her phone. I would have done the same thing but I was relishing the fact that my mom hadn't texted or called in an hour and I decided to let Iris do the Googling.

"Comedy show, ladies!"

I looked behind us. The door guy at the Comedy Cellar was sitting on a bar stool, looking bored. He had his hands on his knees, a tight V-neck showing off his biceps, a dia-mond stud in his nostril. "Ten bucks, two hours of comedy," he said, already looking away from us, directing the pitch at anyone who happened to be nearby. Probably wasn't working off commission.

Iris looked at me and raised an eyebrow. "The internet says the food here is surprisingly good. Could be fun to have a comedy show with dinner."

"Oh sure, laughter is a fun thing. Easily top five on my all-time hobbies list. If I could laugh every day I would."

"You're such a weirdo."

"I just love to laugh, Iris, what can I say," I deadpanned.

We approached the doorman, who very quickly requested our IDs, since apparently you have to be over twenty-one to laugh when you're in the proximity of alcohol. I was about to turn away, thinking maybe Mamoun's again wouldn't be too bad. Then Iris touched my forearm and gave me a look, mouthing a few words that I didn't understand. She pulled out an ID and confidently handed it over to the buff doorman. I tried to act chill about this so as to not ruin our chances, though I had no idea how I was about to get in. Maybe Iris was so cool she didn't have just one fake ID, but a whole slew of them, for everyone she'd ever met.

That's an extraordinarily stupid idea, which proves that I was right to shut up. Iris managed to convince the doorman that I was visiting from out of the country and had not thought to bring my passport along for dinner. He eyed us suspiciously, but halfheartedly, as if he was only doing it in case someone else was watching. Then he said, "Ten bucks," again and waved us through after we handed him the money.

Between the cover charge and the food, I ended up spending way more than I ever should have on dinner. But I realized during a bathroom break why I was so happy to keep the night going, why I could shrug off the financial irresponsibility: I hadn't thought about Leo in hours. You can't put a price on that kind of inner peace (and if you could, forty bucks seemed like an okay deal).

We watched a pretty great lineup of comedians, a couple of which were marginally famous, and one of them a little more famous than that. We got a few weird looks from the other customers and our server kept eyeing us as if we were planning to run out on the bill, but the food was, as the internet had predicted, surprisingly good for a comedy club. When we left, I was a little sad that the night would be over, but thankful that I'd met up with Iris, and that I'd decided not to push the subject of her and Cal so I could have this night. A wave of panic started to build over the fact that I hadn't. Back on MacDougal Street, we could hear a rowdy crowd at Mamoun's, one girl's voice carrying over the street noise.

"This was fun," I said. "I'm glad we met up."

Iris smiled, but then furrowed her brow. "I'm not ready to go home. Stay out with me."

I looked at my phone to check the time. I still had a couple hours until my curfew, and going back home might mean having to face thoughts of Leo and my still-unwritten article. "You make a very compelling argument. Where to next?"

11

SPEAK EASY

Iris and I were crammed into a phone booth at a gourmet hot dog restaurant.

"We might get lucky, since it's a weeknight," I said. I'd read about this spot on *Misnomer*'s nightlife section. At the time, I'd felt it was the most asinine idea for a speakeasy that I could think of, but now that I was standing in the phone booth waiting for some unseen voice to grant me permission inside, I couldn't help but feel like the gimmick was working on me.

The phone rang on my end a few times. Iris was so close to me I could smell her, something fruity and almost musky, covered up by a sheen of cigarette smoke from the comedy club. A hostess picked up the line from somewhere unseen.

We were told in a very snooty voice that it'd be a twenty-five minute wait at least, so we went out to the street and talked about some TV shows we'd binge-watched lately. Three minutes later a text message told us to go back to the phone booth and dial 1, after which the wall gave way to reveal an astoundingly attractive Asian girl in a high ponytail. She eyed us up and down, then grabbed two leather-bound menus and walked us over to the tiny bar. A food menu with secret hot dog options was hanging over the bottles of alcohol, the writing on which was hard to make out in the dark. A few candles in glasses flickered on the bar, casting a pale glow around the closet-sized room. Only a handful of other people were at the bar, their conversations carrying over the lounge techno music playing from the speakers.

"I'm confused as to why hip twentysomethings choose to hang out here," Iris said to me. The hostess looked at us over her shoulder. "Er, fellow twentysomethings," Iris added.

"It's all about wanting what you can't have. This place has room for about seven people, so they're always sold out and it's super hard to get in. Which makes everyone want to be here."

"That's so transparent though. How do people fall for it?"

"Dude, we're here. We fell for it."

"Well," Iris said, looking around. "I've never been to a speakeasy. I was picturing something a lot more…"

"Like a gangster from the '20s?"

"Exactly. I wanted to drink out of a bathtub."

Two napkins landed in front of us. "Lucky for you we serve our gin in tiny bathtubs." We looked up to see another astoundingly attractive employee, this one a Latino bartender. He looked like he was about to burst out singing a deeply romantic ballad and then star in a Mexican soap opera as a doctor with an evil twin and illegitimate quintuplets or something. "What'll you have, ladies?"

This was Daniel, who became the love of our lives. For the night anyway. Especially when he served us without asking for ID, then kept the drinks coming without ever letting his gorgeous smile falter.

"Seriously, how is he doing that? He's been smiling non-

stop for an entire hour and it doesn't even look like he's faking it. He must have the strongest cheek muscles of all time."

"I think they just call them cheeks," Iris said, trying to get
a hold of the curly straw in her tiki drink while not looking
away from Daniel, so her tongue kept feeling around blindly
for it. A couple times she went face first into the glass.

"They can call them whatever they want, those bad boys
are muscles." I looked into the bottom of my glass, scooping
out a piece of fruit with my straw. "Leo has great cheeks," I
mumbled. "I liked rubbing my face on them."

"Who's Leo?"

"Oh, right, you don't know him." I sucked down the last
few drops from the bottom of my glass, feeling light-headed
when I tilted my head back. "It's a pretty astonishing feat that
I haven't brought him up until now. Pete would be proud."

"Girl, who is Pete?" Iris giggled, then motioned for two
more drinks.

"I don't know if I should have more. It's late and I have
to work like two and a half hours to pay for each of these."

"It's on me," she said. "Anyway, I'm not ready to leave
Daniel yet. Now tell me about these boys." When Daniel
had acknowledged her and started working on our drinks,
she leaned her elbow onto the bar, turning her body so she
could face me. The place had filled up as the night went on,
every seat taken by überhip people in unseasonable leather
jackets and plaid shirts.

I told her about Pete first, thinking I'd avoid mentioning
the fact that I think of him as a wise, old uncle, but almost
immediately saying that. "I don't even know how his advice
is always on point, because the dude is technically younger
than me and doesn't even seem to have a life outside of me
and books. Which should make him smart, sure, but just book

smart, right? You can't learn everything from those wonderful papery bastards." I took a breath to accept another drink, thinking it was a really bad idea but also kinda hoping my fingers would brush Daniel's. "There's just no one I feel more like myself around than Pete," I went on. "I'm funnier around him, completely unembarrassed."

"Are you into him?"

"You shut your goddamn mouth," I said. "No. Didn't you hear me say the word *uncle* to describe him a second ago, you freak? Plus, I don't think Pete is really attracted to anyone. We have this game we play at the theater called I Would Bone That Person, and... Well, the details don't really matter. No, Pete's a friend, and he's been my moral compass in this whole Leo thing."

"Still don't know who Leo is," Iris said. The woman sitting next to me shifted in her seat, accidentally bumping me with her elbow and making me take heed of the moment. A subdued pop song played on the speakers, competing with the din of conversation at the bar. At a glance, I could see how Iris and I could fit seamlessly into this crowd. Iris was stylish enough anyway. She was smiley, her eyes glazed over with booze and newfound friendship. For the first time since my breakup, I felt the possibilities of being out and about with strangers, the strangeness of where your life could go, and how easily.

"Leo's my ex. The one who dumped me for the same reason you kind of broke up with Cal."

"Right! You'd mentioned him." Iris pushed herself away from the bar, straightening out and then stretching a little to get her back to crack. "Tell me about him."

I looked down at my drink, rolling little snowballs out of

the napkin Daniel had set beneath the glass. "He's a prick and I love him."

"Great, now with a little more nuance."

I bit my lip and kept rolling snowballs. "He's not really a prick. But I do love him." Bits of conversation from the lady who'd bumped into me kept floating over my shoulder, and it took a lot of effort not to chase after them. She'd used certain words that usually promised a rich eavesdropping session, especially when used within the same paragraph: *cheated, shotgun,* and, most notably (though I have to admit that I hadn't ever heard this particular string of colorful words used together), *that stripper from Alabama.* I turned over my shoulder to get a glance at the woman and whomever she was with, but there was nothing particularly interesting about them, and their conversation got too quiet to overhear.

My pause was excessive, I knew, but I did mean to go on and be open with Iris. But then I took a long gulp from my drink, and then another, and before I knew it the moment had become this awkward avoidance of a topic I was more than happy to talk about. Just, not then. I wanted to enjoy the night.

Thankfully, Iris was better at being a human person, and instead of dwelling on it, she changed the topic, asking me if I'd heard what the people behind me had just said. We finished our drinks right as it was about to turn midnight, which meant I'd have to pay for a cab to get home, even though there was zero chance I was going to beat my curfew. Like clockwork, Mom called just as we left the bar. I didn't want to answer because I was afraid of the background noise and my voice slurring from Daniel's magical elixirs of booze and sexuality, so I let it ring, then texted back.

LU

sorry! at the subway but train's running late. :/ don't
be mad.

MOM

I'm mad. Ur grounded until yur 21. 23 if I have trouble waking up in the mornng.

LU

Har har. You can go to bed now. I'll be home soon,
promise. I'm okay, with a friend.

MOM

Can't sleep. Wht if I Wake up and ur dead?

LU

Mom.

MOM

Good night, Lucinda.

I sighed with a semblance of relief, hoping she really would
go to bed so she wouldn't smell the booze on me when I got
home. There were a few other notifications on my screen,
but reading them made my eyes hate the world, and the fact
that it contained things other than me and Iris and this lovely
night, so I tucked my phone away.

"Was that a sigh of relief I just heard?" Iris did a little
shimmy where she stood, raising her eyebrows up and down
repeatedly as if she was saying something suggestive. "Which
means your mom's probably not going to wait up for you,
which means you're in the clear to hang out a little longer."

I groaned. "How are you that smart? Such powers of de-
duction. I'm gonna call you House."

"What? Is that a weight joke?"

"No, like the TV show about the doctor. You never
watched that?" Iris shook her head and shrugged, pulling
out her own phone and typing out a message. "I binged three
seasons and then had a bunch of dreams that I had cancer."

"Sounds like a blast," Iris said, still looking down at her
screen. Then her phone vibrated and a smile spread across her
ruby-red lips. "C'mon, I've got a cool spot we can go to." She
started walking away before I could protest. Although I guess
that's not quite true. I could have protested at her retreat-
ing back, or maybe protested louder than my initial instinct
would dictate. But anyway, I decided to hold my protest and
just follow her because inertia or psychology or some other
science told me it was easier to do so.

I rushed to catch up to her, noticing that she was smiling as
she was walking. Her hands were in her dress's pockets, and
she had this absolutely serene look on her face, like she was
exactly where she needed to be in the world. I don't know
if I've ever felt that in my life, much less the same day I was
weeping about the heartbreak of a relationship I knew would
be over in August.

The way Iris Castillo walked through New York City made
me envious. I'm not sure exactly of what. Just *her*, I guess. Or
maybe not envious. I was in awe. Which is why I followed
her back up Broadway toward Madison Square Park, avoiding puddles from a rainstorm we'd apparently missed while
at the speakeasy. It almost looked like we were heading *to* the
park, which made me wonder if I should tell her about how
I'd met Cal on that bench. Then she made a turn and started
knocking on the front door of the Flatiron Building. I'd lived

in New York City my whole life and had admired the hell out of this particular landmark's aesthetics, but I had absolutely zero knowledge about what went on within its diagonal walls. For all I knew it was a factory where they pounded iron into flat sheets or something. All I knew then was that it probably wasn't a place two buzzed eighteen-year-olds belonged after-hours.

There were a couple of guys seated at the security station, their faces illuminated by the glow of what were probably—if television had faithfully portrayed security stations even slightly—a dozen different monitors. Iris knocked again, and the Latino one glanced up. At first he scowled, and then he squinted and stood up, approaching the door to get a closer look. His hand went to his nightstick, which is right around the time when I felt like it would be a good idea to retreat. Then his body relaxed, and he took his hand away from the nightstick and grabbed his keys.

He unlocked the door and pushed it open, standing in the doorway, his bulky frame blocking most of the entrance. "Hey, cuz. You here to get me in trouble?"

"Yup," Iris said, dragging out the vowel for a couple of seconds and smiling.

He laughed and shook his head, turning to look at me and then at her. "You guys drunk or something? You know your moms would kill me if I let you up there and you fall to your death."

"Oh come on. My mom's a sweetheart. She's not capable of murder."

"Not literally," the security guard, whose name tag read Hernando, said. "But she'd beat me down with guilt. My life would be over. I'd have to carry that weight around until my actual death."

"We're good, man. I swear we'll stay away from the ledge. Except for when we're throwing stuff."

"Right, the usual rules." He chuckled and shook his head again, then stepped back to let us through. The other security guard, an older black man, looked up from the monitors and started to stand up. Behind us, Hernando locked the door again. "Roy, this is my little cousin, Iris. Gonna let them up to the roof for a bit. If anything happens I'll say I snuck them past while you were taking a leak."

"Fair enough," Roy said, offering a head nod.

We thanked them, then headed up the elevator to the highest floor, taking the stairs the rest of the way, probably too excitedly because when we pushed the door open we were both out of breath. Iris put her hands up behind her head, taking big heaving breaths. "Totally should not have run."

I was taking the hands-on-the-knees approach, trying to appreciate the view while wheezing. "Yeah, that was stupid. Remind me not to ever do that again." When my head and insides begrudgingly returned to normal, Iris and I walked forward to the front of the building, where the diagonal walls converge and look out at Madison Square Park. "Damn."

"Yeah, right?"

Manhattan twinkled all around me. We took a lap around the roof. I looked around for The Strand and my movie theater, the bench where I was supposed to talk to Leo but ended up sitting next to Cal instead. The noise up there wasn't the usual cacophonous orchestra of competing sounds. All the sounds of the city had time to merge together into something more complete, and quieter. (Duh, Lu, it was past midnight.)

"Of course you'd have access to the freaking Flatiron's rooftop."

Iris laughed, leaning her elbows forward on the waist-high

ledge. Her dark curls hung over her shoulder, nearly brush-ing the stones. "What do you mean?"

Below us, I could see some cops in the park, talking to a homeless guy sitting on the curb. An Indian man scrubbed his hot dog cart clean, headphones in his ears. There was that lovely post-rain smell in the air, instead of the usual smell of hot garbage. "You just have that kind of life, don't you? Charmed more than the average." Iris frowned, and I rushed to elaborate in a way that didn't make it sound like I was ac-cusing her of something. "That didn't come out right. It's just…you're so cool. You're going to California because the ocean fills you with calm, you've got a fake ID and flawless style and seem so comfortable with yourself. You're my age and you have the maturity to not delude yourself into think-ing long distance will work with your high school boyfriend, and then the absurd level of maturity to stay with him with a predetermined breakup date." The expression on her face was definitely not the reaction I was going for, like I was still complaining about her instead of the opposite. "I'm not saying all of this to bitch. I'm just saying…it feels like you deserve this kind of life. Like you're one of those people that has it a little more figured out than the rest of us."

A quiet moment followed, which made it feel like I'd messed up this awesome night and probably the rest of my friendship with Iris by being overly earnest. That thought al-most made me want to cry, so I turned my head up to com-bat the threat of tears by having them fight against gravity. I was shocked to see a few stars visible overhead. There's such little sky visible in the city, it almost feels like a waste to look up in search of stars. There's a lot more interesting stuff going on down here.

"Well, I'm glad you think I'm this beacon of awesomeness,"

Iris finally said, breaking the silence. "It's not quite true, but it's nice to be seen that way, I guess."

I found myself mimicking her lean on the ledge, even though I felt like I hadn't looked away from the view in front at all. It was hard to pinpoint what made the sight so beautiful. It was just a different angle of the same buildings and lights I was well versed in. "Which part did I get wrong?"

A breeze blew and Iris tossed her hair over to her other shoulder so it wouldn't hit her in the face. "It's like you're seeing the duck above the surface, but not the feet paddling beneath. Things may look smooth, but there's more to it than that, you know. I'm not saying I have this crazy difficult life. But I'm definitely more than what you've picked up from our two times seeing each other in person."

An urge rose up within me, and I decided I'd try one more time. "So, let me see it. Let me see more of you and Cal, instead of this glossy, romanticized version that's formed in my head."

I thought maybe she'd just walk away, tired of my shit. Or that she'd groan and make a joke about how I didn't quit. Instead she just stood there, looking out at the city, not quite swaying from the booze but not motionless either. "Why do you like writing about love?"

"I just like exploring the topic," I said. No one had really asked me why I write about this stuff before. Maybe they just assumed because I'm a teenage girl that it makes sense, but I never felt like someone who obsessed over love. "This is when a lot of us experience love for the first time, and all we really know about it comes from books and movies and songs, which sometimes offer good advice, or a glimpse of what the experience is like, but it's not the same thing as really experiencing love. We're unprepared, all of us. We see a

filtered version of love in art and media, but what do we really know about it? What have we seen, outside of our parents? And even then, how much is there? I don't know what
your parents are like but mine are divorced, and I have no
memories of what they were like together. They've both dated
other people, but they aren't exactly open about that part of
themselves. And the rest comes from our friends, but they
aren't exactly experts either." Iris's phone buzzed a few times
in her hand. She glanced at the screen then set it facedown
on the ledge, giving me her attention. "I don't know. Maybe
I think it'll make me better at it all."

Iris smiled, her eyes starting to droop with sleep. I was getting tired too, and had an early shift the next day. A yawn escaped me, and I thought of how Leo would make fun of the
exaggerated scope of my yawns, how long they built up for.
He would sometimes try to interrupt them by tickling me.
It got annoying by the end of our relationship, but I remember how much I loved it when we were still just flirting. The
rush of his touch, the intimacy of laughing together. I used
to fake yawns just to get him to do it.

That was gone now. A joy in my life just flittered away.
The thought caused me sadness, but not the kind of sadness
I'd been feeling for weeks now. I didn't think I was healed
from the heartbreak, but I started to realize in that moment,
looking out at a relatively quiet Manhattan, that I would, with
time. A few more nights like this, a few more nights to forget the things I liked about Leo, a few more run-ins where
he acted like a jerk. I'd heal, in the end.

I just didn't know if I wanted to heal.

What We Talk about When We Talk about Talking about Love

By Lu Charles
November 10

Sometimes I wonder how people know that the feeling they're experiencing is the same thing others experience. Like, when I call something "love," am I talking about the same thing a certain boy with sexy stage presence is talking about when he talks about love?

The boyfriend and I exchanged L-words recently. I've written about this momentous stage in a relationship before, but I had no idea what the moment really felt like, could only imagine the layers of thoughts and hopes and fears that rush through a person's mind in the lead-up and afterglow.

I would think it'd be a full relief, something akin to how it felt to finally become uncrushed and enter into that elusive stage of actual dating and kissing. Don't get me wrong, there is joy. An unclenching deep within me. Since the beginning of our relationship, I had been wondering if it was one-sided, if I was deep in the pool while he was sitting at the edge watching me with only his ankles submerged.

Now that we've talked and agreed that we are both in the deep end, I wonder how deep we're talking about. I wonder about the quantifiable measurability of love, and how evenly it can match up. We talk about love, but do two people ever mean the exact same thing when they say they love each other?

It probably depends on your outlook. If you're a romantic, you say of course. If you're a cynic you say we're in actuality always alone and even relationships are an illusion. If you're at a party, you back slowly away from the cynic and come up with a signal with your friends to make sure you don't get stuck talking to him again.

Or. Maybe it's just me. My neuroses. Maybe it's just this relationship. Maybe it's still too new for me to feel complete reciprocity. To trust that it's there. I want that trust, but maybe that's one of those stupid grown-up things that comes with time. Although the most neurotic part of me says that no, that's not the case. Real love doesn't come with a minimum age requirement.

Tell me, readers, is it just me? Does this ring a bell for anyone else, or are these insecurities mine alone?

12

EXCUSES

The next day, as I was walking to work, Hafsah called me. I stared at my phone, wishing I hadn't been a huge tool and missed my deadline. Mornings are hard enough on a day-to-day basis, but I hadn't gotten much sleep the night before because I was out so late with Iris. I'd tried to improvise a last-minute article, but my head started lolling with booze and sleep and I had to succumb to bed. Mom had passive-aggressively grilled me during breakfast, which for sure helped with the whole sleep-deprivation thing.

Other than that, morning phone calls generally made me feel like some alien had zapped my brain and replaced it with one of those flimsy decades-old couch cushions my tita Marian refuses to throw away. So that's the state of mind I was in.

"Hey!" I said, really lingering on the *y* to make it seem like I was totally cool with this phone call and how it would undo my future.

"Where's your column, Lu?"

Small talk isn't the greatest thing in the world, but I would have really loved the opportunity to let my panicking mind ease into the conversation. I sighed, and then decided on a bold, albeit not superintelligent approach. "What was that, Haf? I couldn't hear you!" I even covered up my off-ear to the city sounds, as if it was onlookers in my vicinity that I had to convince.

All that did though was turn up the volume on Hafsah's end of the line. She was so quiet that I could hear the subdued sounds of the *Misnomer* offices gearing up for the day. Interns chatting in the coffee room, office doors opening and shutting, people saying their good mornings. Someone tapped softly on their keyboard, a fridge whirred. I swear I could hear those things. Hafsah was really freaking quiet.

"Can you hear me now?" I could tell she hadn't moved to a different spot in the office or closed her door or anything like that. Which meant she probably could sniff through my bullshit.

Abort, abort. "Yeah, that's better."

"I was expecting your column yesterday. What happened?"

I quickly ran through some possible excuses:

- A grandparent dying. (Too disrespectful to my dead grandparents, too awful to imagine for my still-living grandparents.)
- My dog ate it. (I don't have a dog, and I don't think dogs ever eat entire laptops or, for that matter, someone's ability to access the internet.)
- Someone elbowed past me so hard on the subway that it caused a weekend-long concussion and paralysis in my fingers. (Plausible, but Hafsah would probably ask for a doctor's note.)
- Heartbreak had rendered me wordless and now my future as a writer was over. (Not an excuse that would solve anything for me vis-à-vis losing the job.)

"I need more time," I said. "The couple I'm interviewing just had a busy weekend and they kept canceling our phone call appointments."

Another silence from Hafsah, during which I could physically sense my future falling apart. I was gonna work at the movie theater my whole life. I'd turn into Brad. Except Brad married his high school sweetheart, so I'd probably be a slightly sadder version of Brad, keeping an eternal stockade of notebooks which I would fill only with doodles because I'd never write another word again.

"You should have turned something in, Lu. A draft. A proposal. You're putting me in a bad position."

"It's gonna be really good, Haf. I promise. They're…" I reached around the empty recesses of my brain for a descriptor that would sell Hafsah, somehow landed on "…entrancing. It'll be worth it, but I do need more time. I'm sorry." Were they entrancing? Or was I just desperate?

I was still walking, and at that point I came within view of the movie theater. How this phone call ended could make the next eight hours excruciating or filled with sweet, sweet relief. I stood on the corner of Third Avenue and Eleventh Street, eyes glued to my feet and the sidewalk. I wish I could say I felt a moment of inner peace, knowing that the decision was out of my hands and worrying would achieve nothing. But that's not how my mind works. I focused on a piece of trash rolling along the street, carried by the draft of passing cars.

"Since I needed something by the end of the month, you get one more week. After that, I'm going to look to fill the love column with someone else."

"You are the best person alive. You won't be disappointed. It's gonna be great," I said, my shoulders shimmying with excitement of their own volition.

I hung up and hurried into work. In the back room, I found Pete putting his things away in his locker. I stormed in and slammed my bag into the locker adjacent to his. "All is not lost!" I yelled.

"Oh good. I was worried when you bailed on me last night that you got stuck watching global warming docs. Clearly not the case." Pete grabbed his maroon work polo and slipped it over his head.

"My editor is giving me another week," I said, grabbing him by the shoulders and shaking him as violently as I could. "I get another chance!"

Pete shrugged his way out of my grip. "You're really excited for the extra rope to hang yourself with."

I clapped my hands together. "I'm gonna ignore the rudeness of that comment because I bailed on you yesterday and you're entitled to some snark. But this is good news! My future has not crumbled like the ice caps."

"Now I'm confused. Did you watch documentaries last night?" We walked over to the clipboard on the wall to see where our shifts would start. We were both on cleaning duty.

"No. Iris and I hung out all night. It was actually really cool. We went to the Comedy Cellar and a speakeasy, and even made it to the roof of the freaking Flatiron." Pete's eyebrows went up. "I know!"

We both grabbed a broom and a dustbin and walked out into the lobby.

"Please tell me you're not doing that thing."

"What thing?"

"That '90s rom-com thing where you strike up a friendship for ulterior motives, which eventually blossoms into a real relationship, and then it all falls apart in the third act when the other person discovers the aforementioned ulterior motives."

"Don't be ridiculous" I said. We started making the rounds of the theaters, sweeping up popcorn that last night's cleanup crew may have missed. "I was completely up-front with her about my motives for friendship. But I could use some help in determining a way to trick her into agreeing to an interview."

Pete was a few rows up from me in the otherwise empty theater, sweeping calmly. "Still?"

"Yeah. Get this: they *are* breaking up. But they're delaying their misery by staying together until the end of the summer."

Pete stopped sweeping and looked at me, furrowing his brow. I waited for him to say it was a ballsy move on their part, a bold acceptance of how all good things eventually end, they were living in the avant-garde of romance!

"Weird," Pete said, going back to sweeping. "So she changed her mind about letting you interview them, then?"

"Well, no. She gets sad if she thinks about the breakup, so she didn't want to dwell. But I think she might feel differently if I asked her this morning. We, like, bonded last night."

"Hmm," Pete went. I took that as a sign that his mental cogs and wheels or whatever a brain is made up of were starting to churn. We cleaned six more theaters without saying another word. Except every time Pete made a little noise I assumed he was about to drop some wisdom and I'd perk my ears up like a cat.

By the time we got switched over to concessions, I was getting tired of his reticence. "Alright, dude. You've been brainstorming for a while now. What do you have for me?"

Pete was trying to jam as many napkins as he could in the dispenser. Our record was 258, which I'd set last summer by cheating and taking out the spring-loaded bottom, then throwing that particular dispenser away. "Vis-à-vis…?"

The doors to the theater opened, the first customers of the

day arriving: a group of stay-at-home parents coming in for a matinee that they would not be able to pay attention to because they'd be checking in on their baby and running out to calm the crying. "Have you seriously not been brainstorming this whole time?"

Pete tilted his head at me like a pretty Irish puppy. "In regards to the napkin thing?"

"No, you dolt. A strategy to get Iris to yield!"

"Ah." He nodded once, then muttered something about losing count and went off to attend to the mommy-and-me crowd. I scooped popcorn for him, a little pissed that he hadn't been on the same page as me. We're usually pretty in sync, and it felt weird not to have him on board with me for this. I had to wait fifteen minutes for a break in the first-showing crowd, the whole while berating Pete in my head and trying to keep a smile on my face while toddlers pointed at the candy they wanted and then wailed when their parents opted for anything else.

During the shuffle of actually doing our jobs, we ended up at opposite ends of the concession counter. But people that had been working with us for a while had picked up on the fact that I would do whatever I could to talk to Pete, whether that was talking loudly across the entire row of coworkers or making them switch cashier spots with me, and they usually chose the latter. Brad tried to talk to us about it last summer, but quickly came to the realization that we ended up doing a better job if we were allowed to hang out together during our shifts.

"Okay, you've had more time now," I said once I'd finagled my way down the registers toward him. "What's my approach?"

"Forget about convincing her." He shrugged. "Write about you and Leo."

"I am going to eye-roll you so hard it'll reverse the earth's rotation, sending us back in time to before you were born, so that I can slap your mom about the terrible choice she made bringing you into the world."

"That's rude, my mom's lovely. And you really don't have to go back in time to slap her." He squinted, and looked up and to the right, like he'd just had an idea and was riding the thought off in to the sunset. "Also, the logistics of rolling your eyes so hard that you turn back time is—"

"Pete."

He came back to Earth, leaning against a popcorn machine and then jumping back when it tilted under his weight. "'Sup?"

"Stop suggesting I write about me and Leo. I don't want to think about him. I want to write about Iris and Cal."

He rubbed his elbow, a red welt forming where it had rested against the popcorn machine. "I think you have to accept the reality that this isn't something she wants, and that if you continue to wish for her to just change her mind, you might end up right back where you were the other night, worrying about missing your deadline. My best advice is to find someone else."

"There isn't anyone else," I said, resisting the urge to say it in the whiniest voice possible. Have you ever just sunk into that bratty whiny voice? It's fun. Cathartic, even, like stretching a particularly tired muscle. "My words won't come with anyone else."

"Force them to." Pete shrugged. "You said Iris gets sad when she dwells on her relationship? Allow yourself to dwell too. Write about it." One of the moms ran out from her theater and took the whole stack of napkins that Pete had counted for the dispenser. She cringe-smiled at him then ran back, her sandals clapping against the floor until she hit the carpet portion of the hallway. Pete turned to look at me, his expression kind.

In defiance of what he'd said, I thought of Leo, as if to prove that I could do it without being touched by sadness. I thought of the speech I'd prepared for him, how I still hadn't had the chance to read it. I thought about whether I still wanted to be back with him, even though he'd practically wiped me from his life. The answer was an immediate and resounding yes. I missed getting pho with him, missed walking home from school with him, missed coming up with stupid songs with him. My stomach dropped at the thought.

"God, you really belong as the voice of reason in a third act somewhere." I fiddled with the computer screen on my register, hitting random buttons and then canceling the order, just for the pleasure of the little beeps. "Too bad this isn't a movie and those truth bombs don't do anyone any good. I tried writing about Rachel and Diane, nothing happened. I'm gonna write about Iris and Cal."

Pete bit his lip. Always so damn calm, even when I just dismiss everything he says. Sometimes I wish he'd blow up at me and call me a selfish jerk. But that's not who he is. "I don't know what else to say. Keep trying."

Mom wanted me to stay home after work, complaining that she "hadn't seen me in so long that she wouldn't recognize me walking down the street." I managed to convince her to let me go to the coffee shop down the street from us though, just for a couple of hours so I could work on my column.

"Hmm," she went. "What do you mean by 'a couple'? Is it two or three or just a stand-in for an indefinite number you'd rather not name?"

"Mom, when you sniff out my teenage evasiveness it really makes you unbearable."

"Answer the question."

"I don't know, Mother. Writing doesn't work like that. There's no formula to it. I could be done in fifteen minutes. Or I could be done in fifteen hours."

"You only tell me it's fifteen hours when you want to get away with something."

"Listen," I said. "What I do with my time is none of your business."

"It is entirely my business what you do with your time. That's my job as your mother, above all other business. It is literally the number one item on my business agenda."

I squinted my eyes at her, knowing that I had no ground to respond, but also to convey that I didn't want her to press any further.

"Before I let you out of the house, I'd like to press further. What are you writing about?"

I don't know if my mom reads my column. We don't really talk about it much, but she gets this funny look on her face every time the topic comes up, and then she kind of lets me do whatever I want.

I squinted a little harder, hoping to scare her off. Teenage squints are powerful like that. She clicked her tongue and shook her head, "You think that look scares me." I stopped squinting and instead I activated my second phase of deflection, the I'm-confused-you're-so-weird look. "Fine," my mom said. "I'll respect your privacy. But don't let me slip into the back burner of your mind, or I might burn until I'm nothing but an ashy nuisance crusted into your best pot."

"Goddamn, Mom. Harsh."

"Language," she said.

★ ★ ★

Little Bean is hipster chic, all wood paneling and hanging ferns, string lights draped across the coffee shop like it was the patio at someone's wedding. I bought myself a drip coffee and snagged the only available seat next to an electrical outlet. It's my favorite spot, not just because the outlet gives me freedom to hang out for long stretches of time, but because it's in the corner near the window, allowing me to look out the window at pedestrian traffic, but also at the hip baristas with their septum piercings and couldn't-care-less affectations, and the curious array of customers that came in: those plugged into laptops and headphones, those on dates or friendly meet-ups, those rushing in for a to-go order, a quick detour in their lives.

I opened my computer and brought up the saved blank document that should've been my article, as well as my notebook, flipping to the notes I'd taken about Diane and Rachel. I pulled up Hafsah's last email to me, hoping that seeing her name would intimidate me into inspiration. For the same reason, I pulled up a picture I'd taken of Pete a few weeks back at Books of Wonder. In it, he was holding a graphic novel and eyeing me like I was disturbing the very fabric of his world.

"There! Now I'm ready to work." I would have said it out loud, if I were even more unhinged than I really am. Instead I thought it, and cracked my knuckles for the symbolic effect. Then I did absolutely fuck-all for forty-five minutes. I texted Iris that I'd had a fun night. I texted Pete asking him if he'd had any breakthroughs thinking of ways to convince Iris.

PETE
Dude, I can't even convince you to do anything but pursue these lovebirds, clearly my powers of persua-

BRIEF CHRONICLE OF ANOTHER STUPID HEARTBREAK 135

sion aren't that great. Interview yourself. Or someone else, if you must.

I slouched as low in my seat as a nonslug being has ever
slouched. All the excitement after my phone call with Hafsah that morning had been swallowed up by that unfortunate
whirlpool of writer's block hanging over my head. Then I
spotted them. At a table across the coffee shop sat a blonde
girl and a black guy. They had two different college stickers
on their laptops and they were touching each other the way
you would if you hadn't seen the person you love in months.

Sure, I was making, at the very least, a dozen assumptions
about these two people. They may not have even been a
couple. They could have been having an affair, or displaying
stickers for colleges their parents went to. They could have
met after college. But I was in the state of mind that allowed
me to push away from my seat, grab my mostly empty coffee
cup, and walk over to them.

"Hi!" I said, cheery as one of those people in Times Square
who tries to get you on the tour bus if you look even slightly
like a Dutch family of four on vacation.

The couple looked at me exactly the way they should have.
The blonde girl put a protective hand on her boyfriend's
forearm. The guy retreated slightly, as if I was accusing him
of something. "Sorry," I said, "that was aggressive. I write a
love and relationship column for *Misnomer*, the online magazine." The couple exchanged confused looks. "Anyway, I
noticed your college decals. Do you two happen to be in a
long-distance relationship?"

"Um," they both said, because of course they did.

I was moments away from fleeing and begging Iris to
change her mind, but then the couple said yes.

"How did you know?" the girl asked, half impressed, half still-wondering-how-deranged-I-was.

"Have you ever watched the show *House*?"

They both blinked, and I knew it was time to dial back Normal Lu and call up Journalism Lu. I took a breath, thought of the joys of a column coming together, thought of how good it felt to write again, how this couple might be the ones that broke the block for me. "Let me start over. My name is Lu Charles, I'm a writer for *Misnomer*," I said with a smile that hopefully hid my mental state. "I'm working on a column about dating the summer after senior year, and I'm hoping I could ask you a few questions?"

They looked at each other and smiled, and I knew then and there that I had them.

For twenty minutes I sat with them, interviewing them, pushing my pen furiously across my page, taking note of all the details that made this couple unique, all the specifics of their love lives. I listened to the very best of my abilities, asking questions that would really get to the heart of who they were and how they let love be stronger than the circumstances fighting against it.

Then I thanked them, returned to my computer, and failed to write a single word.

All I could think about was two-person paintball teams, and Iris crying at the fountain in Columbus Circle.

At home, I tried to make my mom happy by not disappearing into my room immediately. I answered questions about my day monosyllabically, faking enthusiasm while slurping through some puttanesca. I watched Jase miraculously switch from murdering people virtually to playing football and virtually causing concussions. I wondered briefly about whether he was interested in romance yet, if he was starting to develop crushes, think about love, dream about people. Probably. But I wasn't about to broach the subject.

After a while of being a decent family member, I opened up my computer. Instead of writing, I perused social media, clicking through pictures of Iris and Cal, which then led me to clicking through pictures of me and Leo.

A text came in from Pete.

PETE
How's the writing going?

LU
Splendidly.

PETE
Mmm-hmm.

Having a friend with ESP is really annoying. I clicked away from my blank document as if Pete might be looking over my shoulder. I had six days to interview someone and write a column. It usually took me at least two days to draft something worthwhile, especially if I was working at the theater. I could probably get some work done on the train ride to Princeton on Friday when Jase and I went to visit Dad, but I definitely needed to have someone locked in to write about by then.

I looked over at my computer screen at a picture of me and Leo from that day we went to Coney Island in the winter. We'd had this notion that it would look beautiful after a blizzard, and it kind of did, but it was mostly miserable and depressing with everything shut down. We'd had fun for about six minutes, taken some selfies, and then gotten the hell out of there as soon as we could. I think we watched a movie at his place that day.

In the picture, the wind is blowing his hair across his face. He couldn't quite get it into the samurai-esque man bun yet. Sitting there on the couch, I tried to remember what Leo smelled like. For some reason I couldn't conjure it up; that particular aroma of his skin and clothes or whatever je ne sais quoi results in the symbiosis of a person's scent. It felt strange not being able to remember his smell.

Maybe that's what made me stand up from the couch, set my computer gently on the coffee table and stare at my phone as if it were buzzing in my hand. What I was really doing was scrolling to Leo's name in my phone. I hadn't done that since the last time he'd stood me up, the day I met Cal.

I tiptoed out of the living room and down the hall to my room, shutting the door quietly as the phone rang.

"Hey," Leo answered. He lingered on the *y* kind of like I had with Hafsah, but not like that at all.

"Hey." I tried to decide between sitting or pacing, then realized my room had about two steps' worth of pacing in any direction and plopped myself down on the corner of my bed. "How goes it?" I asked, which is not how I usually talk, because I'm a normal human person. I swear.

"It's, uh, good."

Someone strike this conversation from the annals of history.

"That's good. So good. Really happy for you," I said. I examined my fingernails and brought my thumbnail up to my mouth to chew on it, even though I had literally never done that before in my life. Through the parted blinds I could see the neighboring building, the column of bathroom windows, one of which was currently lit up. A blurry silhouette was showering, one royal blue bottle of shampoo or conditioner visible in the portion of the window that was pushed out into the night air, allowing mellow billows of steam to waft out.

"So, what's up?" Leo asked. I could hear something on in the background on his line, a reality show, maybe, or a Broadway cast recording.

My showering neighbor reached over for the visible bottle of shampoo, his hand recognizably male. Was I heeding Pete's advice to interview Leo, or was I going against his advice to forget about him? I suddenly wished I'd prepared questions before dialing. Pretty terrible journalistic move to arrive at an interview completely unprepared.

"Leo, I was wondering…"

A long pause from his end. "Yeah?"

I chewed off the corner of my thumbnail, cursing myself when it peeled away into my mouth. I spat it out quietly into my hand and tossed it into the nearby trash bin. My eyes were glued on the showering neighbor, but I'm pretty sure that if a human-sized wolf appeared in the window brushing its teeth and waving at me, I probably wouldn't have reacted at all. I was remembering Coney Island, the excitement of the subway ride there, the quiet disappointment on the ride back. Leo had played a game on his phone, taking the spurned plans pretty well. No matter how I felt, Leo could make the best of bad situations. He was not easily angered or annoyed.

"Can we talk?" I reached for something to fiddle with in my hands, landing on a receipt from the Comedy Cellar from the other night with Iris. I was slightly jealous of teenagers of old and their ability to play with tangled phone cords, tethered to a place but at least free to play endlessly. "About us?"

A quiet sigh from Leo. "I'm not sure that's a good idea."

"Why?"

Leo didn't say anything. You ever hear your past with someone in the pauses they take?

I thought about telling him the real reason I was calling, but couldn't decide if that was more or less weird than just playing the heartbroken-ex card. I crumpled the receipt and then smoothed it out on my thigh. "I just..." I trailed off. "I wish we could talk about it. Analyze things. Figure out what went wrong, what would have gone wrong regardless, what we did right. I wish we could talk about it like it was a harmless thing."

More pauses from Leo. "I'm not sure what to say to that." An awkward chuckle. Not even a chuckle. A throat spasm at best.

"We went through something, Leo. Good or bad, it was *something*. Good and bad, probably. And I was thinking that maybe..."

There was a loud crash on Leo's side of the phone, then some rustling about. "Sorry, I dropped my phone. What was that?"

The receipt was mostly smooth against my leg, so I crumpled it back up and tossed it over to my desk. Across the street, my showering neighbor shut off the water.

"We had love, Leo. Whether it's gone or not, that matters, doesn't it? It's an incredible facet of life and we should be able to dissect it. Share our experiences so that others can learn from them, or at least relate to them." My voice felt small in my room. I wondered if I should have been writing all of this down. I could hear Jase still chatting with his buddies on his headset, though making a concerted effort to be quiet. Through the crack under the door, I could tell the hallway light was off, which meant my mom was getting ready for bed. She'd be in soon to say good-night and ask me for the millionth time what my plans were for tomorrow.

"Um," Leo said, because I was a raving lunatic.

"What did you feel when——?" I asked, at the same exact moment that he said, "I'm pretty beat, I think I'm gonna go to——"

"Sorry," I said. "What was that?"

Leo cleared his throat. "I, uh… I should let you go."

My neighbor turned off his bathroom light. Down on the street, a car zoomed past, then squealed on its brakes. Jase button mashed on the couch, the little clicks and clacks impossible to make quieter, and I thought about going to grab my laptop. It was still on the coffee table, I knew, a yellow light blinking slowly to show it was on but asleep. I wished I could say the same about my writing. It was still alive, still within me somewhere. It just needed to be opened up again.

"Yeah," I said, "you should. Sorry for calling."

Yet another pause. I could picture Leo, if he were in another time, tangling himself up in a phone cord, trying to come up with something good to say. "It's…fine, Lu. It's okay. I hope you're okay." One last pause, this one the briefest of them all. I thought maybe I could slip into that pause. Maybe I could wedge myself between the boy I loved and whatever hesitation had caused him to put us here. Then he said good-night and hung up.

13
STARGAZING

The rest of the week passed by in a series of self-assurances that I still had time. It's only Tuesday, I'd thought when hanging with Iris. Plenty of weekdays left, plus a few of those sweet, sweet weekenders thrown in as a bonus. I told Pete how the phone call with Leo had gone, then shoved down the memory of the conversation, even though Pete said I could still write about our relationship without interviewing him. I could unload myself on the page, he said.

I shoved my empty notebook in his face and told him obviously I couldn't.

Wednesday I had work and then Mom, Jase, and I went over to my tita Marian's in Queens for a family dinner. It was hard to brainstorm backup plans for my column in that situation, because my family is loud and talkative and we have a tendency to end up gathered around the piano singing show tunes. Which was always great, except it was the first time we'd done it since Leo and I broke up. Show tunes reminded me of Leo, the way he looked on stage, the way he'd close his eyes when belting a note. I used to sit in his room pretending to redo homework while he practiced his lines and songs.

He'd catch me staring and blush, which was completely un-called for, because every note he sang was perfect.

At some point with my family, my cousin Cindy—who was living this awesome postcollegiate life in Brooklyn—asked me about how things were going at *Misnomer*. I almost answered honestly, but then Tita started playing a song from *Aida* on the piano and we all lost our collective minds belting out the lyrics. I was reminded how much my family loved Leo because he could belt along with us. Especially because my stupid aunt kept asking where he was.

Thursday I tried to eavesdrop and find another Iris and Cal, but came away with only an exchange which was either a recruitment for a pyramid scheme or a pitch for a cult. My words were nowhere to be found. My deadline approached.

By the end of my work shift, I was starting to get the feeling that I was just going to screw this up again, and that the screwup was almost entirely inevitable now. Even if I wanted to write about Cal and Iris against Iris's wishes, nothing was coming. "You need to forget about these two lovebirds," Pete said. He was throwing on a denim button-down over his black T-shirt as we walked out of the theater. "That's the only thing that's keeping you from writing."

"Writer's block is a thing, Pete."

"So is needless obsession with a distraction." He brushed the hair from his eyes. "You need to go home or are we hanging out?" I cringed and avoided eye contact. "Social cues tell me I'm not going to like what you say next."

"Iris texted me. She wants to hang out. I'd totally invite you but I feel like this might solidify our friendship and I don't want to ruin it with, like, a premature group hang." A trio of people was strolling in front of us, unaware that they were blocking the sidewalk. I sped around them, balancing on the edge of the sidewalk. Pete and I hate getting stuck behind slow walkers, but I was also making a conscious decision to keep him from making direct eye contact with me.

"Glad to see you're taking my advice," he said quietly. We headed toward Union Square, each swiping into an adjacent turnstile without saying much. We were taking separate lines so had to split up soon. It was not yet rush hour, and the station wasn't overwhelmingly crowded. A cute guy walked past briskly, thumbs hooked into his jean pockets like a fashion model. Pete was quieter than usual, and though I could see something bugging him, I didn't ask about it because (a) I was pretty sure I was to blame, and (b) Pete would speak his mind when he needed to.

We stood there for a moment, avoiding eye contact. "Is this gonna be how it goes for the summer?" he asked finally.

"Don't be dramatic. I told you I'll offer a group hang next time. You'll like her."

Pete nodded twice, then looked down at his shoes. "I leave in August too, Lu. You know that." Then he mumbled a bye and headed down the corridor toward the 1 train.

"I said *don't* be dramatic!" I shouted after him, eliciting stares from the fellow commuters not wearing headphones. "The quick departure after a sentimentally loaded statement is definitely a dramatic move!"

Pete turned around as he walked on his heels, giving me a shrug before spinning again and continuing on his path. I watched him go, then found my train to go meet up with Iris.

Iris and I met up at Columbus Circle again, this time going into the Whole Foods to grab supplies for a picnic. "I don't mean to be boring and repetitive," she said, "I'm just gonna miss this park so much."

"I will grieve for you while you suffer in the terrible land-scapes of Southern California."

"Fair point."

I let her lead the way around the store, picking out our snacks. I probably shouldn't have been surprised after seeing where she lived and our adventures the other night, but she didn't seem to pay much attention to the cost of things. A liter of kombucha, a tray of sushi, three mangoes, two vari-eties of organic kettle chips, some artisanal cheeses, a pound of sugar-free granola, about three other items with hyphen-ations in their descriptions.

Part of why Leo had said he didn't want to do long dis-tance was the cost. Neither one of us had a ton of expendable money, even though we worked, and long distance meant more of it would go to trains or buses to visit each other. I'd wanted to oppose this reasoning and remind Leo that love was heaps more important than money, but I'd kind of seen his point. I'd needed a scholarship for my parents to even be able to afford NYU, and I had no idea how I'd visit Leo enough to see him as much as I would have wanted to. If, you know, we were still dating.

Seeing Iris shop so indiscriminately made me think that she and Cal were maybe better suited to staying together if they had chosen the long-distance route.

"By the way, Cal's going to meet up with us."

We were by the self-service spice station, where large con-tainers of cardamom, star anise, and turmeric awaited for cus-tomers who went for that sort of thing in bulk. I said, "Cool," and pretended to read some labels. A funny feeling coursed through my body, or more accurately, my stomach and chest. Writers are liars. Feelings don't ever make it all the way down to your toes. I couldn't put my finger on what exactly it was.

Probably a mix of things, one of them definitely being guilt that I hadn't brought Pete along. But who likes feeling guilty? I shoved that feeling down, making room for the slight thrill I was experiencing that I'd get to see Cal and Iris together.

We paid for our snacks and went out to Columbus Circle to wait for Cal to arrive. I spotted him in the distance, wearing black pants, a maroon T-shirt, and carrying a black backpack. I realized that I hadn't seen him in person since the day of their fight. I'd forgotten how cute he was, how I'd wanted Leo to walk in on us sitting together and feel a pang of jealousy.

Then I remembered that Iris had no idea I'd met Cal already. I hadn't ever confessed the fact that I'd eavesdropped on them, and of course I hadn't ever mentioned our encounter on the bench. I had no reason to.

When he got closer Iris pointed him out and waved, and he smiled at us, then narrowed his eyes at me as he approached. I cringed, kind of hoping he wouldn't recognize me. "Oh my God!" he said immediately. "Bench Girl!"

I narrowed my eyes the same way he did, knowing I should probably just act natural. Problem is, my natural state is human, and human beings are weird. I pretended to search the files of my mind for recognition of his face. Finally, an Academy Award–deserving ten seconds later, I snapped my fingers and widened my eyes. "Holy shit!"

I turned to Iris, who had this confused smile on her face, then back to Cal. "This is so weird! Like, super weird. So incredibly weird I can't believe the improbability of this occurrence of events!"

"Um, what's happening?"

"Is this Lu?" Cal asked, pointing at me. "We sat on a bench together one day. I rambled about paintball teams."

Iris smiled and rolled her eyes. "Damn it, did you tell everyone about that analogy?"

"It's a great analogy," Cal rebutted. Then he looked at me and shook his head. "Even if it turned out to be not entirely true." His grin got bigger for a moment, and then he looked over at Iris and down at the ground.

I wasn't sure where to look so I turned to the French baguette I'd bought as part of my picnic and crinkled its brown paper bag, "Small world, huh?"

Iris had a few follow-up questions about our conversation at the park, which made me briefly panic at the possibility that the two of them could uncover the fact that I'd eavesdropped, but she was quickly sated and Cal soon changed the subject, the matter apparently put to rest way more easily than I could have anticipated.

We dodged a few joggers, heading toward one of the large grassy fields in the park. We picked a spot shaded by a tree, and then Cal unfurled a plaid blanket from his backpack, kicked off his shoes and used them as anchors against the wind. Meanwhile, Iris set out the spread of food she'd bought at Whole Foods, neatly arranging everything on the blanket as if preparing it for a professional photo shoot. We did all snap a few compulsory pics for social media, although in the end none of us posted them. I wonder about those pictures sometimes, the stockade we each have backed up online or on laptops, thousands of pictures of the minutiae of life. Someday, will I see all those forgotten selfies of me and Leo? Will that serve a purpose beyond nostalgia? Or are they just taking up digital space on some unseen server, never to be reexamined, and definitely not reexamined in any meaningful way?

Iris ran off to collect a few wildflowers from the edge of the field, leaving me and Cal alone for the first time since the bench. We made brief eye contact when she left, and I realized that he had beautifully dark eyes. As someone who's been told my whole life by societal representations of beauty that light-colored eyes are the only ones that can be beautiful, I have a deep appreciation for brown eyes that raise a middle finger to those beauty standards and simply slay with their beauty. Leo had eyes like that, and Cal did too, framed by dark lashes that almost made it look like he had eyeliner on.

"She likes a certain aesthetic to her pics," Cal said with a shrug, looking away from me to watch his girlfriend. He smiled after saying it, a smile clearly caused by Iris.

"Weird, the aesthetic I usually go for is not-good-enough-at-taking-pictures-to-be-allowed-to-share-pictures."

He laughed that laugh again, the one from the bench, the one that was like rising bread. "That's right," he said, snapping his fingers, "you're funny. I'd forgotten that."

"Um," I said, because you can't simultaneously confess to a near stranger that you really want to be thought of as funny yet be stricken by the constant insecurities that you're not at all.

"By the way, I've been doing that thing more often. The one I said I wanted to," Cal said.

I blinked at him like he had suddenly switched to a different language, one based on entirely different phonetics than any I'd heard in my life.

"The French tourists," he elaborated. "I've been trying to help people in small ways like that ever since we talked. Nothing crazy. Gave a homeless guy a pair of shoes, carried a lady's bags for a couple blocks. That's it." He scrunched his face up, as if he were embarrassed by this confession. "Both times, I thought of you."

Of all the reactions I could have possibly had, I somehow

smiled at this. "Really?" I looked down at my legs, then reached outside the breadth of the blanket and ripped a few blades of grass from the ground. "Why?"

Cal shook his head. He was sitting with his legs up and crossed, his arms wrapped around his knees. "I'm not sure. I guess because you were there when I thought of it?"

A few moments later, Iris returned with a handful of daisies, arranging them expertly around our spread. We took a few more pics, Iris on a fancy digital camera, then started to eat. The park was busy for a weekday, lots of picnickers and shirtless dudes playing Frisbee, a few women in bikinis taking advantage of the last few minutes of afternoon sun.

Iris said that she'd invited Cal along because she liked hanging out with me, and thought Cal would too. That she liked sharing joys with him.

"You guys are so direct," I said, popping a piece of sushi into my mouth with my fingers, since we'd forgotten to grab an extra pair of chopsticks. "Do you always just say what you mean? How do you function in society doing that?"

They both laughed, not taking offense to my comment. "I told you she was funny," Iris said, raising her eyebrows at Cal.

"You didn't lie." He reached over to rip off a chunk of baguette, pairing it with one of the soft cheeses Iris had brought and a little bit of rose petal jam. "I don't know. Being direct just feels good most of the time. A little uncomfortable sometimes, maybe, but even on the other side of that, there's relief."

"I can't be direct unless I'm making a joke," I said.

"Not true," Cal retorted immediately. "You just did it." He turned over his shoulder as a neon yellow Frisbee landed a few feet away. A tanned white guy with absurdly square pecs jogged up and grabbed it from the grass, flashing a smile at us. "Try it again."

I groaned, then tore a few more blades of grass, twisting them into one thick strand in my fingers. A tightness spread in my chest, which I interpreted as my body not being down for this direct ride stuff. They fell silent though, waiting for me to speak.

A few weeks after I started at *Misnomer*, before Leo and I started dating, I asked Hafsah for some tips on interviewing, since I was afraid every article would be just me ruminating repetitively on unrequited love.

"People are jacks-in-the-box, awaiting the chance to spring," she'd said. "You keep winding that crank."

"Ugh, is that really the plural of *jack-in-the-box*? It's gross," I'd responded.

I ripped my grassy braid into shreds, tossing them into the breeze, pretending I was still thinking. The sun had dipped beyond the horizon, causing the tanners to start to gather their things. Dozens of orange reflections glimmered in the windows of Midtown. "Cal, don't be like that. If she doesn't want to—"

"I'm jealous of the time you have together before breaking up," I said. A pause after, not just because I couldn't believe I'd brought myself to say it, but because I'm a goddamn pro and I know that letting the confession sink in might lead them to retaliate. Screw my deadline and my writer's block, screw Pete's advice, screw writing about Leo. This was the story I wanted. I shrugged at Iris, then looked at Cal, wondering how much Iris had told him about my article. "You guys have chosen momentary happiness, and I'm jealous of whatever it was that allowed you to do that. A lot of people would be."

Another Frisbee whizzed by us. This time a light-skinned black guy with sparse curls on his chest and a white bandanna tucked into his yellow shorts jogged past us, offering a smiling "sorry" before tossing the disk back across the field.

"See?" Cal said. "Feels good, right?"

Iris didn't say anything, her eyes following the black guy's light jog back toward his friends.

"A little bit," I said, watching Iris, waiting for her expression to change. She kept her gaze distant until Cal changed the subject, turning the conversation toward his plans to do as little as possible over the summer, before college and adulthood came around to drown him in responsibilities and the need to pretend to be busy. Iris snapped out of her daze and scooted a little closer to Cal, saying that she was going to walk as much of the city as she could manage before California beat her into its sedentary lifestyle.

"I'll photograph the whole city," she said, smiling at the thought. "I'll need something to look at when I'm missing it."

Other than that moment, they looked completely comfortable in each other's presence, even in front of me. They held hands and smiled at each other warmly without making it feel like they were about to start making out, which is honestly how almost every couple I've seen has ever acted.

I spent more time with Pete than anyone else, and sometimes I still felt awkward around him. Hell, I feel awkward when I'm alone in my room sometimes, like maybe my limbs are at strange angles or I'm doing something weird with my face and the whole world can see. I tried to remember if I was like this with Leo, but I couldn't recall. I remembered being happy with him, and in love, and turned on. But I'm pretty sure you can be all those things and still be awkward.

That two eighteen-year-olds could be in front of a third wheel and make each other laugh without making the third wheel uncomfortable astounded me, especially because I kept remembering the fight I'd witnessed, kept remembering that this was a couple that knew they were going to break up at summer's end. I'd never really looked at two people who were in love. I'd listened in, sure. But every couple I'd ever seen, I'd only glanced at for a few moments at a time. At the movies or at school or just walking down the street. I'd seen people and recognized them as a couple, but I'd never really studied the way two people acted when they were together. I wondered if this was what Leo and I had looked like, at least for a time.

"So, Lu, doing anything exciting this weekend?" Iris asked.

"Does New Jersey count?"

"Not normally, but I'm going to New Jersey this weekend too," Cal said. "Where in Jersey are you going?"

"Princeton, you?"

"No way! Me too."

"Whoa. Weird. Are you visiting my dad too?"

Cal laughed. "Yeah, he and I haven't had a night out on the town in a while, so we figured we'd go tear it up like the old days."

"Cal, be normal," Iris said.

"Do you take the train?" Cal asked.

"Friday afternoon," I replied, stealing some more rose petal jam for my baguette.

"Cool, I was gonna go on Saturday, but I'm sure my mom would love it if I showed up a day early, and a little company on the train is nice. If that's cool, I mean."

My mood was already the best it'd been in a while, and his awkward self-invite made it surge even further.

As the sky turned cotton candy colors and the air got a little less suffocating, Cal and Iris lay against each other on the blanket. He ran a hand through her hair. The noise of everyone else at the park came into focus—the joggers, the cyclists, the cheers from the baseball field nearby—and the three of us fell quiet, watching the clouds. I was starting to wonder how long this would go on for, but I was comfortable, and I wanted to see how quickly my statement would cause them to spring like a jack-in-the-box. I was so ready for them to start talking that I'd already started composing the article in my mind.

Cal and Iris were going to break up. Then they didn't.

The summer before college starts is riddled with the casualties of high school romances. Some couples survive the minefield of long-distance dating and opposing ambitions, some only think they can.

Other people on the field packed up their blankets and their books and Frisbees and went back to their lives. The joggers dwindled, the tourists disappeared. A breeze picked up.

"When does it start?" Iris asked.

"When does what start?" I asked, but too softly and Cal spoke over me.

"Technically, it already has. They say the best hours to view it are right before dawn."

"Cal! My parents will kill me."

"Don't worry, we can leave as soon as we see one."

"And how long's that going to take?"

"Well, we are in one of the brightest cities on Earth, it's a bit cloudy out, and there's a half-moon tonight, so chances are we're not gonna see a damn thing. But you've never seen one, and you've always wanted to. While I still hold the title of Guy Trying to Bring You Joy, I'm not going to let a meteor shower pass us by without you being around to witness it."

"I have questions," I said.

"Oh right." Iris sat up, reaching for a handful of kettle

chips. "I forgot to mention, there's a meteor shower happening tonight. You wanna stick around for it?"

"Um," I said because I wanted to shout "Yes" for six full seconds but wanted to be cool about it, and also probably had to check the time and come up with some excuse for my mom as to why I wasn't coming home yet again.

"Come on," Cal said, propping himself up on his elbows. His hair was messy from lying down, sticking out in the back in two perfect cowlicks. Iris noticed too and tried to comb them down with her hand. "It'll be fun." When his hair refused to comply, Iris chose to instead muss it up some more, and he grabbed at her wrist with a chuckle, his fingers crawling to hers to clasp around them.

I know this is a weird thing to say, but it felt so good to be just near their love. It was complicated, sure. Doomed to end up like mine and Leo's, maybe. But it just felt good to be near them. To be in the presence of a love like that.

I smiled and pulled my phone out of my bag, to text my mom that I was crashing at my cousin Cindy's tonight. "I'm in."

14

LIKE THE MOVIES

I woke up early to Cindy and her roommates getting ready for the day. The smell of coffee was in the air, and I had a vague notion that I'd had a dream about Cal and Iris, though I couldn't recall any details from it.

I already had six missed calls and three poorly spelled texts from my mom telling me to call her as soon as I woke up and that I was an awful sister for leaving Jase alone. What my mom probably meant to say was that I was an awful daughter for having escaped the tight clutches of her umbilical cord.

After calling to assure my mom that I was alive and had no plans to abandon the family, I joined Cindy and her roommates Melissa and Sal in the kitchen. Melissa had been up last night to let me in, and now she asked what I was doing in Central Park until 2:00 a.m. I wanted to tell them, but I thought the details might be a little hard to explain to anyone other than Pete, so I just said I was working on a writing project and left it at that. They shrugged and went on with their morning routines, which was great, but left me with the urge to talk about the previous night.

Okay, so Cal and Iris hadn't quite unloaded on me the way

I'd been hoping, but I'd gotten to see more of their relationship, enough to write about. I'd even written out something on my phone in the middle of the night: **He turns and kisses Iris on her temple, which is the most appropriate word for a body part that Cal can imagine, since the place it occupies feels sacred. What a thrill it is to have someone to kiss every day, someone to watch the skies with, someone to treasure, someone whose happiness is at least as important as your own.**

Not quite the makings of a relationship column, especially since I'd taken the liberty to go into Cal's perspective. Fiction, basically. And a little cheesy. Still. I woke up with the thrill of writing inside of me. I didn't care that it was Friday and I still didn't have my column written, or even a backup plan. The writer's block wasn't quite unblocked, but at least I'd written *something*. I didn't even need their permission, really, if I changed the names.

I poured myself a bowl of cereal, and texted an assurance to my mom that I'd see her at Penn Station before Jase and I headed off to Princeton. Then I chewed happily, a little exhausted but thrilled to be hanging out in the kitchen with Cindy and her roommates. They had already graduated from college but the whole morning had such a college-y vibe to it, or at least what I imagined college would be like, and it made me excited that I'd be going off to college in the fall.

Sal kept glancing at Cindy, and I wondered if anything was going on between them, even something unrequited. The whole world is mad with love, I realized. All the time, if they're not in the midst of it, everyone is seeking it out or hoping for it or recovering from it or looking for a better one.

I worked my morning shift, mostly bored out of my mind because Pete wasn't there. I tried texting him, but he wasn't the most efficient responder, and I couldn't always have my phone on me at work, so I had to keep myself entertained, which almost took the wind out of my I-wrote-something sails. Thankfully, my imagination kept going through my up-coming train ride with Cal, and I thought about how maybe just one more conversation would crack my writer's block. I still didn't have quite enough to comprise a good column without slipping into fiction, and if I fictionalized anything Hafsah would fire me quickly and ruthlessly, like a literal fire. So I needed just a little more.

After work I went straight to Penn Station to meet up with Jase and take the train to Jersey. A bunch of other divorce-lings were huddled by the schedule board with their week-end packs. I'd noticed that more kids came into the city on weekends to spend time with their dads, but there was a good group of us that made the trek out to the suburbs every now and then. Mom was always more of a city girl, having grown up in Manila, and after the divorce, Dad had fled back to Jersey and the quiet he'd always been more comfortable in.

Mom had accompanied Jase to the station, bringing a bag full of clothes for me and several complaints about my life choices. After she kissed us goodbye at the platform, I pulled out my book and settled onto the floor near Jase, scanning the crowd every now and then looking for Cal.

Eventually I fell into my reading, thinking maybe Cal was a late-person who might show up right before the train pulled away. I felt some weirdo take a seat right next to me and ignored him as best as I could, but then the creep had the chutzpah to scoot closer, so that our legs were almost touch-ing. Fuming, I had to keep rereading the same paragraph over and over again, until finally I decided to speak my mind.

Granted, I suck at confrontation, but I give a solid stink-eye, and I figured that would be good enough.

When I put my book down though, I saw that it was Cal, and he was smiling like an idiot. "Wow, that took way longer than I thought."

I closed my book over my finger, responding with my own idiotic smile (to be honest, I don't have many other kinds). "Long time no see," I said, which is a stupid thing people say to each other when they've seen each other recently.

"How is this?" He gestured to my book.

"So far so good."

He leaned forward to take a look at Jase, who had a unique talent for concentrating on whatever was in front of him. I have no idea what he's going to be when he grows up, but, man, is he gonna be a good one. Unless it involves multitasking. Then he's gonna be only partly good.

The train pulled into the station just then, rumbling a few newbies to their feet. The rest of us knew an onslaught of people coming into the city for the weekend were going to take their sweet time and we stayed out of the way. Jase didn't even glance up.

Cal smiled and nodded, then put his knees up and wrapped his arms around them, looking out at the passengers. "How late did you guys stay last night?" I whispered, hoping Jase wouldn't hear me and deduce something he could blackmail me with at a future date.

"Sunrise," Cal said, smirking, but trying to hide it.

I caught myself staring at the side of his face. I wanted to ask him everything about the night but wasn't sure that was a conversation I was ready for. Then he pulled a book out of his bag and started reading, so I tried to do the same, though I kept thinking he was glancing over at me and couldn't focus on a word I was reading. After a few minutes the platform cleared and we boarded the train.

Cal walked behind me and Jase and helped us put our bags in the overhead bins, since I'm tiny and, even though Jase seemed like he was huge to me, he was still only thirteen and couldn't lift his bags without struggling. I plopped down into a window seat, expecting Cal to say bye, but instead he hoisted his own bag over his head, his T-shirt coming up a little and giving me an unexpected glance at his stomach. It was just an inch of stomach or so, nothing of any note, but I caught sight of a faint trail of hair leading up to his belly button.

I turned to look out the window but saw only the tunnel wall and my reflection. Then I felt Cal's weight sink into the seat next to me. Jase was sitting across the aisle, looking for an outlet beneath the seats to plug his phone charger into.

The train started moving, and one of those train guys came by to check our tickets. He punched holes in them without ever looking at our faces. Cal stretched his legs out. We each opened our books, but I found myself rereading the same sentence again. I closed the book, and even though Pete and I have a golden rule never to disturb someone reading, I just couldn't help myself. "Do you and Iris do stuff like that all the time?"

Cal furrowed his brow. "Like what?"

"Picnics at Central Park, watching a meteor shower until dawn. Crazy romantic stuff that people in real life don't do."

He thought for a moment, setting his book down on his lap. "I don't know. I don't think we're all that different from other relationships."

I rolled my eyes. "I'm not the most romantically experienced person in the world, but I do write about relationships. Semiprofessionally. And I'm here to tell you, you are. No one does that. My ex and I once went out for a sit-down sushi dinner, and that was about the pinnacle of our romance." I paused as a couple walked down the aisle wearing huge traveler backpacks with straps flapping all around. I wondered if what I'd said was true. Surely, Leo and I had done something more romantic than that. Nothing came to mind, but I made a mental note to dig deeper into my memories. "Oh, and once we picked a rom-com on Netflix and held hands the whole way through, reaching for popcorn with our free hands."

Cal laughed and sat up straighter. "I think people want to be more romantic. They just keep themselves from being romantic because they don't know that it's actually pretty easy to do stuff like that. All you have to do is open the door."

"Open the door?"

"Yeah, it's this thing I think about often. It's from a story called 'Light of Lucy' by Jane McCafferty. There's this quote Iris and I love about how we all have just one life and every night is numbered and could be more like the movies if only we opened up our hearts, not all the way or all the time, but like you open the door for a cat, just enough to let it out into the open air."

I stared at him. "See? Who does that? Who quotes stories all the time? Both of you have done that already and I've barely even hung out with you guys."

"You don't love quotes?"

"Of course I do, but I can never work them into conversation that easily. Or remember a whole freakin' paragraph." I totally do and can, but it was fun to have a little outburst anyway. It felt justified.

The train came aboveground at that point, the darkness cut by the Manhattan skyline reflecting off the clouds and making the whole sky look orange. Jase was asleep in his seat, his phone dead in his lap. Someone a few rows away was listening to music loud enough for us to hear.

"I'm sorry I'm being weird," I said. "But now you see why I want to write about you, right? You guys do open that door, instead of all of us schmucks who just watch other people do it in movies."

"What do you mean write about us?" Cal asked.

I frowned. "Iris didn't tell you?"

The train screeched to a halt, sending Cal's book tumbling to the ground. He reached down for it, his arm brushing past my leg. A few of the divorcelings got off, their bags bumping into the backs of seats. Jase woke up and asked me if he could borrow my phone, and by the time I'd turned back Cal was looking out the window and it felt like too much time had passed to nudge him about it.

The car lurched forward again, and we stayed quiet all the way to the next station, which was a repeat of the last. A handful of people got off, most of them recognizable divorcelings.

Cal smacked his book into the palm of his other hand, the noise pulling me from my thoughts. "So, you should come to my friend's party tomorrow night," he said, as if the book-smack had obviously been a way to end the conversation.

"Uh, I don't know if my dad will let me." I'm not great at parties. I go to the corner and start writing in my head and I either get all quiet and judgy, or I come up with something good and have to write it into my phone, then everyone thinks I'm an antisocial jerk.

"Okay, I'll talk to him. I'm good with parents. What side of town does he live on?"

"Palmer Square. But, seriously, my dad usually likes us to spend the whole time together. He hands us itineraries when we walk in the door. There's no way he'll let me go to a party with someone he's never met."

"Don't worry. The party's super close to that area. I'll convince him." He pulled his phone out of his pocket and leaned into his seat, putting a foot up on the armrest in front of him. "Iris says you should come," he said, showing me the conversation which had somehow been going on this whole time.

"Okay," I said, not really believing I'd go to the party.

The rest of the train ride, Cal read from his book, occasionally pausing to text Iris. I stared out the window, watching New Jersey towns go by. I usually couldn't stand being on the train without reading or listening to music, but I was strangely at peace, happy with my thoughts.

We got to Princeton and Cal helped us with our bags again, and then he took off to catch a bus. "I'll text you when I'm on the way tomorrow," he called back.

A few moments later our dad showed up wearing his typical khaki pants and royal blue blazer. He gave us one of his patented awkward hugs, Jase first and then me. It started as a side hug, then about a second into it he decided it was too impersonal and went for the full hug. But he assumed that as teenagers we'd be embarrassed by it, so he did it halfheartedly. I missed the hugs we used to get. The ones that felt like he'd spent the whole week missing us. Then he asked about the train ride, like he always does, despite the fact that we have never once answered in an interesting way.

"It was okay," Jase and I both said. Dad picked up my duffel bag but made Jase carry his own, and then we walked toward his car. I kept expecting him to purchase a midlife-crisis sports car, but it was still the sensible sedan he'd had for years. My dad was too broke and responsible for a midlife crisis, it seemed. It would have been sweet to have him unexpectedly fall into some college-tuition-level dough, but apparently Dad was "happy at his position," which is adult for "I have failed to buy into the American ideals of always wanting more money."

We went out for dinner at the one Filipino place in town— Dad's ongoing way to either poke fun at Mom's Italian food obsession, or his way to keep close to her, I'm not sure. These dinners usually consisted of Dad catching up on our lives at school, but because it was summer both of us had very little info to provide.

"How's the writing going, Lu? Is there any more paper- work I need to fill out for the scholarship?"

Ugh. I hadn't even thought of the scholarship in a while. For the past week, whenever my panicky thoughts came, they were still all about Hafsah and blank pages, and they'd been quickly repressed by good cheer and fantasizing about how incredible my eventual Iris and Cal column would be. "It's, uh, yeah. Going well. I pitched this idea for a series to my editor, and she was really into it."

"Taking initiative, way to go. When's it publishing?"

"Er." I stabbed at a comically large piece of chicken adobo and shoved it into my mouth with a little side of rice. "Shmo- moni shmoon," I said.

"Dad, she's so weird," Jase said. "You think I'm kidding, but this is how it is, like, all the time."

"Right." My dad smiled politely. A lifelong academic, he was thrilled for me when my writing led to school opportuni- ties, especially since his lack of tenure meant he had no sway and no money. He loved hearing the details of *Misnomer*, the process I went through with Hafsah, how many views each of my columns got. He especially loved hearing about my scholarship. The writing itself he never really asked about. It probably made him uncomfortable. And I don't really have any complaints. I think I've used the word *boner* two or three times throughout my career. "Well, I'm proud of you, hon. Do I say that enough?"

"Shmo shmuch," I said, still chewing.

"Good. Just want to hammer that point home. I couldn't be prouder of all you've done, and all you're going to do." He smiled, and I think I may have seen a tear glimmer in his eye. Which meant that for the rest of the evening—as we finished our meal and headed home, sat in our usual spots in the living room, tried to remember whose turn it was to pick a movie to watch, went about watching that movie, talked about it when the credits rolled, talked about plans for the next day, said good-night, and finally went our separate ways—I was screaming internally, watching my life teeter on the brink of some nameless abyss, all of it about to fall apart.

15

ATMOSPHERIC PRESSURE

The next morning I woke up to an email from Leo. Well, I woke up to the desire to pee, but then when I got back to bed I checked my email and saw Leo's name in my inbox for the first time in weeks. And right next to it was the subject line: **Do you know that I still...** And then the character limit cut it off so I couldn't see how the sentence ended.

It's a terrifying thing, seeing an email from an ex. Especially when you were kind of managing not to obsess about them lately. Kind of. I stared at it for a long time, wondering if I really wanted to read the message. All day, really, I'd look at my phone and wonder how the thought ended.

Hey, Lu, do you know that I still inexplicably hate sea salt and vinegar chips?

Hey, Lu, do you know that I still really like Nic Cage movies? All of them. A lot. Anyway, have a good day.

Hey Lu, do you know that I still am the most comfortable

**person on the planet, even though you don't get to experi-
ence it, and probably never will again, since I ended things
over four weeks ago and haven't changed my mind at all?
Do you know that I still feel exactly the same way I did the
day I dumped you? Just checking. Best, Leo.**

But, out of bravery or fear, I'm not sure which, I left the
email in the bold font of the unopened. Which was a pretty
freaking impressive accomplishment, because for most of the
day I had my laptop and my phone directly in front of me. I
needed to write. I needed what I knew about Cal and Iris to
come flowing into my fingertips and onto the page where I
was at my best. I needed to forget about Leo.

PETE
How's the writing going?

I needed Pete to shut up.

In the afternoon, Dad said he had to go take care of some
errands, so I had him drop me off at a coffee shop near the
university. Watching people flow in and out of a coffee shop
usually helped stir my creative juices. I brought earphones
with me to help me resist the temptation to eavesdrop, and
as soon as I had set myself up, I looked up as many writer's
block cures as the internet could provide:

Inspirational quotes, advice from some of my favorite authors, ten minutes of freewriting (which resulted in mostly
gibberish, but one really great paragraph about what kind of
homeless person I'll be in my desolate future), taking a walk
(twice around the block), stepping away from my writing to
do anything else (probably hadn't earned that one yet). Nothing worked.

The only strategy that felt slightly good was bashing my fingers up and down on the keyboard as if I were killing a whole slew of spiders, and resting my forehead on the table and making slight whimpering noises. Which definitely made me look like the most with-it person at the coffee shop. But it wasn't quite as productive as I'd hoped. How the hell had I gotten to this point in my life? Why had I even accepted the terms of the scholarship? I should have, like, haggled or something.

I composed several texts to Iris, begging her to change her mind and let me interview her, but deleted all of them before sending.

Another ESP-level text from Pete came in.

> **PETE**
> I think you're going to have to write about yourself, Lu. Just send something in. It doesn't even have to include Leo's perspective, so you don't have to interview him. Didn't Hafsah tell you to write yourself into the pieces anyway? Start with yourself. The rest, whether it's the lovebirds or not, can come later.

> **LU**
> Your texts are entirely too long

> **PETE**
> Trying to help. Not sure how else.

I groaned.

> **LU**
> I know. Sorry. We'll talk later.

I got myself another coffee, used the bathroom, returned to my little self-made hell. It should have been a breeze to write about myself. Just tap into how it felt when I saw Leo's name in my inbox again.

I thought about the day after the breakup. I'd had to work at the theater, which had felt like an unnecessarily cruel blessing. I didn't want to be in public and every moment of it hurt, but I was grateful for all those moments away from my own brain. From the fact that Leo had ended this thing that had been so good.

I remember scooping popcorn into a bucket for a customer that day, my mind lost in the soft swish of the kernels hitting the steel scooper. It sounded like Leo tossing in his sleep, a sound which I thought was going to increase in my life, not suddenly cease. For good reason too. He'd said the words to me.

"One day, we'll be able to do this freely," he had said. It was weeks before the split, an afternoon nap we used to take too many of, forcing ourselves into sleep in the yellow light of day, since our parents didn't allow sleepovers and we weren't going to abstain completely.

He'd said the words into the back of my neck as we spooned, the position in which all the best things get said. "You think we're happy now, just you wait."

"Oh yeah?" I'd rubbed my nose on his forearm to scratch an itch, then let my lips rest against his skin. "How so?"

"Well, for one, we'll be done with school."

"You love school."

"Yeah, but we'll finally have enough free time to record our R & B album," Leo had said. "And once it goes platinum, our parents will come to terms with the fact that our adult lives have arrived and they'll stop freaking out at the idea of us lying down together behind a closed door."

"So in this scenario, we are platinum-selling artists and still live in our parents' tiny Chinatown apartments, but they're now okay with us having sex."

"They've matured so much, haven't they? I'm proud of them."

"Are we still going to college?" At that point we hadn't talked about it yet, and I'd tried to toss the words out casually, broaching the subject because I was hoping that doing so wouldn't ruin the moment but only increase its joys.

"Don't be silly, we have an international tour to go on. We'll be spooning in five-star hotels."

After a couple of hours swimming in memories like that at the Princeton coffee shop, my dad picked me up and we headed back home. *Do you know I still want to go on an international R & B tour with you?*

As promised, Cal showed up at my dad's that night. He'd texted me to get the address, and told me to pretend not to know anything about the party. By the time he showed I was ready to get out of my head for a bit, to surround myself with the distractions a party had to offer, to stop actively resisting opening Leo's email.

Cal knocked politely. He was wearing his usual skinny jeans with a button-down plaid shirt over a plain gray T-shirt. His timing couldn't have been better, as Dad was busting out the Scrabble. Look, I have nothing against Scrabble. But there's something despairing about playing it with your family on a Saturday night.

Dad, bless his optimistic heart, thought I'd invited Cal over to play with us. His face lit up when I introduced them. "I always say this game is best with four people playing,"

Dad said, setting down the board on the dining room table. "Maybe you'll finally lose," he said to me, winking. Winking is the weirdest thing in the world, and no one should do it, especially not middle-aged men.

"Absolutely!" Cal said, before I could argue.

My dad looked thrilled. Jase looked like he did not care how many people were at the table playing as long as the game was over within three minutes or so and he was allowed to return to something with a screen. Cal took a seat, and I just stood there, figuring Cal was buttering up my dad a little, but still not wanting to stay at the house any longer.

I suppressed a sigh and took a seat, hoping I'd be strong enough to resist opening the email even longer. Meanwhile, Cal made small talk with my dad expertly. Jase played the first word: *but*. My dad wrote down the score. "At least we have one literate person in the family," he chided, though Jase didn't care enough to be insulted.

Cal laughed politely. He was pretty good at Scrabble but he was much better at putting on the good kid routine. My dad's not really the overprotective type. Truth be told, he was probably thinking that Cal and I were dating or something, and might have been secretly thrilled about it. I never talked about Leo with my dad, he might not have ever heard the name.

Halfway through the game I was up by a decent amount, which made everyone think harder about the words they were playing, which made the game go excruciatingly slowly. And that was when I finally caved and opened Leo's email.

It was a mistake to do that.

Hey Lu, do you know that I still love you? Thought maybe you should know.

I closed the email, reopened it, closed it again. I wanted to throw my phone across the room but also hug it to me.

For the rest of the game, I had to be reminded it was my turn and played only three-letter words. When we were finally done, I looked eagerly at Cal to make our break, and he seemed to catch on that I was not looking to stick around. He told my dad that we were meeting some friends of his for a movie night.

"I'll have her back before midnight," Cal promised.

We walked quietly in the warm night, our steps loud on the sidewalk until we turned a corner and hit a strip of college bars that drowned out the sound. "Everything okay?" Cal asked.

"So, what's this party we're going to?" I said, pretending I hadn't heard him. "Another Scrabble party, I hope."

"Funny," Cal said, nudging me with his shoulder. "Just a couple of guys I went to high school with. Should be pretty low-key."

Now, in reality, there was about ten minutes of mild-mannered walking and about twenty more after we walked into the crummy frat house before the party really got going. But in a movie they would have totally smash-cut to the scene I saw not all that much later: a group of dude-bros each carrying a case of beer and an iguana on their shoulders. That's four cases of beer and four iguanas. For one party. That's an unreasonable ratio of iguanas to beer, especially in the northeast.

The music got loud, and by extension so did everyone else at the party. The hot tub in the backyard was uncovered and promptly filled up with guys eager to take their shirts off, maybe in the hope that the handful of girls at the party would too. The other girls at the party seemed just as uninterested as I was in joining a six-person hot tub with twelve dudes in it.

Cal and I grabbed some beers, and while I had a strong desire to go off to the corner and watch the madness ensue from afar, Cal ushered me around the party saying hi to a couple people. He was staying with his friends Johnny and Raul, but had clearly made more friends since his arrival.

It was a distraction, exactly what I needed to keep myself from repeating Leo's email in my head all night, or even worse: responding. I did not trust myself to say anything coherent or sane, much less something that I would feel good about having said in the morning. My first instinct was to gush back, tell him everything that I'd been planning on telling him at the bench that day, and all those other times before. Then what though? He hadn't written anything about getting back together. Could I handle another instance of him not showing up, emotionally or otherwise?

Since I didn't have that skill some people seem to have for being able to hear things when the music is too loud, I mostly sipped from my beer and nodded while Cal chatted with his friends. I didn't really drink often, so I tried to pace myself, but when you're just being quiet and listening as best you can to a conversation that's being drowned out by a bassline, it's hard to keep track.

The frat house was run-down. I'm getting ahead of myself here. It was a *frat house*. Greek letters were plastered all over the place, numbering almost as many as the stains on the gray carpet. The only person I even slightly knew was Cal, who was still somewhat of a stranger, though one whose love life I felt completely immersed in lately. In the moment that didn't make any sense to me. There were drinking games to my left, dudes dancing like idiots to my right, and here I was obsessed with a relationship that wasn't even mine. I looked over Cal's shoulder as he talked casually with a group of girls, seemingly impervious to the music.

A half hour into the party I'd reread the email about seventeen times. **Do you know that I still love you?**

No, goddamn it, Leo. I did not know that.

Because he hadn't talked to me in weeks, and the last time he had, save for one stupid, heart-wrenching exchange when I was at work and he was my customer, was when he told me he didn't love me enough to stay with me, in so many words.

Why now?

I drank more from my beer and read the email and thought back to our 0.9% of a life together. I thought about how many times he'd said something as sweet and charming as he had in this weeks-too-late email that contradicted all of his actions.

It was hard to count, because it felt like a time in my life so far-removed from the present, but maybe also because of the beer. But as I stood there in a darkened frat house, surrounded by freakin' iguanas and conversation, I thought to myself that it hadn't been enough. And suddenly I was angry. I felt like Leo hadn't meant a word of his email, but had only missed me for a moment, had only felt the guilt of his actions and thought a stupid confession like that would help.

I felt like I was a receipt that had stayed in Leo's pocket too long; proof of something he once thought worthwhile but no longer needed. What I really needed to do was text Pete. He would get me through this.

Except when I tried to do that, I just ended up reading the email another eight million or so times and stewing.

I decided to put my phone away and see what else the party had to offer. Wandering away from Cal, I stepped through the door that led outside. Immediately one of the hot tub dudes beckoned me over to the steaming cauldron of germs and general grossness.

I thought about Cal and Iris at Central Park the other night, thought about how good those months with Leo had been when they were good, and how quickly it had all gone away. Could either of those relationships ever come from me allowing myself to be beckoned into a hot tube by some dude at a frat party? Maybe I'd throw caution to the wind. Just kiss the first cute boy I saw. Not in the hot tub, of course. But some other more presentable cute boy. I looked around the party but my eyes didn't really land on anyone. My beer was empty all of a sudden, so I put the can down and went hunting for another.

Oh, look. There was one. Not a beer. A cute boy. He was leaning against the wooden pillar of the little hand-built-patio thing they'd put the hot tub on. White T-shirt and blue jeans, sneakers that had somehow managed to stay clean at the party. He had dark brown skin and a small afro, a silver bracelet on his left wrist. He looked bored, but in a content way. Like he understood boredom was transient and a part of life and he was just patiently waiting for someone to come along and pull him out of it. I could be that person. I'd wait for eye contact and then just strut my little self confidently over there and kiss him, forgetting about Leo entirely. I'd take him by the hand and say something, like… I don't know. Something really…mmph! It would come to me.

Oh no, he'd looked at me. Dead on, eyes-on-eyes, pupils, irises the whole thing. Had he smiled too? Holy shit, that was intimidating. I was definitely not going over there and kissing him. Who the hell did things like that?

I went back inside, running from my embarrassment, and found another beer in the fridge.

Scanning the room, I spotted Cal talking to yet another group of people. I felt my phone in my pocket, the email basically poking me in the thigh, like Jase used to do when he was smaller and wanted attention. Not to be outdone by an email, the fact that it was Saturday and I had another deadline on Monday exploded into my mind too, burning a hole in my thigh. Or the thigh part of my anxiety. Anxiety is human-shaped, therefore has thighs, right?

Maybe I'd had enough beer.

I checked my phone, reread the email.

Okay, one more beer and then I'll go, I thought to myself. *I'll stay up all night writing about myself, fueled by beer and the terrifying proximity of my deadline. Catharsis after catharsis will find me in the middle of the night, bathed in only the gentle glow of my computer screen, the way all brilliant writing happens.*

There was a cute Asian guy on the couch, but his face was zoned in on his phone. I pictured him reading an email from an ex too, feeling the same things I was feeling. Does love ever come up from two people just trying to stick it to someone that's left them behind? If not love, I'm sure there had been good make-out sessions founded on just that. Except I kept looking over in his direction and trying to catch his eye, but he was only interested in his phone.

I didn't know what I had expected from that party. A distraction from thinking about love and its absence in my life? Time spent with Cal? Normal teenage behavior? Then I felt that unique tingle of my cheeks going into blushing-drinking mode, looked around the party, and realized I was tipsy.

I'd only been at that stage a couple of times before, and I'd forgotten how downright pleasant it could be, at least physically. I looked over at the guy on the couch and he actually looked back. I wanted to smile at him but I guess I wasn't quite there yet. I drank a little more.

Now, I'm not one to condone teenage drinking or anything. But at that moment? I was ready to condone the hell out of it. If I drank a little more, maybe I'd even be able to smile at Couch Guy. I should have really texted Pete already. Pete was great. He'd talk me through this party. He'd convince me to delete Leo's email before I could respond to it, before it burrowed itself into the scars that had somewhat healed, ripping them apart anew.

I pulled my phone out and sent him a message, waiting for the ellipsis that said he was writing back. Meanwhile I took another sip from my beer and watched the party, this time not scanning for cute boys, or being too judgmental of bathtub bros, just watching the sight of a hundred or so people interacting. Five minutes later Pete hadn't even checked my message yet, but I was feeling all warm and chatty, so I found Cal and worked my way into the little circle he was standing in.

This took a little work. First, I stood by and waited for him to notice and open up the circle. When that didn't work, I tried to catch what they were talking about and chime in with my own comment. But they were talking about some people they knew, and so I just pretend-laughed whenever they laughed. Then I realized I wasn't sure what my real laugh sounded like, so I had to practice laugh a few times, which is what finally made Cal notice I was there.

"Are you drunk?" Cal asked.

"Probably," I conceded when I caught my breath from my practice laughter.

Cal and I stood quietly for a while, watching the party unfold. An uncomfortably grindy dance party had broken out, the music getting even louder than it was before. Several couples around the party were deep into make-out mode, the beer pong table was surrounded by people who seemed to have a moral imperative to high-five every eight seconds.

Cal leaned in so I could hear him over the music, his mouth close to my ear. "How do you feel at parties?"

I tilted my head at him, then leaned in to him, our shoulders touching as I shouted to be heard. "Awkward and buzzed. Why do you ask?"

"You don't feel this deep curiosity about everyone? Like, this amazement that humanity is a thing that exists in the world, and that you get to be surrounded by it?"

"Cal, there are literally six dudes peeing against the fence in the backyard, and another one passed out in the dirt."

Cal turned to look and laughed. "Still."

Somehow, this led to us deciding we'd go around the party talking to as many people as possible and introducing each other as someone else every time.

The first few attempts went horribly, since I was still in quite the giggly mood, and Cal tried to introduce me as his newly adopted sister, then as his newly adopted daughter, then as an extraterrestrial refugee that his family had taken in until the war ended on my planet. The last one didn't have much of a chance of fooling anyone, even without my giggling.

Cal pulled me aside as I recovered from my fit. "Come on, Lu," he said, a little giggly himself, but managing to put on a straight face. "You need to get it together. A lot is on the line here."

"Like what?"

Cal grabbed me by the shoulders and shook. "*Like what? The joy of fooling someone!*"

"That doesn't sound like a very honorable mission."

"It isn't!" Cal cried out, a smile breaking through. "But

what of the memory of tonight? Remember, you have but one life, and this is one night in that one life." He pulled his hands away then gestured toward a couple that had just walked in. "Perfect. There are two people neither of us know, and who we won't ever see again. Now, what are we going to do?"

"Lie to them?"

"Exactly! We're going to bring fiction to life. Follow my lead."

He took off across the house and I followed behind, starting to get a little stumbly, but otherwise feeling great. The only thing on my mind now was not writing or Leo, but just this comparatively simple task of not giggling while lying to strangers.

Cal reached the couple and put his arm around the guy, who was tall and muscular, with one of those chiseled jaws that always make me think of action figures and cartoon superheroes. "Norton! So great to see you again."

"Uh, my name's not—"

"And, Matilda, darling! How are things?" Cal stepped away from the guy and gave two Italian air-kisses to the very confused girl. I stood by, focusing on not laughing the same way you try to resist a sneeze in class.

The couple got understandably wide-eyed. "You've got the wrong people, man. We're not—"

"Nonsense!" Cal said. He stepped over to me and put his arm around my shoulder. "Don't you remember us, old chap? We're the Kaminskys! The safari last year? Dar es Salaam?"

"We shared a tent," I said, not really knowing where the hell the improvisation was coming from. Maybe it was from Cal's arm on my shoulder, which gave me a little rush of warmth and joy. "The sound of hyenas kept us up at night, and we each confessed our secrets to each other, so that we wouldn't take them to the grave."

"What the hell?" the girl said, grabbing her boyfriend by the arm and trying to pull away from us.

Cal sidestepped and blocked their path. "You don't need to worry, Matilda. Your secret's been safe with us. No one will know about the homeless man you murdered."

"Or about your fear of chickens," I added, putting a reassuring hand on her shoulder, which she immediately shrugged off. "We haven't told a soul."

They made a few more evasive maneuvers around us, managing to sneak away, casting furtive glances back at us. "You gave us the best night of our lives!" I shouted.

When they disappeared into the crowd, Cal and I turned to each other and immediately burst into laughter. Then we decided that we probably didn't need to have any more beer, and that it was a good note to leave the party on. I stepped outside to get some fresh air while Cal went around saying bye to his friends. It was perfect out, unlike the mugginess of Manhattan summer nights, a cool breeze blowing in through the trees lining the street.

The last time I'd had this much fun was with Iris, and I gave a quiet thanks to past me for being in the right place at the right time and meeting these two. They hadn't saved me from my writer's block, but they kept saving me from nights thinking about Leo. I hadn't even checked my phone in a while, and had no desire to now. A minute or so later Cal came out, stumbling a little bit and smiling widely.

"God, that was fun," he said.

"Yeah. It reminded me of being little." We walked down the driveway and turned in the direction of my dad's house.

"Playing pretend. It's like childhood's one big game of improv that we lose the skill for when we hit puberty."

"At least the cringing sticks around," he quipped. "Kind of sad though. Why do you think that happens?"

I shrugged. "Hormones and society. I don't know." I laughed and looked up at the sky. There were way more stars out than there had been at the park that night, but I somehow felt like even if there was a meteor shower today too, we wouldn't be lucky enough to see any. Only Iris and Cal would. I glanced at Cal, a little surprised by how well we'd gotten along all night. "I like to think there's an unexpected explanation for it. Not something reasonable, like self-consciousness or social norms or anything like that. Something sillier."

"Like what?"

I thought for a while. "Piggyback rides."

Cal burst out into laughter, and I wanted him to keep on laughing the whole way back. "God, I love that idea. That if we just gave each other piggyback rides more often we'd find our inner children."

I didn't say anything. I was happy. Even if I knew part of it was the alcohol. Happiness is always chemically induced, whether the chemicals are naturally occurring in your head or ingested. I slowed down my pace, not just because I was swaying to the point that every now and then I'd bump into Cal, but because I wanted to prolong this walk back to my dad's. I didn't want the feeling to go away, didn't want to be alone at home, didn't want to think about Leo's admission that he still loved me.

"Give me a piggyback ride!" Cal shouted out suddenly into the night air.

I laughed. "Cal, my legs are so stubby they can barely support *my* weight. I don't think it's a good idea to load you on top. No offense."

"Okay," he said, undeterred, "then let me give you one. I'm sure giving a piggyback ride is as effective as getting one for the purposes of being a kid again. And if that doesn't make any sense, just pretend it does." He smiled, and his eyes were wide and gleeful. I like to think that, somewhere deep down, in whatever part of me was still sober, I knew it was a bad idea. I like to think that I hesitated, that I was at least initially responsible and intelligent, even if that wasn't the part of me that won out.

But the truth is that as soon as the words were out of his mouth, I was ready. I wasn't just ready. I was thrilled. The happiness I'd felt just a second before had in an instant multiplied, if happiness is a thing that *can* be multiplied. Whatever. There was more happiness than there was before. I was elated. I was thrilled. There was nothing in the world I wanted to do more than to jump on Cal's back and have him carry me down the street, laughing.

"That is such a good idea!" I cried out, even though— heavy-handed foreshadowing here—it wasn't.

We laughed into the night like a couple of cartoon villains, and then Cal turned his back to me, flexing his knees, ready to take my weight. I took a few steps back to get a running start, which made sense at that point. Like, I was short and I thought I needed that running start to jump high enough. I landed with my arms wrapped around his neck, his hands holding my legs on either side of him.

"Hold on," he said, and then he shifted a little, readjusting me on his back. My arms weren't all the way up on his neck anymore, but secured tightly against his chest. "That's better." He turned over his shoulder to look at me. "Ready?"

I nodded, holding on, feeling my heart pounding against his back.

"And away we go," he said, and he took off running.

The air rushed past me, like we were going way faster than we possibly could have. I pictured my hair flowing in the wind and closed my eyes for a second, basking in that breeze. When I opened my eyes again, trees were blurring on either side of us. We were either accomplishing impossible feats, or I was kind of drunk. A curb was coming up ahead, and I braced myself tighter against Cal. I became aware of my hands against his chest, the skin and rib cage that I could feel through his soft T-shirt.

Cal hopped off and landed without a problem, running on with another one of his doughy laughs. I let my chin drop to his shoulder. I could see a bead of sweat forming at his hairline, right behind his ear. I forgot about everything else and watched as it traced down his neck, around the curve of his collarbone, soaking into his shirt. Without a clue as to why the hell I was doing it, I leaned into him. Nothing obvious, but just enough so that our cheeks grazed against each other.

"Oh shit," he said, a breathless whisper. Then I felt us start to tumble forward, gravity tugging at us.

The next thing I felt was a shooting pain on the side of my face. I closed my eyes, dizzy, and when I opened them again I saw Cal's head framed by trees and the New Jersey night. His face was drawn with concern.

"You're okay," he said, moving his hand to wipe hair from my face.

"How bad is it?"

"Not bad at all," he said. He took off the plaid button-down he was wearing over his T-shirt and bunched it up into a ball. Then he pressed it against my face, and the pain came to life again. I couldn't tell exactly where it was coming from.

"What happened?"

"I lost my balance. I'm so sorry."

I blinked a few times, and I could feel tears forming in my eyes. One of them scuttled down, focusing the stinging pain on my cheek.

"Come on. Let's get you home and cleaned up."

"Okay," I said. Then I let out a giggle. "You shouldn't piggyback under the influence."

He smiled, still dabbing his shirt at my face.

Then he helped me up and held my arm as we walked the ten blocks or so to my dad's house. I was dazed and in pain. I was worried about the fact that the pain was coming from my face, and how I would explain that to my dad. I was worried about permanent damage, scarring, a concussion. But Cal kept saying reassuring things to me, one arm around my shoulder, and it was helping. The tears were flowing, but it was more of a physical reaction than sadness or worry or panic. Somehow, a trace of the night's joys remained, and maybe that worried me too.

When we got to my place all the lights were off except for the one at the front entrance. Cal shut the door softly behind us. We went upstairs quietly to the bathroom connected to my room. I kept Cal's shirt against my face when I turned on the lights, not wanting to see the damage quite yet.

"Am I gonna freak out?" I asked him, lowering the shirt and motioning to the mirror without looking.

"Umm. I don't know if you're the freak-out type. I won't lie, it looks kind of bad. But I think maybe you should let me clean it up first. There's dirt and stuff that's making it look worse than it is."

I turned to the mirror, covering up the right side of my face again. That half of my reflection looked normal, aside from my eye being red from crying, which I guess shouldn't have been a surprise. I lowered my right hand and gasped inadvertently. There was a long scrape going from cheekbone all the way to my upper lip, bloody and flecked with dirt. The tip of my nose and my chin were bright red, and there was a deeper gash below my nose that was also bleeding.

Through the mirror, I saw Cal wince, whether at my pained reaction or at my face, it was hard to tell. "I thought you said it wasn't bad," I said, trying to keep my voice even.

"It's not. I really think it looks worse than it is."

I leaned in closer to the mirror, watching blood start to pool on my upper lip. There were little specks of gray in there too, like the force with which I'd hit the ground had guaranteed that I'd have a piece of that sidewalk with me forever.

The tears started flowing again, so I turned away from the mirror and sat on the lid of the toilet while Cal grabbed a washcloth and ran it under the tap. He kneeled down in front of me and tilted my head up by the chin.

"I'm never giving anyone a piggyback ride ever again," he said.

I managed to chuckle, tasting tears, but then he pressed the washcloth to my cheekbone and the pain shot through again. "Sorry if this hurts." He steadied my head with one hand as he kept cleaning off my cheek. His eyes were focused and concerned and a lovely shade of brown, tinged with yellow, I now saw. Like autumn leaves. It did hurt, but I looked at Cal's eyes and it wasn't all that bad. It was hard to tell what I was more aware of: the sting of the scrapes or the light touch of his hand.

"Your elbow's bleeding," I said.

"I got off light." He dabbed the washcloth on my nose a few times then moved to my lip. "When I felt myself losing my footing I tried to turn so we'd land on our backs. I think I messed that up." He stood up and rinsed the washcloth off, then opened the medicine cabinet and rummaged through the bottles. "You have some really gross diseases, Lu."

"Shut up," I laughed, which made my face hurt more, which made me tear up again.

He took a seat on the edge of the bathtub this time, a tube of Neosporin in his hand. I watched him unscrew the cap, studied his fingers for the first time, followed them down to the sinewy length of his arms, faintly muscular despite his thinness. "Neosporin is the greatest thing on the planet," Cal said. "It'll make your face all better."

"Maybe we should put some on your face too, then."

He laughed and shook his head, then squeezed some of the ointment onto his finger. Then he paused and looked at me. "I'm sorry I slammed you into the ground." His eyebrows arched at that perfect apologetic angle, and I almost felt bad for how bad he felt.

"It was a stupid idea and you shouldn't have suggested it," I said. "But I agreed to it. Don't feel bad."

"Okay. I'm probably going to feel bad anyway, but I'm glad you don't hate me for it."

"No, I don't hate you. I actually had a really good time with you tonight. Before you assaulted my face."

He smiled, then brought his finger up to my cut lip and spread the Neosporin. Goose bumps tingled down my arms, and I tried not to shudder, though I wasn't sure if pain or relief was to blame. He had a light touch, caring. Was Iris constantly being touched like this? Constantly cared for, treated as precious, goose bumps tingling down her arms?

I braced myself for the familiar feeling of my cheeks reddening, but maybe they were already too red from the booze or the pain. Cal kept applying the ointment with a natural tenderness, and when he touched a spot that hurt, I reached out and put my hand on his leg, squeezing his knee. "Ow," I said, to distract him from what I was doing, or maybe to distract myself.

The atmospheric pressure in the bathroom increased.

Okay, I don't really know much about atmospheric pressure and how it works, or if it could shift based on the feelings of people in a room. But something increased. "So," I said, trying to get that something to return to normal. "I have a question. About you and Iris."

"Shoot," Cal said, still dabbing gently at my scrapes.

"Why break up? Why not let the relationship run its course? If it ends, it ends. But why force it?"

I take back my previous statement about atmospheric pressure not being affected by feelings. Because oh boy did that room get tense.

Cal didn't respond for a moment, his eyes clouding over with what could have been sadness or focus or just too many drinks. "I told her whatever I could so that we would stay together as long as possible."

Now it felt like there was a full-on storm brewing. Like, if for some reason my dad had a barometer in the bathroom, it would be going berserk right now. It's amazing the impact words can have on the feeling inside a room. For a moment it even felt like we should switch roles, like I should be tending to his wounds, instead of the other way around.

"I want to interview you," I blurted. Cal stopped for a moment, and we made eye contact. The house was so quiet otherwise, no city sounds like I was used to, the constant whir of life outside. Once the words were out it was all I wanted to talk about. "Iris seemed hesitant but maybe you could convince her that it's okay. I just think you guys have something special worth writing about. I could do it without your names, but I'd rather be allowed in."

Cal bit his lip while I talked, saying nothing, his eyes reddened by the beers and lack of sleep.

Maybe those same things were responsible for me continuing to talk. I told him about my writer's block, about eavesdropping being the only stand-in for writing since my breakup. Then I told him that I'd eavesdropped on their conversation outside The Strand. As soon as I said it, I braced myself for him to run out.

"That's why I found your wallet. I was there. But I swear that's just a coincidence. I am no creepier than what you've seen in person."

Thankfully, he laughed that comment off, which made me want to confess even more. So I told him about the scholarship too, and how I was probably going to lose it, since I didn't have a single thing written yet.

He paused, which confirmed my immediate fear that I'd unloaded too much and he was seconds away from sprinting, leaving a cartoonish human-shaped hole in the bathroom wall.

"I'll talk to Iris," he said, and I was shocked I'd ever felt fear that he would run.

We went to my dad's backyard with full glasses of water, sobering up, looking out at the leaves rustling lightly in the night breeze. Every now and then we turned to look at each other, maybe to check that we hadn't fallen asleep, maybe for other reasons, and we'd break out in laughter that we'd try to contain. Mostly, though, we were quiet. I tried not to think

of the pain radiating from my face, tried not to think of anything at all. I just wanted to stare out at the dark with Cal,
and watch the night cement itself into the past.

16
PROBABLY SWITCH GAMES

On the train back to the city, I took a window seat. My laptop was open, but any sentences I attempted sputtered halfway through, like cars breaking down and dying along the side of the road.

Cal was sitting next to me, his head lolling as the train rocked. Jase sat across the aisle, staring at his phone, every now and then casting strange looks my way. My face had healed surprisingly well, considering it hadn't even been a full day. Much better than I thought it would. All hail Neosporin.

Dad had wanted to rush me to the ER first thing in the morning, but I'd managed to calm him down, insisting that at the current rate, my face would look better than new in a matter of hours. My story had been that I had slipped on ice on the sidewalk. It was an awful excuse, because summer. But I spun a masterful tale about a careless restaurant and a very narrow cold front caused by an AC unit pointed in the wrong direction, and my dad had ended up calming down. Instead of going to the emergency room I had spent the rest of the day thinking about stuff other than my face.

Namely, Cal. His touch. The fact that he got my sense of

humor perfectly. That damn doughy laugh. How I hadn't been able to stop watching his fingers or his eyes as he took care of me.

How much of last night had been shared, I wondered, and how much had I made up?

For the life of me, I tried to remember what I had been like with Leo, but it was as if the memories had been wiped out. Or not the memories themselves, since those were still popping up when I didn't want them to, the good and the bad alike, but who I was during those memories. What I'd actually felt. Had there been this much doubt, this much uncertainty? Had the joy always been tinged by something else, or was that just in the beginning?

Every now and then Cal's screen would light up with a notification, bringing to life the picture of him and Iris cheek-to-cheek that served as his background. I watched time tick away in the corner of my computer screen. I didn't need to read Leo's email again, its entire stupid contents were probably graffitied somewhere in the folds of my brain.

Do you know that I still love you?

What was I supposed to do with that? Return to a boy who'd fled?

On the train, back at home, at the coffee shop, at home again, I tried to write. Nothing. It was like some force field had been set up on my keyboard, or around my brain.

PETE
Dare I ask?

LU
Please for the love of god don't. I'm broken. Will you spare change when I'm homeless?

PETE
You're not going to be homeless, Lu.

LU
I certainly won't be homefull.

PETE
That doesn't make sense.

LU
SEE?!? I'm broken.

PETE
Want me to come over for a pep talk?

I sighed and told him that I probably shouldn't invite any more distractions, and that I'd talk to him after I'd sent in the column, or during the end-time, whichever came first. Moments later, another text came in.

LEO
Hey can we talk sometime

So much for avoiding distractions. Something in my chest fluttered, but I didn't feel the way I might have if the text had come a couple of days earlier. Before, I probably would have called Leo back right away, hoping to get my face on his face as soon as possible. But now my reaction was to let out a quasi-humanoid groan and put my head on my desk again. Which caused me to groan again, this time in physical pain, because of the whole piggyback accident.

A few seconds later there was a knock at my door. I looked

up and saw Jase standing just inside my room. "Mom sent me to check on you. She's worried about the noises you're making and wants to know if you're hungry."

"Does she think I'm making those noises *because* I'm hungry?"

Jase shrugged, a video game controller still in his hand. "Should I say you're okay, then?"

"Sure, just make sure to mention that the fabric of my being is slowly unraveling and I will soon be a pile of mush, vaguely shaped like the human I once was."

Jase widened his eyes and stared for a second. "'Kay," he said, then started walking away. I called after him, sitting up. "Yeah?" he asked, reappearing in the doorway.

"Don't say those things."

"Yeah, I know. You were kidding."

"Oh. Sometimes it's hard to tell if you get me."

He shrugged again, the most thirteen-year-old expression there is. "Sometimes you're hard to get."

I nodded. "Fair enough." He turned to go again, but I called him back one last time. The controller in his hand was starting to shake. Withdrawals, probably. "I'm sorry, I just..." I trailed off, thinking that maybe he was far removed enough from my weird situation to be able to chime in with something helpful. Some bit of unexpected wisdom that would jar me into inspiration and productivity, saving me from myself.

"What's up?"

I turned to my computer screen. My Word document wasn't blank anymore, just littered with the corpses of false starts and random paragraphs that I didn't feel brave enough to delete. "What would you do if you were stuck and didn't know how to move forward?"

Jase looked down at his feet. "Like, physically? Is it glue?

Or did I go into a small tunnel? Because if I was in a tiny tunnel I'd just die. That is the scariest thing I can imagine and screw you for putting that in my mind."

"Wow, you are more my sibling than I give you credit for." I shook my head, tried to put it in a way that Jase might understand. I ran a hand through my hair, fluffing it out the way Iris did. "Okay, so what if you were playing a video game and you were trying to get past this level. And you knew what you had to do, like, all the steps you had to take, the exact bad guys you had to shoot down. But you just couldn't beat it. And you've looked online and talked to all your expert buddies that have advice, but you still can't seem to get past it. No matter how hard you try."

My brother leaned against the door frame for a moment, looking lost in thought. He scratched his chin and made a face like he was hurting a little bit, which momentarily filled me with confidence that my unexpected-nugget-of-wisdom theory might actually play out, because he was looking solidly pensive. Then he shrugged and said, "I'd probably switch games."

I squinted at him, trying to find a metaphor in his response. He stared back, jiggling the video game controller more violently now. "That doesn't help me at all. I don't have another game to switch to. I could theoretically stop playing altogether, I guess, but quitting in this scenario has intense real-world ramifications."

"I don't know what we're talking about."

"Me neither!" I shouted, returning to my forehead-on-the-desk position a little too violently, sending shooting pains from my scrapes and bruises. And that's how I stayed for most of the evening. I gobbled down some lasagna Mom made, then went back to my room, slammed my face on the desk, stared at my computer screen, and stewed in my own uselessness.

Before going to bed, as my deadline approached single-digit-hours, I emailed Hafsah. It was the most concise thing I'd written in weeks. **I'm sorry. I suck.—Lu.**

When I woke up drenched in sweat and dread, I looked at my phone and saw that I had a missed call from the *Misnomer* offices. A creeping sense of shame oozed down my arms. Yes, oozed. I felt gross with regret. The thought of calling Hafsah back brought tears to my eyes. But I couldn't just leave her hanging. She'd been the first person who made me feel like I was a real writer. She'd given me a platform, given me readers, given me confirmation that I could really do it, not just for myself, in the privacy of my notebook.

I took a long sip of water, rubbing the sleep from my eyes. Then I sat up, trying to rouse myself into a semicoherent state by scrolling through various social media feeds. I had a handful of texts from last night I hadn't responded to, but I wasn't quite ready to dive into that can of worms. After some time, I clicked on Hafsah's name in my recently contacted list. Each time the phone rang it felt like the breath was getting sucked from my lungs. It rang four or five times, then finally there was that terrible click which told me I was going to have to speak.

"What happened, Lu?"

I was instantly choked up, which kept me from saying a single word. I bit my lip and looked out my window, trying to will away the tears. Unfortunately, my blinds were closed, and all I could see were little freckles of gray light, the hint of a cloudy sky. More time than I realized must have gone by, because eventually Hafsah broke my silence.

"Look, I'm sorry, but I'm gonna find someone else to take over your column. I wish I didn't have to, but I need someone who's reliable and—"

A sob escaped me, taking me by surprise. I hadn't known it would feel this way, hearing Hafsah say the words out loud. Like I was losing a part of myself. It felt like getting dumped.

It must have taken Hafsah by surprise too, because her speech trailed off, something which rarely happened. I looked around my immediate vicinity for a tissue, but couldn't find any. Somehow, Hafsah's silence only made me cry harder, and I lowered my head, hiding my face behind my hand.

It hadn't even been like this with Leo. We'd been in his apartment, sitting on the fire escape like we sometimes did, watching the city while behind us his family argued over the sounds of the television. Leo'd been quiet and distant all day, something clearly off. It had taken him about fifteen minutes of beating around the bush, during which I had plenty of time to prepare for the actual words. When he said we should break up, I'd stood up so that I wouldn't be able to see him at all. After a couple of minutes, I shook my head, told Leo he was making a mistake, then stormed out, muttering a goodbye to his family, not a single tear shed to show my pain.

Now I couldn't stop the tears, and I knew that Hafsah wasn't making a mistake. I'd messed up, and this is what I deserved.

"Lu," Hafsah said, her voice all soft with concern.

"I'm sorry," I managed to eke out between my sobs. "You can hang up if you want. I know you're busy."

For a while I assumed she had. I slunk back into bed, not even thinking of my scholarship and my sudden inability to afford college. I was just thinking of my column, and how I'd miss the act of writing it every week. Going to the coffee shop, transferring my thoughts onto the page, tweaking them until they said exactly what I wanted them to say. The stupid, superficial, but absolutely wonderful moment when I'd check *Misnomer* to see my name up there. The "likes" and comment count rising, people tagging me on Twitter when they shared the column. More than all of that though, I was afraid. That it was gone: my ability to comprehend the world through my writing. That Leo had stolen *that* away from me too.

Then there was a loud intake of breath on the phone, and Hafsah spoke again. "One more week, okay, Lu? I love your writing and want you to stay with us, but I can't stretch it any more than that."

My breath caught. "Wait. What?"

"Just get me anything. It doesn't have to be what we talked about. But send me something. End of day Friday."

I blinked, the tears suddenly stopping. My blinds fluttered with a breeze, which sent a trickle of refreshing cool air through my room. "Really?"

"Last chance, Lu." She stayed on the line for a second, then hung up.

I dropped my phone in my lap and rubbed my eyes clean. Hafsah was too good for this world. I went to the bathroom and splashed water on my face, telling myself that I was going to take advantage of this second—er, third—chance.

I started by calling Pete and telling him the news. "I just wanted to let you know I'm not gonna waste this opportunity, and I want you to remind me I said that."

"Does that mean you're done obsessing over the lovebirds?"

"Probably not, but I'm not gonna try to write about them," I said. "I'm gonna take your advice and write about me and Leo." I hesitated, wanting to tell Pete about Leo's email, but not sure I was ready to talk about it. "There've been some developments. I can tell you at work though."

"Alright. And can we hang out after? I feel like I haven't seen you in several millennia."

"I don't think that's accurate," I said, the first smile of the morning creeping onto my face. I suddenly became excited about the day ahead. Working and shooting the shit with Pete, having him help me brainstorm, maybe even writing something out at work and getting his feedback. Still on the phone, I double-checked to make sure I had one of those pocket-size notebooks I could carry with me throughout the day, and plenty of pens in my bag.

"Pretty sure it is."

My phone buzzed in my hand. "Alright, dude, my phone's blowing up because I'm extremely popular and people clamor for my time. I'll see you at work." I figured it was a social media notification or something, or some follow-up pep talk from Hafsah, so after I hung up with Pete I went out to the living room and had breakfast with my mom and Jase. I only checked my phone again right before heading to work. It was a text from Cal.

CAL
You can write about us. You can interview us. Whatever you need, we're in.

At work, I found Pete in a projection room, changing over from one film to another. I walked up to him with my phone out, showing Cal's text message.

He stared at me, his eyes wide. "Whoa."

I thought he was reacting to the text message and so I nodded and smiled. "I know!"

"I'm talking about your face. Goddamn, Lu, that looks worse in person. How did it happen?"

"Oh that." I waved my hand. "Drunken piggyback ride, you know how it goes. It's healing quickly. But read this text."

"You're definitely gonna have to elaborate on 'drunken piggyback ride' in a sec." He turned his attention to my phone and read. Now, I wasn't exactly expecting an over-the-top reaction. I didn't need Pete to do somersaults and shoot confetti out of his butt or anything. But some overt expression of joy would have been nice. A smile or a high five or something. Instead he shuffled around the projection room, checking switches that we never had to look at before. "Interesting timing," he mumbled.

"Interesting my ass. This is perfect! I have their permission, right during my last chance. It's all going to be okay."

Pete brushed the hair out of his eyes and kept fiddling with the projector. "You said there were developments with Leo? He didn't do that, did he?" he asked, motioning at my face.

"What? No. It was Cal."

Pete nodded. "Right. I have no follow-up questions." He looked up at the official theater clock on the wall, then started the trailer reel and we headed out of the booth. "So, what happened with Leo?"

"I don't want to talk about Leo. I'm finally forgetting him and moving on from him, like you wanted. You should be excited for me."

"I am," he deadpanned. Oh, I got it. He was joking. We walked out into the theater lobby and saw Brad walking by, clipboard tucked under his arm. "Brad! We need responsibilities!" Pete called out.

"Hot dogs and popcorn," Brad called back, barely missing a beat before disappearing into the back office.

I belched a groan out as we shuffled our way to the concession stand. Throwing more hot dogs into a fake rotisserie thingy and reloading kernels and prepackaged popcorn into a machine wasn't the worst thing in the world, but we long ago decided it was the worst part of our jobs. Then I realized Pete wasn't joining me in the exaggerated parade of complaints we usually indulged in.

We fell into a silence, heavy only because of its timing. We'd never loaded the popcorn machine without making some sort of guess as to what they made the fake butter out of. "What do you think?" I asked. "Liposuction extractions, hippopotamus eye boogers, Saint Bernard drool?"

"Those are repeats," Pete muttered. He shut the glass door for the popcorn machine, then pulled out a package of hot dogs from the freezer. "What do you wanna do after work?"

"Er, did I not scroll down from that text message I showed you? Because there were more."

Pete pinched the bridge of his nose. "You're hanging out with the lovebirds again."

"You can come if you want!"

As Pete and I moved on to the second popcorn machine, we muttered a hello to our coworker Rahim, who was manning the one open concession register, a handful of people lined up waiting to be served. "I'm gonna be interviewing them for the article, so you'll totally be a fourth wheel, but it might help to have you there. I think you'll like them. Iris is doing a little photo shoot in Brooklyn, so at least it'll be a change of scenery."

Pete crossed his arms in front of his chest. He had his pouty face on. It wasn't a full pout, just a hint of sadness behind the eyes. I think it might be an Irish thing, pouting with your pupils.

"Don't get all broody on me. It's bad timing, but it's not like I'm spending every waking moment with them." Rahim turned over his shoulder at us, clearly hearing the conversation. I finished refilling the popcorn machine and lowered my voice. "You know how important this column is to me. Once the column is written, I promise we'll return to our regularly scheduled time-killing activities."

Pete nodded his head quickly, offering me a tight-lipped smile. "You're right. I'm happy for you. Not sure if I'll make the trek out to Brooklyn, but I'm glad you've got another chance." He sighed and uncrossed his arms, running a hand through his hair. "What game are we playing today?"

The Sound of Settling

By Lu Charles
November 21

What did couples do before movies and television were widely available from the comfort of your home, flashing from a computer screen set up in a bedroom while you pressed yourselves against each other?

I'm not being facetious here, I'm seriously asking. What did we do as a species to pass the time in the company of someone we loved? When the conversation dries up after months together—not entirely, obviously, not for good, but for now—and economic limitations prevent you from going out into the world, when the mental and physical onuses of senior year have taken their toll, and it's exhausting to do anything but lie around and be entertained by stories, what did couples do? Did they have to do anything? Do we?

I'm asking less out of a sincere interest in the dates of the past (no pun intended), but because, as my relationship has settled itself into comfort, I find myself wondering about options. I'm not knocking the Netflix-and-chill approach to modern romance. Few things sound more romantic to me. I've just been asking myself, is this all there is? Am I falling too deep into comfort and complacency?

When these thoughts float across my mind, it's hard for the questions to contain themselves to the literal. I start thinking that the questions are not just directed at the activities my boyfriend and I choose to partake in for our dates, but at the relationship itself.

I get a thrill when I see him for the first time in a few days after I've spent a weekend in New Jersey. I get a thrill when we fall asleep on one of these Netflix-and-chill dates and he wakes me up with a kiss on the temple. I get a thrill when I make a joke I'm sure is stupid enough to be grounds for a breakup and he responds with honest laughter, the sound rising up from his sexy belly, which juts out in a way that makes me think of teacup pigs.

But these thrills are few and far between now. Three months later, I don't keep myself awake all night texting him, thinking about him, writing him into my AP English essays just for the chance to talk about him. A natural part of the whole relationship thing, maybe. I've heard of this so-called honeymoon phase, and I think it's stupid to think feelings should lessen, even if I believe it's a real thing and a natural part of being a human.

Love that isn't thrilling is still love.

But thrills are nice too.

Maybe the only thing that happens to relationships as they go on, is that we forget that variety is the spice of life. We seek the same thrills from the start of the relationship, but those have been tired out, and don't provide the same jolt they used to. Or we've elevated those experiences in our minds, colored them gold with nostalgia, so that any new thrills that enter our lives feel lesser in comparison.

But there are new thrills to be found, right? We just trick ourselves into thinking that a relationship that has gone on for a while has tired them all out. We are blind to the possibilities because we're complacent.

What I'm saying is: I could find more thrills for me and my beau (ew, sorry, I won't repeat that term again) to partake in. From you, maybe. Thrills that you've tired of might hold some novelty for us.

Comment below with thrills you've experienced, so that someone (cough, cough) might try them out for herself.

17

OUT OF SHAPE

Cal and I stood leaning against a brick wall by the Dumbo waterfront while Iris walked around us, finding the best angle for the Brooklyn Bridge, with Manhattan coloring the background. It had been overcast all day, but a few rays of sunlight poked through the clouds now, as if the skies had parted just for Iris.

"Face looks good," Cal said. I started to blush, even though I knew what he meant.

"All hail Neosporin," I responded.

Iris waited for some tourists to step out of her shot. She was in another pinup-style dress, red with white polka dots. Again, I thought about how she seemed entirely at home in New York, but I could also picture her fitting into California perfectly. She moved through the world like she belonged in it.

I slipped my pen inside my notebook, where I'd been scribbling notes for the past hour or so. Not just my questions and their answers, but the way they looked at each other, how many times Iris reached out to put a hand on his forearm, anything they said that might have been an inside joke. I wanted to capture anything that could have been a key to answering why they survived and Leo and I had not.

"How'd you convince her?" I asked.

Cal squinted against the sun and shrugged. "I didn't try to convince her. I just told her that it would be a gift to have a little reminder of us. We might be splitting up come August, but what we had—what we *have*—is special. I don't want time erasing that, don't want myself thinking in the future that what I feel today was an exaggerated teenage feeling. That it wasn't actually love." He shifted his stance, resting one foot against the wall and turning to look at Iris, who was changing her camera lens. "Iris told me that it was silly, that we already have two years' worth of exchanged emails, texts, Tumblr messages, mementos like that receipt that was in my wallet you found. Plus, two years' worth of memories.

"But I want more than just memories. I wanted a love story. Our love story." If Pete were around, he might have burst out in laughter at the earnestness with which Cal said this. But there was something to how he said it that made my heart break on his behalf. "I just want an account. Something I can turn to months/years down the line and relive." He shrugged again, a very different gesture than when Jase shrugged at me while standing in my doorway. In the distance, Iris fluffed her hair and checked her camera's display, then turned to us and raised a finger to say she'd be a minute. "Maybe," Cal added quietly, almost like he didn't want me to hear the thought, "I could even use it as a way to figure out what went wrong, and how to fix it."

Then he turned and smiled at me, motioning at the notebook. "What's next?"

It took me a second to recover from his little speech. I couldn't even remember what I'd asked. I flipped my notebook open again, looked at the questions I'd scribbled throughout the day at work and on the subway ride over to Brooklyn. Nothing seemed pertinent or poignant enough. "Tell me about your first date," I said, right as Iris caught up to us.

"Ooh, I love telling this story."

Cal smiled. "Go ahead."

We started walking away from the waterfront, Iris switching up her lenses again as she started to tell the story.

We turned down a random street, me and Iris in front and Cal walking behind us. I turned over my shoulder to glance at him. He had his hands in his pockets, a little smudge on his glasses, which he didn't seem to mind or notice.

I kept quiet as Iris described reaching for Cal's hand for the first time outside of an Indian restaurant in Hell's Kitchen. I had to open up my notebook and start doodling while we walked in order to distract myself from the memory of holding hands with Leo. Not for the first time, but the last. How we'd lain in bed with our fingers limply intertwined, the air in the room so clearly heavy, though I had no idea why at the time. A few hours later we were out on the balcony ending things.

We'd been walking along Flushing Avenue, getting close to Williamsburg. Leo lived nearby, which was something I would have rather not thought about. Thankfully, Iris had been giving plenty of details about their date, her memory almost suspiciously good, providing me with plenty of fodder to occupy my mind. I checked my phone to make sure my mom wasn't getting pissed and threatening to hunt me down, but all I had was a text from Pete asking if I was still in Brooklyn. I texted back, Yes, hanging around Dumbo interviewing the lovebirds, and then added a string of random emojis because I couldn't think of what else to say as an apology for bailing on him again.

"I don't mean to bring down the mood after that lovely reminiscence," I said, "but I just have to know, why are you guys breaking up?"

Iris slipped her hand away from Cal's, shoving her hands inside the pockets of her dress. "You wanna take this one?" she asked. I tried to detect bitterness in her voice, tried to detect pain in the air around them. But there wasn't anything so obvious as that. Cal fiddled with his rolled-up shirtsleeves, trying to even them out.

"We just know the path that we'll likely end up on if we stay together," Cal said. "We're not one of those couples that assumes first love is last love. Everyone knows it's irrational to think that, but they also believe they're one of the exceptions. It's better to end things on a good note."

I made eye contact with Cal, certain I'd see some of the hurt I'd seen the other night. I listened for his voice to waver.

"We know it sounds ridiculous," Iris added. "And we know it's not necessarily avoiding any pain. But we're avoiding the ugly parts, the sad unraveling. Everyone that doesn't marry their first love has it ruined by the breakup."

With just those few lines, I probably had enough material to put together into something Hafsah would accept. All I had to do was arrange it into something semicohesive. I couldn't tell if I was officially past my writer's block, but I felt close enough that a sigh of relief was appropriate.

Before I could, though, I felt a tap on my shoulder.

I turned around and when I saw who it was I let out an exasperated, "Of course!"

Leo furrowed his brow, then turned to look behind him, as if I might have been talking about someone else. "Hey," he said.

I searched the scene for further context as to why the hell he was standing in front of me right now. Then I saw his parents and sisters standing outside of a restaurant across the street. Cheryl, his younger sister, looked over at me and waved. She went to our school too and seemed to think I was cool. The rest of his family didn't seem to give me much thought.

"What are you doing here?" I asked, although I'd picked up enough context to guess.

"You never answered me," he said, scratching at his neck. He looked over my shoulder at Iris and Cal, who'd picked up on the fact that something awkward was in the works and had taken a couple of steps backward. "I texted Pete, and he said you were around here."

"So you convinced your entire family to stalk me?"

I expected him to flatly reject this statement as me being ridiculous, but he combed a tress behind his ear and looked down at the ground. My stomach lurched. Why wasn't I throwing my arms around his neck, telling him that I still loved him too? Wasn't this exactly what I'd wanted? "I was just hoping to see you. I convinced them to go for Italian." He smiled. He had such a great smile, the prick. "It's been harder than…" He trailed off, looking again at Iris and Cal. "Wow, new friends already?" He forced a smile, then awkwardly waved.

Cal and Iris waved back, and then I saw Cal lean into Iris to say something, but their exchange was interrupted by Leo shouting his name at them, like a child with a weak grasp on social etiquette. Before Cal and Iris could respond with a slew of questions about his understanding of how the world works, Cheryl jogged across the street toward us.

"Our table's ready," she said to Leo. Then, turning to me, she smiled and waved. "Hi, Lu! How've you been? I haven't seen you in a while." My eyes flitted toward Leo, whose downturned eyes made it obvious that he hadn't told her we'd broken up. Maybe he hadn't told any of them.

"I'm okay," I said. "Just, you know. Hanging. Say hi to the rest of the family for me," I added, making a point to say it to Leo.

Iris, Cal, and I walked away, wandering through Williamsburg as the sun dipped down. Iris stopped every few blocks to take pictures of buildings, a group of friends hanging out in stoops, two guys taking a smoke break from unloading a beer truck. They looked at the camera, one of them staring blankly, the other smiling, his hands resting on his hip. I could picture Iris printing this shot out, hanging it up in her California dorm, a shrine to all things New York.

"Was that the ex?" Cal asked.

I nodded, feeling physically exhausted from thinking about Leo. It was like I'd been in shape for a while, lifting that heavy load week in and week out. But since hanging out with Iris and Cal, I'd slowly lost my conditioning, and now the slightest exercise got me winded.

"I may not know what you're feeling now, but I can confidently say the dude made a mistake." Cal turned to look at me, pushing his glasses up the bridge of his nose, looking a lot more tenuous than the person who spoke about love and paintball teams to strangers on benches. He gave me a little smile. "You're great, Lu."

About an hour later, riding back on the J/M/Z toward Manhattan, the city lights starting to flicker on as twilight grew, Leo texted me again, telling me he missed me. If only I had the strength to delete it. Instead I stared at it for a long time, wishing it hadn't come, or that it had come from someone else.

18

THE SUBTEXT SNEAKS IN ANYWAY

What should have been a night of feverish writing and transcribing all I'd learned about Iris and Cal, unleashing all that pent-up desire to tell their story, unpacking everything I'd been wanting to say about relationships through the specific lens they existed in was instead spent curled up in bed trying to empty my brain of thoughts. My laptop was set up on my laundry hamper playing cartoons on Netflix, my notebook forgotten beneath a cup of water and some discarded tissues. I'd purposely left my phone charging in the bathroom.

The next morning, all I wanted to do was see Iris and Cal. Even in passing, from afar, for a single moment. It was strange how specific that desire was, almost like a craving for a favorite dish at a restaurant.

At work too I was thinking about Cal, reliving our night in New Jersey. Or I was thinking about Iris, and our adventures in Manhattan. Or I was thinking about them stargazing, kissing on the sidewalk, cardamom and the heat of vindaloo on their lips. This is what inspiration felt like, and if it hadn't been for Leo, these thoughts would have already turned into writing. I just needed to give it a little more time.

Thoughts of them slipped in between my breaths, in the space between my words when I was talking to customers, in the accidental brushing of fingertips when I handed people their change or their popcorn. It was hard to focus on anything else, and I wondered how the hell the world was in such relatively good shape, if everyone who was in love was constantly distracted like this.

Not me. Them. Everyone out there, constantly in the throes.

Or maybe those people weren't in love either. Maybe that's why teenage love got its reputation for being more intense and all-consuming, and "adult" love was tapered and comfortable, focused on compromises and commitment. Teenage love was the real version, but the world wouldn't be able to function that way. People gave up on it after the first time or two, because they couldn't get anything else done. They opted for something that left room for other activities. Like breathing, and conversing with people who are present, and purchasing movie tickets. They loved in a way that made the heartbreak less severe, in a way that made the love less suffocating.

I spent my shift not in the least bit present, constantly being nudged back to attention by Pete and other coworkers. Pete acted normal for the most part, although the fact that we were avoiding each other felt as obvious as if we were both dressed in lucha libre outfits. Or I guess I wasn't aware enough of my surroundings to really say that for sure. Pete could have been talking at me all shift. Come to think of it, when I snapped out of it, he was standing right next to me, looking expectantly, as if maybe he'd said something that, in a typical social interaction, might have elicited a response.

"Sorry, what?"

"Your plans today?" He leaned back and shoved his hands in his pockets, staring at a crowd of people letting out of a theater, a trail of spilled popcorn at their feet. His eyes followed along with someone, and I turned to see who it might be. An attractive group of girls, an attractive group of guys, some dude in a tracksuit to add to our running tally (544). Hard to tell, it had been a full theater, and everyone had exited at the same time. "Starla said she got some advanced copies of winter releases and that we can go sort through them."

"Coolio," I said.

Pete eyed me sternly, then sighed. "Don't invoke the holy one's name when you're clearly not Coolio. You haven't listened to a word I've said all day."

"Whaaat? I'm a great listener."

"Name three words in succession that I've said today."

I bit my lip. "That's so many words though." I looked around the theater for ideas. "Oh! I know. 'That'll be eight dollars.'" I smiled smugly, sure that he at some point said that, since it's what most of our concession items cost.

Pete looked around for a moment, as if looking around for someone, then stuck his hand in the nearest popcorn machine and tossed a fistful at me. "Hopefully that'll snap you back to our reality."

"One of us is gonna have to clean that up, you jerk."

"No, one of our coworkers will. We're off in fifteen. Seriously, where've you been all day?"

I had a miniflashback to the daydreams I'd had throughout our shift: me, Iris, and Cal riding bicycles through a meadow, happy pop music playing in the background. The three of us in a car with the windows down and our feet sticking out, sunlight dancing on our toes, wind getting whipped around everywhere as we headed somewhere vague yet adventurous, happy pop music playing in the background. There was even one fantasy I had—brief, and quickly dismissed by the rational part of my mind, even though it was fun to be in its illogical clutches for a while—where the three of us were living in the same Brooklyn apartment, exposed brick on the walls, sparsely but tastefully decorated, so comfortable with each other that all of us walked around in our underwear without batting an eye. Happy pop music, of course, played in the background.

Pete waved a hand in front of my face. "I mean, what happened, Lu. Did you get hypnotized?"

"What? Sorry. I've been...um...brainstorming. You know I've got this column due. I'm just an utmost professional and it's been hard to think about anything else."

Pete cocked an eyebrow at me, then rolled his eyes. "Right. So, should I tell Starla we're swinging by?" He raised his phone up to show me the texting screen he was on. I knew I'd been a less-than-ideal friend lately, and I'd been spending plenty of time with Iris and Cal and should probably let them have a day off from me. But I wanted to have my damn cake and eat it too.

"Sure," I said because I'm considerate but also a coward. Plus, I hadn't talked to Iris and Cal all day, so assuming that they'd be down to hang out would be a little presumptuous, even if it felt like we'd been hanging out all day in a golden montage of carefree, adolescent good times.

When we clocked out, I called my mom to let her know I wasn't going to be coming straight home.

"Is that you, Lucinda? It's been so long, I can hardly remember what your voice sounds like," she said because she's a goddamn comedian.

"Very funny, Mom."

"I'm not being funny."

"Well, then, you're being dramatic. I'll be home for dinner," I said. Then added a quiet, "Probably."

"Now you're being funny. I know it's been a while since you saw me, but I haven't aged enough that you can sneak in that 'probably' and expect me to miss it. What are you doing that's so important you're abandoning the woman who cares most about you in this world?"

How to begin? "Well," I said, choosing to go with the easy answer first, "you know how Pete's leaving for school in August? I want to make sure I'm being a good friend and spending time with him."

There was a pause on the phone, and I thought maybe she would complain about the fact that I was making time for Pete and not her. "I hate to admit it, but I did a good job with you."

"Why would you hate to admit that?!?"

"Anyway, since I've been granted the generous gift of your voice, at least over the phone, tell me, how are you?"

"I'm good, Mom."

Another pause, which meant either Mom was getting distracted or she was gearing up for some sort of lecture. Since I was hoping for some leniency during the afternoon, I motioned to Pete to give me a second. He mouthed, "Tell her I say hi and also…" And then he quietly continued mouthing a speech about—I think—US foreign policy.

"Lu, are you depressed?"

"Um," I said, because Mom had just taken the conversation from about a three to a nine.

"Because I know that boy broke your heart, and if you have to get out of the house a little more to help with it, that's okay. But I want you to know that you can stay home and talk to me about it too. Or stay home and not talk to me about it. Whatever you need."

I felt that pressure behind my eyes that could only mean that my emotions had also gone from a three to a nine. I turned away from Pete, who was still mouthing words, so that he couldn't see me tear up. Instead of staying at a nine along with my mom, though, my stupid brain somehow decided that what it really wanted to do was deflect. "So I can go to that all-night warehouse rave with all the drugs? Thanks, Mom, you're the best!"

My mom sighed. "Very funny. That'd be a great way to get disowned."

"Love you too, Mom," I said.

After I hung up, Pete and I went to The Strand and loitered at the information desk with Starla. Pete sorted through advanced copies while Starla leaned her chair back against the wall. I stood by, trying to remember if there was something specific I was supposed to be doing other than aching to hang out with a couple I'd met recently.

"What's with the notebook and the idle pen, girly?" Starla asked.

"Right, that's what I'm supposed to be doing."

I opened it up randomly, landing not on the pages of scrawled notes from the other day, but on the one lame attempt at a poem about Leo I'd written post-breakup. *Eyes the color of desert cliffs.* Ugh. I'd never even seen desert cliffs. I threw the notebook down on the help desk.

"You gonna tell me what happened with Leo?" Pete asked, halfheartedly reading the back cover of a fantasy novel. "You can't throw around the word *developments* and then not fill me in for a whole day. It's too loaded."

"Are we still talking about fart boy?"

Pete widened his eyes and nodded dramatically.

"Such a lingerer," Starla said, wrinkling her nose.

"To be fair, I think last time we talked we'd decided that I was the fart. Or my pain was. I don't know, I'm foggy on the details." I uncapped my pen and started fiddling with it, just to give myself something to do. I didn't want to talk about Leo, he had delayed my writing long enough. And if I brought up Iris and Cal, Pete would probably disown me, if that was a thing that friends could do to each other. "Friendship breakup" doesn't seem like an adequate description.

"Also, I don't want to be rude," Starla said, looking at my face in a way that made it easy to guess what she was about to say next. "But what happened to your face?"

I propped my elbows on the desk, then rested my chin in my hands, cupping slightly so that my cheeks pressed together and muddled my words when I answered. "Drunken piggyback ride."

"Oof. Kids these days, so irresponsible. When I was your age we—"

"Had the highest ever rate of drunk-driving accidents?" Pete chimed in.

"Probably. Stop being clever around older people, we don't like it." Starla smirked. She stopped as a customer approached the desk, putting on her professional smile. But the customer had a change of heart and awkwardly walked past us, pretending to check her phone as if she'd just gotten a text that instructed her not to talk to us. "Lu, you were saying?"

I mumbled some more into my hands, not wanting to reduce the memory of that night to a funny, somewhat embarrassing story.

Starla furrowed her brow, clearly not understanding my mumbling. She turned to Pete and asked him if he wanted to translate. He shrugged. "I don't know this story yet. We haven't had the chance to catch up."

They both turned to me expectantly, and since it would at least allow me to talk about Cal and Iris (or at least Cal) without judgment (er, mostly), I told them about the party and the regrettable transportation choice we'd made on the way back to my dad's place. There were moments from that night that I didn't share, of course. The way Cal had cared for me. Sitting out there on my dad's back porch with him, my face sore but tingly with Neosporin, the hum of summertime bugs in the New Jersey night, the deliciousness of a cool glass of water nursing me back into sobriety. I wasn't embarrassed by these moments or anything, I just didn't know how to include them without causing some intense eyebrow raising.

"Wait, do I know who this Cal person is?" Starla asked, her bracelets jingling as she gestured.

"I don't even know this dude. One of her eavesdropping victims. It's this whole thing."

My phone dinged with a text message at that point, which was cartoonishly good timing because it was the exact moment that I was struck by a brilliant idea. "Pete, you are so right!" I said, as cheerfully as I could manage.

"Um," Pete said, backing away a step because I'm not a normal person. "What's that thing your voice is doing?"

"You *should* get to know Cal. That's a great idea." I grabbed my phone and unlocked it. "What a crazy coincidence, Cal *just this moment* texted me to see what I'm doing." This wasn't true. It was my mom sending a string of emojis that equated to: Every moment you're away from me breaks my heart. "Why don't you and I go hang out and you can get to know him! Yay friends coming together!"

Pete looked legitimately scared. He turned to Starla. "I think she's been body-snatched."

"Ooh, you know *Body Snatchers*? Good flick. You just got old people points." She held out her fist, and Pete tapped it.

While they did that, I texted Iris and Cal in a group message.

LU
Sorry to be clingy, but I'm thinking I need just a little more for my column. Are you guys free?

IRIS
Hmm. When/where were you thinking?

LU
Now-ish? Wherever you guys can. I'm the worst, sorry.

CAL
Sure! We were about to learn real-world skills making spaghetti Bolognese at Iris's.

LU
No way. My mom cooks that like twice a week. You could basically call me Spaghetti BoLugnese.

LU
Please don't call me that. Please delete that text.

IRIS
Ooops we just screenshotted it and tweeted it and now that's your official nickname. See you soon!

LU
Okay if I bring a friend?

CAL
👍

When I looked up from my phone, Starla was typing some-thing into her computer, helping a young Asian woman find a book. Pete was flipping through more of the advanced cop-ies, avoiding eye contact with me.

"Pete."

"My head's in a book, Lu. You're breaking our rule."

"Your eyes aren't even moving across the page." I could see him suppress a smile. "Now they're moving way too fast. You're gonna give yourself a seizure." I reached out and low-ered the book from his grip. "I promise that this is the last time I'll do this. After today, I have to write the column or I'm for sure fired and my life is over. Then I'll move on. And I'm really sorry I bailed on you before. That's why I want you to come with me now."

Pete chewed on his lip for a while, eyes up, flitting around the store. "Please tell me they're not excessively PDA. They sound like they make out more than they breathe." He brushed his hair out of his eyes and glanced over at Starla, who'd stood up and was going to walk the customer over to find a book, which was our cue to back away from the help desk.

"They kiss so rarely, they're practically mouth virgins."

Pete winced. "Don't say mouth virgins." He sighed, and we started heading toward the exit. "I'm going to come with you," he said. "But I want you to know that if it sucks as much as I think it's going to suck, I reserve the right to complain about it for the rest of our friendship."

"Pete, darling—" I hooked my arm into his, leaning my head on his shoulder as we walked out onto Broadway "—I will listen to you complain about anything you want."

When Pete and I exited the subway uptown, the late afternoon light was golden and dazzling, shaping the people around us into nothing more than silhouettes, the cars and buildings nothing more than glares, everything a canvas for the sun. The air was magically fresh, a slight, natural breeze that carried no humidity and none of the city's sour summer smells. I noticed leaves swaying gently, people laughing with friends, an old man in a suit whistling as he strolled by, his fingertips trailing the sides of buildings as if reminding himself of the pleasures of touch.

We got to Iris's building and I rang the apartment number, expecting the world to literally become rose tinted at any moment. An unfamiliar voice answered, only slightly pulling me out of my daze. I told the intercom that I was Iris's friend, then struggled to open the door when they tried to buzz me in, because intercoms are hard.

When Iris opened the door, she revealed a much different scene than when I'd first come over to return Cal's wallet. The TV was tuned to a baseball game, and a set of twin black-mop-haired boys were at the dining table wielding crayons like swords and speaking to each other at an inhuman volume. Iris's mom was at the table on a computer, looking like she was somehow managing to get something accomplished despite the ungodly noise of two seven-year-olds interacting. Her dad was on the couch, and he glanced over and waved.

"Hey!" Iris said. She gave me a quick hug then looked to Pete, extending a hand and introducing herself. Then she introduced us to her family as "some friends," said something in Spanish, and we went into the kitchen. Cal was seated at the island, looking intently at his phone. When he looked up and saw me, he smiled. I'd forgotten how it felt to be smiled at just for my presence.

"Your face!" Cal said, still smiling. "It's healing so well. It's like magic."

He just called my face magic, I thought, triggering my stupid, blushing blood vessels. I turned away so he wouldn't notice, gesturing toward Pete. "Cal, Pete. Pete, Cal."

I let them shake hands and walked around the island to the counters, where tomatoes, garlic, and onions were resting on a wooden cutting board. A pot with water sat on the back burner, the flame set to high.

"I should have told you not to trust his piggyback rides," Iris said, joining me at the counter. "I've seen him drop glasses of water he was holding with both hands. He should not be trusted to carry a human being, ever. If he ever gets married, we'll have to warn the girl not to go for any of that carrying the bride nonsense."

Cal laughed, and I heard the rattling of Pete pulling out the stool to take a seat next to Cal. "So, what are you guys up to?" Pete asked. He was making a concerted effort to be normal, I could tell. If this were me, or random people he didn't care about, he would have cracked a joke, or settled deep into himself without attempting to interact.

"Researching spaghetti Bolognese recipes," Cal said, taking up his phone again.

"Lu, we should call your mom and tell her to join us." Pete turned to Iris and Cal. "She makes the best spaghetti."

"Do it," Cal said, still looking at his phone. "I want mom-quality spaghetti, not whatever spaghetti-like food we're about to come up with." He sighed as he scrolled, his glasses re-

flecting his phone screen, his pretty eyes narrowed behind
the lenses. "Reading some of these recipes is like doing AP
Physics homework. Blanch the tomatoes? Mince the garlic?
Reduce the sauce? What are these words? What kind of magic
spells do chefs use?"

"You guys want me to help? I've picked up some stuff from
my mom over the years."

"Actually," Iris said, "I'd rather you didn't help. I want to
learn, and I do better if left to my own devices." She stood
up and grabbed one of the saucepans hanging over the stove,
then started filling it with water. "I mean, if you see us doing
something incredibly stupid, stop us." She chuckled warmly,
and I found myself thinking: *like bread baking.* That's what her
laugh sounded like to me, tasty and nourishing. Which made
me think, somewhat sadly, of Cal's doughy laugh, and how
perfectly suited they were to each other.

Cue the fun cooking montage.

Except, instead of a fun montage of us getting flour on each
other's noses and making an eggy mess while laughing, it was
me and Pete sitting at the kitchen island, watching Iris and
Cal work through a fairly simple online recipe. Cal dropped
half an onion on the floor, and some of the sauce bubbled
over onto the counter, but there were no shenanigans. I kept
my notebook within reach, since my reason for being there
was ostensibly to take more notes for my column. Instead, I
watched them cook. Cal would look over at Iris's chopping/
mincing garlic technique and imitate it for the onion he was
attempting to dice. She watched his oniony tears and then
dropped her knife, walked over to him, and moved him away
from the cutting board by placing her hands on his hips and
gently repositioning him farther down the counter. They
blended blanched tomatoes with basil and then Cal stuck a

spoon in the not-quite-sauce, tilting it to taste-feed Iris. She looked into his eyes as she tasted, thought for a second, then announced she had no idea if it was any good. Both of them burst into laughter which did not include me or Pete.

God, how does anyone leave a relationship when they have that? Even if love itself is gone, how do you step away from that? How does happiness dissipate from something that looks so effortless? Was that what Leo and I'd looked like?

The four of us ate in the kitchen, since Iris's dad was still watching baseball on TV and the twins were still screeching their way through some indecipherable game which involved the dining table. Somehow, Iris's mom managed to eat, continue to work on her computer, and keep the twins from wreaking complete havoc. Iris and I sat on the bar stools, while Pete and Cal stood next to each other and across from us, leaning over their plates as they ate.

"So, Pete," Iris said, adding some more parmesan cheese and a tablespoon of red pepper flakes to her pasta. "What's your story? Are you a writer like Lu?"

"Nope, I'm just a cinema employee. We met when we started working at the theater, and I haven't been able to rid myself of her yet."

"Rude," I interjected. I knew he was kidding, of course, but there was something to the comment that felt a little passive-aggressive. Aggressive-aggressive, maybe. Or whatever it is you call a comment that isn't meant to be cruel but just sort of strikes at your insecurities.

But I didn't say anything else, not wanting the conversation to turn toward me and Pete. I wanted to sink into Iris and Cal, in all of their Iris-and-Cal-ness. We all fell quiet, slurping at our pasta in our different ways.

Iris's parents brought the twins by the kitchen to say good-

night to Iris and Cal, then told us we could use the living
room if we wanted.

Cal stood first, clearing our plates and rinsing them off.
"You guys up for a movie?"

"You don't have to do those," Iris said. "Just leave them
in the sink."

"It's okay, it'll make your mom happy," Cal said. I checked
the time on my phone, and even though my mom had been in
I-miss-our–umbilical-connection mode, I thought to myself
that I had plenty of time to get back home and see her. Plus,
Pete's departure was only a few weeks away, and I hadn't yet
cashed in on those pity points.

"I'm up for a movie!" I said. I looked at Pete, giving him
a look that I'm sure conveyed that I wanted him to stay too.

"I dunno," he said, looking away from me. "I have to open
tomorrow."

"Dude, our shift starts at ten, and it's only 7:30 p.m. That's
practically the afternoon."

"Seven o'clock is definitely not the afternoon," Pete said.
"It's evening."

"Maybe in this prudish country. I have it on good authority
that most countries don't consider night to have fallen until at
least 8:00 p.m. Or, you know," I said, gesturing to the open
blinds in the living room, where the floor-to-ceiling windows
showed a beautiful pretwilight skyline, "until it's dark out."

We looked at each other for a moment, trying to commu-
nicate through eye contact the way most best friends have
attempted. This took place through a series of eye widen-
ings, squinting, and eyebrow movements. And we clearly had
zero clue what the other was trying to say, because we both
ended with our heads tilted and our foreheads creased with
furious confusion.

"Well, I'm up for a movie if you guys are," Iris said, pushing away from the island. "My mom's a huge movie buff, so we've got a crazy collection. Some of them are even hard to find on the internet."

So, Pete and I may have failed at the silent eye-convo thing a second earlier, but we did get the same thought at the same exact time. *"Troll 2!"* we shouted, then realized there were two seven-year-olds probably trying to sleep and we shouldn't be assholes, so we cringed.

"Sorry," I said. "But please tell me you have *Troll 2*."

"What's *Troll 2*?" Cal asked from the sink, setting plates into the drying rack.

"Legend has it, it's one of the worst movies ever made," Pete answered.

"It's so hard to find online unless you pirate it, and we've been holding out hope that we could watch it legitimately. And this night has been lovely and all, but literally all of my nights that don't end in watching *Troll 2* are a complete failure and add to the general meaninglessness of my life."

"Wow, that's a little heavy," Iris said. "Fortunately…"

Four hours later, we'd watched *Troll 2* twice back-to-back, and my whole torso was sore with laughter. Iris hadn't quite made it through the second viewing, and was currently curled up on the three-seater, her feet just barely resting on Cal's thighs.

Pete was yawning too, looking at his cell phone in a super obvious way that made it clear he wanted us to leave. I'd barely even bothered checking my phone since the break between viewings, and then it was just to tell my mom that I'd be home late (and a few follow-up texts to convince her not to disown me and that I still loved her).

"I don't think I understood any more of it the second time around," Cal said. His hand was resting on Iris's exposed calf, fingers lightly rubbing up and down. I wondered if Iris could feel that in her sleep.

An idea crept into my mind. "There's only one possible thing we can do, then."

Pete lolled his head in my direction. "Please no."

Cal, though, was nodding vehemently. "Yes."

"Too much *Troll 2*," Pete moaned.

"No such thing," Cal and I said at the same time.

The end credits rolled again. Pete was snoring now, and Iris was so deep into her REM cycle that she hadn't even flinched when Cal and I burst out laughing yet again at the scene where the kid stands up on his chair in the middle of dinner and pees directly onto everyone's food.

Cal and I shared a look, as if we'd just gone through something life-changing together. Which, honestly, jury was still out on, because maybe we had. Watching that movie with anyone is a life-changing experience.

That was probably around the time I should have woken up Pete, called a car service or whatever back to Chinatown. Except Pete looked so peaceful snoring with his eyes slightly open and that adorable stream of drool in the corner of his mouth, and I didn't want to disrupt him. I stood up and stretched, then caught the door that led to the balcony with the corner of my eye.

"I think I spoke too early. There is such a thing as too much *Troll 2*." I tiptoed over to the balcony door, looking out at the buildings across the street, the city lights. I couldn't see a huge stretch of the city like Iris and I had seen at the Flat-iron, but it still felt magical. I looked back at Cal, who was drinking from a glass of water. "You think it's okay if we go out there for a little bit?" I asked, turning my voice into a whisper. "I think I need some fresh air to recover from that marathon of madness."

There were two patio chairs on the narrow balcony, arranged at angles so that they could fit, pointed half at the railing and half at each other. We plopped down after shutting the door gently behind us to keep out the sounds of the city.

"I wasn't too pushy, was I?" I asked, stretching my feet out and resting them on the railing.

"About what?"

"Forcing everyone to watch *Troll 2* all those times. I sometimes get carried away and don't want things to end, so I force everyone to hang out longer than they want to."

Cal chuckled. "I know what that's like."

Most of the lights were off in the building across the street. I hadn't looked at my phone in a while, and I could only guess what time it was and how much trouble I was in with my mom. She might actually ground me. Which wouldn't be the worst thing in the world, seeing as how I had two and a half days to send in my column and after that my life would be over anyway. My chest tightened with the realization that it was technically Wednesday already, but I managed to quell the panic by turning to look at Cal.

"Are you talking about paintball teams again?"

He snorted. "I wasn't going for subtext on that one."

"And yet it snuck in there anyway."

Cal put his hands on his thighs, rubbing them up and down as he let out a long breath. "Funny how that happens more and more as the days go by. It's like everything is suddenly steeped in symbolism. I saw a poster for a missing dog the other day. It said, 'Missing: The Best Thing That Ever Happened To Us.'" He made a sweeping motion with his hands to show that that was the headline. "Then under that it had a picture of a cute dog, whose name is, get this…"

"Oh my God, are you about to tell me that the dog's name was Iris? That'd be some heavy-handed symbolism right there. Like, come on, universe, have you heard of subtlety?"

"Well, no. The dog's name was Sir Barks a Lot."

I stared at Cal, maybe extending my reaction a bit because he was really nice to look at. "Human beings are the worst."

"Yeah, I know. But below the name it said, 'Without her, love has left our lives.'"

"Wait, *Sir* Barks a Lot is female?"

"I guess. But my point is—"

"I mean, I respect the refusal to adhere to society's oppressive gender rules, but that's really a mouthful of a name. Do they like, call out the whole thing when they're out looking for her? Ugh, they probably have a really gross, cutesy name that they use more regularly. Something like Barksy. Or Lottie." I noticed that Cal was staring at me with his eyebrows up. "Sorry, not the point. Yeah, that's harsh."

Cal sighed. "You're telling me." He yawned, stretched his arms out, and rested them behind his head. Then he leaned back in his chair and put his feet up on the railing, his left shoe resting against my ankle.

God, how much comfort could come from a touch like that. I remembered all those instances of first contact with Leo. How they lost their meaningfulness after a couple of months of dating, but never their comfort. Never the joy of being touched by someone whose presence you wanted near you all the time. How sometimes Leo and I would be lying down together in his bed, touching almost our entire bodies together, and yet we'd want to get closer and closer. We'd press ourselves tighter, feeling all our skin. Even through clothes, touch was something to marvel at.

I wondered briefly when the next time I would do that with someone would be. Then I thought, in a quick flash, about all the things Leo had said in the last few days. His email, his texts, running into him. What had felt like finality a few weeks ago had suddenly opened up, like a knot coming undone. There were all these loose strings flapping around now, and I couldn't even see how far they extended, what they might lead to.

"I can't believe she's leaving this city," Cal said, softly. "She's gonna miss it so much."

"Hey, Cal?" I said, making my voice go soft.

"What's up, Lu?"

"Do you think that, maybe, in the statement you just made, 'the city' might be a stand-in for something else? An easier way for you to say a difficult thing? I'm not claiming I have any proof." I raised my hands up in mock-defensiveness. "I'm just, you know, reading into things."

"I don't know what you mean," he said, then tapped his shoe against my ankle, giving me a smile. It was like we were back in New Jersey, except my face hurt a little less.

Then the balcony door opened behind us, making me jump in my seat. "Jesus, Pete. Don't sneak up on a girl after she's watched *Troll 2* three times in an evening. You're liable to get peed on."

His hair was ruffled, his eyes droopy with sleep. "I'm gonna take off, you want to come with?"

I looked beyond Pete into the living room. The TV was still on, and I could see Iris now fully stretched out on the couch. From the sounds of the city, and the number of neighboring apartments with their lights off, I could tell it was much later than I'd thought.

I realized that I'd slipped my legs from the guardrail, which meant Cal's shoe was no longer resting against my ankle. I didn't want to leave, but I couldn't find a normal-human reason for staying.

"Yeah, sure," I said, standing up. Cal remained seated, looking up at me and Pete.

"It was really nice meeting you," Pete said.

"Back at you. Sorry it was in such a weird setting. We don't always just hang at home trying to improve our cooking skills. I swear Iris and I are normal."

"No they're not," I said.

"Yeah, sorry, man." Pete ran a hand through his hair, trying to get it back in its usual sweep across his forehead. "I've heard too many stories about you to believe that."

Cal shrugged. "Fair enough." Then he held up a hand to wave goodbye, which I mistook for a call for high fives, then tried to play it off like goodbye high fives were a thing I regularly did by high-fiving Pete too, even though we were obviously not saying goodbye to each other.

"Well," I said, when the air around us had grown sufficiently awkward. "I guess all good things come to an end."

"Jerk," Cal laughed.

19

THE MOMENT THEY
FIRST KNEW

Pete and I entered the nearly abandoned subway station. Two white guys wearing untucked button-down shirts sat on a bench, both looking at their phones. At such a late hour you can reasonably expect at least one drunk person to be stumbling about, or if not that, then at least someone doing something shady. I guess the Upper West Side got less of that though.

We'd been quiet since leaving Iris's building, which I'd assumed was a normal 2:00 a.m. silence. But then Pete, apropos of nothing, looked at me with those piercing, soulful eyes of his as if we'd just been in the midst of a meaningful silence. I knew that look well. He was about to say something honest and tactless.

"You're getting a crush on this guy."

I scoffed and combed my hair back behind my ears. "I got scared there for a second. You went into your nugget-of-wisdom voice. It sounds exactly like your having-an-aneurysm voice, which is clearly what's happening right now."

"You're denying it?" His hands dropped to his sides.

"I don't find the need to deny preposterous statements. If you called me a fish, I wouldn't really worry about correcting you." I turned my body away from him, scanning the tunnel for any oncoming trains, even though the signs overhead clearly said the next one would be arriving in thirteen minutes.

"Fine, deny it. But I've got an official prediction for this— it doesn't end well for you."

"What's the 'it' in that sentence?"

"Your emotional well-being."

"And the west will always be at war with the east. Bold pick, Nostradamus."

"Don't get defensive, Lu. I'm not saying anything bad about Cal or you or Iris or any of it. I'm just worried that you're setting yourself up for more heartache."

One of the dudes in the button-downs looked away from his phone and toward us, staring for a moment and then glancing too-quickly away to show he hadn't meant to hear anything. I could spot the maneuver with ease because I employed it often when I was eavesdropping.

"I don't have a crush on anyone, Pete. I'm writing about a couple. And, yes, becoming friendly with them. But that doesn't mean I suddenly wanna bone him. Or her, for that matter. Or them." I was going for a laugh, but Pete didn't provide one. He kept his Irish brooding up at full capacity. "They're interesting, cool people. I think they might be my friends. That's what's happening here."

Pete clicked his tongue. It looked like he wanted to say something else, but then he just leaned back against the wall and crossed his arms, looking everywhere around the station except at me. I mimicked his pouty stance, hoping again to defuse whatever this was with a laugh.

The minutes ticked away. The train arrived with a rumble and a sweep of stale, warm air. We climbed into a different car than the buttoned-down white guys, into one with only three other people in it. Pete and I still had about fifteen stops or so to go though, so when we took our seats I thought I'd try to convince him that he was reading too much into things.

"I know it looks like I fell into a weird friendship with them really quickly. I get that it's weird I've been spending so much time with them. But remember what happens if I lose my job? I don't qualify for the scholarship? My whole world falls apart? I spend the rest of my life at the theater, mumbling about the life I could have had. Like a high school athlete reminiscing about the glory days."

Pete had a Gaga-level poker face going. I sighed and leaned my head back against the train window. I closed my eyes, a wave of tiredness spread over me like a blanket.

I don't know how long it was before Pete spoke up again. I wasn't even sure he had spoken at first, since the rumble of the train was so loud. I opened my eyes and looked over at him to find him glancing down at me. "Maybe that's how it started, Lu. You were interested in them. And I'll grant you the fact that they're cool people. I liked spending time with them tonight. But you're pursuing this so diligently because of him, probably as a stand-in for Leo, and I think it's gonna cause you pain. Or at least sadness."

I put my hand over his. "Pete, hon. You're wrong. You're imagining things."

He looked at me for a long time before turning away. "Good," he said.

★ ★ ★

Over the next two days, I kept meeting up with Iris and
Cal. First together, then individually. Despite pages of notes,
I still didn't have a column written that I could send to Hafsah. When I tried at the end of the day to sit down and get
something cohesive written, my thoughts refused to focus. I'd
start thinking about Leo's eyes. I'd start thinking about sex.
About when I'd have it again. I'd start thinking about college
breakups, and even about the very idea of love and what that
meant. God knows you can't write something concise with
that kind of shit on your mind.

All this felt increasingly terrifying, especially when I received an email from the foundation that was giving me my
scholarship. They needed some paperwork from me. I'm not
sure exactly what paperwork, since I panicked when it all
started feeling too real and closed out of the email.

Iris and I met up first. She was still spending her days pho-
tographing as much of the city as she could, and making her
way around Brooklyn on Wednesday. We met in Bushwick, at
a hip Caribbean restaurant with a sweet rooftop patio, which
made me look forward to the days when I had enough money
to spend at rooftop patios in Brooklyn. Well, I did do that,
but I couldn't afford any of the food. Not after our last foray
out on the town.

It was, if I'm being honest, the most journalistic I'd been
around her. I came with a specific list of questions prepared,
everything that I thought could flesh out that goddamn column which should have been written weeks ago. I was focused, and had even arrived at the restaurant with the idea
that it was a professional meeting and not a friendly one.

I tried not to be too enamored with her cool composure,

the way the pain of her oncoming breakup seemed to roll right off her, not in a callous way, but because she seemed to understand pain was a natural and often transient part of life. I tried not to imitate that hair-fluffing thing she did, or appreciate how well she continuously pulled off her pinup model look. Instead, I tried to pry as much as I could. I wanted to get stories from their relationship, not just facts.

"When did you first know?" I asked her when we were done with our food, our plates pushed to the side in defeat.

Iris stirred her virgin daiquiri, beads of condensation dripping off the glass and forming a ring on the wooden picnic table. "Know what?"

"That you loved Cal."

She paused, did that hair-fluffing thing, then told me that it had been such a tiny thing that made her realize that she had almost missed it. It was just like joy in that way: if you didn't pay attention you might not know it was ever there, or believe that it had been there at all.

Cal had borrowed his mom's car for a date, and they'd driven out to Long Beach for the day after a recent snowfall. The idea had been to build Calvin and Hobbes–esque snowmen near the shore. They'd purchased thermoses of crappy gas station coffee near Montauk, then wrapped themselves up in their best snow-proof gear and trekked out to the beach.

"Look!" Cal had called out. "White sand beaches!"

They'd done their best to re-create the grotesque snowmen from the books they'd both loved as kids, mostly failing.

The cold reddened their noses and stiffened their joints, and whenever they would stop to kiss, the warmth of each other's mouths kept them close for long periods, almost causing them to forget the snowmen entirely.

They went back to the car and turned down the music, rolled up the windows, and got the heat started. A quiet moment passed, their breathing normalizing from the mayhem and the laughter, fogging up the glass. Iris looked at Cal's face and felt something within her shift. He was smiling, leaning back against the headrest. Then he pulled his glove off, warmed his hand against the vent, and then moved it to Iris's knee. He sighed pleasurably, as if he were punctuating their day.

"That's when I knew. At the sound of his sigh, with his hand on my leg. It was a feeling before I knew what to call it. As distinct as hunger, originating somewhere similar, but entirely different. Only a moment later the words came to identify what it was, and as soon as they were there, I moved my hand over his, and leaned back into the seat, knowing what it was I'd found."

"And you're letting it go," I said. Not a question, but a crowbar, meant to slip into the crack and unleash all she might be hiding. Tears would be good, or maybe even a confession that the feelings she felt weren't actually as strong as how she described them. That a part of Iris and Cal was the version of themselves they portrayed to the outside world. A fabrication on par with books and movies. That the love they had did not really exist. And if it did, it wasn't ending for the same reasons that my and Leo's comparatively muted love had ended.

In that moment, when I had that thought, I tried to dismiss it. I tried to tell myself that the love I'd experienced wasn't muted just because someone else's sounded more romantic. But then I had this little flashback, if that's what you'd call it. It wasn't a specific memory, just the recollection that, every now and then during our relationship, I'd look at Leo—while he was joking around with his friends, while he was staring at his phone, while he was kissing my stomach—and wonder what it was about him that I was drawn to. It was as if every now and then, I'd simply forget that I loved him.

Iris didn't cry or confess after my question. She simply shrugged. "We are."

When I met up with Cal the next day after his shift at the coffee shop where he worked near Washington Square Park, I wasted no time in asking him the same question.

"Jeez. Firing on all cylinders. So much journalism. I'm impressed."

"Answer the question," I said, sliding my phone closer to him. I'd taken to recording our conversations because (a) it made me feel cooler, and (b) not sure you've noticed, but my mind tends to wander and that leads to poor note-taking.

Cal leaned forward on the table, his elbows almost halfway across the wooden surface toward me. He cracked his neck and looked over to the register, as if wanting someone to call him back over to work. Then his eyes met mine, and goose bumps shot down my arms.

Just because I knew he was about to tell me another incredible story. Not for any other reason.

Cal let out a breath and clasped his hands together into a double fist, which he brought down gently onto the table. "She came over to my house for dinner, and to do homework together. At that point I hadn't known what exactly we were, but I knew I loved *that*. Sitting at the kitchen island with Iris, each of us focused quietly on our own thing, music playing from Iris's computer. Knees touching, cheesy as that is." He chuckled, as if no one had ever acknowledged that touching knees is a cliché of love that we all nevertheless indulge ourselves in.

"The thought came quickly. Just like that. I can't even tell you what spawned it, at what time, how long into our night. Just that I knew. Without a doubt, all at once. What I'd previously thought was true is wrong. Soul mates are not about finding the one person meant for you. 'The one' does not mean *the only one*. It's just that…there are others, but they are lesser. They have their qualities, but if you add them up they don't equal the qualities of this person you've found, this one person who has so many things you crave, so many joys to provide. Not all the things you crave, but more than anyone else does." He took a sip from the coffee he'd ordered when he arrived.

"*I did not know love would be this calm*. That was my thought."

I stared, because, duh. How was I the first to write about these people? How had Cal not already been featured in numerous *Misnomer* articles and Jane Austen novels? I set my pen down. "I think I have all I need."

Cal raised his eyebrows, smiling. "Yeah? Article's all done?"

"Probably. Just needs typing," I said. I even tucked my notebook away inside my bag and set it at my feet. I looked at my phone. "I still have time to hang, if you do."

Cal shrugged. "Sure." He took a sip from his iced-coffee-frappe-concoction thing, which he'd loaded up with extra flavors and caramel drizzles because he got them for free. "So, now that you've gotten what you need from us, you're gonna stop hanging out, huh?"

"Oh, one hundred percent. You guys are lame."

"I guess it makes me feel special in a way. That I've been screwed over by a writer, my trust betrayed."

"There's a support group that meets Tuesdays at Jefferson Market Library."

"Damn it, I'm busy Tuesdays."

"Ha! I screwed you again."

Phrasing, Lu.

The door to the coffee shop opened behind us, letting in the noise of Washington Square Park, along with two girls that walked in talking about whatever meal they'd just had. For some reason I was blushing again when the door shut and Cal looked back at me.

"So," he said, his voice trailing off. His eyes caught the light coming in through the windows, a pretty glint of auburn in his irises. I remembered the bathroom again, and found myself reaching up to the scrape on my cheek. The scab had subsided to the point where I felt the urge to pick it away, bit by bit. What is it about scabs that make us want to peel them off and leave scars behind? What evolutionary purpose could there possibly be for that? "What should we do now?"

20

DOING NICE THINGS WITH CAL

There's something about walking aimlessly with a person that passes the time like nothing else. That could be another instance where movies have worked their influence on me. Watching characters talk as they wander, smooth cuts that make it seem like they've been transported to a whole other place in a city. *Before Sunrise*, which is basically ninety minutes of walking and talking, is one of my favorite movies because that's the basis for how everyone falls in love, the basis for humanity. I think 90 percent of our existence is spent walking and talking.

We left the coffee shop, talking for the first time without my having to worry about writing everything down or even remembering it. Then we were passing through Canal Street's jam-packed sidewalks, stores overflowing with knock-off sneakers, loaded up with electronics and racks with cheesy T-shirts aimed for a very specific kind of tourist. Before I knew it, we had ended up at the South Ferry piers, sweaty from walking in the heat. "Why is lower-back sweat the worst feeling in the world?"

"Ugh, I know," Cal said. "We should start a summer fashion trend where T-shirts have that part cut out. Get a nice draft going back there."

Without thinking about it, I reached for the back of his T-shirt and gave it a tug, pretending I was trying to rip it.

"Oh my God, yes. You just gave me a little draft. That felt so good." He stopped walking and spread his arms out, his eyes closed.

I held on to his shirt, fanning it gently. We were at Pier Eleven by the water, near a pretty stretch of colorful flowers that had been landscaped into the structure. A breeze hit us, and Cal smiled, his eyes still closed. The breeze blew a little stronger, and Cal almost seemed to lean into the draft. My knuckles, gripping the inside of his shirt, brushed against his lower back, which did not feel sticky with sweat, but warm and thrilling. I gave myself the liberty to keep them there for just a second, just long enough to let the sensation sink in and take hold of me. Then I pulled away, letting his shirt drop. Pete didn't know what he was talking about.

"A-plus draft making, Lu." He opened one eye and smiled at me, and we kept walking to the edge of the pier. There we leaned against the guardrails and looked out at the sun shimmering on the Hudson, and the boats zipping their way across the river, streaks of white in their trail. New Jersey in the distance, an uninteresting skyline of drab buildings. Even Jersey was looking pretty good.

"Do you think human beings are overly obsessed with love?" I asked.

"Overly?" Cal shrugged. "It's better than a lot of other options, I guess. We're obsessed with plenty of other things."

"Like porn?"

"Yeah, I was thinking of porn specifically. So many types." He chuckled. "What makes you ask?"

"It's just been on my mind lately. I have a weekly column where I get paid to share stories about love, or just my thoughts on the subject. And people read it. I'm far from the only one too. It's all over the world, almost every story you hear, love's at the core."

"What else would be worthy?"

I turned my back to the water, wanting to make eye contact without craning my neck to see him. "Piggyback rides?"

"Definitely."

"Doing nice things for others. Helping bring joy into others' lives. That's a pretty worthy obsession. Have you been keeping up with it?"

He grimaced. "Not as much as I'd like."

On the pier, a handful of people milled about, same as everywhere. Tourists, mostly. "What about one of these fine folks?" I gestured to the crowd.

Cal smiled, then turned to face the same direction as me, leaning his elbows back against the railing, scanning the pier.

"What do you look for when you're trying to find someone to be nice to?" I asked.

"People with signs that say Help Me are ideal. French tourists looking at maps." I smiled at the memory. "It's kind of hard to find obvious ways that people need help. I gave my shoes to a homeless guy, which is an easier one to figure out, but I only have so many pairs of shoes." He pushed off from the railing and we started walking again down the pier, toward the street.

"Have you tried just asking people if they need help with something?"

"No, Lu, I've got social skills."

"Well, then, it's probably not a surprise that you haven't done as much of the being nice to strangers thing as you wanted to."

"But just approaching and talking to people is terrifying. They'll think I'm selling them something."

"Yeah, but you get used to it. I do it all the time for my pieces." We walked off the pier, strolling along the path near the water. There were plenty of joggers out, and a few people sunning themselves on the grass. "When Iris still wasn't on board for the column, I was getting close to my deadline and panicking about not having a topic, so I was at a coffee shop kind of harassing everyone who looked remotely like a couple."

"Judging from the fact that you haven't had an article in a while, I'm guessing that didn't go well."

I stopped walking. "How do you know that?"

"Oh, it's this thing called the internet. It allows you to find out stuff about people's lives. Crazy, right? You should check it out."

"You've read my stuff?"

He squinted as if I'd just suggested something immensely stupid. "Yeah, dude. I showed it to Iris and it helped convince her. You're a great writer." He took up the stroll again, hands in his pockets, turning his head back and forth as he gazed.

I had to jog to catch up to him. "Thanks."

He may not have heard me though, because as soon as I said it, Cal approached an elderly Asian couple that was walking hand in hand toward us, shuffling their feet, adorably wearing matching long-sleeve shirts and floppy hats. "Excuse me," he said. "Is there anything I can help you with?"

They looked at each other and then at him. "What?"

"My friend and I are just wondering if there's anything we could do for you." He gestured to me, probably trying to show he wasn't a murderer, like his introduction suggested. "See?" his gesture meant to convey, "here is a person I know whom I have not murdered. Now please answer my normal question."

The man furrowed his brow. "Like what?"

"Oh, could be anything," Cal said, putting his hands on his hips. "Give you directions somewhere, write a particularly difficult email that you've been having trouble writing, clean your house."

"You want to clean our house?" the man asked in a monotone voice.

"If it would make your life easier, sure!" Cal smiled warmly, and I tried to match his smile, though it was hard not to cringe instead.

Not surprisingly, the couple shuffled away without another word. Cal turned to look at me, eyebrow raised. "That went well."

"Eh, at least they stopped and heard you out. Most people will do anything they can to avoid talking to a stranger on the street. It's surprising they didn't just keep walking."

"I don't know if I can handle that."

"I'll take the lead on the next few," I said.

A group of women pushing strollers, a guy standing on a street corner flipping a sign that advertised a good deal on cell phone plans or something stupid like that, a cook taking a smoke break in an alleyway. Every single one of them looked at us like we were exactly as socially challenged as we seemed.

We kept tweaking our approach, trying to be as unintimidating and normal as possible.

My legs were sore and sweaty, even with the sundress I was wearing. I thought about suggesting we go get ice cream, but

I didn't want to break our momentum. My mom had already called and given me a hard deadline of 7:00 p.m. for dinner, which was too quickly approaching. Heading away from the Hudson, we started meandering through the streets again, passing near Wall Street and its onslaught of suited bros hitting up the bars after work.

"I don't know how I feel about helping out finance dudes," Cal said.

"I mean, me neither. But helping someone is helping someone, right? Someone here might be really struggling with something heavy. Like, that guy," I said, pointing to a semi-attractive white guy in a blue suit, the top shirt of his button undone, his tie just a little loose, like he'd given it one good yank as soon as he left the office. "Maybe he's second-guessing his career, and really hates the environment he's put himself in. Maybe he's begging for someone to tell him it's okay to leave. Or maybe his parents are sick, maybe he's lonely and..."

"Okay, I think I get the picture. Wall Street bros are human too."

"Don't put words in my mouth." I walked up to the guy, who was looking at his phone outside of a generic Irish pub. I tapped him on the wrist. "Hi. Sorry to interrupt, and this is going to sound weird, but please don't let the weirdness undermine the sincerity of the question. Is there anything nice I can do for you today?"

He blinked, like so many others had. "Something nice?"

"Yeah. Maybe something you can't do for yourself. It doesn't have to be big, just something that could help make your life a little better. Even if it's just for today."

He looked at Cal. "Is she serious?"

"Super serious. Me too."

Wall Street Dude considered us for a second, then reached

into the breast pocket of his jacket and pulled out one of those unabashedly douchey vaporized cigarettes. He inhaled slowly and thoughtfully, then exhaled a huge puff. To his credit, he turned his head so that he wouldn't blow it directly into our faces. "Actually, yeah. There is something." He craned his neck back toward the bar, which was not quite full but getting busier. He could have been there alone, or a part of any of the groups hanging out in booths and those high-top tables that don't have seats, but are only meant to rest your drinks on. "There's a bartender in there. Charles. Tall, fit, cute as a button." He took another pull from his e-cig. "I've been in love with him for months. But I don't want to make him uncomfortable by hitting on him at work, and I'm not sure if he even knows I'm gay. I'm only ever here with coworkers, and it's not like it comes up."

Of course it would be love related. Cal's eyes were practically gleaming with joy. "Yeah, we'll help. What can we do?"

"You tell me, kid."

Cal bit his lip and looked sideways at me. "What do you say, love columnist? Have any ideas?"

For a second, I thought they were messing with me. The solution felt so simple that I couldn't help but roll my eyes. Then Cal and Wall Street Dude shared a look, and I realized that they really didn't know what to do. People can be so stupid about love. I sighed, and walked into the bar.

"Where's she going?" I heard Wall Street Dude say to Cal, a hint of worry in his voice.

The bar was as equally loud with music as it was with chattering. There were two male bartenders working, and it became clear quickly which one was Cute As a Button. He, however, was busy punching something into the electronic tablet that served as his register, so the other one noticed me first.

"No!" I said when he locked eyes with me. "The other one."

The bartender continued his approach. "What?"

"I said the other one!" I pointed at Cute As a Button, or whatever his name was. "Bring him to me."

The guy looked like he wanted to ask me for my ID. Then someone else approached the bar and so he shrugged, tapped the other bartender on the shoulder, and tended to the new customer. Meanwhile, my phone started ringing. I checked to see who it was. Leo.

"ID," Cute As a Button told me, as soon as he saw me.

I hit Ignore on my phone. "That's not important right now," I said, waving him away. "Do you see that guy outside?" I pointed toward the door, where Cal was standing with his hands on his hips, looking so happy that just the sight of him made me break out into a grin. Wall Street Dude had been staring a moment ago, but as soon as Button looked over, he pretended to look at something very important on his phone.

"Who? Scott?"

"Sure," I said. "He has a crush on you but is iffy about hitting on you at work. Are you interested in him?"

He didn't even have to answer. His smile said it all. "Great," I said, matching his grin. A little flutter shot through my chest. "You want to write down your number or something? He seems like he's so nervous he might run away waving his arms in the air at any moment."

I left the bar and handed Scott the napkin I had with Button's phone number on it. "Wow, the classic digits-on-a-napkin," Cal said. "I feel like no one's done that since the early 2000s."

Scott grabbed the napkin, staring at it with mild disbelief, holding it gently, as if it were a butterfly that could flitter away at any second. "He says to call anytime," I said.

"That's all it took?" Scott said softly.

"'People are vines, awaiting the chance to cling.'" Both he and Cal looked at me with eyebrows raised. "It's a quote. From *Look at Me* by Jennifer Egan." Scott returned his gaze to the napkin, but Cal kept his eyes on me, a slight smirk on his face. My chest flutter grew. "What? You and Iris are allowed to quote stuff all the time. I can be deep too."

Cal laughed, putting his hands up to say he wasn't judging. Scott thanked us, a big smile on his face and a new glow to his skin, even though his hand was shaking when he took his next puff. Cal and I waved goodbye and started heading back to Chinatown toward my place.

"You feel that?" Cal said, when we were a few blocks past the hectic streets of downtown.

I did. I wasn't sure if it was exactly the same thing Cal was feeling, if he meant just the fact that we'd helped Scott out, or if he meant something else. "Yep," I answered, leaving it at that.

"That was surprisingly simple. If we ignore the six thousand failed attempts before this one."

"We got lucky that it was love related."

"Why's that?"

"Because love's pretty simple to figure out."

Cal laughed. "Is that right?"

"Not always. But when you're outside of the situation, hell yeah. It's easy to see the solutions to someone else's problems. Especially an early stage. This was just the approach. Things may get messy later, but the approach is easy. You have feelings for a person, you try to see if they reciprocate. Then you get closer to each other."

"That's all it takes, huh?" Cal said, scratching his chin.

"In a nutshell."

Again, that stomach flutter returned. I checked my phone to see how I was doing on time, if I could stretch the day out any more, but I had about fifteen minutes before my mom threatened to disown me again, and we were ten minutes away from my place. Also, there was a voice mail on my phone. Probably from Leo. Which made sense, because who even left voice mails anymore, other than ex-boyfriends intent on making your life more confusing than it had to be.

For the rest of our walk, Cal and I were quiet. I was wondering how much of what I'd said was true, that love is easy when you look at it from the outside. Like Iris and Cal. For me, it was easy. They should stay together. They should extend the rare thing they have until it can't be sustained, not give up on it because there were obstacles in the distance. Was there some easy solution for me that I was failing to see? If there's an easy solution for love, is there an easy solution for heartbreak too?

"Well, this is me," I said because that's the thing everyone says when you're walking and you arrive at your house. It's practically a law that those are the words that leave your mouth.

Cal looked up at my building because that's what his role dictated he had to do. Then he smiled at me. "Well, Lu, thanks for hanging out and doing nice things with me today. It's always great hanging out with you."

"You too," I said, averting my eyes in hopes of quelling

my overactive blushing mechanism. Pete's accusation flashed through my mind, not for the first time that day.

Then Cal took a step toward me. "Are you a hugger?"

I shrugged. "I could be." I stepped forward into his arms.

Goddamn, was it a good hug. I could feel it on me long after it was gone, long after we'd said goodbye and I went upstairs and had dinner with Jase and my mom. It clung to me like a scent, like a feeling, refusing to let go.

In my room, later that night, I listened to the message Leo had left on my voice mail. His voice was cracked with hurt and regret, which was enough to convince me that the words he was saying were honest. "I fucked up, and I'm sorry, and I think I want you back. I don't think, I know. I want you back." A beat on the phone, no static because the quality of the call was good, but I could imagine it hanging in the silence, just like I could still feel Cal's touch on me. "I can't believe I'm leaving soon and that I might not see you again." He sighed into the phone. "I hope it's not the last time. I'm sorry."

Then, a click.

21

WHY NOW?

How had I arrived back on deadline day without having written a word?

Well, Lu, as soon as you find yourself in an emotionally healthy state, ready to tackle the task set before you, your idiot ex-boyfriend says or does something that throws you back into a confused place where thoughts are the last thing you want to face.

Also, your words have probably left you for good, revealing to the world that all you are is a love-obsessed teen. You don't pay enough attention to your family, or your closest friend. You allow a job, and therefore a scholarship, and therefore your ability to attend an institution of higher learning, to slip through your fingers. Because of something as superficial and, frankly, nonexistent as writer's block. Writer's block is nothing but cowardice. The fear of facing what you should really be writing about, or the fear that what you will write won't be good enough to meet some lofty and vague standards that only you yourself have set. Either way, you put yourself here, so don't blame stupid Leo and his change of heart.

Blame, maybe, the memory that lingers of that incredibly

silly, stupid, and wonderful thing he used to do when you found yourselves in a room all alone. He'd rush over to your backside, place his butt against yours, then do a little side-to-side shimmy.

Blame, even, the fact that every story about heartbreak you've ever read has made you expect his smell to cling to your bed. Except he only lay on it a handful of times, and never slept in your room overnight, so no matter how much you burrow your nose into the pillow, you cannot reclaim those moments spent lying next to him.

Blame your stupid desire to address yourself in third person.

It was Friday. The morning light slipped in through my blinds, weak and gray. I woke up right before my alarm went off. It felt like I was waking up from a bad dream, but the truth was that I was waking up *into* a bad dream. This was it. I was going to lose my job and my scholarship. My whole life from that day forward was going to look very different from what I had imagined, and it was all because Leo suddenly agreed with me that he was an idiot and that we shouldn't have broken up.

I hadn't responded to him yet, but as soon as I'd had a sip of water and had a moment to adjust to being human in the morning, I grabbed my phone.

LU
Why now?

Someone started knocking on my door.

"Lucinda, are you awake?" my mom shouted, clocking way too many decibels for the morning. "You have work, right?"

"Yeah, Mom, I'm awake and capable of meeting my responsibilities, thank you!"

"Except for making yourself available for an adequate amount of family time!" Mom yelled. "Come have breakfast before your brother eats it all."

I kicked the sheets off and stumbled to the shower, putting on a podcast so that I wouldn't have to listen exclusively to my thoughts. That didn't work out great though, as I just ended up peeking my head out of the shower every thirty seconds when I imagined I heard my phone buzz. I wondered if Leo would respond at all, or if in the course of the night he'd changed his mind again.

My mom knocked on the bathroom door this time. "Lucinda Philomena Charles, stop wasting water and come out to have your breakfast!"

"Mother, you named me, and you know that's not my middle name."

"I'm trying to annoy you so that you come join us." She knocked again. "Love you!"

I toweled off and went back to my room to get dressed, pausing the podcast and rewinding it to the beginning so that I could actually listen to it some other time.

Mom had made strawberry-basil French toast. If you need something to further illustrate the state I was in, I only managed to eat two pieces. Jase ate the other fifty-one.

I kept doing math in my head, trying to figure out how much time I'd have to write my column (not counting the previous three weeks or so). My shift would be over at three, and Hafsah had given me until the end of the workday, which ostensibly meant 5:00 p.m. I could maybe stretch it to six, but it probably wouldn't behoove me to stretch anything at all with this last chance I'd been granted. I could also add thirty minutes for my lunch break, plus a few stolen trips to the bathroom which could be productive, especially if I came in announcing I'd eaten a bad kebab and was feeling queasy and could sneak away to the bathroom more than usual.

Oh right. Faking an illness. That was a thing people did.

"Mom," I said, "I'm not feeling great. I think I might call in to work."

"You better be sick, to only eat two slices." She stopped doing the dishes and walked over to me, placing the back of her hand on my forehead. She frowned, then touched my cheek. "You don't have a fever."

"I think it was something I ate."

My mom gave me a look that I was breaking her heart.

"Not the French toast. Or last night's dinner. I think something before that."

She put her hand over her heart and started looking seriously wounded. "You ate something before dinner? Do you not like my food?"

I said it wasn't that, and then stammered to think of some other thing I might have eaten between leaving the house and coming back for dinner, but my brain was still not in tip-top shape and I failed. Then my mom took a seat next to me, her eyebrows angling with so much worry I was afraid that if I kept thinking up excuses, she might never recover from the heartbreak. "So you are depressed, then. Should I call Leo and yell at him? You want Momma to do that?"

Oh good, I wasn't going to have to fake throwing up. The thought of my mom confronting Leo made me queasy but also strangely emotional. There were too many feelings happening for the time of day. I didn't have time to deal with feeling things.

I groaned. "Never mind. I'll go to work."

"You sure?"

"Yes, your food is wonderful, I'm okay."

"Okay," she said, still pouting. She put her hand back on my forehead. "Should I be worried about you?"

I thought about the shitstorm that would come when I lost my scholarship, how I could possibly explain the reason why I had failed to deliver one stupid measly column. "No, I'm fine. I think I'm just gassy."

"Gross," Jase mumbled as he chowed down on three slices of French toast at the same time, syrup dribbling down his chin.

"Yes, I agree, chemical reactions are gross when they occur inside my body." I pushed my chair out. "I guess I'll see you guys later when my life is over."

"Sounds great, honey. Drink a mineral water when you get to work, it'll help." Mom smiled at me then went back to the sink, slipping on a pair of blue latex gloves. Jase was already deep into a game on his phone. I gave one last wave to my former life, then grabbed my bag, slipped my computer in, just in case I found time to type up the column, and headed out the door.

It was a slow walk to work, since I had my notebook open, trying to write as I weaved around other pedestrians (or, if I'm being honest, as I let them weave around my annoying, slow-moving self). I did manage to write a paragraph on the fifteen-minute walk though:

This is an introductory paragraph about a very interesting couple who I thought were breaking up but aren't really. This is their story. Did you read that in a *Law and Order: SVU* kind of way? Because I wasn't going for that at all. Tonally, it's just not what I write. I write about love and stuff. You probably used to read my stuff, but then I stopped writing because love messes you up like that.

Good, right?

I pushed the door to the theater open, that familiar blast of AC hitting me, yet offering no relief. A second later, Pete came in behind me, a backpack slung over one shoulder. He brushed the hair away from his eyes. "What's with you? Did you not hear me calling your name for the last block?"

I blinked at him, then showed him the notebook. "I was working."

He read silently. For like six seconds because I hadn't accomplished all that much. "Jesus, Lu, this is all you have? You can't send that in to Hafsah."

"Oh really? I thought I might pitch a new relationship column written by a toddler."

He shook his head. "I dunno about that. Hell of a vocabulary for a toddler." We crossed the lobby toward the employee room. "I don't mean to pour salt on a clearly gaping wound, but what the hell have you been doing for the past week? I thought you had more than enough material."

"It got complicated."

"What, you're in love with Cal?"

I smacked him on the chest, harder than I would normally. "Shut your face, man. I'm not in love with anyone."

"Right." Pete slipped his work shirt over his head and threw his backpack into a locker. "So where's the complication? Write a few paragraphs about how they're hanging on to love while they can and that you and Leo couldn't and then move on."

"Wow, that's really reductive. It's harder than that to write something compelling. You just threw together a sentence about the main idea. Not even the right one. *A* main idea."

Pete rolled his eyes. "I apologize. So why haven't you written more than one borderline toddleresque paragraph?"

"Leo's still in love with me."

Silence filled the employee room. I looked at Pete, begging him to just say the right thing again, like he always used to. Just tell me what to do, what to say, what to think, how to live. "Oh no," he said. "Have we gone back in time? Are we still at the start of the summer? Has your obsession switched back?"

"This isn't wishful thinking or delusion. He told me."

"Your ex-boyfriend, Leo Juco, said those words."

"Yes."

"I'm gonna need you to run those exact words by me."

We walked over to the computer system where we clocked in for the day. "Beginning quote from Leo Juco, in an email sent last Friday at eight thirty in the morning: 'Do you know that I still, dot, dot, dot—'"

"He said 'dot dot dot'? Just wrote out the words like that?"

"No, it was in the subject of the email, so the ellipsis naturally popped up."

"Ah, got it. 'Do you know that I still, dot, dot, dot.'" He motioned for me to continue with his hand, and his eyebrows, and basically his entire body.

"'That I still love you.'"

Pete raised his eyebrows the farthest they could go. "Those were the words he wrote?"

"In their entirety. Oh wait, he also added, 'I thought maybe you should know.'"

He relaxed his facial muscles, and we walked over to the whiteboard to look at our shift assignments. "Who's the 'I' in that email?"

"Pete, focus."

"This happened last week? These were the developments you mentioned? How the hell did you keep this all from me for a freaking week, Lu?" I waved the notebook in front of his face. "Right, the lovebirds." Pete rolled his eyes, then used his wiry index finger to trace his name along the clipboard that listed our duties. "Yay, box office."

I checked to make sure I was there too. "Oh thank God. I'll be able to work on the column during the lulls."

"I take it this means we won't be hanging out after work."

"We'll get back to our routine soon enough," I said, opening the door to the box office for him.

"I've heard that one a few times this summer," he muttered, plopping down into the farthest chair. The shutters were still down on the box office window, so I flicked on the lights, then powered on the register computer. "What'll be the next obsession that keeps me from hanging out with my best friend before I move five hours away?"

"Come on, that's not fair."

"I agree. I tried to help you get over Leo, I tried to help you find topics to write about. Instead you jumped into this unhealthy obsession with the lovebirds and I've spent the summer twiddling my thumbs waiting for you to be available." Pete was raising his voice a little, which he never did. He was also resolutely looking away from me, even though he'd already logged in and there was nothing to see on his computer. I was about to respond when Brad came in, jiggling his keys.

"Hey, gang," he said.

"Gang?" Pete and I responded in unison. We shared a look then fell back into silence, a tension building that I wasn't expecting.

"Yeah, that felt weird to me too." Brad whistled a little bit, searching through his comically large key ring, until he found the one needed to automatically raise the metal shutters. They were painfully slow, creaking with every inch they moved.

"Why are these even automatic?" I said, tossing a pen at them. I was hoping Pete would laugh or smile or something, but he seemed to be stewing in his annoyance at me. By the time Brad finally left, Pete was exemplifying textbook restless leg syndrome and brushing the hair out of his eyes so regularly it was as if his movements were guided by a metronome.

Obviously, he was upset, but I wasn't really in the mood for a Pete diatribe. Tactless honesty would have to wait until after my column had been sent in. "Wouldn't it be great if Brad started talking in really outdated slang? Which decade do you think he'd pick? I'm picturing him speaking like someone who was a little cool in the '50s. Calling people 'cats' and saying 'neat-o' and stuff. That'd make this place a little more lively, huh?"

No response from Pete. He even pulled out his phone, which is not something he usually did at work, or at least not to the same extent as most of our coworkers. I could see him scrolling through Twitter, then closing out of it, and immediately opening it back up.

I scooted my chair closer to him, using the pen I'd tossed at the shutters to poke him in the ribs. He swatted at me. "Read the room, Lu."

"I did, and the mood didn't appeal to me, so I'm trying to move it in another direction." Pete sighed and set his phone facedown beside the computer mouse. "Come on, give me a decade of slang for Brad. Maybe '60s grooviness? Early '80s hip-hop?"

Pete chewed his lip, which gave me hope that I'd successfully turned the room in my favor. But he just kept staring out the window at the intersection of Third Avenue and Eleventh Street. The stoplights went through a couple of cycles.

A homeless man with a mess of dreads and dangerously low-riding pants shuffled by. No one approached our window.

I leaned over and poked Pete again in the ribs. "Will you help me with my column?"

Suddenly, Pete pushed away, smacking the pen out of my hand. "For fuck's sake, Lu! Take a hint."

I froze, feeling my jaw succumb to cliché and gravity. The hurt kicked in a moment later. "Fine," I said. "Whatever." I faced forward like he was, grabbing another pen from the holder in front of me. I twirled it in my fingers, tapped it on the edge of my notebook, remembered that I had a deadline that afternoon and I was going to need every second that I could get to formulate something deliverable that wouldn't cause my life to unravel.

I looked around for any approaching customers, then opened my notebook to a fresh page and pressed the ballpoint tip to the first line. But now I had that goddamn restless leg thing going on, and the only thoughts in my mind were definitely not deliverable to Hafsah. I put the pen down and turned back to Pete. "I get that you're upset, but that was messed up, Pete. All I'm doing is—"

Pete swiveled his chair to face me. "Is what, Lu? Please, I'd love to know exactly what it is you've been doing all summer."

I scoffed, tears unexpectedly rushing to the brink. I had to look away to keep them from coming. Some guy carrying a closed umbrella was standing on the corner, looking up at our showtime display boards while texting. "Writing! At least trying to. It's how I process the world, Pete. And it's what I want my future to be, a fact that becomes infinitely less likely if I don't get this column done. So I'm sorry if I haven't been lavishing you with attention while I work on that."

"Oh bullshit. You're not processing a thing. You're

using this column as an excuse to do the exact opposite."
Pete glanced outside, probably thinking like I was that the
umbrella-toting guy better hold off on his desire to purchase
a ticket until we were done. "You've spent all summer clinging to the notion that because Iris and Cal survived their precollege breakup, then so can you. You've been in denial about
Leo, and instead of writing and processing your heartache,
you've plunged yourself into this weird fantasy where they
are the golden standard of love, and you're hoping that their
love will somehow rub off on you." Pete took a long breath,
then exhaled through his nose. I couldn't help but wonder
how long he'd been holding this in.

"That's not what I'm doing." My voice came out as a whisper. Umbrella Guy chose that moment to walk up to my window. I went through the motions of getting him his ticket,
and dropped his change onto the floor when I tried to slip it
into that little slot beneath the window.

"You haven't written anything, Lu. You're not processing
the world around you. You're trying to distract yourself from
your pain. And I get that. Of course I get it." Rather than
brushing the bangs out of his eyes, Pete ran his hand through
all of his hair, mussing it rather spectacularly. "I've been here
just wanting to help you in whatever way I could. Instead, I
get left sitting at home waiting for texts from you, while you
feed an unhealthy crush on Cal."

"I don't have a crush—"

Pete waved his hand in the air. "That's not the point." He
swiveled his chair from side to side, our eyes not meeting.
His leg had stopped shaking. Outside, the clouds parted and
a beam of light hit the building across the street. "You know
I put in my two weeks here, right? And that a week after that
I leave the city? You know that all I wanted for this sum-

mer was to hang out with you as much as I could, to enjoy
your company while I had it? And you've acted like that
doesn't mean a thing to you. You could have listened to me.
You could have written about anything else, like the heartbreak that's causing all of this. But you've chosen not to. You
brought this on yourself."

I couldn't look at Pete anymore. My stomach started churning, like maybe I really had gotten food poisoning at some
point. I stared out our window, begging everyone who entered my periphery not to approach. I waited for my retort to
come, but all I could feel was the stinging threat of oncoming
tears, and a queasiness in my gut.

So I grabbed my notebook, rushed out to the lobby to find
Brad, told him I was sick, and then fled the theater.

Indie Folk Album

By Lu Charles
April 17

You ever have one of those days where you feel like you're stuck in a particularly sad indie folk song? More like one of those weeks, maybe.

I've discovered loneliness is still something you can feel in a relationship. I think we're all taught to believe that love inoculates you from certain unpleasant feelings, but that's either a lie or I'm still bad at this whole love thing.

I guess that's to be expected. I'm doing it for the first time, and it's no longer just in my head, where everything can go swimmingly all the time. There's someone else involved, and that always complicates things. As a writer I understand this discrepancy between what's in your mind and what shows up in real life. It's just a little more difficult to deal with when it's, you know, not just writing.

Like in writing, it's hard to know whether the problems are real or just in my head. I'm critical of myself when I write, and so I guess the same could be true of my relationship. I don't know if the silence I've felt this week has a reason behind it, or if its significance is imaginary.

It's not like anything tangible has changed between us. Our touches don't feel lesser in any way, our silences aren't heavier, none of the usual indie-movie indicators that something is astray are present. We're still saying I love you and spending time together, and I couldn't point at anything in our relationship that I would change. But I feel a weight somewhere, just off on the horizon, like a storm brewing, and I have no idea what it is.

I'd ask him if he feels the same way, but calling attention to it might just reveal my insecurities. So I'm putting them here, where I can have strangers tell me whether I'm being silly. And if he's reading, he can bring it up (Hi, babe).

I've gone back and read my previous columns, searching for clues as to how to help myself. I've also gone through the vast resources of relationship advice columns, self-help blogs, that wonderful archive of human emotion that is Tumblr.

Nothing's helped. Maybe because this is a wave of emotion that will pass. It has no specific cause, and therefore no specific solution. Or maybe the problem is specific but I can't put a name to it, and so, like an undiagnosed disease, it's impossible to know what solution will work.

Maybe it's too much for us to expect an instruction manual for love. It's a complicated thing, and even those who have loved before and loved well cannot promise us a step-by-step guide.

I'm only a chronicler, in the end. Take in what I see, process it through my particular lens of experiences and insecurities, spit it back out at you to do with what you will. Just because the experiences are a little closer to home now doesn't mean I'm suddenly an expert. This is my one relationship, and it looks like no others, can be treated like no others. The human heart is layered and complex, and it'd be foolish for even a love columnist to pretend she knows exactly what goes on within its thin walls. (Are heart walls thin? Probably not. All the cardiologists reading this feel free to go nuts in the comments.)

All I can claim to do is see what happens to us teenagers in love and share it with the world. I'm content with that, at least.

22
A FLIGHT TO NAIROBI

I found myself at Madison Square Park, eavesdropping on a woman's phone conversation with what sounded like her grown son. She was wearing traditional Orthodox Jewish garb and picking at a blueberry muffin that she'd laid out on her lap, the crumbs attracting pigeons which she would intermittently shoo away with a lethargic wave of her hand.

"Did you call your landlord about it?" she asked, brushing crumbs from her skirt.

I wrote down her words out of habit, out of a desire to shut my brain up.

"Mmm-hmm," the woman continued. "Right. Yeah, no, I know. But what about asking him again? You have to bug him a little or he'll never do anything about it."

Really compelling stuff, I know. I kept writing, filling almost two pages with lines from her conversation and the meaningless details of the park surrounding us. The scruffy brown pigeon that looked a little diseased and was unperturbed by the woman's halfhearted attempts to make it go away. A dumpling food truck was parked behind us, and every

now and then the girl working inside called out a name and
an order.

I tried to remember if I was on the same bench where I'd
met Cal, but I hadn't quite taken note of it at the time. I'd
taken note of his attractiveness, and the way he talked, and
of Leo's absence.

My pen stopped moving. I moved my notebook beside me
on the bench, rested my elbows on my knees, rubbed my face
a few times, tried sighing to get it all out. Then I buried my
head in my hands and begged the tears not to come.

Thankfully, at that moment, my phone buzzed. God bless
these little computers we carry around with us, and their
ability to pull us far away from our thoughts and pains and
public meltdowns.

IRIS
Hey! Doing anything tonight?

My mind flashed forward to me on my bed weeping while
Netflix played a cartoon for no one.

LU
No set plans. Why, what's up?

IRIS
Cal and I are going to a party, wondered if you
wanted to come.

IRIS
It's in Washington Heights. 7 pm.

I looked at my phone. It was barely ten in the morning.

LU

Sure! I'm in. You guys wanna get dinner or something first? Lunch? Coffee? Piggyback rides?

LU'S CONSCIENCE

Hey. Aren't you forgetting something?

LU

Shut up, I'm not talking to you.

IRIS

Haha. Sure, let's keep in touch. Either way, I'll send you the address and let you know when we're on our way?

LU'S CONSCIENCE

Dodged a bullet there. You need to gety our column done.

LU

WTF. How are you sending out typos?

LU'S CONSCIENCE

It's been a weird day. Just write your column, will you?

LU

Sounds good! Thanks for the invite!

The good news was that I'd now weaseled myself out of work, and could focus the next few hours on keeping my entire life from falling apart. So, naturally, I went to Cal's coffee shop. Look, it was nearby, and sometimes when you can't decide where to go for a writing session you end up wandering around being nitpicky and wasting entirely too much time, so it was a very responsible decision on my part.

I walked there listening to that same podcast from the morning, still not listening to a word of what was happening, but happy to have some other noise blasting directly into my brain. Also, it made me look super casual when I walked in, as if I didn't know where I'd stumbled into. A cute black girl with a septum piercing was at the register, not the cute bespectacled white boy I was hoping for. I ordered a regular coffee which came with refills, set up my computer in a spot that hit all of my checklist items (outlet, view), and only then looked around the coffee shop for Cal. And I swear to the god of reliable narrators that he walked in at the exact moment I turned to the door.

Which, of course, meant I started staring intently at my computer, setting my fingers on the keyboard and chewing my lip like I was reaching desperately for a word, or mired in the internal suffering of a true artist. My Word document wasn't even open yet, and I'd paused the podcast, so there was nothing distracting me from the fact that I could see Cal walk toward the register, pause, do a double take, then head my way.

It was hard to not burst into a smile when he arrived at my table, but I managed to keep the charade going. Then he reached out and tapped my shoulder. I jolted out of my fake focus—my fauxcus—taking a moment to process who'd dared to interrupt my intense work session. He was wearing a gray button-down shirt with his sleeves rolled up, the strap of a laptop bag slung diagonally across his chest. He smiled

BRIEF CHRONICLE OF ANOTHER STUPID HEARTBREAK 269

at me and waved, and I made a show of raising my eyebrows in surprise and taking my silent earphones out.

"Hey! What are you doing here?"

"Hey! I wasn't sure if you'd be here today or not," I said. Then I pointed at my computer. "It's deadline day, so I pretended to be sick at work and came here to put the finishing touches on the column."

"Oh man, that's exciting. I can't wait to read what you really think about us." He leaned over to sneak a glance at the screen, which made me almost panic and throw the laptop to the ground. Thankfully he didn't seem to really process the blank Word document I had open.

"It's a scathing indictment of your relationship."

"I'd expect nothing less." He chuckled. "I'll let you get some work done, then. Iris says you're coming to the party later?"

"Yup!"

"Awesome. No piggyback rides though."

"Aww, come on. It's my turn to give you one."

"Fair enough. By the way, your face?"

"Magic, I know."

We smiled at each other, and then Cal went back into the kitchen and reemerged behind the counter wearing an apron. I put my earphones back in and stared at my computer screen, feeling so much better than I had all morning.

For the next two hours or so, I proceeded to accomplish absolutely nothing, even with my phone buried deep in my bag to avoid distractions. I typed a bunch, but it was mostly gibberish or freewriting so that if Cal glanced in my direction I would seem like I was really getting work done. My leg didn't stop nervously shaking. I flipped through the notes I'd taken over the last couple of weeks, rereading them at least two or three times. Every now and then, I allowed myself glances at Cal steaming milk and grinding coffee beans, chatting amiably with customers and coworkers.

I checked my email obsessively, half hoping that Hafsah would message and say that she was actually super busy and could I hold off on sending the column until next week/next month/whenever I was ready? I also looked up flight options that combined the cheapest possible ticket with the farthest possible location. I even worked out a formula in a spreadsheet where I'd plug in all the numbers so I could rank the flights in order of cost per mile. I drank so much coffee that my stomach hurt and I got heart palpitations.

When I looked down at the right-hand corner of my computer screen and noticed what time it was, a fresh wave of panic washed over me. Why the hell had Pete chosen today to pick his little fight with me? Why had Leo left his stupid voice mail last night? I could have been at work focusing on writing. Instead, my brain was mush and the only thing that helped me feel semicoherent was looking up at Cal. I closed out of all my internet windows, put on my favorite playlist to write to, closed the spreadsheet, angled my body a little bit so that I couldn't look over at the coffee counter without craning my neck.

I cracked my knuckles because that's a thing that helps according to writing montages in movies. "Okay," I told myself, "no distractions, get this thing done." Then I got up to use the bathroom because I'd had approximately twelve cups of coffee and my bladder was not happy with me.

To get the key to the bathroom, I had to go ask someone working. So of course I found myself talking to Cal. "How's it going over there? You look like you're in the zone."

"I'm in a zone alright."

"Almost done?"

"Is a piece of writing ever really done?"

Cal used a dishrag to wipe down part of the super fancy espresso machine beside him. "Yes?" he asked, cracking a smile. "I think yes."

"I was asking philosophically, you philistine. You know—" I made air quotes "—'Art is never finished, only abandoned.'" I fidgeted with the silver ladle that they had attached to the key to keep people from forgetting it inside the bathroom.

"So is that the stage you're at now? Editing and perfecting?"

My mind flashed to the image of my computer screen, the word count on my document. "Ish."

Cal smiled, and then his coworker with the septum ring came over and said something to him, pulling him away so that he could complete some task or the other. I used the bathroom and then returned to my computer. It was only about noon, so I still had five hours to figure out how to do the thing that had eluded me all summer. No big deal.

Plus, anytime I let my guard down for a moment, my treacherous thoughts returned to what Pete had said. To what Leo had said. To how he still hadn't answered my text message. To all the angles and cracks of my stupid heartbreak.

I looked over at Cal, trying to examine what it was I felt for him. Yeah, he was cute. He was great to hang out with. But a crush? I chewed on my thumbnail and shook my head to rid myself of those thoughts. Of all thoughts. Instead, I looked back down at my notebook and flipped through my notes. Maybe what I could do was start the column with something Iris and Cal had said during that first eavesdropped conversation.

We have love. What else matters?

Or, no. What if I started the column with an introduction to them?

I would have called bullshit on the whole thing from the beginning if I didn't see both Iris and Cal get the same look in their eyes. Constantly. When Iris hums to herself as they walk hand in hand, when Cal insists on doing the dishes at her parents' house, when she underlines whole paragraphs in novels then simply has to voice her appreciation for what she's just read, and how he'll stop whatever he's doing to listen, even if he clearly has no idea what she's talking about.

One eighteen-year-old gets that look, you start feeling sorry for them. Two of them give that look to each other and no matter what kind of cynic you are, you start thinking only teenagers really understand love. How insane it's supposed to be.

Ooh. That wasn't bad. Except Hafsah wouldn't let me get away with using *bullshit*. I deleted the word and brainstormed possible replacements for it. Which led me to click over to the internet for a few seconds to find a thesaurus, decide that I could just use *bull* instead of the full version, but then continuing to click around the internet instead of going back to my Word document. Before I knew it I was plugging more flight options into my spreadsheet.

There was a crazy cheap flight to Nairobi out of Newark leaving the following month, which I'm not entirely sure how I found. I had enough money saved up to get myself on the flight and then maybe pay for a place to stay for a couple of weeks, and pay for meals, according to a quick search on the currency exchange rate and cost of living in Kenya. It was satisfyingly far away, and I had a fantasy of getting a job as a tour guide, wowing Americans with all the Kenyan knowledge I'd accrued over the course of a few short months, how seamlessly I'd slipped into the culture, my nuanced understanding of how things were different and how they were the same. My familiarity with the best restaurants and food stands in the city would become legendary, and my tour group would become highly sought after as an exploration of Nairobi's culinary highlights. On one of these tours, I'd meet a boy. A Spanish boy. Sparks would fly. We'd spend a night walking around the city talking, ending up on...quick Google search for the best views in Nairobi...the roof of the Best Western Premier hotel, watching the sunrise as we made out. He'd cancel his flight back to Madrid to stay with me a little longer. We'd become more and more intimate, eventually coming so close to one another that we could really *see* who the other was. Until one day he finally brought himself to ask me about what brought me here, what did I run from in America. I'd go really quiet and stare off into the distance. He'd put his hand over mine. "Hey, it's okay. You can talk to me." A single tear would drip down my cheek, and he'd rub it away with his knuckle, softly palming my cheek and moving my head so I could look into his beautiful brown eyes. "It's in the past. Whatever happened, it's okay. It's over. You have me now."

Then I snapped out of my fantasy, wondering what I would do for the next month until that flight. How would I hang around the house without telling my mom that my scholarship was gone? I checked for a flight leaving tomorrow. The price went up three thousand dollars. Damn it.

I clicked back to my Word document, reread my introductory paragraph, feeling okay about what I had until I saw the time. One o'clock. Four hours to go.

I slammed my forehead down on the table.

At four forty-five, I shut my computer.

I had just emailed Hafsah, and did not want to think about the contents of that email, or the lack thereof. Another apology, another failure to save myself. I finally pulled my phone out of my bag to distract myself. Within the slew of notifications I saw Leo's name, and I clicked to that first.

LEO
Idk. I'm sorry. Can I see you sometime?

I typed out a dozen different responses, deleting them all as soon as I read them back to myself. The longest-lasting one was, **Do you really still love me?**, which I stared at for almost a full minute, my thumb hovering over the send button before I decided that I was in no condition to be thinking about this stuff. I threw my phone back in my bag and walked up to the register, where Cal was counting out tips from the two different jars (one of those cutesy do-you-prefer-this-or-that ploys which I always fall for).

"Finally taking off," I said.

He looked up from the pile of singles and quarters. "Yeah? The column's done?"

"Oh, I'm done alright."

"I can't wait to read it," he said. "Wait, what time is it?" He pulled his phone out of his pocket. "Oh sweet, I'm almost off. You doing anything between now and the party?"

I shook my head.

"You mind waiting? I'll be done in like ten. Iris was trying to think of what to do before the party. Maybe we could grab something to eat to help soak up the booze."

"You're such a responsible drinker."

He laughed, rubbing the side of his face with his hand and then taking off his glasses to clean them on the hem of his shirt. I don't know why, but I had the sudden urge to help him. I wanted the familiarity of being able to reach over to him, gently pull them off his face, and clean them for him.

"Okay," I said. My voice came out soft and shaky, like I'd just been woken from a dream. "I'll wait for you outside."

Cal and I rode the subway all the way up to the 103rd Street station. Our knees didn't touch, not really, but we were sitting side by side, and other parts of us were in nearly constant contact. Not that I was hoping for that, or whatever. But I did notice. I'll grant Pete that. I noticed Cal's laugh too, and how I felt like myself around him.

We met up with Iris at Xi'an Famous Foods on Broadway, not too far from the party. When we saw her, Cal's eyes lit up with joy, but a little bit of sadness too. Which made sense. She looked fantastic, but he'd soon be me.

He leaned in and gave her a kiss on the cheek, and we headed inside for some insanely delicious hand-pulled noodles. We sat at the counter looking out at the street. Somehow I got the middle seat, which meant I didn't feel like a third wheel at all. I felt like I was the center of their attention. It felt natural, and comfortable, like by writing about them (or at least meaning to) I'd somehow carved out a little place for myself in their relationship.

It was exactly what I needed, eating spicy noodle soup with Iris and Cal. They didn't pry about the column, they didn't bring up Leo, they didn't even touch on the not-so-

distant future in which they'd be broken up and I'd be dropping out of college before I could even begin. August 4 was
three weeks away, but rather than delve on that future heartache, they knew how to appreciate the happiness they had in
front of them. They joked, talked about each other's days, laid
hands on one another in small but deeply affectionate ways.
There was no subtext to the conversation, just two people
who loved each other. I was in awe and thankful of their presence. It would get a little more complicated than that by the
time the night was over, but at that point, I didn't want to be
anywhere else but by Cal and Iris's side.

23

THE TRUE MEANING OF PARTYING

The party was at a swanky apartment with its own rooftop terrace. It wasn't huge, but there were about thirty or forty people around, split up evenly between the living room and kitchen inside, and the terrace outside.

A blue-haired girl with a pixie cut let us in without much fanfare, and then Cal and Iris led us straight to the kitchen where the bottles of booze and soda were lined up.

"Mmm, alcohol," Iris said, wiggling her eyebrows at me. "'Drink up, young man, it'll make the whole seduction part less repugnant.'"

"Solid reference," I said.

"Wow, first time someone's caught that," Cal said, reaching for a bottle of whiskey and the stack of red plastic cups.

I eyed the bottles for what I should drink. Again, I swear I don't go straight to the bar at every party, and I'd definitely been given reason to think twice about doing it now. I didn't even believe that drinking could drown your sorrows or worries. Those jerk feelings are good swimmers and will just be there to greet you in the morning. But if there was any night in my life that I needed an artificial way to push them down, it was that night. "So, who do you know at this party?" I asked, pouring myself some tequila and grapefruit soda, which is a concoction Cindy discovered while doing a semester abroad in Mexico.

"Not a soul. Pretty smooth party crashers, right?"

Iris smacked Cal on the shoulder. "Don't listen to him. It's our friend Monica's party." She pointed across the room to an Asian girl wearing jean shorts and a plaid shirt sitting on the couch's armrest. Just then, Monica looked over at us.

She stood up and waved. "Clarice! You made it. Come play twenty-one with us!"

We finished pouring our drinks and went over to her, where hugs and excited hellos were thrown around briefly and then I was introduced to Monica and a handful of others around. "Why Clarice?" I asked.

"Eh, I'm into couple names. Cal and Iris don't really mesh well with each other, so I had to really stretch for one. It stuck, though."

"That's not true," Iris said, "no one else calls us that."

"I didn't say it stuck universally, did I? Just with me. Which counts." Monica smirked, and then she led the group over to the dining room table. "Okay, everyone who's going to play twenty-one, come now!" She called out over the music, which was playing loudly but not ridiculously so.

About ten people gathered around the table, six of us sitting down, the rest standing or squatting wherever they could. Cal had been sitting next to me and Iris, but gave up his seat for a guy with crutches, and ended up standing on the other side of the table, where I could slyly stare at him every time I drank or made a joke or just kind of wanted to.

I tried to follow the rules of the game, which involved counting to twenty-one one by one as a group, but every time we succeeded, the last person had to come up with a new rule for a number. For example, Cal came up with the rule that instead of saying "four" you had to name a city that started with the letter *F*. And for "twelve," Monica came up with the rule that we all had to stare silently at each other for five seconds without laughing. Any time someone messed up a rule or the wrong person counted, we all drank and had to start over.

Needless to say, my goal of forcing my sorrows to swim in a deepening pool of alcohol went pretty well. Now, we all know people that put "I love to laugh" on their social media profiles and senior yearbook pages and online dating profiles, and hell has a special eye roll reserved for those people. But holy crap did laughing on that particular Friday feel like a godsend.

The game was nonstop hilarity. I can't recall accurately whether it was merely drunken hilarity or an honest-to-goodness great time, but who really cares about the difference when you're in the moment.

Eventually the game lost its steam, as we'd all become sufficiently sloshed, at least for that time of the night. We were now ready to party.

And by *party* I mean stand near Iris and Cal all night and joke about whatever came up and look out at city lights twinkling in the Manhattan night while a few people around us talked and shot the shit with their preferred subgroup and some of them danced a little bit.

"How would you guys define *party*?" I asked. I was on my nth cup of tequila and grapefruit soda.

"A festive gathering of people, usually to celebrate a specific occasion," Cal said.

"Okay, Merriam-Webster. Now using your own words. Also, I meant the verb. Like, someone saying, 'we're going to party tonight!'" I added a wooh for effect.

"Hmm." Cal thought for a little bit.

Iris peeled the label off a beer bottle. "It means dancing." She'd asked Cal if he wanted to dance several times throughout the night, but he said he wasn't feeling it. Since then she'd been eyeing the improvised six-person dance floor inside the apartment with a palpable sense of longing.

"Not a universal definition, but respect for working in that subtle dig." He rubbed Iris's back. "I'll dance with you later. Right now I'm feeling more of a buzzed stupid conversation kind of partying."

Iris rolled her eyes, then put her beer down on a nearby charcoal grill, which was already a graveyard of abandoned bottles and red plastic cups. She kissed Cal on the cheek. "Well, I'm not. Lu, care to join?"

"Sorry, I'm with Cal on this one. To party is to banter while buzzed."

"Lame."

We watched her go back inside and join the modest dance floor with three other girls and two guys who were way more skilled at moving their bodies than I would ever be. I looked around the terrace, trying to come up with more definitions. Another summer thunderstorm was brewing in the distance, lightning flashing in the clouds on the horizon. "Thanks for inviting me to this. I needed it."

"Oh yeah?" Cal said, taking a pull from his whiskey ginger. "To celebrate finishing your column?"

I drank to buy myself time to come up with a good answer.

"I don't know. I just like spending time with you guys. It's been an easy part of my life at a time when life isn't so easy."

Cal frowned. "Sorry if this sounds flippant or naive or presumptuous, but what in your life isn't easy?"

I stared into his eyes for a moment, then took a sip. "No, it's nothing. Nothing that I'll have to move to Kenya to escape from anyway."

Cal laughed. "Okay, good. And I'm sure this goes without saying, but just because you're done writing about us doesn't mean we have to stop hanging out. You know that, right? We like hanging out with you too. I'm gonna need a friend to help me take my mind off the heartache of my oncoming breakup."

His words brought to mind my conversation with Pete. I took another gulp. Drown, stupid sorrows, drown. I winced, then turned to Cal. "I feel like we haven't put this *party*-definition thing to rest yet."

"You're right. I think we should take a piggyback lap around the party, I hear it's a great brainstorming activity."

"Come on now, we've done a piggyback joke today already. Don't get lazy on me, Cal," I said, giving him a little hip bump, trying real hard not to leave my hip on his. Then I had to add some more liquid to my sorrow pool. "Broaden the definition. Regardless of *how* someone chooses to party, what's a definition that's all encompassing, whether it's dancing or buzzed banter or yelling 'woooh' repeatedly."

Flashes of lightning made us pause for a second. A few people at the party oohed, but most didn't seem to notice. Monica was on a lounge chair making out with the girl with the blue hair, and there were a few other hookups happening. Most everyone was just kind of standing, talking, laughing, drinking, sitting, not drinking.

"I guess I'd say that to party is to live in the moment," Cal said.

"Hold my drink, I have to throw up on you."

"Yeah, I'd like that stricken from the record. Permission to rephrase?"

"Granted, but do it quick, my stomach is lurching."

Cal laughed his rising-bread laugh, then took a seat on the ground, resting his back against the wall and stretching his legs out in front of him. He patted the floor next to him, and I was more than happy to oblige. We were at the far end of the terrace, with the railing at our left, the inside of the apartment at our right, and the whole party in front of us.

"I think the true meaning of partying is..." He gestured vaguely with his hand, then dropped it into his lap. "I was going to say 'living in the moment' again. It sounds so lame, but I think it's kind of true. Parties aren't necessarily about celebrating life or anything like that. I mean, some of them are. Birthdays and New Year's are quite obviously a celebration of still being alive. But, parties in general, their biggest goal is to provide enjoyment, right? To be aware of the joys of the moment." He brought his drink up to his lips. "Whether it's in the form of a chemical buzz, or..." he pointed at Monica "...the chance of meeting new people you can create a bond with, or..." he motioned toward the mini dance party "...letting loose with your body..."

"That's a weird way to say 'dancing.'"

"Those are all acts of enjoying the moment. Forgetting the not-easy parts of life in the company of others, just for a night, just for a few hours." He crossed his legs at the ankles and leaned his head back against the wall, his eyes glimmering with joy and alcohol, and I want to say "moonlight," but it was overcast to the point where the city lights were reflecting off the clouds and the shimmer in his eyes probably came from a nearby lightbulb.

That's when I felt it. Or, I should say, that's when I recognized the feeling for what it was. The warmth in my stomach, the inability to look away from his face, the desire to keep the conversation going all night, the slight appreciation for the fact that Iris had stepped away to dance and had left us alone. Pete was right.

"Somehow I don't feel like throwing up anymore," I said quietly.

What a realization, to know that you are in love with someone. Even if it was just a crush, even if it was ill-advised, even if it was confusing. It was still some degree of being in love. Cal was appreciative, attentive, shared my sense of humor. He was warm, thoughtful, *good*.

He wasn't a distraction from my heartbreak over Leo. He was the cure. Hell, these were things I missed about Leo that now felt like qualities Cal had in excess. And he didn't like me only after making the mistake of leaving me behind. He liked spending time with me, he'd just said so.

I put my drink down on the ground suddenly feeling like I didn't need it anymore. I could see Iris in the apartment, moving to the music, her hands in her thick, curly hair as she danced. She looked so happy. Like these were the only moments that mattered, not whatever was to come. I wondered if I would have been happy if I'd known the breakup with Leo had been coming. I wondered what would happen on August 4, after Iris had left, after Leo had left, after Pete had left, when it would only be me and Cal together in the city.

But then I pushed the thought down. I stole another glance at Cal, then watched the partygoers standing around, drinking, flirting. "Do you think you can identify the people at this party who are in love?" I asked.

Cal made a little humming noise somewhere between a laugh and the noise people make when they want to indicate that they're thinking. "I dunno. Probably not. Do you think you can?"

"Yeah," I said, nodding. "It's pretty easy. All of us here. Everyone, all the time. Just walking around being in love. It's what people do. We can't get away from it, no matter how much we try."

The song playing on the speakers inside changed to something slow, and the dance party broke away. Iris moved to the kitchen and grabbed herself a fresh beer, apparently forgetting the one she'd set down on the grill. Monica and the blue-haired girl had stopped kissing and were now just holding each other on the lounge chair. Another flash of lightning overhead, this time followed closely by a loud rumble of thunder. Cal turned toward me and our eyes met, the song getting louder in the background. A few seconds later the first few drops of a light rain started to come down.

"No complaints from me," Cal said.

24

NORMAL HEART THINGS

I hadn't looked at my phone all night, so I wasn't sure at what time I got home. I fumbled with the key for a little bit, finally creaking the door open as quietly as possible. My mom was asleep on the couch with the TV playing quietly, her phone resting on her chest. I turned off the TV and the floor lamp that was still on, got myself the largest glass of water I could find, and went into my room quietly.

I took my laptop out of my bag and set it on my desk, opening it up but not moving past the log-in screen. For a long time, I sat on the edge of my bed, staring at the screen. I still hadn't changed the background picture away from one I'd taken of Leo in front of our school. It was hard to reconcile the image I saw with who I was now. High school already felt like so long ago, and so did Leo. Even the breakup felt long ago.

While I considered whether or not to log in and attempt one last-ditch effort at the article, or at the very least change the background image, my door creaked open. Under normal circumstances I might have jumped in fear or surprise, but I guess my reflexes were mellowed by the night of drinking. I turned to see my mom in the doorway.

She looked at me for a moment and yawned. "You have fun?" she asked in a whisper.

"I did," I responded.

"Good. That's the last fun you get to have until you can afford to pay rent somewhere in Manhattan."

"Yeah, I figured as much."

"I'm not sure if you've heard, but Manhattan is expensive. You'll probably be here until you've graduated from college, and had at least two to three jobs. I fully intend to ground you that whole time."

I gave her a smile. "Fair enough. At least I'll eat well."

She scoffed and walked over to me, planting a sweet kiss on my forehead. "Suck-up." On her way out, she paused in the doorway. "Are you okay?"

"Yeah, I think so." I bit my lip and looked over at the picture of Leo. She stood there for a while, waiting for me to continue, or maybe trying to figure out just how drunk I was, and whether her bit about grounding me until college graduation was hyperbolic or not. "Mom, how highly would you rank love on your list of priorities?"

She chuckled and walked back over to me, putting her hand on my shoulder. "You're not just asking to get out of your punishment?" I shook my head, and she sighed in response. "In theory, I'd say it's the most important thing. But that downplays the complications that surround it. I'm sorry I don't have a clearer answer for you."

"Yeah, I could have used a clear-cut 'number one.'"

"Sorry, love." She kissed my forehead again. "If you need to talk in the morning, please do. I don't hear enough about your life. You know I want more than just to feed you and complain that you're not home, right?"

Then she left my room, leaving me in the glow of my computer again. I stood up from my bed and closed my laptop with a cathartic click. It felt like letting go of a rope I'd been clinging to for way too long, and the relief in my metaphorical knuckles made me want to sing.

Or maybe that was the booze still in my system. I stumbled to the bathroom, brushed my teeth, washed my face, and came back to my room. I pulled my phone out of my bag and plugged it into the charger, finally looking to the screen to check for notifications, but it had died at some point during the day, so I laid it facedown on the nightstand and slipped into the cold comfort of my sheets. The room was threatening to spin, but I let out a slow exhale, took a long sip of water, and managed to keep it at bay. As soon as my head hit the pillow, I closed my eyes, and allowed myself to dream of Cal.

In the cruel, cruel morning, my serenity had evaporated and left in its place a headache, nausea, and a drained pool where all of my sorrows were now walking around and making it known that the alcohol had not drowned them even a little bit.

I reached for my water, but found that I'd drank the entire glass at some point in the night. "Blurgh," I said into my pillow, which only made my terrible breath waft back toward me, sending my nausea into high gear. "I hate life," I said out loud, hoping that voicing my opinion to the universe would cause it to make some adjustments.

Somehow, I managed to stumble out my bedroom to the bathroom across the hall, grabbing my phone from my nightstand before I left. Opening the door led to a barrage of noises: Jase's video games and the accompanying button mashing and smack talking into the headset, my mom cooking some-

thing and the accompanying pans clanking around and blend-
ers going. I swear there was more than one blender going.
"Ahhh," I said, trying to keep this complaint under my breath
at least until I made it into the safety of the bathroom.

As soon as I shut the door though, it felt like the noises all
got louder. Maybe I was imagining it, but I'm pretty sure Jase
was yelling, "I swear my mom wants me to do this! I don't
know why! I know I'm screaming! Shut up, Jerry!"

Immediately afterward, there was the hellish sound of
someone pounding on the door with the full force of their
open palm. "Morning, honey!" my mom shouted at the top
of her lungs. "How are you feeling now?"

"Not great, Mother!" I shouted back, very quickly regretting expending the energy it took to do so. I groaned and
turned on the faucet, drinking hungrily from the cold Manhattan water. Mom kept pounding on the door. "Why?" I
moaned.

"This is your punishment," she shouted, somehow hearing
me through the cacophony she was creating.

I shut off the faucet, then crawled to the floor and curled up
into a ball, pressing my cheek to the cool tile, staring through
one eye at my phone and yesterday's barrage of missed notifications. "Why don't you just ground me?"

"Because of your speech last night."

"What speech?" I felt like crying and puking at the same
time.

"Okay, not a speech. You asked me about how highly I'd
rank love on my list of priorities. My guess is you didn't just
pull that question out of nowhere but were asking for a reason." She blissfully stopped pounding on the door for a second. "As much as I believe you should stay indoors for the
rest of your young adult life so that I can keep my eye on

you, I'm your mother and want the best for you, and I have a sneaking suspicion you being relegated to this apartment all summer might cause more harm than good."

"Wow. That's actually really cool of you. What's with the noises though?"

"I want this hangover to be so traumatic that you think about it next time you drink." She resumed the pounding while I scrolled past more Leo texts that I didn't want to think about. "Now take a shower to wash your shame away and come out to have breakfast. I finally made Filipino food like you asked. Dinuguan."

"Blood stew? Are you fucking kidding me?"

"Hey! Language. And it's not part of the punishment, it's actually a great hangover remedy. I'm having fun with your misery, but I'm not a monster."

"Where does one even find blood to cook with...?" My voice trailed off. I'd found an email from Hafsah from exactly five o'clock yesterday. **I'm disappointed in you.**

"A butcher, dummy." She pounded one last time on the door, then her footsteps sounded down the short hallway.

My shower was long and painful and provided almost none of the comfort I wanted from it. I kept wanting to lie on the floor of the shower and just fall back asleep under its wet blanket of warmth, but managed to resist.

I'd screwed up so bad. I'd lost my column. I was going to lose my scholarship. I'd wasted my summer away being heartbroken. I'd sullied my remaining time with my best friend in pursuit of a stupid idea that only resulted in... Well. It *had* given me Cal. And it was a weird situation, but the only thing that felt okay during that shower were thoughts of Cal. The fact that he was staying. Everyone would be gone, except for him.

I turned my face into the water, closing my eyes, trying to find a way to make everything okay again. Instead of solutions though, all I got was a montage of the time I'd spent with Cal over the past few weeks. The bench, the subway, the party in New Jersey, the pier, last night.

What if I didn't have to make *everything* right?

What if I just held on to one good thing the summer had provided for me? This boy who was part of a ridiculously romantic, albeit doomed relationship. What if the reason I'd met him wasn't to write about him and Iris?

I opened my eyes again, my heartbeat starting to quicken, a smile managing to break through my hangover's defenses. A closed window means an open door, right? People say something like that? What if a bunch of facets of my life were coming to an end, but something else was set to begin? A cliché, maybe, but who cares about lacking originality if a cliché leads to joy?

After I toweled off and ate my bloody breakfast (way too rich for my queasy stomach, but surprisingly tasty), I sat on the couch while Jase played his video games at full volume, trying to think of what my next course of action would be. I wanted to reach out to Pete, but he hadn't texted me at all yesterday after I left the theater, and I had the sneaking suspicion he wouldn't be on board with my plan to salvage my summer/disposition/love life/life.

I brainstormed to the best of my ability under my current conditions. It actually wasn't all that bad, because at long last I didn't have the pressure of trying to write. That part was over now. It hadn't exactly been a quick pull of the Band-Aid, but I no longer had to worry about it. I could let my writing come to me whenever it was ready. The way love did. Or something.

In the end, I decided that I didn't need a big plan. I just needed to see Cal, maybe talk to him openly, see if he felt the same way I did. He had to. The way he'd cleaned up after me after slamming my face into the ground. How well we got along. He called my stupid face magical. That meant something, didn't it?

Under normal circumstances I would have stepped far away from someone in a relationship. Especially someone as clearly in love as Cal and Iris were. But these weren't normal circumstances. They themselves had decided that the love was secondary to timing. In the space they carved out for that sensibility, I could see how feelings for me could sneak in. Even if he didn't know it yet, there had to be something there, right?

LU
Good times last night. Thanks again for the invite.

CAL
To party would not have been the same without you.

LU
☺
Are you as hungover as I am?

CAL
I was, but then I went for a run. It works every time.

LU
A run. While hungover.
You either have incredible mental fortitude or are a way bigger idiot than you make yourself out to be.

CAL

Say what you will, but I am now hangover-free.
What's your go-to remedy?

LU

Er. I had blood soup today.

CAL

Ugh. Sounds offal.

LU

Clever. Wasn't bad, actually. Wouldn't recommend
while hungover, but I'd try it again.
What are you up to today?

CAL

Relishing my non-hangoverness by walking around
the city.

LU

Coolio. Iris too?

CAL

She holds similar views to you about running after
a party, so she's still in bed.

LU

Want some company?

CAL

Sure!

The High Line was unsurprisingly busy. After yesterday's late-night thunderstorm, the sky was a brilliant blue and the heat had been momentarily washed away, leaving a cool breeze in its wake. I was in my favorite gray dress, carrying nothing with me but my phone, keys, and a few five-dollar bills. No notebook, no laptop, not even the earphones I usually jam in as soon as I leave the house. Physically, I was still feeling less than perfect, but mentally and emotionally I was feeling... Okay, still less than perfect. I was still in deep, deep shit, and suddenly on a life path that I had not planned on.

But I was going to see Cal. And I would get to keep seeing Cal. I took a seat on a long bench that looked out at the water and was near a stretch of food kiosks and coffee stands. To my right, a couple speaking in Spanish were toying around with a selfie stick, laughing tirelessly at their poses and private, whispered jokes. I wished I understood enough Spanish to pick up on some of the details of their conversation, but could only catch the occasional word.

The foot traffic was constant, tons of people holding iced coffees and popsicles and each other's hands. I looked around, hoping to see a couple on a date to eavesdrop on, or even a couple breaking up, since last time it hadn't gone so bad, in the end. I didn't spot anything like that, but I was content to look out at the parade of humanity passing by in front of me.

Every now and then my thoughts turned to Cal, and what I should say. Should I have a speech prepared? Should I wait until August 4? Would it be a completely selfish and inconsiderate thing to want him the way I did, to burden him with these feelings I'd developed? Or would I be doing what I'd been told to do by nearly two decades' worth of art: following my heart, putting love above all else? Would I be doing what Iris could not do for him?

I didn't want to think about Iris. She was letting him go. I liked her and admired her and wanted to keep her as my friend. Maybe she would understand. It was love. I turned my attention back to people watching, emptying my thoughts, still feeling a little physically miserable but nevertheless enjoying the sun on my skin and the breeze in my hair and my ass going numb from sitting on the wooden bench too long.

Cal took a seat even before I had noticed him approaching. Which was awesome because it totally saved me from spotting him and then trying to figure out if I should pretend I hadn't or if I should hold his gaze the whole time.

"You look very content for a hungover person," he said, squinting into the sun. He had an iced coffee in his hand and looked freshly showered, his hair too damp to take on its normally tousled look.

"I *am* content," I said, by way of a greeting. I felt like reaching out to grab his coffee and take a sip, but withheld the intimacy for the time being. "It's a beautiful day out. I got drunk without someone pile-driving me into the concrete, so—"

"I think it was more of a suplex last time."

"I'm hanging out with you. My worries, however big or small, will be dealt with some other time, by a future version of myself that is more ready to deal with worries because she's already had this little moment of joy."

Cal smiled at me and took a sip of his coffee. "I can tell you're a writer." Then he lifted his cup at me like he was offering a sip. I tried to maintain my short-lived reputation for being chill by not knocking it out of his hands as I rushed to grab it.

"How's your day going?" I asked when I handed back his drink.

"It's good. Again, the run helped. It's a cool feeling to

defeat a hangover. Like a superpower." He swirled the ice cubes in his coffee, then looked around the park. "I've actually been thinking a lot about the…" He trailed off, making a halfhearted motion in the air with his hand. "You know, the breakup."

I know people describe all sorts of nonsense things that they think their hearts have done. Backflips, somersaults, lurches, skipped beats. That's ridiculous. Hearts just beat until they don't. Contract and expand. Pump blood in and out. Maybe an arrhythmic beat here or there due to a medical condition. But when he said that, I almost understood what they meant. I twirled my hair as nonchalantly as I could manage. "Oh yeah?"

Cal bit his lip, scooted back on the bench so that he could lean all the way against the backrest. I had noticed he was not the most relaxed sitter, often falling into poor posture. Now he looked at ease. He crossed one leg over the other and set his drink on the bench between us. I could see little indents of teeth marks on the straw, and I thought to myself: *He's a straw biter. That's a thing you know about him now.*

"Yeah," he said. "And I feel strangely at peace about it."

My heart upped its non-heart-like activities. "Really?"

"Not, like, thrilled or anything."

"Of course not. No one expects that."

"Yeah, but not… I don't know. Not devastated. Zen, almost. Like, I know it's going to hurt more than this at some point. Probably a lot more. But I had a lot of joy over the last two years with her. And this isn't the last I see of joy in my life." He turned to look at me as he said this, holding eye contact with me for far too long for it to not mean something. I smiled at him.

"No, it's probably not."

"Yeah," Cal said. He picked up his drink and looked away from me, toward the water. "And it's weird to come to terms with that. That I'll have joy again, it just won't be coming from her. It'll be from someone else." For good measure, another glance in my direction. I hadn't bothered even pretending to look away, so our eyes met again. Now it was my entire body doing un-body-like things. Chills, waves of goose bumps, floating. All the possible hyperbolic descriptions people use. "It's weird, you know? Thinking like that. But I know it's true. Here comes another quote for you. 'Love was not a quantifiable substance. There was always more of it somewhere, and even after one love had been lost, it was by no means impossible to find another.' That's from—"

At that moment, all my questions flittered away. All my doubts about what I should do, what things could mean, whether he felt the same way. It was clear to me that he did. That we would be each other's unquantifiable new love. I cut the distance between us, parting my mouth and waiting for the beautiful, inevitable moment when he would part his too and kiss me.

But it never came.

Cal pulled away. He stood up. His brow furrowed. He looked like a skittish animal about to bolt across a meadow. "What was that?" he asked.

My heart went back to doing normal heart things.

"Lu, what was that?"

"I thought..." I started. But nothing else came. I couldn't look at him. I pulled my knees up to my chest and stared at my shoes. The Spanish-speaking couple next to us said something in their beautiful quick tongues, then stood up. A family of four squeezed into the space they'd occupied.

It felt like several groups of people took a seat, enjoyed

themselves, then made way for someone else. The earth rotated several times. Cal and I didn't say a word. He stood there, clearly not knowing what to do with himself. "Lu," he said, tenderness in his voice. But not the tenderness I was expecting. Or hoping for.

"I'm sorry," he said. I dared to look up at him. He had one hand on the back of his head and was looking up and down the pathway, like he was worried someone had seen, like he didn't know how to proceed.

Then his eyes met mine. I didn't know what to do with that gaze. Whether I should plead or apologize or avert my eyes so that he wouldn't have to. I didn't have to second-guess much longer. He walked away, leaving me alone on the bench.

25

DARK DAYS

Dark days were ahead.

Well, not literally. They were bright, summer days that stretched way too late into the evening and started well before I was ready for sunshine.

I went to work and came back home, leaving my phone buried in a drawer so that I could stay far away from all the people in my life. Pete and I severed our attached-at-the-hip workplace relationship, and Brad or one of the other managers must have noticed the tension because they stopped scheduling us for the same shifts and the same duties. When we did see each other at work, we didn't say much. Pete's jaw was perpetually tensed, like he was trying hard to hold back all the wise, honest, tactless things he wanted to unleash on me. One shift we sat together in the box office, each of us staring resolutely out the window, or down at the books we'd brought with us and kept hidden on our laps.

At home, I helped Mom cook. I sat with Jase on the couch and asked if I could play a game with him. I did all I could to keep my mind off the topics of love or writing or human relationships or the future or escaping to Kenya.

It didn't really work.

As soon as I let my guard down, my mind attacked itself, entering loops of the same stupid thoughts repeated over and over until I had to go to the bathroom and pretend I was taking cold showers to combat the heat. I barely ate, claiming I'd been tasting so much while cooking with my mom that I'd filled up on spoonfuls of marinara sauce and bites of meatballs.

For some reason, Mom didn't call me on this obviously terrible excuse. She smiled and said, "Okay, honey. Thanks for helping." Every now and then she'd ask me if I was okay, if I wanted to talk, but I didn't. I wanted to never talk again, since I obviously couldn't be trusted to understand other people in the slightest. I especially didn't want to talk to anyone about love, since I was in no way qualified to do that. Honestly, Hafsah should have fired me a long time ago.

Every now and then in bed I found myself tearing up suddenly, feeling like the world was too much to handle. Or I'd start to tear up because I was just another stupid teen going through another stupid heartbreak. But knowing that didn't help ease the pain at all. I wasn't even sure anymore who I was feeling heartbroken about, Cal or Leo or Iris or myself or my writing. Most of the time though, I tried to go numb. That's all I really wanted. I listened to songs like "What Happens When the Heart Just Stops" by the Swell Season and "To Wish Impossible Things" by The Cure for the comfort of their mopiness, but couldn't even handle listening to the lyrics, so I tuned them out as best as I could.

There was also that small matter of figuring out how the hell to tell my parents that I was about to lose my scholarship. A few times I came close to confessing to my mom, when she was looking at me super sympathetically like she'd already guessed everything I'd gone through. But then I'd

have to talk about it all. That felt like something Future Lu
was better equipped to handle. I decided to wait on that particular disaster when it naturally arrived in the form of a notice email or repo men showing up to take back that NYU
sweatshirt I'd bought when I'd gotten accepted, or however
it would happen.

I got one text from Cal, which I never responded to.

CAL
I'm sorry I bolted like that. But that really took me
by surprise.
    Things between us aren't like that, Lu. I care about
you, but not romantically. I'm not mad or anything.
Love is weird and hard. I know. And Iris isn't mad
either. Maybe the three of us should meet up and
talk this out?

I had a few texts from Leo too, most of them classic ex-
boyfriend texts like:

LEO
You up?

LEO
Hey, hows it going

LEO
I've been thinking about you.

LEO
Please answer me Lu. I miss you. I'm sorry.

LEO
I'm trying here, but you're not making it easy.

About a week and a half after my disastrous decision to unravel my own life and scatter the pieces like an oversize game
of Jenga, I was at work taking tickets. It was a Wednesday
night, and since I was tearing tickets I had few ways to get
my mind off of the tiny, not-at-all-overwhelming mistakes
that I had made.

Pete was working that day, but thankfully he was at concessions behind me. I was trying to keep myself entertained
playing one of our people-watching games, I Would Bone
That Person. Unfortunately it being a Wednesday night meant
there weren't all that many people coming in, and every time
I tried to play out a fantasy with an attractive person who
came by, my daydream would turn to me fleeing the country well before it progressed to anywhere sexual.

So I made up a new game for myself called I Would Be
a Completely Normal Human Being around That Person
and Not Act like a Total Weirdo. There was one inherent
flaw in the game, which was that I didn't come up with any
rules and wasn't playing with anyone, and so I just thought
the name of the game every time a person came to hand me
their ticket, and that's where the game ended. I put my elbows on my little podium and leaned forward, making it tilt
as I sighed. Maybe I could count how many popcorn kernels
were on the floor. Or how many times the ugly pattern on
the bright red carpet repeated itself within my periphery. Or
how many scholarship dollars I'd lost.

Then a wave of panic would creep in, reminding me that
I was alone and jobless (well, kinda) and when I'd made a

friend who I felt like myself around, I'd proceeded to embarrass myself by projecting my feelings of affection onto him.

"Girl, you look like you're a million miles away."

I looked up. Starla was standing in front of me.

"Hey, Starla." I took her ticket and handed her back the stub. I wanted to follow her into the theater, sit in darkness for two hours while a story took over my mental functions. "No work today?"

"What's going on with you?" She tossed the ticket stub into her open purse and then waved her hand around like she was tracing the outline of my body. "You do not look as sprightly as usual."

The mere fact that she asked me the question threatened to send me into a tailspin of tears. I wanted to leap into her arms and weep into her tattooed bosom while she shushed me and told me everything would be okay.

I blinked back my neuroses and tried my best to fake a smile. "I'll admit I'm not feeling peppy. What are you watching, by the way? I didn't actually look at your ticket. Don't tell my boss."

"You are not just sidestepping that conversation that easily, girl." She moved aside to let a group of high school boys come through. When guys my age come through, I usually do a little scan for attractiveness, or at least try to recognize attraction for me in their eyes. This time I just took their tickets and waved them through, not bothering to count how many tickets they'd handed me. "What's got you upset? Who do I have to beat up? Is it Fart Boy?"

This time tears did fight through to the surface, and I had to take a deep breath to not let them loose. Starla reached out and put her hand on top of mine, her bracelets cold against my skin. She didn't break eye contact, her look kind but unrelenting. I looked over my shoulder toward the concessions and caught Pete watching the exchange, an eyebrow raised until he realized I'd caught him and he pretended to be doing something else.

When I looked back at Starla, I realized how little I knew about her life. We talked about books and bounced one-liners off each other, but I knew nothing about this cool woman I'd been seeing consistently for two years. Other than what she looked like, her place of employment, and her reading tastes, I didn't know her story at all. I knew she wasn't married, but I didn't know what kind of love she had in her life, if at all. I didn't know the shape of her life outside the bookstore at all, and at the realization that I hadn't ever bothered to ask, a couple of tears fought through my weakened defenses and trickled down the bridge of my nose. I wiped them away with the back of my hand, then saw Brad walking in my direction, looking down at his clipboard as he crossed the lobby. Starla noticed me eyeing him and she gave a little nod with her head, motioning me away from my duties.

I called out to Brad and begged off for a fifteen-minute break, which he acquiesced to quickly.

Starla and I sat on a bench by the bathrooms. "I feel bad. It's like Pete and I have just been mooching advanced reader copies from you for years and unloading our teenage drama on you without asking you about you."

Starla gave a little chuckle. "Are you kidding? I love having you guys around and not having to talk about myself. You're more interesting than I am. Plus, I go to therapy once a week, not to mention the therapy sessions forced upon me every six to eight hours when my mom calls to check in on me."

"I don't know, Starla. You have tattoos and have lived like four times as long as we have. You *must* be interesting."

She pointed her index finger at me and mock-scowled. "Check your math, girl. But fine, I'll say stuff about me first, if that's what you want. Ask away. But then I need you to open up the way the Red Sea parted for Moses or the way my legs parted for anyone with a pixie cut when I was nineteen."

"Wow, okay, that's already quite a bit of info." I looked around the theater for a bit, wondering what exactly I wanted to know, wondering if I was just trying to delay talking about myself. I shrugged. "I don't know, I guess I just want to know your story."

As it turned out, Starla was much more interesting than she'd let on. I don't know how she'd ever managed to keep this from me and Pete, but she had been married for five years not long after college. Then her husband got sick and his health deteriorated even quicker than the doctors had expected. By thirty she was a widow. She'd had an office job before that, but after her husband died, Starla's main comfort came in books, so she decided to surround herself with them. Hence, The Strand.

"Wow."

"I see that look on your face," Starla said. "Save your comments about not being able to complain about your life now that you've heard about mine. A terrible thing happening to me doesn't mean your pain isn't valid."

I stammered for an excuse a little, then, like with every other situation in my life, opted for a stupid joke. "No, I was just wondering if your husband had a pixie cut."

Starla laughed, then smacked my leg lightly. "Your turn."

I told her everything. How the summer started with Leo dumping me, then my writer's block, eavesdropping on Iris and Cal, the whole of the past few weeks recounted so easily it was hard to believe that it had all happened to me. Once it was all out, I didn't know whether I felt any relief, or if I was closer to tears than I had been at the start. "I know this probably sounds stupid and juvenile," I said, looking down at my lap. "But…I just don't know how I got here. I don't know if anything I've been through is worth this feeling."

At that point Starla put her hand on my knee and raised her voice. "Hon. Wishing you weren't suffering is a whole other beast than wishing you hadn't experienced anything good. Just because I will never stop grieving my husband doesn't mean I'm going to erase our life together. The bad cannot possibly erase the good."

She looked around, waiting for the people coming out of theater seven to clear out. "That couple? They have the right idea. A weird way of doing it, but they've accepted the bad will come, and that it won't cancel out what they have. My only surprise is that they didn't agree to you writing the column earlier."

"Why's that?"

Starla sighed. "A few years after Larry died, I moved. The memories that I was clinging to at our old apartment had turned more painful than comfortable, so I got out. Along the way I lost a photo album we'd been keeping since we started dating. Mostly of our travels, little paragraph descriptions on the back of each picture. The whole trip summarized into a few lines."

"Oof. I can't imagine."

"You can." Starla gave a tight-lipped smile, then patted my leg. She stood up. "Maybe to a lesser degree, but you understand the feeling, I'm sure. If there's one possession I'd love to have back from all my life, it's that photo album. Just because it's gone doesn't mean the memories are gone. But having a tangible reminder of something that's no longer around means being able to return to bygone comforts. It's proof that what was once gone did exist, however briefly. A reminder that you *were* granted that time, and that can never be lost. If I were that couple, I'd beg you to write the column." She gave me another smile, then checked her wristwatch again. "Perfect. Just in time to catch my movie."

I stood up too, not wanting to go back to actually working. I wanted to sit there and soak in the conversation with Starla. I was afraid if I moved away from the area, I wouldn't absorb some of it, whatever *it* was. The lesson in all she'd said. The wisdom she'd passed on that I was still too hurt and ashamed to fully feel. I wished I'd brought my notebook with me or recorded the conversation. I had the notion that what she'd said deserved its own column too, though I no longer trusted myself with the ability to capture anything of importance.

"Take care of yourself, kiddo. Don't let the heartbreaks silence the love." She reached out and ruffled my hair, then disappeared down the hallway toward the theaters, her bracelets jingling as she walked.

26

JUST HOW LOVE KIND OF WORKS

I spent the rest of my shift deep in my thoughts rather than trying to escape them. When it was over I stood outside the theater and waited for Pete to come out. He had his earphones in and almost walked past me, but then we made eye contact and he stopped in his tracks, pulling out his earphones and wrapping the cord around his phone. "Hey," he said.

For a moment, I tried to read whether he was angry. I'd never known Pete to hang on to a grudge for a long time, but I'd never seen him as frustrated as he had been the other day. I'd missed his presence in my life. Our banter, his advice, the mere fact of his company. The past few days had been the most emotionally draining of my life, and I knew that part of that was because he wasn't around.

"You were right," I said, afraid he might walk away before I got the courage to unburden myself. "You were trying to help, and I'm sorry that I was stubbornly resistant to that. I was..." I chewed on my lip for a second, looked across the street at the sushi restaurant, reached for a word. I couldn't land on one though, and when I looked back Pete was nodding gently.

He pocketed his phone and brushed the hair out of his eyes. "Have there been developments? Your face looks like there've been developments."

"Yeah, but I want to do this first. You mean a lot to me, and I've always trusted your judgment. I don't know why I didn't this time." I shrugged, less of a gesture expressing my quandary and more to show Pete and the universe that I was really at a loss. A moment passed, during which I was afraid Pete would be thoroughly unimpressed by my apology and decide he was done with me. Traffic rolled by, people entered and exited the theater, a bike messenger sped past behind me, blasting music on speakers rigged hidden within his backpack. "Did you know I think of you as my wise, old uncle?"

Pete smirked. "That makes a little more sense than it should."

"I should have listened to you, and I didn't. I went further down the rabbit hole with Iris and Cal, and ended up in a sort of nightmare situation that could have easily been avoided if I'd just paid attention to you. If I'd admitted what was going on. If I'd spent the amount of time I normally spend with you so that your wise, old, avuncular qualities would rub off on me and I would stop being such an idiot."

Pete smiled, then motioned with his head. "I need to get home soon. Walk with me? Or was that it? Because I'm ready to forgive."

Tears rushed to the corners of my eyes again, persistent little fuckers. "I don't know if I deserve to be forgiven yet."

"It's okay. I was hurt and wanted all your attention. I could have done better too. I could have been more supportive."

We started walking down Third Avenue, our gaits slow.

Night had fallen already, and the restaurants and bars we passed were filling up. Our shadows stretched behind us as we walked, then receded when we approached the next street-light, then shifted ahead. "I wasn't the easiest person to be supportive of," I said. "I was obsessed, like you said."

I filled him in on what had happened since our fight, my realization that he was right about my feelings for Cal, how I'd missed my deadline again. That goddamn attempt at a kiss, and the look on Cal's face afterward. Leo.

"I just kind of lost it, you know."

"Oh, I know." He nudged me with his shoulder.

We'd walked past at least two subway stations that Pete could have taken to get home, so now it felt like we were committing to the whole walk to his place on the Lower East Side. "At least you don't have to worry about writer's block anymore, right?" Pete said. "I kept thinking through-out this whole ordeal that you could easily write, if only you weren't so tied down to one idea. It sucks about the job, and the scholarship, and—"

"And the rest of my life falling apart as a result."

"Yeah, that. But at least you don't have to carry this bur-den of writer's block around with you anymore, you know. You can just write when you feel compelled to do so, about whatever topic is in your heart."

"Yeah," I sighed. We passed by a busy strip of bars, where of course there seemed to be a disproportionate number of couples, people flirting, making out, smearing love and dat-ing and sex all over each other. That was a weird way to put it. "Rub it in, assholes!" I yelled.

Pete laughed. "Been holding that in for a bit?"

"Is it that obvious?"

He laughed, and we slowed our gait even more, looking in

at bar after bar of people laughing and pawing at each other. "You never talk to me about your love life," I said. "I don't wanna just unload all my stress on you and make this a one-way friendship. You can lay it on me too, you know. I don't even know what kind of people you're attracted to. I can't believe I've never asked."

Pete shoved his hands in his pockets and shrugged in the same motion, which I filed away as a really poignant gesture which I wanted to use in some future conversation. "I haven't really found anyone that inspires that in me," he said. "Male, female. I don't know if I really have that same drive you and your readers and the rest of the freaking world have."

"Now I get why you suck so much at I Would Bone That Person."

Pete laughed. "Yeah, I figured you might have picked up on it by now."

"I'm sorry, that was shitty to say. Don't let me make you feel bad about that. I'm gonna try to be a better friend. Starting, like...now."

Another laugh, which made feel like I hadn't immediately screwed things up again. "It's okay, I don't always feel like I want to talk about this. It's just not something that's on my mind all the time. I like people, and intimacy. But I don't find myself wanting anything more than what we have, you know? I don't need romantic love, or sex."

"I wanna say you're lucky, but I don't know if that's a stupid thing to say too."

He reached out and gave me a little side hug. "We can go back to our normal dynamic and not talk about me. I kinda like dishing out advice on what to do. Being the wise, old uncle."

"Okay," I said. "But if you ever want to. I'm here, you

know. I may suck at it because I'm self-indulgent and self-centered and terrible. But I'm here."

He gave me a little shoulder bump. "Thanks, Lu."

We walked in silence for a few blocks, or at least the relative silence Manhattan can provide. We weaved through a crowd standing in front of a kebab truck, a group of smokers standing outside a bar, a man walking four dogs on a leash. "So, what are you gonna do next?" Pete asked.

"Beats me. Any ideas?"

"You could try to find another writing gig. I bet Hafsah would still write you a decent recommendation. Maybe you still have time to save your scholarship."

"Yeah, I don't know if she will. She might have a soft spot for me, but she won't abide what I put her through."

"Just send in writing samples to other publications, then. Everything that you've been through doesn't erase the fact that you're still a damn good writer."

"Thanks. I'm gonna miss *Misnomer* though. It's so…hip. I don't know if I'll ever be that hip again."

"True. But you don't need to be hip."

I laughed. "Yeah, I guess if I'm being honest it just felt good to fake it. I'll always write for myself. And I'm okay with that because I have no choice but to be okay with that. But the validation feels good. It makes me feel like it's okay that this is how I process my feelings and the world around me."

"Dude, just start a blog, then. Outside validation doesn't have to come with a paycheck. Hell, I'll be your outside validation. You have Twitter followers. You have the internet, and you have talent. Forget about everything you can't control, and just do this thing that comes naturally to you. Everything else will fall into place. Maybe not the exact place you had in mind at the start of the summer, or even a week ago.

But there's no use in worrying about all that. Just, you know, keep writing."

I smiled at him. "There's the Uncle Pete I know and love."

We said goodbye with a long hug, and then I made my way back home and ate Mom's food, and sat with Jase and gave him shit. Mom even joined us on the couch and jumped in on berating him about not contributing to the household. Before she went to bed, she gave me a long forehead kiss and asked me if I was doing okay. I didn't think I could answer with a flat-out yes, but I nodded my head and told her that I was doing better. "Good," she said. Then she told me and Jase she loved us and to keep it down, then disappeared into her room.

We still didn't talk about love deeply, but we'd established a sort of trail, some stepping stones that might someday lead to conversations about it.

Jase turned down the volume on the TV, and I sat there for a while longer, feeling the simplicity of that joy. What a marvelous thing it is, to feel like you've marooned yourself on an island, surrounded only by worries and regret, most of your own making, then suddenly find that the island is an illusion. That you have people there with you, and that they're constantly offering lifeboats.

It still hurt me to think of how wrong I'd gotten things with Cal. I still felt like I wanted to repeatedly hit the undo button on my decisions with the column, just go back on each missed deadline and have a chance to redeem myself. I still felt heartbroken that Leo had left me, and confused about what he wanted us to be, what I should do with his change of heart. But I no longer felt like I was on an island.

A little while later, I said good-night to Jase, went into my room, and opened up my computer.

Iris and Cal

By Lu Charles
July 20

I would have called bullshit on the whole thing from the beginning if I didn't see both Iris and Cal get the same look in their eyes. Constantly. When Iris hums to herself as they walk hand in hand, when Cal insists on doing the dishes at her parents' house, when she underlines whole paragraphs in novels then simply has to voice her appreciation for what she's just read, and how he'll stop whatever he's doing to listen, even if he clearly has no idea what she's talking about.

One eighteen-year-old gets that look, you start feeling sorry for them. Two of them give that look to each other and no matter what kind of cynic you are, you start thinking only teenagers really understand love. How insane it's supposed to be.

This started out as a plan to profile a series of couples dealing with the question of what happens to a relationship the summer before college starts. When I first pitched it to my editor, it was very timely, since it was the start of summer. Also, I'd just been dumped.

The weeks have gone by though, and my goal of helping out those couples who might have needed some outside perspective is now mostly moot, as I'm sure most of you have also been dumped. If not, good for you. Or maybe bad for you, I don't really know.

Then I met Iris and Cal. Rather, I should say that I eavesdropped on what sounded at the time like their breakup. They were happy, but worried about the challenges of being long-distance, and how that could mar this wonderful thing they had between them. Iris worried that they were too young to survive it, that four years apart was too much. Cal responded with almost the same thing I responded when I'd been dumped by my ex: "We have love. Isn't that enough?"

They went their separate ways. I assumed they'd fallen victim to the precollegiate breakup like so many eighteen-year-olds do. I thought about my ex. I thought, no, it's probably not enough. Not when you're eighteen. Then, through a twist of fate in the form of a dropped wallet, I saw Cal and Iris again.

They were still together.

With a caveat: they were going to break up at the end of summer.

Like any good journalist, I became single-mindedly obsessed over this decision, and convinced myself I had to write about them. Mired in writer's block since my breakup, I convinced myself that they were the only thing I could write about. I had to explore all the nuances of their decision, of their unique relationship, the love that they wanted to hold on to but were okay eventually letting go of. Under the guise of this column, I started spending time with them, eventually forming a friendship based on the mere fact that being in the proximity of their love made me feel better about love itself.

I kept expecting to see dramatic flare-ups caused by their unique arrangement. I kept expecting their self-imposed expiration date to strain the way they were with each other. But somehow they resisted the dramatic. I saw them both struggle with the thought of losing the other, but throughout the past few weeks, I've also seen them dive into their love so deeply that they achieved what we all hope to achieve—everything but the love faded to the periphery.

Iris has impeccable vintage style, and the confidence to pull off her pinup-model aesthetic. She's funny and insightful, and knows exactly what she wants to do when she goes to school—she's already declared as an international business major at Pepperdine, a school she knew she wanted to attend as soon as she saw the campus.

Cal is charming and considerate, less sure of what he wants from life, but certain that he loves New York too much to leave it. He's got a hipster aesthetic and a few cheesy tastes, but is to his core a good soul that wants the best for others. He'll attend Columbia in the fall.

Together, they make storybook love feel possible. They actually go out of their way to remind me that it is. "It's all about keeping the door open to the possibility," Cal says, quoting a short story, a habit they both share, though it's unsure whether they're drawing on the same material or each have come into this admirable quirk separately. They go on dates to Central Park in order to watch meteor showers, even on overcast days, because Cal doesn't want Iris to go through life never having seen one. Their first date would be the envy of even the swooniest contemporary YA novels. They learn how to cook pasta together, even when they know it's a skill they won't get to share together for long.

In my mind, if I managed to capture the magic of their relationship in one of these columns, then I would be better off. I would have learned something valuable about love, understood relationships better, gotten marginally better at this thing we're all walking around obsessing over all the time. Maybe I could help some of you avoid the same fate I'd met by teaching you to hang on to whatever love is in your lives.

What I managed to do was miss my deadline a bunch of times, lose this job, lose my scholarship, neglect my friendships, neglect my family, fall in love with Cal, and not know what to do when my ex succumbed to my silent wishes and changed his mind, begging to see me again.

This is the point in the column where I tell you how I learned to let go of my broken heart and move on from my ex, how Cal and

Iris taught me that love that ends is, even with that bitter end, still love. Or I tell you Cal and Iris's secret for maneuvering the mine-field of the summer before college. I tell you how they succeeded where I—and maybe many of you—failed.

Except love isn't that tidy. You've all seen that, if not firsthand then at least in this column. Spending time with a couple doesn't mean I know how they've cracked the secret to love. Hell, the fact that they're happy and facing a difficult decision with levelheaded maturity doesn't mean they've cracked the secret to love at all. It doesn't mean they've learned how to avoid heartbreak.

Did I learn a lesson through all this? Kind of. It didn't come from Iris and Cal, but from a bookseller named Starla that I've become friends with. Love that ends was still love.

Have I absorbed that lesson deep in my heart so that it can fight off all the hurt swirling around inside? No, not really. I think that's just how love kind of works.

I finished the column, finally. It wouldn't run, but I guess I needed someone to read it, and that someone may as well have been Hafsah. It wouldn't fix anything, but at least I'd know that I had turned something in, in the end. I shut my computer and creaked open my window, then slipped into bed. Somewhere nearby, I could hear neighbors arguing, their voices carrying through enough that if I truly listened, I could have made out what they were talking about. Instead, I closed my eyes, and let the conversation fade into white noise.

27

YEAH WHATEVER

The weekend passed by uneventfully, a definite weight off my chest now that I'd managed to write again. Not that my chest was particularly weightless.

I went to work, happy that I could do so next to Pete again. Afterward, we jumped around from bookstore to bookstore. We hung out with Starla for a bit. Then I went back home and had dinner with Mom and Jase. It was supposed to be another New Jersey weekend for us, but Dad had to take a last-minute trip to a conference in Denver, which was fine by me because I don't know if I was ready to face New Jersey again, or his questions about my scholarship.

I resisted texting Cal or Iris, the shame creeping down my spine every time I even looked at their names in my phone. It was weird to miss not just Cal, but Iris too. And on top of that, I couldn't ignore the fact that Leo was still in love with me. I couldn't help but imagine being by his side again, doing it better this time. Going on Cal and Iris–esque dates in Central Park, keeping the door creaked open for life like the movies to sneak in.

On Monday morning, as I was walking to the theater for

a shift, I got an email from Hafsah. I didn't want to get my hopes up, but hopes are rebellious little buggers that do what they want. I clicked on the email immediately.

Hey Lu,

I'd guessed there was a reason for the missed deadlines. Wish you would have channeled some of those frustrations and heartache into writing, but I understand that's not always how it works. I talked to the team and we decided we will run this column next week. I've attached my notes.

Unfortunately, it will be your last column, as I've already filled the position. If you have any pitches for one-offs in the future, please do reach out.

Take care,

H

That felt like something. I didn't know what, exactly. But it was something.

Later that night, I found myself with Pete traversing the particular circle of hell that is Times Square. "I can't believe Leo is holding his going-away party at Dave and Buster's," Pete said, avoiding contact with one of those dudes that dressed up like the methed-up nightmare version of your favorite superhero.

"I think he's doing it tongue in cheek."

"But you're not sure."

I sighed, avoiding accidentally photobombing about six different selfies happening at the same time. "No, I'm not sure."

We pushed open the doors and entered the adolescent casino. Baseball and soccer games were on every one of the approximately three hundred television screens around the bar/restaurant/arcade. Dudes were running around holding their twenty-ounce beers and jumping from machine to machine like they never wanted to grow up. I couldn't blame them much. I scanned the crowd, looking for a place Leo and his group of dweebish friends might be hanging out, and spotted them at a long table littered with half-drunk sodas, half-eaten nachos, and fully eaten chicken wings. Leo himself was not far off from the table, at one of those basketball games where you have to shoot a tiny ball into a tiny hoop to get a tiny amount of tickets.

"We could leave," Pete said, looking around the room, clearly uncomfortable at the abundance of noise and absence of books.

"As much as I want to, I should probably have this interaction. Closure, and all that."

"Alright. Want me to come with? Or should I go pretend I know how to play Skee-Ball, kind of keep my eye on you and watch for some sort of signal that it's all going terribly so I can come intercede?"

"Yeah, the second one." I watched Leo shoot small hoops for a while. He was wearing the outfit I thought he looked best in, his black jeans, a light green T-shirt, and his gray hoodie, which he brought everywhere with him even in summer because he hated intense air-conditioning. I remembered wearing the hoodie a few times, its oversize sleeves feeling like Leo himself was wrapped around me. I remembered the first night we'd ever kissed, how he was wearing a similar outfit, but with a couple of added layers because of the weather. His skin had been warm, his cheeks flushed from the fleece and body contact. The night we'd broken up he was also wearing those pants, only with a tank top instead of a T-shirt. And he'd pulled away as soon as I'd tried to touch him, so there wasn't a clear memory of how his skin had felt.

Pete clapped a hand on my shoulder. "I don't mean to be an unsupportive friend right now, but can I borrow five dollars for tokens?"

I sighed and gave him the money, then crossed the mayhem of the arcade to approach the stupid, beautiful jerk of an ex-boyfriend who'd landed me in this predicament in the first place. He was next to his friend Miguel, who saw me approaching and thankfully peaced out.

"Lu," Leo said, combing his hair back behind his ear. I wondered if he knew what my name in his mouth did to me. "You came."

I crossed my arms in front of my chest, now wondering if this was a good idea. I tried to look anywhere but into his beautiful brown eyes. There's much to be said about the attraction of new people, but so much more to be said about someone whose eyes hold history for you. "Yeah, I thought it'd be best to say goodbye in person."

Leo rubbed the back of his neck. "Oh. Yeah. Right. I'm glad you're here." Then he broke into a wide smile, his eyes shimmering with what could well have been tears. "Can we go somewhere a little more quiet?"

I looked around. "We're at a Dave and Buster's, I don't know if that exists here."

He chuckled, then walked over to a Jurassic Park shooting game where you could sit down in your own little private booth thingy that was maybe meant to represent a car. He pulled the curtain aside and peeked in. "This is open."

I bit my lip, thinking of sitting in an enclosed, private place with Leo again. I turned over my shoulder and saw Pete playing Skee-Ball, but then spilling a handful of tokens out of his shirt pocket as he tossed a ball. He leaned over to pick them all up, not looking in my direction. "Sure," I said to Leo, stepping inside the booth.

"So, you're leaving."

"Next week. This was just the only day that worked for everyone." He put his hands on his knees, fidgeting. I'd never known him to be a fidgeter. I was the restless one between us, the one who didn't know where hands were supposed to go, didn't know if at any point I looked like a weirdo who thought too much about where to put her hands. A couple of kids ran past the game, causing the curtains to flutter a little. Outside the booth, there was incessant dinging and shouting and simulated explosions. But inside the noise seemed to fall away. "I'm sorry about all the messages. It's just that—"

"It's okay," I said, cutting him off. "I'm sorry I didn't respond. It's been a crazy few weeks."

"Anything to do with those new friends?"

"Partially," I said. Then I took a breath, readying for what I'd come here to say. Pete had helped me figure out exactly what I needed to get off my chest, and I thought the words were on the tip of my tongue, but I suddenly didn't know anymore if I should even bother. He was leaving, my life would continue without him. I looked at the screen, which was in demo mode, outdated but still pretty decent graphics of velociraptors getting shot. I should leave, I thought, let Leo have his fun day with his friends.

Then Leo scooted closer to me, reaching for my hand. I was surprised, but managed to look him in the eyes instead of running out terrified. "Let's try again," he said. "I'll do better. I don't want to lose you." Then he moved his hand to my cheek, and leaned in to kiss me.

God, it was so hard not to accept the kiss. His voice sounded so sincere and tender, and I had no doubts that the regret I could hear was authentic. I'd have his company, even if it was only a couple of times a semester, or in text form. Someone who'd ask after my day, make me feel attractive, funny, loved. I'd have love back in my life. My words were back. Now all I needed was this.

But somehow, I managed to shut up that part of my brain. I pulled back and put my hand on Leo's chest. And as great as his chest felt, the thrill of touching someone, the memories of slipping my hand beneath his shirt and feeling his skin for the first time, all the times I'd laid my head on his chest while we watched TV, I pulled my hand away.

"I came here to say bye, Leo. That's it." I saw his lip quiver for a moment, and then he turned his head away. "You hurt me when you broke up with me. I wanted us to have a chance. I thought we did. But the truth is that it was probably the best decision. We had what we had. It's over now. We're obviously both struggling with that, but that doesn't mean we should try to erase our hurt. We just have to move past it."

Leo turned his head even farther away, and that annoying part of my brain was momentarily moved and flattered that he could be crying. "Yeah, whatever," he said, his voice almost breaking.

On the screen, the demo started again, all the same dinosaurs getting shot in the same spots. A stegosaurus swung its tail, and the computer simulation failed to shoot at it, so Leo's side of the screen flashed red and he lost a life.

"Yeah," I agreed. "Whatever." I reached over and gave his hand a last squeeze. Despite his tears and terse dismissal, his fingers quickly weaved themselves into mine. He wasn't just regretting the breakup out of loneliness, I knew. He loved me. Still, this felt good. Our love had run its course. We weren't

Iris and Cal, weren't a storybook love. What we had was real, but it was also over.

"Take care, Leo," I said. Then I slipped my hand loose, and left the booth.

28

AIRED LAUNDRY

It was mid-August. The heat had only gotten worse as the summer stretched on, but on this particular day another morning rainstorm had cooled the air down, so I decided to go to Madison Square Park and do some people watching and maybe a little bit of eavesdropping. I had to go to work at the theater in an hour, so I wanted to enjoy the nice day as much as I could.

I got myself an iced coffee from a street cart and found a spot on a bench with a good view of foot traffic. I kept my notebook within reach, but still tucked away in my bag. It was one of those days where I felt okay with losing my *Misnomer* gig. Some days weren't as easy going, especially as I was still getting emails from NYU trying to prepare me for the fall semester, which I wouldn't be attending.

My parents had not been thrilled to hear that I'd lost my scholarship, but after a few days of tension, anger, and apparently brainstorming, my mom had come up with the simple solution to defer for a semester or two until I found another job that would allow me to keep the scholarship. If that didn't happen, I'd look for other grants or take out a loan. "You are young, with your whole life ahead of you," my mom had said. "Starting college six months or a year after other people will not change anything. And it'll keep you at home longer, which I'm perfectly happy with." My dad was a little slower to come around, but he still deferred to my mom's judgment on almost everything, and if he was still pissed, he hadn't shown it on my last visit to New Jersey.

I looked around the park, trying to scope out any potentially interesting interactions. Most people were on their own or talking quietly to each other though, and I was kind of happy just watching instead of actively listening. There was a cute boy on the bench across from me too, and he was laughing every now and then at whatever he was listening to through his earphones. He had a great smile, and really clean shoes, which I know is a weird thing to look at but I somehow always notice it first. I wasn't about to go talk to him or do anything outrageous like that, but I was okay sticking around and just watching him laugh and eat his way through a bag of chips until he got up and left or I had to go to work.

My phone buzzed in my pocket, and I pulled it out to see that Pete was trying to video chat me. I answered, holding the phone up to my face but switching the camera function so that it was showing Pete the cute boy instead of me.

"Lu?"

"I'm here. Just showing you this cute guy sitting across from me at the park. Look at how much he's laughing. He's so pure."

"Are you at Madison Square Park scoping out cute boys on benches again? I thought you were morally opposed to reboots. This feels like one."

"I'm not scoping anything out, I was just sitting here having a coffee." I switched the camera again so Pete could see me.

He was on his dorm bed, his pillow propped up against the wall. I could see the corner of a *1984* poster above his head. "How's your institution of higher learning treating you? Is your roommate still sleeping twenty-six hours a day?"

"He got up and had a meal the other day, so he's officially not hibernating," Pete said. Then he filled me in on how his orientation and first week of classes had gone. He complained about the paltry number of bookstores in his college town in Rhode Island, and then we bickered for ten minutes because I said him leaving meant I could now legitimately call dibs on Alice.

Right as I was about to hang up, I looked over the edge of my phone to get another glance at the cute boy on the bench, when I saw something else entirely. "Oh my God," I said.

"What? Is someone doing something surprising even by New York standards? I miss the unexpected sights of the city. Nothing here is surprising. Lu? What's happening? Your jaw is doing that clichéd dropping thing that we agreed never happens in real life."

I glanced down at the screen to give Pete a look, then returned my gaze to the couple entering the park. I hadn't been sure at first, but now they were close enough that I had no doubts. It was Iris and Cal, holding hands.

"Pete, I think I'm gonna have to call you back."

Right as I said that, Iris looked up and made eye contact with me. She paused and tugged at Cal's arm, and then they started walking toward me. That was a good enough sign. They weren't fleeing from me or storming at me with rage in their eyes.

"Yup, definitely hanging up now. I'll tell you more later," I said, and put my phone away, wondering if I could also fit my entire body into my purse. Cute boy laughed again, and

I silently begged him to rescue me from the interaction I was about to have. My prayers worked well enough that he looked up at me and smiled, but not enough to get him off the bench.

"Hey," Iris said.

Cal squinted through his glasses, avoiding eye contact. I couldn't help but stare at their clasped hands. If they noticed they didn't say anything. "Hey," I said finally. "You're still here."

"Yeah, I changed my flight," Iris said. "We haven't heard from you in a while." I looked at Cal, wondering if he had somehow kept it a secret what I'd done, forgetting for a moment that he'd texted after my stupid kiss attempt and said there were no hard feelings.

"Sorry," I said lamely. "I just..." I let the statement peter out. I looked down at my lap, but their shadows were cast in my direction, so it was hard to pretend that they weren't there anymore.

"It's okay. It'd be awkward, I get it. I almost didn't come over here, but I wanted to say that I read your article," Iris said. I could feel myself blushing right away. My heart was thumping in my chest, my hands sweaty right away. "It was really good. It felt weird to read about ourselves like that. I felt a little naked, equal parts proud and embarrassed."

I finally looked away from my lap, and through the space between the two of them I could see the cute boy laughing again, shaking his head a little. I kept my eyes on him. "Thanks," I said. "I'm sorry if I stuck my nose in your business too much." Like, all the way in Cal's face. "I got carried away."

"You don't have to apologize, Lu," Cal said, speaking up for the first time. I didn't have the guts to look up at his eyes. Over the past couple weeks, I'd thought of what would happen if I ran into them again. What I would say to them. Shame still crawled down my spine anytime I thought about them, but I still couldn't help but fantasize about a redemption. I'd even fantasized about thanking them. If they hadn't come along I might still be moping around about Leo, mired in writer's block and swearing off love entirely.

"I probably should," I said. "I was inappropriate. And clingy. Then I aired out all your laundry for the world to see."

"At least it wasn't the dirty laundry," Iris said with a laugh. "You were pretty complimentary. Made us look more interesting than we really are."

I examined my fingernails, looked back at cute guy. He was looking at his phone, no longer laughing, his brow furrowed in concentration. "Anyway," I said. "I'm sorry."

We didn't say anything for a few moments. It was hard to tell how much time had gone by. It could have been ten seconds or ten minutes. I was suddenly sweaty, like I had been all damn summer. So much for a refreshing day. I noticed Cal rub his thumb against Iris's hand, tried not to dive into memories of his touch. "So, when's the new breakup date?"

Again, the thumb rub against the soft flesh Iris's hand. I'd been avoiding thinking of Cal romantically at all, but it was hard not to want that. I forced myself to look up, see their faces when they answered. The sun was shining behind them turning them into more silhouettes than human faces. Seemed fitting, and I was glad to not see Cal's eyes.

"We've postponed it," Cal said. It sounded like he was trying to restrain a smile. Behind him a cotton-candy cloud moved in the way of the sun, and then I could see his eyes clearly again. "Indefinitely."

"Really?"

"After reading your article, how could I let go of what we

have?" Iris said. She was definitely smiling. "If it goes sour, if we can't survive the minefield of long distance, so be it. But we're gonna try. We have you to thank for that."

Behind us, a woman shouted out something that could have been my name but was probably one of a million words that end with the same "oo" sound. I looked back, trying to hide the fact that tears were coming to my eyes again. I took a breath, gaining control of myself. When I faced them again, I noticed cute boy looking in our direction. I tried smiling at him, but his eyes flitted away, guilty at being caught.

"I don't know why that makes me feel good," I said. "But it does. I'm happy for you guys. You really are..." I bit my lip. "I want to find a better word than *special*."

"Cheesy? Hopeless? Treacle? Naive?" Cal said.

"Hey!" Iris said, letting go of his hand to smack him across the arm. "We'll take *special*."

We shared a laugh, and I felt something within me relax. "I should be the ones thanking you anyway. You broke me out of my writer's block funk." I noticed my iced coffee sitting beside me, forgotten, sweating beads of condensation onto the bench. I picked it up and took a sip. "This is going to sound cheesy and treacle and naive, but seeing what you guys have let me hold on to romantic ideals. Maybe a little too much. But I think it's better than the alternative. I want to believe that love can be special at this age. And you guys showed me that it can be. So, thanks."

Both of them were smiling now, and I could sense my cheeks blazing up to a fiery red. Iris fluffed her hair out, and Cal pushed his glasses up the bridge of his nose. "Well, we were gonna go meet up with friends for coffee," Iris said. "You want to come with?"

I considered it for a moment, before the smart part of my

brain nudged the rest of me and suggested that maybe it wasn't a great idea to dive back into obsessing over them. "I have to go to work," I said, nodding with my head in a direction, even though I wasn't entirely sure that it was the right direction for the theater.

"Cool," Iris said. "It was nice seeing you again."

"Definitely."

"Don't be a stranger," Cal said. "We can still be friends."

I chewed on my straw a moment. The cloud that had moved over the sun blew away, and the two of them turned into silhouettes again. "Yeah," I said. "Maybe someday."

They nodded, and then we gave each other awkward hugs that still felt emotionally fulfilling, even if the physical aspect was a little more complicated than that. I didn't stand up all the way, and tried to keep my body away from Cal's, even though it felt good to be in his touch. I counted to three on both hugs, wondering if I was squeezing too hard or not enough. When the hugs were over it felt like they'd been entirely too long, and not nearly long enough. Then they took their leave, and I watched them cross the park, hands clasped back together.

My phone buzzed in my pocket, Pete asking what the hell was going on. I waited to respond until I couldn't see Iris and Cal anymore, and even then I kept looking in the direction they'd walked off, trying to catch sight of them. Before I could respond to Pete, I felt a shadow pass over me. I looked up, and Cute Bench Boy was standing over me.

"This is gonna sound weird," he said. "I couldn't help but overhear your conversation. Do you mind if I join you?"

★ ★ ★ ★ ★

ACKNOWLEDGMENTS

Since I've started writing, this book has been the one that has taken the longest to fully form. It couldn't reach this final stage without the help of a ton of people. First of all, my agent, Pete Knapp, for guiding me to the heart of the story. To TS and the team at Inkyard Press, for giving Lu a home, and for continuing to give my writing a home. I'm lucky I get to keep doing this, and that's thanks to the hard work of the editorial team, the publicity team, marketing, sales, design and many more. Thanks to all those who help make my books a reality.

Thanks to the hundred people who filled out my survey on what teenage love feels like. Your answers helped remind me, as well as tap into experiences I did not have.

Thanks to Laura for constant inspiration and for helping me leave behind a lot of the crappy things about love and break-ups that I wrote about here.

To Drea Walter, Leah Kreitz and Marianne Reyes for help with representation matters.

To my family for their love and support and absurd group chat messages.

And of course, to you. I get to do what I love to do because you have this book in your hands, and I'm very grateful for that.

CHARLES W. CHESNUTT

AMERICA'S FIRST GREAT
BLACK NOVELIST

BY

J. Noel Heermance

ARCHON BOOKS
1974

© 1974 by The Shoe String Press, Inc.
First published 1974 as an Archon Book,
an imprint of The Shoe String Press, Inc.,
Hamden, Connecticut 06514

Printed in the United States of America

Library of Congress Cataloging in Publication Data

Heermance, J.   Noel.
    Charles W. Chesnutt; America's first great Black novelist.

    Bibliography: p.
    1. Chesnutt, Charles Waddell, 1858-1932.
PS1292.C6Z7   813'.4[B]   73-14595
ISBN 0-208-01380-6

TO MY FATHER:
  THE REAL AUTHOR
  IN THE FAMILY

Contents

Preface

Although research is, implacably, a matter of solitude and self-immersion in one's special sea, before the scholar becomes totally submerged, and as he occasionally surfaces, it is often the people on shore and in the water around him who make his venture both profitable and fun. For this reason the author wishes to acknowledge the following beacons and personal life rafts:

Mrs. Ruth Hodges and other members of the Fisk University library staff, for their vital early assistance;

Mr. Bennett Webb for making that Nashville summer fun;

Dr. Arthur P. Davis, for the expansive sense of freedom and understanding he showed throughout the manuscript's original development;

Dr. Greg Rigsby, for some much needed summer "slack";

My father, for some equally needed winter comments;

Mss. Jennie Stewart, Jackie Horton, Ernestine Patterson and Bettie Kennedy, for their concern and diligence in the manuscript's later stages.

Finally, with a deeply personal sense of wonder and awe, the author is indebted to the cosmic sea of art itself, which has made Chesnutt come alive for him each and every time he has ventured out into the waves.

J.N.H.

Introduction

Each writer is forged in his own environment—the world he grows up in, the world he later writes to. Initially, he is influenced by his parents, and his early attitudes are generally formed in the family atmosphere. As he leaves the home, he stumbles upon—and over—and into—all the social/political/economic/cultural ramifications of life we call "society." Some of these reinforce the family's early training; some expand it; some contradict it. All, however, influence the writer, and in their diversity his strength and complexity are born.

Such was true of Charles W. Chesnutt, America's first great Black novelist; and for this reason it is crucial for the modern scholar to view Chesnutt's artistic greatness within the context of his total environment. Art does live for and in itself, of course, but the artist behind it is, finally, only a man. Greater knowledge of this man, therefore, leads to a greater—and more sensitive—understanding of his work. In Chesnutt's case, it ultimately leads to a greater appreciation of both the work and the man. Hence the genesis of this book.

At the same time, there is a second reason for delving so deeply into Chesnutt's surrounding milieu. Cultures, as well as writers, are forged in their early "environments"; and modern America has been strongly molded by the same environment Chesnutt found himself fighting in 1901. His world of prejudice, Big Business, and social indifference seem all too similar to the world we find around us today. Indeed, the problems he faced and the solutions he offered then are almost identical to the problems and hopes we see today. Only the names have been changed to . . . . In short, his world is our world, because his roots are our roots. And those roots, also, are what this book is about.

There are, as we are beginning to see today, really *two* American Dreams. The first is the original religious-democratic Dream of early New England. Put forth in the Mayflower Compact, Declaration of Independence, and Bill of Rights, this Dream asserted the sanctity of the individual, the cosmic brotherhood of all men. It has been kept alive most strongly over the last two centuries through the struggles of the Abolitionist and civil rights movements.

The second, "bastard" Dream is that of material wealth and power. Inspired by this country's great national resources, it was soon sanctified by Cotton Mather and personified by Ben Franklin. Throughout the centuries, it has tended to obscure the original Dream, and has led to a whole series of shabby moments in which this country has sold out its original moral values for simple, greedy profits.

These "sell outs" are generally too voluminous to mention, but some stand out as especially symbolic. There was, for example, Article I of the *Constitution,* which defined slaves as "three fifths" of a "person" because it was politically expedient to do so. There was the corresponding prostitution of moral values after the Civil War, when Reconstruction was consciously allowed to die because Big Business stood to enrich itself from a rapid settlement of social issues in the South. And there was—and is—our own voracious military/industrial complex today, devouring so many of our major resources while basic humanistic needs in this country go untouched.

Chesnutt, of course, was directly fighting that Reconstruction "sell out," and he dedicated much of his writing to that fight. Thus the study of Chesnutt is both an appreciation of a unique artist and an investigation of a whole culture. It simultaneously takes us into the past and leads us into our present selves. For

Chesnutt and his world mirror very closely the frailties and strengths of our own turbulent times.

Charles W. Chesnutt

What Chesnutt Was Pitted Against

The Physical Scene

Contrary to popular belief, "Reconstruction" of the South after the Civil War did not re-construct very much. It was generally not harsh—and certainly not effective. In fact, its so-called "harshness" began largely in the minds of Southern politicians and was successfully spread by the pens of Southern writers. The truth, unfortunately, was quite different from the myths these men created.

In April of 1862, the surrender of New Orleans introduced to Lincoln's mind the need for a Reconstruction policy. The resulting policy in 1862 and 1863 was very lenient in restoring citizenship and political activity to the secessionists, and it laid little stress on rights of any sort for Blacks. In fact, Lincoln's original Proclamation of Amnesty and Reconstruction of December 8, 1863, excluded all Blacks from "oath-taking, voting, and holding office." And only once, in a March 13, 1864, letter to the newly elected Louisiana Governor Hahn, did Lincoln even "barely suggest for your private consideration" that "some" Blacks be allowed to vote: "for instance, the very intelligent, and especially those who have fought gallantly in our ranks." It is not surprising, therefore, that one of Louisiana's first state resolutions, after its temporary readmission under Lincoln, stipulated that "the legislature should never enact a law permitting Negroes to vote"[1] despite the fact that Louisiana had a very advanced and intelligent Black population.[2]

Congressional reaction to this leniency and to Lincoln's alleged overuse of Presidential authority resulted in the stronger Wade-Davis Bill of July, 1864. This bill generally sought to exclude more ex-Confederates from the Southern political scene. Indeed, it demanded sweeping oaths of past as well as future loyalty from a majority of the electorate as a condition of restoration to the Union. Lincoln's reaction to this was a pocket veto, plus a Proclamation in which he stated his interest in the Southern states returning to "their proper practical relation in the Union."[3]

At Lincoln's death, no reconstruction had been officially accomplished. In 1864 and 1865 Congress had refused to seat congressional delegations from Louisiana (1864), Arkansas (1864), and Tennessee (1865): the various "Lincoln states" which had sought readmission to the Union under Lincoln's mild policy. Now Andrew Johnson sought to develop his own plan for "restoration"—a term, significantly enough, which he preferred to "reconstruction."[4]

As a man from the border state of Tennessee, Johnson was basically of Southern thought regarding states' rights. Yet, as a "poor white," he personally hated the planter class whose reckless policies he believed to be responsible for secession and war, a war whose burdens quickly fell on "poor white" shoulders. Thus Johnson's general policy of readmission was also lenient, with the single exception that one specific group was not allowed the general pardon. This group consisted of all Southerners whose estimated property value exceeded $20,000. Johnson made these wealthy Southerners apply to him personally for pardon. With his social class hostility purged by this direct deference, however, he was extremely generous in granting pardons, and reconstruction was smoothly and softly on its way.

One further aspect of this leniency was the early withdrawal of Federal troops from the Southern military provinces. As John Hope Franklin notes,

The complaints of many white Southerners that the army of occupation was large and that the many Negro troops in the South were there for the purpose of insulting and humiliating the former Confederates were withought justification. . . . Even casual examination of the report of the Secretary of War for 1865 and 1866 clearly establishes the fact that postwar demobilization was rapid and that only a skeleton military force was in the South by the end of 1866.[5]

Regarding the political rights of Blacks, Johnson, like Lincoln, suggested to Southern leaders that some Blacks be given the vote. But he, unlike Lincoln, was not really concerned about any of the Blacks mentioned or about any of those rights. Rather, as he suggested to Governor Sharkey of Mississippi, he favored "a token enfranchisement of Negroes for tactical purposes," so that the Radicals "who are wild upon Negro franchise will be completely foiled in their attempt to keep the Southern states from reviewing their relations to the Union."[6]

It was at this point that Northern congressmen began to advocate the need for guaranteeing Black suffrage as the only effective means by which Blacks could protect themselves. Thus there soon developed the belief that suffrage for Blacks should be a prerequisite for the readmission of former Confederate states.

Equally disturbing to these congressmen was the implicit defiance entailed by the rapid return of former Confederate soldiers and politicians to power in their home states. Officially elected to the 39th Congress in December, 1865, were the former Vice President of the Confederacy, four Confederate generals, five Confederate colonels, six Confederate cabinet officers, and 58 Confederate congressmen. Of further alarm was the atmosphere in which they had been elected. In Louisiana, for example, all the candidates for offices, including doorkeepers and clerks, printed on their tickets "Late of the Confederate" in seeking votes—and every man in that group was subsequently elected. Symbolically and perhaps most distressingly, in both houses of the new Louisiana legislature former Confederate officers openly wore their uniforms.

The most ominous form of "legal" defiance was the blatant discrimination against—and reenslavement of—the freedmen, as legislated through the "Black Codes." Within a year of Appomattox they were in effect, and they soon spread across the South. Though they recognized the rights of Blacks to hold property, to sue and be sued, and to have legal marriages and offspring, they limited the ability of Blacks to testify in court only to cases where one or both parties were Blacks, and they made intermarriage between the races a heavily punished felony.

Yet far more significant than those judicial and social discriminations were the sections in the "codes" designed to control the freedmen's economic possibilities and thereby provide once more the humble, dependent, cheap labor upon which the South had come to rely. With Mississippi leading the way, these codes provided strict controls on contracts between Black laborers and white planters—sharecropping contracts which most often took advantage of the illiterate former slaves with no capital.[7]

Mississippi, for example, enacted laws similar to the antebellum fugitive slave laws. These new laws authorized any person to capture and return any Black man who left his employer before the expiration of his contracted term of labor. The reward for this was $5.00. Furthermore, most states had strong provisions against enticing or persuading Black workers to seek new positions before the expiration of their present binding contracts.

Most important in these codes was the development of the Southern vagrancy laws that were soon to provide plentiful, cheap labor for decades to come.[8] The vagrancy section of the Mississippi Black Code for 1865, for example, stated that

> All freedmen, free negroes and mulattoes in this State, over the age of eighteen years . . . with no lawful employment or business, or found unlawfully assembling themselves together . . . and all white persons so assem-

bling themselves with freedmen, free negroes, or mulattoes
. . . shall be deemed vagrants, and on conviction thereof
shall be fined in a sum not exceeding in the case of a freedman, free negro, or mulatto, fifty dollars, and a white man
two hundred dollars, and imprisoned at the discretion of the
court, the free negro not exceeding ten days, and the white
man not exceeding six months . . . and in case any freedman, free negro or mulatto shall fail for five days after the
imposition of any fine or forfeiture upon him or her for violation of any of the provisions of this act to pay the same,
that it shall be, and is hereby made the duty of the sheriff
of the proper county to hire out said freedman, free negro or
mulatto, to any person who will, for the shortest period of
service, pay said fine and forfeiture and all costs.[9]

Similar laws soon sprang up in the other ex-Confederate
states.

Coupled with this defiant determination to reestablish a form
of legislative slavery in the postwar South was a parallel attempt
to return freedmen to their former slave status through organized
and semi-organized bands of terrorists. Violence had always been
a basic Southern approach to Blacks and to much of life itself.
Now there was even greater license offered the nightrider. For
the first time, Blacks were "independent" and no longer the un-
touchable property of some powerful planter. Nor did they have
anyone else of importance to offer them protection. They were
alone and powerless in a society that was itching to compensate
for Appomattox, a violence-oriented society that saw Blacks as
the source of all its problems, the psychological and physical
release for all its frustrations. In a few years it would be the highly organized Ku Klux Klan; now it was merely sporadic
groups like the Regulators and the Jayhawkers.

In short, it was as if the war had never happened; as if, from
the Northern point of view, that war had been fought and won to
kill a cancer, and that cancer was now as virulent as ever. Clearly
the south could not—or would not—exorcise itself. It was at this

point, therefore, that the Northern, Republican Congress decided to step in and provide its own format for reconstruction.

At this moment of Congressional intervention, young Charles Chestnutt was an impressionable nine-year-old. It is interesting to note his retrospective evaluation of "Andrew Johnson's policy of reorganizing the Southern States" as one that "threatened to prove so disastrous to the free people that it was replaced by the reconstruction as we know it."[10]

Early defiance, therefore, was what brought on Reconstruction as we think of it today. It consisted merely of the Fourteenth and Fifteenth Amendments and of the earlier established Freedmen's Bureau. Significantly enough, these provisions were neither "radical" nor particularly harsh. Indeed, the very gradual nature of their enactment and the fact that they later needed the Second Civil Rights Act of 1875 to enforce them show how gently they were carried out.

Thus, despite all the rhetoric that has persisted over the "radical reconstruction" enforced by a Northern "occupation army,". Reconstruction did not attempt to reconstruct anything more than the social and political patterns entailed in citizenship, education and suffrage. In fact, as W.E.B. DuBois noted concerning the Freedmen's Bureau, in the final analysis

> it failed to begin the establishment of good-will between ex-masters and freedmen, to guard its work wholly from paternalistic methods which discouraged self-reliance, and to carry out to any considerable extent its implied promises to furnish the freedmen with land."[11]

This last point was crucial, because redistribution of land—as proposed by such congressmen as Thaddeus Stevens and his famous "forty acres to each adult freedman"[12]—would have begun profound reconstruction. It would have created a class of Black, and white, small landowners. This program, however, appeared too revolutionary to most Republican leaders. Hence the vast majority of ex-slaves remained landless, and the opportunity for significant, lasting reconstruction was lost. Nor was this a minor loss. As DuBois noted in 1903,

> those men of marvellous hindsight who are today seeking to preach the Negro back to the present peonage of the soil know well, or ought to know, that the opportunity of binding the Negro peasant willingly to the soil was lost on that day when the Commissioner of the Freedmen's Bureau had to go to South Carolina and tell the weeping freedmen, after their years of toil, that their land was not theirs, that there was a mistake—somewhere.[13]

In its full assessment, therefore, "Radical Reconstruction" was not at all radical. Nor were even the more conservative of its "reconstructive" provisions rigorously enforced. Nevertheless, the South fought it with an open resistance and white-heat dedication to violence that thereby set the tone and atmosphere for the world that Chesnutt was to grow up in and finally write against. It is no coincidence that his final and most outspoken novels, *The Marrow of Tradition* and *The Colonel's Dream*, attained their power and their depth of tragedy by confronting stark violence as the major medium of expression for the Southern people as a whole.

Though inadequately enforced, the restrictions of Radical Reconstruction nevertheless drove the Southern states closer together. Emboldened by President Johnson's sympathetic attitude, they continued to reject the Fourteenth Amendment as late as 1867. Through blatant defiance and violence they rejected Reconstruction completely.

Georgia, for example, was most direct in its design. As soon as federal authority was withdrawn from that state in 1868, the Conservative Democrats attacked the three Black senators and twenty-nine Black representatives in the state legislature. After failing to expel the Black senators as a group, the Conservatives immediately launched new attacks on them as individuals. They soon expelled all three. Nor were the Black representatives safe. In August, 1868, resolutions to expel them were passed by a vote of 83 to 23, with the Black members abstaining. The next month, the Georgia legislature formally declared all Black members ineligible to sit in that body. When Georgia topped even this performance with her outright rejection of the Fifteenth Amendment in 1869, Congress finally stepped back in. It understandably put Georgia under military rule once more, and made ratification of the Fifteenth Amendment a condition for her readmission.

As the century continued and Reconstruction completely died out, the South's defiance became more open. In the extensive United States Senate debate on the Lodge "force" bill in 1890, Senator Pugh of Alabama "warned that in regions where there were large numbers of Negro voters, no power—no public opinion, state, federal or military force—could stop whites from preventing Negroes from voting." Senator Vest of Missouri, waxing strongly Darwinian in his rhetoric, asserted that the White race was the dominant race in the world and that the "tiger blood" in its veins could not be "tamed or chained."[14]

The various disfranchisements of Blacks in the 1890s essentially marked the culmination of this period's "legal" defiance. In 1890, Mississippi dramatically revised its constitution for the express purpose of disfranchising most of its Black citizens. This action was clearly in violation of the readmission oath that every Southern state had had to take, stating that its constitution should never be

> so amended or changed as to deprive any citizen, or class of citizens of the United States of the right to vote, who are entitled to vote by the constitution [of 1868] herein recognized, except as punishment for such crimes as are now felonies at common law.[15]

Equally in violation of the readmission oath was South Carolina's disfranchisement amendment in 1895, Louisiana's "Grandfather Clause" in 1898, and North Carolina's constitutional amendment disqualifying virtually all Black voters in 1900.[16]

The South, obviously, no longer felt the need to disguise its plans for Blacks and its outright obstruction of the social changes for which the Civil War was fought. In many ways, Southerners felt that the war was still not over. Hence the South's return to violent repression.

> History does not furnish an example of emancipation under conditions less friendly to the emancipated class than this American example. Liberty came to the freedmen of the United States not in mercy, but in wrath—not by moral choice but by military necessity—not by the generous action of the people among whom they were to live, and whose good will was essential to the success of the measure, but by strangers, foreigners, invaders, trespassers, aliens, and enemies. The very manner of their emancipation invited to the heads of the freedmen the bitterest hostility of race and class. They were now free, and hated because of those who had freed them. . . . It was born in the tempest and whirlwind of war, and has lived in a storm of violence and blood.[17]

When we come to discuss the tremendous amount of violence that played a predominant—and continous—role in "re-enslaving" Southern Blacks during Chesnutt's lifetime, we are discussing a thick and fiery thread that is woven into every aspect of Southern culture. As such, it played a large role in Chesnutt's decision to become a socially crusading writer.

To begin with, violence was a basic form of Southern expression,[18] having deep roots in both the Southern frontier and in the Cavalier traditions there. The isolated nature of plantation geography and the correspondingly unchecked power a master had over his slave were the basic ingredients. Important also was the aristocratic, Cavalier ideal of "honor" which both "farmer and cracker admired and shared." Indeed, it is not difficult to see how the tradition of fisticuff, the gouging ring, and unregulated knife and gun play tended rapidly, from the hour of their emergence, to reincarnate itself in the starched and elaborate etiquette of the code duello . . . so that one of the notable results of the spread of the idea of honor, indeed, was an increase in the tendency to violence throughout the social scale.[19]

With physical violence so pervasive a means of personal and social expression, it soon became a significant political force as well. Most descriptive of this directly political violence was Senator Blanche K. Bruce's March 31, 1876, speech in the United States Senate regarding the "conduct of the late election in Mississippi." As a Black leader and senator from Mississippi, Bruce spent much of his time in debates on election frauds and violence. His speech here documents the disorders which occurred in the 1876 election.

The evidence in hand and accessible will show beyond peradventure that in many parts of the State corrupt and violent influences were brought to bear upon the registrars of voters, thus materially affecting the character of the voting or poll lists; upon the inspectors of election, prejudicially and unfairly thereby changing the number of votes cast; and, finally, threats and violence were practiced directly upon the masses of voters in such measures and strength as to produce grave apprehensions for their personal safety and as to deter them from the exercise of their political franchises. . . .[20]

Less descriptive but more forceful was Frederick Douglass's later summary of the same period:

Under the fair-seeming name of local self-government, they were shooting to death just as many of the newly made citizens of the South as was necessary to put the individual states of the Union entirely into their power.[21]

And of greatest significance is the fact that it was the blatant savageness of the Wilmington, N.C., election "massacre" in 1898 which awakened Chesnutt to the very real dangers of the Black man's position in the South.[22]

At the same time, a large portion of this violence was not directly political. Much of it took place at night and in rural isolation, and served to intimidate the general Black population by ruthlessly killing or maiming specific individuals. The targets of this violence were numerous, including freedmen, Freedmen's Bureau members, Northern teachers, the Heroes of America in North Carolina, the Lincoln Brotherhood, and numbers of similar organizations set up to help and to educate the freedmen.

By 1869 this violence and harassment were so bad that the Reconstruction governments in the Southern states applied for power to organize state militias in order to defend themselves. Significantly, as much as Congress did not want to see militias in Southern states ever again—which is why it had recently passed a law "forbidding the former Confederate states to organize and use militias"—Congress repealed its own recent law and allowed the recreation of the militias.

As Reconstruction continued, the political violence and the more covert intimidations soon merged and became organized. Before the war, lynching parties and nightriders had assumed an organizational form not unlike the "loose yet definite" volunteer fire departments still common today. In the same way, violent terrorizing groups sprang up after the war, all essentially symbolized by the Ku Klux Klan.

With the institution in late 1865 of the Klan in Pulaski, Tennessee, this phase of organized Southern violence began. It created and disseminated the myth of "the brute Negro" and used it to play upon the fears of many whites that the freed slaves would now seek physical revenge on their former masters. The Klan thereupon set itself up as an institution of "chivalry, humanity, mercy, and patriotism," sprung from the "instinct of self-protection" and the determination "to act purely in self-defense."

Acting "purely in self-defense," however, assumed some curious forms.

It involved the murder of respectable Negroes by roving gangs of terrorists, the murder of Negro renters of land, the looting of stores whose owners were sometimes killed, and the murder of peaceable white citizens. . . .

Meanwhile, the personal indignities inflicted upon individual whites and Negroes were so varied and so numerous as to defy classification or enumeration. There were the public whippings, the maimings, the mutilations, and other almost inconceivable forms of intimidation.[23]

In short, it is obvious that the Klan's basic appeal and purpose were not against Radical Reconstruction indignities forced upon the South, but were, rather, against the determination on the part of the Blacks and their Radical colleagues to assume and wield political power.

Despite a network of local anti-Klan laws across the South, a series of special Presidential messages to Congress, a number of Congressional inquiry committees, and the anti-Klan Enforcement Acts on the national level, the Klan continued unmolested. It did, admittedly, "dissolve" itself in 1869, but that was merely a tactical maneuver to allow it freer reign as a truly "Invisible Empire." Thus, as late as September, 1876, President Grant's attorney general could write to the new president, Hayes, that

it is a fixed and definite purpose of the Democratic party in the South that the negroes shall not vote, and murder is a common means of intimidation to prevent them.[24]

As we look at it now, it is clear that only a very determined reassertion of military power by the federal government could have successfully combatted the Klan's influence. However, under Grant and especially Hayes, the Federal government was more and more content to leave the South to its own devices. Thus, in the final analysis, violence won "the peace" for the South after the war itself was officially over. The abolitionists were dead, the Union Army dispersed, and the "Invisible Empire" was left alone on the battlefield—master of all it surveyed.

If a capsule summation of this period were sought, we would
need to look no further than "Pitchfork Ben" Tillman's speech
before the Senate in 1901, where he boldly discussed South
Carolina's disfranchisement of Black voters:

> We have done our level best . . . we have scratched our
> heads to find out how we could eliminate the last one of
> them. We stuffed ballot boxes. We shot them. WE ARE
> NOT ASHAMED OF IT.[25]

Why did the North let the South win the peace after losing the
war? Where did its prewar moral fervor go when meaningful
postwar social change was so clearly within reach? It was the
North that had pushed the debate on slavery into a civil war in
the first place. It was to be expected, therefore, that the North
would pursue and enforce the reconstruction of the South for
which the war was fought and won. But it didn't.

There were many reasons in the North for the loss of the old
abolitionists' moral fervor and the growth of general indifference
to the conditions of the Blacks in the South. There was, first,
the Northern desire for peace at almost any price. Partially this
was the natural reaction of any nation after a long war, even when
successful. But mostly it was a result of the Northern businessmen's interest in the South and its economic potential.

> Their interest transformed itself into a strong desire to
> attain certain specific goals for the South. One was the
> achievement and maintenance of law and order. . . . They
> wanted governments that would insure this safety; and if
> they could facilitate the establishment of such governments,
> they would certainly do so.[26]

Accordingly, when it soon became clear that enforcing the
freedmen's rights in the defiant South would require considerable
effort and physical upheaval for several more years, most Northern businessmen favored forgetting those rights and working in-

stead to build harmonious commercial relations with the white South.

As soon as the South realized how much the North wanted to avoid a new war, it very quickly took advantage of the fact."Let the be White Leagues formed in every town, village, and hamlet of the South," shouted an Atlanta *News* editorial of September 10, 1874,

> and let us organize for the great struggle which seems inevitable. . . . We have submitted long enough to indignities, and it is time to meet brute-force with brute-force. Every Southern State should swarm with White Leagues, and we should stand ready to act the moment Grant signs the civil-rights bill.[27]

By 1877, it was a Southern governor, Wade Hampton, who was waving the famous "bloody shirt" as he accompanied President Hayes on a goodwill speaking tour of Southern cities. While Hayes stressed the theme of peace and harmony, Hampton grasped Hayes's fear of war and immediately began to suggest the possibilities of renewed war if Hayes pushed for the South's adherence to the Constitution and all its amendments.

When Hayes crumbled under the implied threat, his "Let-alone" policy was born, and Black hopes began to die. Needless to say, this policy, with the complete removal of all Union troops in the South earlier that year, left Blacks without any protection at the hands of a violence-prone South.

Most noticeable in this period of searching for "peace and prosperity" was the loss of the old Abolitionist moral fervor. Men like William Lloyd Garrison were getting older and running out of energy by the 1860s. By the 1870s, even those Northern leaders who had pressed for the Radical Reconstruction legislation of 1867 were leaving the scene. Thaddeus Stevens was dead, and there was no replacement for his relentless championing of the Reconstruction cause.

More important than the aging and death of the deeply committed Abolitionists was the loss of moral commitment to the freedmen's cause by the country as a whole. "A great deflation of ideals occurred," Gunnar Myrdal has noted.[28] Money and economic investment now came to be the new American "commitment," as the Muckrakers would show us most incisively thirty years later.

Significantly cnough, economic considerations warped many of the men who had once expressed strong moral convictions about the freedmen's plight. Edward Atkinson, a longtime reformer from Boston, now shifted his attention to business interests and promoted reconciliation with the South for admittedly business considerations. Similarly, Whitelaw Reid, the New York journalist who had found the South arrogant and defiant in 1865, was much more charitable five years later—perhaps because he had recently made heavy investments in Louisiana plantations.

In short, the vigor of Radical Reconstruction had been replaced by a mood of compromise and reconciliation in order to facilitate economic investment and growth. Economic investment and industrialization had become the chief idols of the postwar North, and the South was one of the major vineyards in which this religion was soon spread.

One final aspect òf the national postwar scene is of interest. This is America's empire-building during the end of the century. What makes this interest so important is the two major effects it had on the North's relationship to Blacks in the South. First, it helped direct much of the energy and concern of businessmen and politicians away from civil rights and toward economic gains in other lands. Secondly, many of these foreign lands were populated by different and often darker races. Thus America's seemingly "natural" superiority over those races and its patronizing assumption of the Anglo-Saxon "white man's burden" soon was transferred to the darker, less educated race here at home—all of which seemed to reinforce many of the myths which Southern apologists were spreading about Blacks.

By 1870 and Chesnutt's twelfth birthday, therefore, the position of most Blacks in America was at its lowest point since slavery. In the South, were 90 percent of Black Americans still lived, they were being subjected to a wave of violence and brutality which sought to destroy whatever social and political gains Reconstruction had tentatively managed to introduce. The South also saw Blacks fighting an uphill economic battle, without land, without independence, and without the necessary capital to do anything other than farm as sharecroppers on white-owned land: doing all of the work and receiving almost none of the crop. Furthermore, those Blacks who did possess mechanical and semi-technical skills were deliberately excluded from such skilled jobs, as the South sought to industrialize itself for the benefit of its poor whites and to the calculated detriment of its Blacks. Indeed, there was considerable truth to the suggestion that all Emancipation had meant to the slave was that now he was "free to starve."

Blacks in the North during the period were only somewhat better off, simply because they were subjected to fewer lynchings and had somewhat greater social and political freedom. Yet the North as a whole was far more interested in commercial and territorial expansion than it was in guaranteeing civil rights for Black people anywhere—in the South or North. In short, this period truly was "The Nadir" of the Black man's physical position in American life, a period which Charles W. Chesnutt found himself pitted against.

The Literary Scene: Romance and Rhetoric

By 1900, not only was the Black man's physical position in America at its lowest point in the country's history, but his condition on the intellectual and literary scene was equally precarious. Ignorance, indifference, and hostility all combined to obscure his plight and denigrate his personality and basic human worth.

There were no real Black voices on the literary scene:

At the time when I first broke into print seriously, no American colored writer had ever secured critical recognition except Paul Laurence Dunbar, who had won his laurels as a poet. Phyllis Wheatley, a Colonial poet, had gained recognition largely because she was a slave and born in Africa, but the short story, or the novel of life and manners, had not been attempted by any one of the group.[29]

It was to fill this void that Chesnutt set out to write: to "crusade" against the "subtle almost indefinable feeling of repulsion toward the Negro, which is common to most Americans"[30] and to overcome the general indifference and romantic ignorance which the country had been taught by the basically well-meaning, but naive, white writers who had written of the Black man during the period.

There had been many novels dealing with slavery and the Negro. Harriet Beecher Stowe, especially in *Uncle Tom's Cabin*, had covered practically the whole subject of slavery and race admixture. George W. Cable had dwelt upon the romantic and some of the tragic features of racial contacts in Louisana, and Judge Albion W. Tourgee, in what was one of the best sellers of the day, *A Fool's Errand*, and in his *Bricks Without Straw* had dealt with the problems of reconstruction.[31]

More prevalent and pernicious than the above ignorance, however, was the hostile polemic of those novelists and politicians who deliberately sought to undercut the Black man's image in America.

Thomas Dixon was writing the Negro down industriously and with marked popular success. Thomas Nelson Page was disguising the harshness of slavery under the mask of sentiment. The trend of public sentiment at the moment was distinctly away from the Negro.[32]

This, then, was the literary scene which Chesnutt faced as a developing and mature writer.1

In any discussion of the sentimental romances of Southern novelists, we must realize first that we are dealing quite obviously with a form of propaganda. On its most general level, it was an attempt by a defeated region of the country to win the peace after it had lost the war. On its more profound level, it was an attempt by the South to convince the North—and itself—that slavery never had been evil; that the "peculiar institution" over which the war had been fought actually had been a benevolent one; and that the outcome of the war had not been a moral judgment on the South at all. In fact, so the claim went, the defeat of the gallant, hospitable, Cavalier South by the metallic, money-grabbing North had actually been a grave injustice to the cosmic moral order. These were the didactic themes implicit in all the Southern romances.

The question now arises as to why this major aspect of the propaganda struggle took the form of romance rather than of direct rhetoric. There are several answers.

Romance had always been a characteristic expression of the South. Much of this was probably due to the geographic atmosphere of the region—a landscape of rich, luxuriant foliage swaddled in soft, languid air. Much of this was also probably due to the Medieval-Cavalier tradition which the South had long subsumed as part of its heritage. This was a tradition which not only stressed myth and romance as a pervasive ethos, but one which pretty clearly was a myth all in itself—since it is hard to believe that very many real Cavaliers would have willingly given up the refinements of civilized London for the savage wilds of early Virginia. In any event, Romance did flourish in the South, and it did become a major medium of thought and expressions.

Accordingly, when, in the early 1830s, the South found itself pierced and raked over by the sharp glare of Northern Abolitionists, it needed something to defend the "peculiar institution" from those hostile, inquiring eyes. Needed also was some sort of varnishable structure behind which to hide the shame and guilt which the South itself sporadically felt. The outcome of these needs was the creation of new romances, greater myths, and finally hard-core stereotypes which would "logically" support or emotionally sentimentalize that un-Christian and undemocratic system.

Of all those fictions which were created, the most inevitable was that which formed the backbone of the whole Plantation Tradition—the assumption that every planter was a gentleman. Primarily this myth sprang from the Southerner's own self-delusion about his "Cavalier, aristocratic" ancestors, and it was sculpted to help temper—or isolate as "exceptional"—the many reports of slavery's brutality which constantly made their way North and to Europe. Furthermore, it laid the foundation for the paternal myth of the benevolent, concerned, fatherly slaveholder who tenderly looked after the cares of his childish, infantile, "Sambo" slaves.

Significantly enough, the myth also had a unique effect on the South's relationship with the North. It enabled the South "to wrap itself in contemptuous superiority, to sneer down the Yankee as low-bred, crass and money grubbing, and even to beget in his bourgeois soul a kind of secret and envious awe." In short, "it was a nearly perfect defense mechanism."[33] For reasons which we shall discuss later, the North accepted, and even developed deference for, the myth.

At the same time, most of the myths that were developed in the romances set out to debase and render ludicrous the Southern Black man. So much of the South—both in terms of past guilt and present comfort—was wrapped up in its relationship with the Black man that it was almost imperative that he be depicted in as many degrading stereotypes as possible This was the major function of most Southern romances.

The most significant and pervasive of these stereotypes was that of the happy, irresponsible "Sambo." Slavery itself was brutal and ugly,

> But the South could not and must not admit it, of course. It must prettify the institution and its own reactions, must begin to boast of its own Great Heart. To have heard them talk, indeed, you would have thought that the sole reason some of these planters held to slavery was love and duty to the black man, the earnest, devoted will not only to get him into heaven but also to make him happy in this world. He

was a child whom somebody had to look after. More, he
was in general, and despite an occasional spoiled Nat Tur-
ner, a grateful child—a contented, glad, loving child. . . .

Mrs. Stowe did not invent the figure of Uncle Tom, nor
did Christy invent that of Jim Crow—the banjo-picking,
heel-flinging, hi-yi-ing happy jack of the levees and the
cotton fields. All they did was to modify them a little for
their purposes. In essence, both were creations of the South—
defense-mechanisms, answers to the Yankee and its own
doubts . . . [34]

The fusion of these two mythic stereotypes—the large-hearted
aristocrat and the infantile "Sambo"—did not come until after
the Civil War. At that time, the South needed to defend itself
against those "Radical Reconstructionists" who still carried the
moral torch and had not let commercial interests sway their
humanitarian concern for the ex-slaves. It also gave convenient
rationalizations to those commercial interests in the North who
wanted to make moral and racial "reconstruction" as transient a
period as possible, so that they could get back to business as
usual. For them, the rationalized belief that nothing had ever
really been wrong in the South was the quickest route to reconciliation. Simultaneously, the South needed this romance to assert its past pride and regional independence in the face of the
victorious, overbearing Yankee.

At this moment, a number of additional Black stereotypes
were created. As Sterling Brown has enumerated them, they fall
into seven discernible categories: the Contented Slave, the
Wretched Freedman, the Comic Negro, the Brute Negro, the
Tragic Mulatto, the Local Color Negro, and the Exotic Primitive.[35] Implicit in each of these was the concept of the Black
man's inherent inferiority, and perhaps we can assume the
promulgation of that concept to be their basic *raison d'etre*.

These stereotypes did serve several specific, immediate purposes as well, most of which are obvious from the names themselves. Some, like the Contented Slave, sought to show how

comfortable and friendly the antebellum period of slavery was. In deliberate contrast, the Wretched Freedman sought to show how hard and inhospitable was the slave's lot once he was emancipated and set out on his own. A stereotype like the Tragic Mulatto attempted to define racial intermarriage as somehow cosmically impossible, leading only to the most dire consequences.

One stereotype, the Brute Negro, was somewhat special in the harshness of its creation and the intensity of its use. For this reason we will look at it in greater detail later. Yet even in its specialness it shared the common purpose of all these stereotypes: it sought to debase the Black man as a human being and thus mitigate any claims that he had on the white Southern citizens, who claimed to espouse democracy and Christianity. If the South could define the Black man as subhuman, then Christian brotherhood and social equality need not apply to him. In some ways, of course, this "logic" lay at the core of all these myths.

Of primary importance here was the fact that all these romances restored an atmosphere of tranquility to the South and to the nation—an atmosphere which the North craved for two major reasons. On the one hand, tranquility and peace were the *sine qua non* of the economic investment and industrialization which the Northern businessmen hoped to effect in the South. On the other hand, after Radical Reconstruction showed itself to be a failure, the North began to fear a re-establishment of the war. Accordingly, as we have already seen, it began to develop the equivalent of a "peace at any price" philosophy. The romances of Page and Joel Chandler Harris, therefore, did much to soothe the atmosphere of hostility and return the country to the concept of "Southern hospitality," as did those stories and plays which were intersectional romances in their symbolic love affairs between Northern soldier and Southern belle.

A somewhat deeper reason for the North's acceptance was the fact that, with the abject failure of Radical Reconstruction and with the obvious betrayal of the Black man in the Hayes Compromise, many Northerners felt a certain guilt now. It was comforting for them to "learn," therefore, that slavery really never had been evil and that they in the North really never had had any moral commitment in the first place.

There was still another force at work: the physical condition of the North itself. The North's world—especially in the industrial cities—was becoming complicated, dirty, and corrupt. Hence many found a great satisfaction in reading of, and believing in, an idyllic agrarian time—a time when gentle manners, smiling countenances and uncomplicated lives still existed, in a country-side of sweet magnolia and fragrant honeysuckle. To the Northern reader in the mechanical, money-grubbing gilded age, the concept of pastoral serenity and warmth was very enticing indeed.

These were the major reasons for the North's acceptance of the Plantation romances in general. The question is why it accepted so readily the Southern stereotypes of the Black man. This question is exceptionally important, since these stereotypes made their way so pervasively into the Northern consciousness, where Chesnutt so strongly sought to combat them.

To begin with, most of the North did not know a great deal about Black people from either occupational or social contact. In 1880, in fact, there were only 412,715 Blacks to 25,285,891 whites in the fourteen Northern states east of the Mississippi River. Even when there was some contact, the Black man very early learned not to reveal his inner self to a potential white threat and often played instead one of the "acceptable" Northern roles sanctioned for him. Therefore the average Northern white had very little real awarness of Blacks as people.

At the same time that there was ignorance, there was also curiosity, fed by biased anecdotes, cartoons and jokes; and it was amplified by the Northerner's own feeling of responsibility and guilt for the Black man's position in the South. Yet the curiosity was there, and it sought out and devoured the many romantic myths and stereotypes of the period. Thus the Southern romances came, the stereotypes were seen, and the plastic Northern minds were conquered.

In more than a quarter century of giving ear to Southern politicians, Klan speakers, and preachers . . . I came to believe in something of reincarnation, or the more likely fact of numbing unoriginality of minds prejudiced by race.

Now and then someone came along . . . who raised the act of irrelevance, vulgar invective, and demagoguery to preposterous heights of entertainment. But even they were playing their own arrangements of original composers.

. . . ideas, blasphemies, prejudices, sophistries, syllogisms, phrases of invective, and theories. . . . The words and phrases have for years been floating in the South's political air, like motes in sunlight, to be breathed in and expelled.[36]

In these 1963 words of Ralph McGill, we see the seemingly eternal world of Southern racial rhetoric and myth. Its method is one of "invective," "sophistries," and "demagoguery"; its substance is prejudiced ignorance at best, vicious slander at worst. What is significant for us is that most of these myths in rhetoric were in full use after the Civil War and were, in large measure, much of the world of prejudice which Chesnutt was determined to "live down" and eventually "crush out."

When we come to discuss the direct and extensive use of this rhetoric, we discuss once more the background which made this form of expression so pervasive and effective. Interestingly enough, there is a very strong link between this direct rhetoric and the indirect "propaganda" of the Plantation and local color romances.

It was in such a light that W.J. Cash saw "the Southern fondness for rhetoric."

A gorgeous, primitive art, addressed to the autonomic system and not to the encephalon, rhetoric is of course dear to the heart of the simple man everywhere. . . .

But in the South, to recapitulate, there was the rising flood of romanticism and hedonism clamoring for expression

. . . . Thus rhetoric flourished here far beyond even its
American average; it early became a passion—and not only
a passion but a primary standard of judgment, the "sine
qua non" of leadership. The greatest man would be the man
who could best wield it.[37]

Being more social and explicit in its message than were the "messages" to be found in the romances, rhetoric quickly found its
medium in the political arena. To speak of "the love of rhetoric,
of oratory," suggested Cash, "is at once to suggest the love of
politics. The two, in fact, were inseparable."

Thus the politics of the Old South was a theater for the
play of the purely personal, the purely romantic, and the
purely hedonistic. It was an arena wherein one great champion confronted another or a dozen, and sought to outdo
them in rhetoric and splendid gesturing. It swept back the
loneliness of the land, it brought men together under
torches, it filled them with the contagious power of the
crowd, it unleashed emotion and set it to leaping and dancing, it caught the very meanest man up out of his tiny legend
into the gorgeous fabric of the legend of this or that great
hero.[38]

With this as social/psychological background, we can understand how romance and rhetoric developed so strongly in the
South as soon as the pressure from the North began over slavery.
Even as early as the 1830s, the mythopoetic faculty was being
called to the fore to protect the South from outside ideas and
criticism. And, looking at the 1830s, we can see just what purpose
the rhetoric was developed to serve. It sought to solidify the
South's mind and spirit, to desperately draw its intellectual
wagon train into as tight a circle as possible. As such, it, and its
postwar successor, formed much of Chesnutt's world.
  As with the romances, the direct rhetoric was concerned with
developing myths and stereotypes for internal and external

consumption. Ranging from the nature of Reconstruction to the basic nature of Blacks, these fabrications were presented outspokenly and with force. Furthermore, with the exception of the violently polemical novels of Thomas Dixon, they depended mostly on politicians and newspapers to achieve their circulation.

Similar to the romances, the rhetorical myths and stereotypes fell into two discernible categories: those which dealt with the general world of politics and those which dealt with the basic nature of "the Negro." Most important of those myths in the former category was that concerning the "large occupation army" which supposedly stayed on in the South after the war, bullying and harassing the helpless inhabitants until the 1870s. Despite the vast mileage of rhetoric which the myth produced, however, it was only a myth.

A more crucial myth for our understanding of Chesnutt was that which encouraged the belief in a New South. Mixing pathos with heroism, romance with rhetoric, the concept was sounded and resounded throughout the country by Southern spokesmen from 1868 on. In this way, it was a major propaganda weapon for obtaining in the South a "hands off" policy by the Federal government.

The greatest and most famous statement of this "doctrine" was that delivered at the annual dinner of the New England Society in New York in 1866 by Henry W. Grady, one of the editors of the Atlanta *Constitution*. In his oration, Grady spoke eloquently of the New South's pitiful, femininely metaphored plight. He suggested to his Northern audience that never "was nobler duty confined to human hands than the uplifting and upbuilding of the prostrate and bleeding South, misguided, perhaps, but beautiful in her suffering, brave and generous always." He reiterated the warm welcome which the South offered Northern industry and stressed how "we have learned that one northern immigrant is worth fifty foreigners, and have smoothed the path to southward, wiped out the place where Mason and Dixon's line used to be and hung out our latch-string to you and yours." In short, he pictured a pitiable but courageous and willing Southern damsel, softly waiting to be helped across the stream of life by whatever gallant—and profit-minded —Sir Walter Raleigh might be willing to cast his industrial cloak upon the water.

When he came to discuss the question of the Black man's treatment in the South—a treatment which had deteriorated infamously by 1886—Grady was especially eloquent and convincing. Asking himself rhetorically whether the South had progressed toward a solution of the problem, the record would speak for itself, he suggested. No section showed a more prosperous laboring population than the Blacks of the South; no laboring class revealed more sympathy with the employing and landowning class. The Black man shared in the school fund and had, so Grady claimed, the "fullest protection" of the law and, of course, the friendship of the Southern people. As a result of all this, Grady made his plea that the South be allowed to handle its own race problem.

So moving and eloquent was Grady before this Northern—but willing to be convinced—audience that he was frequently interrupted by applause. When he sat down, he was given a standing ovation, and the band played *Dixie*. In short, he had been a resounding success, and from this time forward the myth of the New South was an established and convincing piece of fiction.[39] Significantly enough, it was this myth to which Chesnutt finally addressed himself in his final and most forceful novels, *The Marrow of Tradition* and *The Colonel's Dream*. By then Chesnutt had become convinced— after the various disfranchisements in Mississippi, South Carolina, Louisiana and North Carolina, and after the grotesque election massacre in Wilmington, N.C.— that the "New South" was a completely hollow myth which was not going to correct itself.

Related to these general Reconstruction myths were those concerning the Black man in Reconstruction and the "odious," "incompetent," and "dishonest" role he supposedly played therein. Developed as an outgrowth of the "Sambo" stereotype, these myths basically served to promote the concept of the Black man's inherent inferiority. They enumerated in harrowing rhetoric the oppressive amount of "Negro rule" and "Negro misrule" supposedly took place in the various Reconstruction governments. The truth, of course, was quite the opposite, as historians of the period now see so clearly.

By far the most vituperative and pervasive "Negro" stereotype spread by this Southern rhetoric was that of the "Brute Negro." It was spread by the eternal Southern demagogue, prefacing his diatribe with the equally eternal "Would you want your daughter to. . . ." It flooded the novels of Thomas Dixon, whose works have been defined by C. Vann Woodward as "the perfect literary accompaniment of the white-supremacy and disfranchisement campaign, at the height of which they were published."[40] It surfaced daily in the newspapers and magazines of the period in both North and South.

The effect of these media was immense. "Then as now," notes Rayford Logan, "most Americans made up their minds about local affairs and their relations with their fellow men on the basis of news articles, many of them slanted, and the other less weighty ingredients of the paper, such as anecdotes, jokes and cartoons . . . ."[41] And while most of the anecdotes, jokes and cartoons were generally given over to expression of the "Sambo" and various "comic Negro" stereotypes, a great weight of the slanted news articles set out to create and emphasize the "Brute" and "Criminal Negro."

On its most basic level, this biased coverage indulged itself in an overall tendency to stress "Negro" crimes. A newspaper such as the New Orleans *Picayune*, for example, had a column called "Southern States Items," which almost daily featured articles about crimes committed by Blacks. Other newspapers featured such crime in headlines and as sensational front page news.

More important than the extensive reporting of "Negro" crime *per se*, however, was the *kind* of crime that the newspapers so dramatically reported and expanded upon. Crimes of violence and stories about "razor-toting" Blacks were common. So was the most inflammatory crime a Black man could be accused of— the rape of a white woman.

Throughout the period of Reconstruction and after, a large number of articles appeared in both local newspapers and national magazines, developing the latter crime. In this slanted "developing," the editorial and tonal reaction was quite clear: the general "Negro" had "violated the chastity of white women with appalling frequency and under circumstances unutterably shocking to human nature."

Most significantly, beneath the expressed horror and outrage at this "criminal act" was the implicit statement that this brute creature had no conceivable business being anywhere near the romantically pure Southern belle. This was implied by its being so "utterably shocking to human nature." Hence every display of shock at the concept of "Negro" rape was actually a stressed reiteration of the Black man's biological and somehow cosmic inferiority.

To a certain extent the "Brute Negro" stereotype was developed as much by the language of these articles as by their frequency and prominence. Such words as "colored" and "negro" were constantly reiterated in these stories. Equally important was the use of debasing, inflammatory language. The typical newspaper description of a Black suspect accused of rape very often pictured him as a "black wretch" or "big, burly negro."[43] Similarly, perjorative terms like "negro ruffian" and "colored cannibal" were used for Blacks accused of other offenses. The rationale behind this overall "Brute-Criminal" stereotype was clear, even if it was not always on the surface. It was racial and political propaganda, meant for both internal and external consumption.

Internally, the South sought to substantiate and perpetuate many white fears that the newly freed slaves would seek physical revenge on their former white masters. The introduction of this violent stereotype motif was designed to draw all whites back into a "solid South" political group. This was especially important to the planting class when it faced the dreaded possibility of the poor whites and poor Blacks joining together against the landowners under the aegises of the various Populist movements of the 1880s and 1890s. By attaching this fear of violence to the extremely sensitive "racial purity" zone of the Southern psyche, it was invested with even more emotion.

Of greater importance, perhaps, were the effects of the myth on the North and other outside observers. On the one hand, it was an attempt to obliterate some of the un-Christian and undemocratic cruelty with which the North equated slavery. Once the Black man was defined as nonhuman and bestial, the white Christian had no moral commitment to treat him as a brother. In political terms, if the Black man really were less than human as, indeed, he had been defined in the original Constitution (where he was defined politically as "three-fifths" of a "person"), then there was no compelling need to extend democracy's political rights to him either.

Furthermore, the stereotype was especially revived in the late nineteenth century in order to justify to the outside world the reincarnation of those white Southern violence groups which had traditionally offered sadistic "recreation" and warped ego-building to the region's poor whites. With the resurgence of groups like the Ku Klux Klan, the South needed a rationale to justify this rebirth of cruelty and violence. The myth of the "Brute Negro" was just the answer.

Whether romance or rhetoric, sentiment or vitriol, the "literature" of the postwar South was almost completely propagandistic in purpose and effect. As such, Chesnutt saw it as a major weapon being used against Blacks in this country, and he sought to combat it through his own creativity and literary talent. It was towards this goal that he dedicated most of his literary life. For he knew—as we see so clearly today—that

> The Negro has met with as great injustice in American literature as he has in American life. The majority of books about Negroes merely stereotype Negro character.[44]

CHAPTER II

Chesnutt's Basic Nature: Middle-Class Riser

> I believe that life was given to us to enjoy, and if God will help me, I intend to enjoy mine.[1]

Influences

As we have seen above, America after the Civil War was a nation of materialistic concerns and conquests. It was not until 1889 that Andrew Carnegie sanctified this pursuit by evangelizing the "true Gospel concerning Wealth,"[2] but the revived national interest in money and middle-class values was evident long before Carnegie's article. In fact, this interest in business as a vehicle of cultural expression went back as far as the early 1700s, and it very much became the standard American conception of success.

In its basic form, the "gospel" went all the way back to the days of Cotton Mather and Benjamin Franklin. For Mather, a Christian had two "callings." The "general calling" was "to serve the Lord Jesus Christ" and the "personal calling" was to develop a certain Particular Employment by which his 'Usefulness' in his neighborhood is distinguished."[3] In short, a man must not only be pious, but he must be productive as well.

Even though this gospel of "callings" began as a worship of God, it soon took on overtones of personal wealth, hard work and profit.

> Would a man "Rise" by his Business? I say, then let him "Rise" to his "Business". It was foretold. Prov. 22.29, "Seest thou a man Diligint in his Business? He shall stand before Kings;" He shall come to preferment. And it was instanced

by him who foretold it; I Kings 11.28. "Solomon, seeing that the young man was industrious, he made him a Ruler" . . . Let your "Business" engross the most of your time.[4]

Soon this concept of industry and profit almost displaced God altogether. As Mather's philosophy tended to unfold, "a Christian should for the most part spend most of his time" on his earthly calling "so he may glorify God" by doing of "Good" for others and by the getting of "Good" for himself.[5]

Made popular by Franklin and Poor Richard, this ethic of industry, profit and thrift soon became the dominant philosophy and concern of the slowly developing American middle class, especially on the Eastern seaboard where the Revolution was to take place and the economic/social center of the country was to mature. Nor did this way of thinking remain merely a colonial seaboard phenomenon, for in the nineteenth century it was caught up by Francis Asbury and spread by his Methodist circuit riders throughout the continent's interior. Its advice to the young men was emphatic: work and slave, if you would win the game of life and would honor the God Who made you. Soon "Work, for the Night is Coming" became a popular hymn of evangelical Protestantism.[6]

With the tremendous flourishing of industry and capital during and after the Civil War, it is not surprising that this driving force received such tremendous impetus—an impetus that was clearly to affect a boy like Chesnutt, who was six years old when the war ended and therefore at a formative age when the postwar industrial surge intensified. Not only were the concepts impressed on him in his middle-class home and in his early schooling, but they abounded in the outside American scene as a whole. Textbooks, pulpits, and even popular literature echoed the good word.

"We are not of that number who inveigh against wealth," the general textbook of the period usually stated, and then continued to explain just what it was advocating in outspokenly religious terms:

If "the 'love' of money is the root of all evil," the proper use of it is productive of measureless good; and as the world grows wiser, and business becomes more or less largely consecrated . . . money will become one of the most effective means in hastening the benign advent of "the good time coming."[7]

"By the proper use of wealth," wrote D.S. Gregory, author of a textbook on ethics used during the 1880s in many American colleges,

> man may greatly elevate and extend his moral work. It is therefore his duty to seek to secure wealth for his high end, and to make a diligent use of what the Moral Governor may bestow upon him for the same end. . . . The Moral Governor has placed the power of acquisitiveness in man for a good and noble purpose. . . .[8]

"To secure wealth is an honorable ambition, and is one great test of a person's usefulness to others," said a Baptist minister in Philadelphia, Russell H. Conwell, whose popular lecture, "Acres of Diamonds" was said to have been repeated throughout the East and Middle West six thousand times.

> Money is power. Every good man and woman ought to strive for power, to do good with it when obtained. Tens of thousands of men and women get rich honestly. But they are often accused by an envious, lazy crowd of unsuccessful persons of being dishonest and oppressive. I say, Get rich, get rich! But get rich honestly, or it will be a withering curse.[9]

In 1900 the Right Reverend William Lawrence solidified this philosophy on both social and philosophical grounds:

> Material prosperity is helping to make the national character sweeter, more joyous, more unselfish, more Christlike.

> That is my answer to the question as to the relation of material prosperity to morality.[10]

and, more profoundly, he suggested that

> . . . in the long run, it is only to the man of morality that wealth comes. We believe in the harmony of God's Universe. We know that it is only by working along His laws natural and spiritual that we can work with efficiency. Only by working along the lines of right thinking and right living can the secrets and wealth of Nature be revealed.[11]

The ultimate truth seen by Lawrence was that "Godliness is in league with riches."[12]

As if textbooks and pulpits weren't enough, a corollary of the gospel of wealth during this period was the popular formula of success. "The stream of success literature which appeared after the Civil War," notes R. H. Gabriel, "became a flood by the end of the century."[13] Success, as taught by such men as Horace Greeley and L. U. Reavis, depended on a few simple rules:

> Don't be Discouraged. Do the Best You Can. Be Honest, and Truthful and Industrious. Do Your Duty, and Live Right; Learn to Read, then Read all the Books and Newspapers You Can and All Will Be Well After Awhile.[14]

And it was quite evident to fellow youth moralists of the period that

> . . . religion requires the following very reasonable things of every young man, namely: that he should make the most of himself possible; that he should watch and improve his opportunities; that he should be industrious, upright, faithful, and prompt; that he should task his talents, whether one or ten, to the utmost; that he should waste neither time nor money. . . . Indeed, we might say that religion demands SUCCESS.[15]

Soon this expository formula found its way into the popular fiction of the period, especially the juvenile literature, where it was acted out continually in the adventures and successes of the heroes who populated the novels of Horatio Alger.[16] Through Alger the success-ethos had a tremendously broad and constant impact on the youth of this country. As R. E. Spiller notes,

> No writer of juveniles has been more widely read than Horatio Alger, Jr. . . . It is supposed that no fewer than 20,000,000 copies were published in the Ragged Dick Series (1867 ff.), the Luck and Pluck Series (1869 ff.), and Tattered Tom Series (1871 ff.), etc.[17]

There is no proof that Chesnutt read any of Alger's stories. There is no mention of Alger in his *Journal,* nor does he allude to Alger in his brief description of his library in *The Quarry.* Nor are any of Alger's books to be found in the library collection of books which Chesnutt's daughter donated to Fisk University. None of these criteria is, of course, conclusive; and, in a more profound sense, they may actually be irrelevant. For the point is that the middle-class concept of success completely pervaded the American scene in the 1870s and 1880s, and it is obvious that Chesnutt came into contact with it thoughout his early years. In his Journal of March 12, 1881, he mentions reading Greeley directly and invokes the twin gods, Franklin and Greeley, when he makes his major manifesto of economic determination to "go to the Metropolis . . . and like Franklin, Greeley, and many others, there will I stick." (Journal, April 23, 1879) He similarly becomes quite infatuated with Thomas Macaulay and his middle-class beliefs, and even notes in his *Journal* that

> Macaulay's Life is very interesting. . . . His was a great and glorious career. If I could earn a tenth of his fame, or make a tenth part of his money, I would have good cause to be content. (January 15, 1881)

Perhaps more enlightening is the fact that Chesnutt begins his whole Journal (July 1, 1874) with extensive quotations from "A Handbook for Home Improvements"—the text of which directly parallelled and echoed the various rules of "success" that we have just seen put forth in Reade, Reavis, Thayer, and others.

In short, whether it was Macaulay and Alger or Greeley and a success manual makes little difference here. The point is that Chesnutt was very much exposed to this way of thinking that dominated America during his early youth; and it is clear that he was greatly influenced by it.

While the national consciousness was being oriented in the direction of material "success," the ambitions of the somewhat separated Black communities were similarly spurred by the same philosophy. The concern of Black for land and material assets that had come alive long before the war developed most strongly right after it.

Before the war, the major way to acquire wealth for free Blacks was the ownership of land or other real estate. In such Northern states as New York, Pennsylvania, and Ohio this process began as early as the end of the eighteenth century. Somewhat later, as the plantation system of agriculture became unprofitable in such Southern states as Maryland, Virginia, and North Carolina, plantations were broken up into small farms and some of the growing numbers of free Black were able to buy the smaller ones. Thus in Chesnutt's North Carolina, for example, where the plantation system was never as extensive as in the states further south, by 1860 slightly more than 10 percent of some 30,000 free Blacks in that state were listed as property owners. In short, the middle-class regard for property had considerable currency among the free Blacks in the South even before Emancipation and the end of the war.

During this same antebellum period it has been estimated that "the free Negroes accumulated $50,000,000 in real and per-

sonal wealth. . . ." Far more important than the material
wealth here, however, were the underlying economic attitudes
that Blacks acquired during this period.

> The savings and business undertakings on the part of the
> free Negroes reflected the spirit and values of their envi-
> ronment. Through thrift and saving, white American arti-
> sans hoped to accumulate wealth and get ahead. This spirit
> was encouraged among the free Negroes by their leaders,
> one of the most distinguished of whom has been described
> as a "black Benjamin Franklin." In fact, these free Negroes
> were trained in the "old style" bourgeois spirit represented
> by Benjamin Franklin.[18]

During and after the war this exposure to middle-class values
increased for a large number of Blacks. During the war, banks
were established to enable Black soldiers to save all or part of the
allotments that the government made to them and to their
families. Furthermore, as the war drew to a close, an army pay-
master and a Congregational minister devised a plan for setting
up a bank to encourage thrift on the part of the newly emancipated freedmen. This plan finally resulted in the establishment of
the influential—though ill-fated—Freedmen's Savings Bank, and
it is not unimportant to note the influence this economic institution did have, short-lived though it was.

Although Black leaders like W. E. B. DuBois have suggested
that the "crash" of the Freedmen's Savings Bank dramatically
damaged the emerging Black saver and that, with the loss of his
money, "all the faith in saving went too, and much of the faith in
men,"[19] E. Franklin Frazier thinks otherwise. As he sees it, "the
bank succeeded nevertheless in giving Negroes training in business and in implanting in them bourgeois ideals." Frazier notes
how

> The literature distributed by the bank was designed to
> teach them how their savings would increase through inter-

est and how thrift would bring them the things they desired. Booklets containing pictures and poems, which provided homely advice on thrift as the means to riches, were widely distributed among Negroes.[20]

The Freedmen's Bank and its booklets were not the only means urging thrift and industry for Blacks. There was also Frederick Douglass. Associated with the bank and later its president, Douglass had long stressed those middle-class virtues to his fellow freedmen. In fact, we need only look at his major oration, "delivered . . . in Elmira, N.Y., August 1, 1880, at a great meeting of colored people met to celebrate West Indies emancipation," to realize just how committed he was to these principles, even two years after the Freedmen's Savings Bank had collapsed.

In this address Douglass began by noting how difficult life had been for slaves set free without land, friends, or any initial means of supporting themselves. He then moved to a discussion of the present position of Blacks in 1876, advocating the course that they should follow to succeed in American society.

Let us, then, wherever we are, whether at the North or at the South, resolutely struggle on in the belief that there is a better day coming, and that we, by patience, industry, uprightness, and economy may hasten that better day.

As if to drive home the point completely, seven paragraphs later he returned to this theme and made his middle-class ethic even clearer.

Pardon me, therefore, for urging upon you, my people, the importance of saving your earnings, of denying yourselves in the present, that you may have something in the future, of consuming less for yourselves, that your children may have a start in life when you are gone.

With money and property comes the means of knowledge and power. . . . This part of our destiny is in our own

hands. Every dollar you lay up represents one day's independence, one day of rest and security in the future. If the
time shall ever come when we shall possess, in the colored
people of the United States, a class of men noted for enter-
prise, industry, economy, and success, we shall no longer
have any trouble in the matter of civil and political rights.
The battle against popular prejudice will have been fought
and won, and, in common with all other races and colors,
we shall have an equal chance in the race for life.[21]

Besides the influence of Frederick Douglass, the Freedmen's
Savings Bank, and the bank's extensive literature, the postwar
Blacks of Chesnutt's generation were influenced by yet another
prophet of wealth and bourgeois success: the schools.

> From its inception the education of the Negro was
> shaped by bourgeois ideals. The northern missionaries, who
> followed in the wake of the Union armies as they overran the
> South, established schools which taught the Yankee virtues
> of industry and thrift.

Furthermore, since most of these schools were supported by
Protestant churches in the North, "they sought to inculcate in
their students the current ideals of Puritan morality."[22] And
when we realize that, as far back as Cotton Mather, Puritan
morality was closely linked with the Protestant ethic of hard
work, thrift, and respectability, we see how middle-class values
did impinge on postwar Blacks: ex-slaves and "old issue" free
men alike.

When we come now to discuss "old issue" free Blacks, we
come directly to discuss the parents of Charles W. Chesnutt and
the immediate home environment of his impressionable youth.

Both parents were "free colored people" of North Carolina
who had met as they fled from the state in 1856, journeying from
Fayetteville to Cleveland in the same wagon train. His mother,

Ann Maria, "was a born teacher" who "had been secretly teaching slave children to read and write" at a time when "such teaching was becoming very dangerous." Indeed, this was one of the reasons why she and her mother left Fayetteville. Andrew Chesnutt, on the other hand, was a man who worked at various trades. Driver-conductor for a horsecar line and wheelwright assistant in Cleveland before the war, he then became a teamster in the Union Army and finally returned to Fayetteville after the war as a storekeeper and, finally, farmer.[23]

Charles Chesnutt, therefore, was an American youth reared in the dream of attaining economic and social success through diligence and hard work. It was his mother and his first public school teacher who affected him most in this direction. At his birth, Ann Maria's plans for her son's future were clear and determined:

> . . . her boy should have every advantage that any child could have, a happy childhood, a good education, opportunity for mental and spiritual growth. He should stand upright and fill a man's place in the world. He should become a scholar and a gentleman, and all the dreams and hopes that in her own case had been unfulfilled should come to full fruition in this child of hers.

Therefore,

> In his early years, she endeavored to fill his heart with fine ideals and lofty principles, to imbue his mind with the spirit of courage and high endeavor. (*CWC*, pp. 2-3)

Later, when the Chesnutts returned to Fayetteville after the war and young Charles entered a newly created Freedmen's Bureau School, he came under the influence of its principal, Robert Harris, a man who seems to have been strongly oriented toward the same American middle-class success values held by Ann Maria.

He was a man of irreproachable character and high ideals. His position in Fayetteville was, on a smaller scale, like that of Booker T. Washington later. . . . By his tact and moderation he won and held the good will of all classes of the community. He enjoyed the confidence of the leading men of the town as well as that of the parents and the pupils themselves. His example and precept promoted among the colored people a higher standard of morality and good conduct than existed in almost any other southern town of that period. Ann Maria's children were fortunate to come under the influence of the remarkable man and Ann Maria was thankful for it. (*CWC*, p. 5)

When Ann Maria died in 1872 and Charles was appointed "pupil-teacher" at the school, he "now fell under the direct influence of Robert Harris, who encouraged in him the aspiration and hopes with which his mother had inspired him."

If this seems to imply that his father was a lesser influence on his ambitions and concepts of success, the implication is correct, and yet incomplete. For while it is true that Ann Maria and Robert Harris gave Chesnutt middle-class values in a strong, class room dose, his father's life also made a strong impression on Charles. In some ways it reinforced the ethos of personal climb up the political-social mountain, as Charles saw his storekeeper father become a county commissioner and justice of the peace for Cumberland County. In another light, his father's later years further impressed on Charles the Puritan virtues of thrift and carefulness with money, as he saw his father fail " in the storekeeping business because of having given too much credit to his customers." This failure, followed by the years his father then spent scratching out a bare living from a small farm with poor soil, went far to make the boy conscious of obtaining, and holding on to, money and economic security.

Chesnutt Himself

Regardless of what outside national, racial, or familial influences affected Chesnutt, it is clear that he soon internalized them and determined to pursue them on his own.

Throughout his life he was very conscious of the value of money as it affected his own comforts and enjoyments.By the time he was twenty, he had decided to go North because there, "although the prejudice sticks . . . yet a man may enjoy these privileges if he has the money to pay for them." (Journal, October 16, 1878) Only half a year later, returning from a trip to Washington, D.C., he noted in his Journal (Summer, 1879) how "Colored people have a great many 'privileges' which they do not possess further South; but it requires money to enjoy them to any considerable extent"; and he observed further in the entry that "the advantages of city life can only be fully enjoyed by the wealthy, while the poor feel the full weight of the discomforts." On the same trip and in the same Journal entry he came to understand his future success in similar terms.

> I shall hereafter devote myself to my studies and my profession. By modesty and economy I shall raise myself still higher in the estimation of my fellow citizens, and with a permanent situation and an increased salary, I hope to be somewhat independent in five or ten years.

When it came to using and enjoying his money, Chesnutt was equally at home. In 1880, at age twenty-two, he became principal of the Normal School in Fayetteville and received an even larger salary than Robert Harris had had for the same position. With this new money the young Chesnutts—noe Charles, Susan, and their two children—quickly moved into "a home of their own," "bought an organ," and "spent the summer months up in the mountains." Equally indicative of his enjoyment and sense of economic status was the fact that their comfortable circumstances meant that immediately "Susan was able to have a woman help her with the housework." (*CWC,* pp. 25-26)

After they moved to Cleveland in 1884 and the Chesnutt stenographic reporting business began to prosper, he was ready by 1889 to buy a lot in town and have a new house built on it. (*CWC,* p. 48) Almost immediately Charles and Susan "were invited to join the Cleveland Social Circle . . . a very exclusive organization. . . . (*CWC*, pp. 244-247)

In her biography of her father, Helen Chesnutt suggests that much of his concern for money and economic success was the result of "intense pressure" to satisfy his family's economic aspirations. With this in mind, Miss Chesnutt announces, in discussing the financing of the new house, how "Susan had all the pride and pleasure of owning a comfortable and adequate home in a pleasant and friendly neighborhood." (*CWC*, p. 80) However, this is an oversimplication, though basically correct. For while it is true that Susan was far more socially and economically oriented than Charles was, and thus did demand certain economic comforts as befitted her sense of station in life,[24] her interests alone do not account for the real sumptuousness of the library in the new house, and the expensive trips that the family—and sometimes Charles alone—took through the United States, Canada, and Europe. Nor do they fully explain the purchase of two new automobiles by 1917, nor the many years of summer-resort renting, culminating in the building of a new summer home in the Michigan resort area at Idlewild, in 1925, (*CWC*, pp. 273-295)

As a further example, it is almost impossible to miss the stance of the complacent, successful, bourgeois gentleman that dominates Chesnutt's letter to an old Fayetteville acquaintance in 1916:

> You ask about my family and myself. . . .I have enjoyed for many years an ample income, from the standpoint of a moderately successful professional man. . . . Of my four children, all are college graduates, two of my daughters from Smith College, at Northampton, Massachusetts, one from the College for Women of Western Reserve University, and my son from Harvard. . . .
>
> Not only have we been well treated in a business and professional way, but in other respects as well. I am a member of the Chamber of Commerce, the Cleveland Bar Associa-

tion, the City Club, and other Clubs of lesser note, and also of the very exclusive Rowfant Club which belongs among the Clubs, membership in which is noted in Who's Who in America, which includes among its members half a dozen millionaires, a former United States Senator, a former ambassador to France, and three gentlemen who have been decorated by the French Government. . . . Indeed in this liberal and progressive Northern city we get most of the things which make life worth living. . . . (*CWC*, p. 268)

Still, it is true that much of his economic pursuit was done for the sake of his family. Expensive silk dresses, the housekeeper in Fayetteville, the new house in a comfortable section of Cleveland, the constant summer vacations in the mountains, in Europe, and at American resorts—all were the sort of things which appealed to Susan and the daughters. In fact, one merely needs to read Helen Chesnutt's "Silas Lapham" sort of description of the new house (*CWC*, p. 48) to realize just how much this purchase appealed to the girls and to the feminine side of the family. Nor is it surprising that by the time the girls entered Cleveland's Central High School in 1893, Ethel and Helen were able to convince Charles that they felt it necessary to "have a dressmaker make our clothes." He concurred, and the result was soon "a procession of excellent dressmakers." (*CWC*, pp. 66-67)

That he acceded so easily to the "need" for dressmakers is quite predictable, for not only did he share many of his family's success-appearance values, but he was also very conscious of a man's duty to his family to provide as many comforts as he could. In turning down an 1889 offer to be George W. Cable's personal secretary and work with him on the Open Letter Club and its racial crusade, which was designed to bring the plight of Blacks to the mind and conscience of the American public, Chesnutt cited the loss of income such a change of jobs would entail and declared that "my duty to my family, and other considerations which would perhaps not interest you, constrain me to decline the offer.[11] (Letter to Cable, May 3, 1889) And two years later, when he was at a resort in Point Chautauqua, N.Y., he noted to his wife:

> When I see the cute and pretty and polite children, I want to send my own to dancing school, want to get rich and give them a chance to enjoy the brighter side of life. (*CWC*, p. 65)

And then years later, in a letter to Ethel, he contemplated his future as a writer and saw it in economic terms. After *The House Behind the Cedars* failed to come anywhere near Chesnutt's expectation of sales, he was now releasing *The Marrow of Tradition* and discussed his future in that light. Thus he noted to Ethel that

> You must join me in hopes for the success of my book, for upon its reception will depend in some measure whether I shall write, for the present, any more "Afro-American" novels; for a man must live and consider his family. (*CWC* p. 175)

Then, while he was initially "trying to decide whether he could afford to give up his business and devote himself to literature," he and Susan sat down and discussed the economic aspect of the matter because

> The income from his literary productions at that time could not possibly support the family, and this was always his first consideration. (*CWC* p. 118)

Of some interest here is the range of reasons why Chesnutt so highly valued money and property. Most importantly, as we have seen above, he valued wealth for the comfort and excitement it could bring to him and to his family. He also occasionally stressed the importance which wealth could have in favor of the Black race. In an unpublished letter to the *Christian Union* in 1879, he found himself discussing the progress of American

Blacks and saw it in the middle-class aspiration terms that Chesnutt himself so clearly subscribed to. As he states his position,

> The security of property encourages the acquisition of real estate, and as the colored people constitute the majority of the laboring class in the South, not only in the more menial employments, but in the mechanical trades, it is from them that the influential "middle class" will be largely recruited in the future. (Journal, April, 1879)

On another level twenty years later, he put similar thoughts in the mouth of one of his major characters in "The Web of Circumstance":

> "I tell yer dere ain' nothin' like proputy ter make a pusson feel like a man."[25]

In fact we hear his basic manifesto on this and on money in general stated in a May 16, 1913, letter of reply to one David Gibson:

> Your philosophy in the main is sound, although I would suggest that personal prosperity, the affairs personal to ourselves, are not necessarily trivial and foolishly selfish, for upon them depend very largely, in the scheme of things, our relations to others and to the race.

The echo here is obvious. For whether the terms dealt with race, family, or self, one-third of Chesnutt's basic nature believed that "life was given to us to enjoy, and if God will help me, I intend to enjoy mine." (Journal, July 16, 1878)

The question that now concerns us is how Chesnutt set out to accomplish his economic success, and the answer lies in the traditional bourgeois ethos of hard work, determination and thrift.

That Chesnutt was a hard worker was clear throughout his life. In describing his youth especially, his Journal is crammed with Franklinesque work-lists and plans for personal improvement.

This week has passed very well. I have made tremendous progress in algebra, almost finished Natural Philosophy, read *Universal Education*, and think it splendid. . . .

When I finish that *Elementary Algebra*, and try for a *Peck's Mechanics*. I would like to get a *Bryant and Stratton's Bookkeeping* but books cost a great deal of money. I think when I finish my algebra, I shall take up Latin grammar again, for if I have the remotest idea of studying medicine, a knowledge of Latin is very essential. . . . (August 13, 1875)

I am home again. I shall follow my inclinations during the summer and devote myself to study. I have formed a general plan—one hour daily to Latin, one to German, and one to French, and one to literary composition. I shall continue to practice shorthand. An hour's work in the garden, miscellaneous reading, and tending to the baby will occupy the remainder of my time. In this manner, I expect to pass a very pleasant summer. . . . (Summer, 1879)

I shall continue my studies as best I can. . . . I shall read Latin, French, and German, with history, biography, and shorthand thrown in for lighter hours; composition and music shall not be forgotten; domestic economy, practically applied to housekeeping, will fill up another portion of my time, and with these friends and companions, silent but eloquent, I shall try to spend the summer pleasantly, and with profit. (June 25, 1880)

Accompanying this dedication to determined self-improvement was the fact that he very clearly recognized this bourgeois way of planning and the role it played in his basic nature—both mental and physical.

There are just two courses in life open to me. One is the pursuit of pleasure; the other is mental activity, constant employment of the mind and purpose toward some good end,

—culture, mental and spiritual. Neither my tastes nor habits incline me to seek more animal enjoyments. . . . My mind is so constituted that it cannot remain idle. (May 29, 1880)

Thus, as he planned his trip North for the opportunities that lay there, "work, work, work!" was the dominant and forceful theme. In later years, the same rigor and the same hard-work approach governed most of Chesnutt's time. Unlike Susan, who was very much socially oriented, he very rarely gave in to his own impulses for social relaxation. By 1897, he was both working as a stenographer and writing almost around the clock: "His short-hand business was very absorbing; his writing had to be done at night and on Sundays." (*CWC*, p. 76) And two years later we find him working equally hard, socializing only when Susan refused to go out alone.

> So Chesnutt, not yet forty years old, worked at his business in the daytime; worked at his writing late into the night, when the house was not filled with company; kept Neddie up to the mark in his studies; accompanied Susan to those social functions to which she refused to go alone; enjoyed the developing personality of his little daughter Dorothy, and wrote frequently to his other daughters. (*CWC*, p.88)

Such a full list of activities at age forty echoes nicely the same list of planned activities followed in his earlier years.

Perhaps strongest proof of such rigor is to be seen in the later condition of Chesnutt's physical health. As early as 1882 he had realized the potential danger of overwork when he wrote in his Journal, of March 7, 1882, "Can work procure success? Then success is mine. My only fear is that I may spoil it all by working too much." And, in time, the overwork did catch up to him as several major strokes overwhelmed him.

In 1910 he suffered his first stroke, the effects of which lasted through 1911. Ten years later he suffered a second "serious ill-

ness" which "left him with his health impaired." From that time
on "his activities were greatly curtailed." Seven years after that,
in 1927, a third serious illness struck him as the "unsparing ex-
penditure of energy in his younger days was taking its toll."
(*CWC*, pp. 238-297) He died five years later in 1932.

Nor was Charles the only one hurt by the Chesnutt family's
approach to work and to ambitious aspirations. In her senior
year at Smith, his daughter Helen began to experience severe
headaches and eye trouble, and, as her elder sister and roommate
Ethel wrote of it to him, the cause of this was the same bourgeois
rigor which was to cause Charles's first stroke nine years later.
Ethel's letter is remarkably explicit on this point.

> Helen is in a frightful state; she has had headaches nearly
> every day lately, and today she is in despair. If you want
> your Helen a total nervous wreck, just keep on in the way
> you are going. She is too proud, too ambitious, to act sensi-
> bly. She cannot keep on with the work; every time she does
> anything of any consequence she collapses with one of these
> headaches. . . . The girl is on the verge of nervous prostra-
> tion and no one seems to realize it. At home you are all
> under a fearful nervous strain all the time; you do too many
> unnecessary things and you talk and discuss too much, and
> Helen has got to have rest somewhere. She has got to stop,
> and future questions can be settled at future times; if she
> comes home she must not be troubled with questions as to
> what she shall do in the future. . . . Please try to realize
> these things. She cannot keep on at college at present. Helen
> Chesnutt needs complete rest of mind and eyes for a long
> time and I propose to step in now, and see that she gets it.
> Pride and ambition are all right within certain limits but
> I don't want them to kill or ruin Helen. I should imagine
> from all I hear of you that you had better call a halt on
> yourself, too, or you will collapse. No matter how much will,
> ambition, pride you have, you can't strain Nature very long;
> something will smash somewhere and you are living too
> strenuously. (*CWC*, pp. 166-167)

Chesnutt was very much aware of his drive for success, and it is clear from his Journal that he was strongly determined to pursue this course in life as energetically as possible.

As early as 1878 he realized that the South with its many restrictions on a Black man was no place for him, and he characteristically decided to assert his independent nature and seek his success in the North, where he strongly committed himself to "live down the prejudice" and "crush it out." Related to this strong dedication to success was an equally strong sense of self-reliance, traditionally a strong, "aspiring" American virtue. In Chesnutt, this self-reliance was largely the result of his lonely and severe course of self-instruction as a youth. Having "no learned professor or obliging classmate to construe the hard passages and work the difficult problems," he tells us of his studies, "I have perservered until I solved them myself. (Journal, October 16, 1878) And, along with such self-reliance, there developed a definite self-confidence to support his determination. "I am confident that I can succeed," he notes in his Journal, as he discusses his plans to become a writer. "My three months vacation is before me after the lapse of another three, and I shall strike for an entering wedge in the literary world, which I can drive in further afterwards," he noted.

> "Where there's a will etc," and there is certainly a will in this case. (March 20, 1881)

Furthermore, lest we think that this desire motivated Chesnutt only to literary success in those early days, the October, 1900, issue of the *State Normal Magazine* in Greensboro, N.C., is a significant testament to the contrary. In an article on "The History of Shorthand Writing In North Carolina," written because the college "devotes much attention to preparing young women to positions of stenographers and reporters," a whole page is given to Chesnutt as "one who is entitled to a place in the foremost row in shorthand work of native writers up to the end of the century." As the article continues, we learn that "Mr. Chesnutt has reported many important conventions" and that "until his retirement from his business in 1899 to devote himself to literary work, he conducted a reporting bureau through which was done most of the business of the state and federal courts in the city of Cleveland, and its vicinity." More impressively, we find that "Mr. Chesnutt served two terms as president of the Ohio State Stenographers' Association."[26] In summary, it is clear that this determination to rise was a major force in all of his activities.

Having seen how the middle-class concepts of hard work and determination ruled both the writer and stenographer in Chesnutt, we also need to note how his industrious acquisition of wealth was complemented by a thrifty concern for retaining as much of it as possible. "He was making money and saving much of it," (*CWC*, p. 76) Helen noted by 1897, and this was in direct conflict with his own enjoyment of basic self-indulgences—and in mortal combat with the heavily socializing and spending natures of his wife Susan, and the girls.

We see this thrift and this conflict expressed in his many letters to his daughters at Smith, where they had asked to go for their college education. Though he had expected to send them to Western Reserve in Cleveland and now realized that "Smith would be far more expensive" and though he himself wanted to accumulate enough savings to be able to "give up business and devote himself entirely to literature," (*CWC*, p. 70) he nevertheless let them enroll. At the same time, however, his letters to them dramatized the concern he had for the money they were spending. Hardly a letter went out from him in which he did not inject some plea for economy.

In the early days of their college experience, his letters to them were fillled with allusions to the need for thrift:

> Write me all the interesting things and take care of yourselves, and be economical.

I am quite willing to see you properly started off, and have you keep up with the fair average standard of the place. Of course, you cannot compete in expenditures with the daughters of the rich, of whom I suppose there are at least a few there. The expense account you send me is not bad; I shall expect you to keep up the custom. . . . These letters are to you and Helen jointly; be good girls, be economical. . . .

We are all glad to know that you and Ethel are enjoying yourselves, but I trust you will not forget the serious side of it all. My primary object in sending you up there, at some personal sacrifice on my part and your mother's I will assure you, was that. . . .

I think you labor under a misapprehension as to all the Cleveland girls there being the daughters of rich parents; some of them I know are the daughters of professional and business men who work as hard for what their daughters spend as I do. (*CWC*, pp. 81-83)

Even after this initial onslaught, subsequent letters sporadically returned to the eternal theme:

Send me a memorandum of the amount necessary to clean off the slate and bring you home for Christmas. I haven't begun to draw any considerable revenue from my writings yet, so do not touch me any harder than necessary. (*CWC*, p. 125)

The reviews of the new book *The House Behind the Cedars* are coming in, and are very favorable. . . . If this keeps up, the book will be a genuine success, and my next book a howling success. . . .

I do not, however, expect to get rich out of it, and I therefore have not sent a great deal extra in the check I enclose

herewith. I'm afraid you are "Spread"-ing too much. I guess
you can worry along with this awhile. (*CWC*, pp. 154-155)

Nor was all this counseling on thrift lost on his daughters, or
the family at large. Thus Helen, desiring to teach in Washington,
D.C., instead of coming home to Cleveland after graduation,
points out that she can earn more in Washington than she can
by part-time teaching in Cleveland. And she clinches her argument by noting how

> You and Mama are always talking about the need of
> saving money and economizing; therefore I do not see the
> sense of your undertaking to support me for another year.
> (*CWC*, pp. 164-165)

When his only son, Edwin, was graduated from Harvard and
went to Europe to repair his health and escape America's pernicious racism, he too received correspondence stressing economy
and thrift. Thus, after encouraging Edwin to "Keep your health
always first in mind" because "It is that for which I sent you
abroad," Chesnutt concluded the thought on the usual note:

> Have as good a time as you like, within the limits of strict
> economy, remembering that I am not carrying you, but
> merely boosting you along. . . .(*CWC*, p. 213)

So ingrained was this approach in Chesnutt's outlook that we
even find it in a letter from him to Susan in 1915, when they
were both in their late 50s and hardly to be confused with spend-
thrift teenagers.

> I have your letter of October 10. I cannot say it was un-
> expected. I quite appreciate that life is expensive, and have
> no doubt that you have spent your money wisely and I hope
> you have gotten value for it. I certainly have given value for
> it, in good work. (*CWC*, pp. 264-265)

Chesnutt himself was not a lavish spender, though he did enjoy purchasing basic comforts and luxury items. But this was not a dominant part of his nature. It is characteristic, then, that on a 1900 trip to Boston, his letter to Susan in Cleveland noted that "The Touraine is a 'swell' hotel, *so* I may not stay here long . . . ." (*CWC*, pp. 144-145; italics mine) And a full dozen years later, while touring Paris with Helen, he again wrote to Susan that the "Continental is a fine and expensive hotel, *but* Helen wanted to stop here and enjoys it very much." (*CWC*, pp. 254-255; italics mine)

Clearly, then, economizing was a very strong part of Chesnutt's basic nature, just as acquiring money lay near the heart of his concept of "success." Both these aspects of his nature were so obvious that they were referred to by W.E.B. DuBois in his 1903 article in *The Booklovers Magazine* about "The Advance Guard of the Race." Selecting the ten most eminent Negroes in America at the time, DuBois set out to present them in as favorable a light as possible in order to dispel white America's "ignorance of the work of black men." Yet even here we find that DuBois feels compelled (with, perhaps, a touch of snide acidity) to discuss Chesnutt's acquisitive interests that came before his desire to write or crusade.

> Here in America three artists have risen to places of recognized importance—Dunbar, the poet; Chesnutt, the novelist; and Tanner, the painter.
>
> Widely different are these men in origin and method. Dunbar sprang from slave parents and poverty; Chesnutt from free parents and thrift; while Tanner was a bishop's son. To each came his peculiar temptation—to Dunbar the blight of poverty and sordid surrounding; to Tanner the active discouragement of men who smiled at the idea of a Negro wanting to paint pictures instead of fences; and to Chesnutt the temptation of money making—why leave some thousands of dollars a year for scribbling about black folk?[27]

As we see, Chesnutt's propensities were as clear to his contemporaries as they are to the retrospective historian today. He was the product of American middle-class society in a period that strongly stressed material values. Hearing the American success story's call, the middle-class man in Chesnutt answered.

Chapter III

Chesnutt's Basic Nature: Isolattoe

Intellectual Isolattoe

To understand the career and writing of Chesnutt, we need to delve more deeply into his basic nature and interests. To begin with, he was an intellectual—a man concerned with ideas and thoughts both for their immediate value in the tangible world and for the companionship and link they offer to a higher, better world. And, as an intellectual, he suffered the basic ostracism and isolation that all intellectuals and artists face, which in some ways drove him even more into his own privately created world of books and thoughts.

As historians today, we find it rather easy to see how this side of Chesnutt's nature was so fully nurtured and developed. From the very beginning his mother "endeavored to fill his heart with fine ideals and lofty principles, to imbue his mind with the spirit of courage and high endeavor," essentially so that he "should become a scholar and a gentleman." (*CWC*, p. 3) Thus he was a pupil-teacher at fourteen and well-read and scholarly at sixteen, deciding eruditely in his Journal, after a fruitless search for a summer teaching job, that "I ought to make 'Nil desperandum' my motto." (July 3, 1824) By the time he was twenty, he told his Journal "I want to be a scholar" (January 15, 1881) and even pictured his ideal world in these terms, asserting that "If all the men who have a high ideal could reach it, the world would be full of scholars and saints." (Journal, July 21, 1881) Significantly enough, he received the principalship of the Fayetteville Normal School in 1881 largely because the Commission of Education in Raleigh also realized that he was a "scholar and gentleman." (Journal, February 27, 1881)

In his own early activities, Chesnutt clearly showed a tremendous interest in books and reading. Even as a nine-year-old boy, "every moment that Charles could spare from his busy life was spent in browsing in the bookstore, and every cent that he could call his own he spent in buying second-hand books." (*CWC*, p. 6) His absorption into this world soon became profound, as we find whole chapters from "*A Handbook for Home Improvement*, published by Fowler and Wells, New York" (July 1, 1874) and "Dr. Todd's invaluable Student's Manual" (October 7, 1878) copied verbatim into his Journal.

More significantly, we find in his Journal that all of his early stories and poems show a strong dependence on book-learned situations, descriptions, and dialogue. "Lost in a Swamp," for example, "my first real attempt at literature," is complete with croaking frogs, howling wolves, and "gloomy reflections" as a first-person narrator verbally shudders his way through the experience of being "Lost in a Swamp." (August 14, 1874) "Frisk's First Rat," the story of young kitten's triumph in seeking out and and killing a large rat, Chesnutt's second story, is also bookishly artificial in trying to capture dramatic effect from the "literary" world where "His breast heaved . . . his eye flashed fire" and where "in his bosom burned a desire to distinguish himself" and achieve a "glorious victory" over a "fallen foe." (August 23, 1874) Likewise, Chesnutt's third story, "A Storm at Sea," is equally encumbered by a reliance upon book-learned dialogue and identification. (August 25, 1874)

By 1881 Chesnutt was so at home in books that he read "King Henry the Sixth" to relax on a night when he was "too lazy" to do anything else. (Journal, December 31, 1881) Yet perhaps the ultimate proof that Chesnutt was tremendously engrossed in books both early in and throughout his life is to be found in the description of his home in his basically autobiographical, final novel, *The Quarry*. Written when he was seventy, it seems reasonable to infer that, in its autobiographical dependence upon setting, Chesnutt would select those elements in his home for which he most wanted to be remembered; if this assumption is true, it is no accident that the library of Senator Brown is that part of the house which received the most elaborate and detailed description.[1]

As well as being a book lover, Chesnutt was also a person who enjoyed thought *per se* and the very process of thinking. Those rigorous study schedules which were cited above represented both a Franklinesque determination to prepare for success and an intellectual's love of that preparation as an end in itself. Chesnutt himself saw this intellectual energy as basic part of his nature. On one level, as he discussed it in his Journal, this seems to have been a sort of flighty mental wandering in his youth

> I have a fatal propensity for building air castles—"Aerial Architecture" you might call it—a fault very common to youth. (summer, 1879)

Its existence on a more profound level, however, is our major concern here. As Chesnutt analyzed himself in that same Journal entry, he noted that "My mind is so constituted that it cannot remain idle," and "is always active"—so much that its "activity is sometimes burdensome, and at times I long for some means of escaping from my own thoughts." In a June 5, 1890, letter to George Washington Cable, Chesnutt reiterated this same awareness of his constant intellectual energy, especially when it contemplated the contemporary American racial scene:

> Pardon my references to myself—they are not meant to be egotistical, but when I first began to think, circumstances tended to make me introspective, self-conscious; latterly, I fear they have tended to make me morbid. It may be weakness, but my mental health and equipoise require constant

employment, either in working or in writing. If I should
remain idle for two weeks, at the end of that time I should be
ready to close out my affairs and move my family to Europe.

With this basic inclination towards thought, it is not surprising
to find that Chesnutt had specific theories of thought, believing
that "only debate, argument, interchange and criticism of opinion
can give one that skill and judgement which is necessary to select
the valuable and reject the worthless." (Journal, May 29, 1880)
It is in this light that we understand his August 11, 1903, letter to
Booker T. Washington in which he dissents from Washington's
position on the Black man's status in the South and notes the
"limitations" which seem to attend "You Southern educators
[who] are all bound up with some cause or other, devotion to
which sometimes unconsciously warps your opinion as to what
is best for the general welfare of the race." As he further noted
in the letter, what limits the mind in such cases is "the zeal of the
advocates, before whose eyes his client's case always looms up
so as to dwarf the other side." With this letter and his general
opinion on debate and argument in mind, it is not surprising to
learn in an October 18, 1911, letter to George E. Bellamy that a
major innovation which Chesnutt brought to Cleveland's Hiram
House meetings was to have each discussion after an evening lecture begin with someone who would "lead off in the opposition."
   Related to this interest in debate was Chesnutt's concern for
critical, analytical thought, and this lay at the heart of his writing
literary and social reviews throughout his life. Beginning with
his reviews of Booker T. Washington's *The Future of the American Negro* for the *Saturday Evening Post* and *The Critic* in 1889,
he was concerned with this line of analytical thought throughout
his life, on general as well as racial topics. Until his second serious illness in 1920, he enjoyed writing critical papers on such
topics as "Francois Villon, Man and Poet," "The Dairy of Philip
Hone," and "The Autobiography of Edward Baron Herbert of
Cherbury" as part of his membership in Cleveland's Rowfant
Club. Indeed his daughter noted even further how "When his

turn came to contribute to the Saturday night program he was delighted, and spent a great deal of time in research and in writing." (*CWC*, p. 289)

Yet perhaps the most important aspect of Chesnutt's intellectual nature was the ultimate realm to which it brought him. "Castles in the air" may have been where it started, but it soon assumed greater and more profound proportions.

> I hear colored men speak of their "white friends." I have no white friends. I could not degrade the sacred name of "friendship" by associating it with any man who feels himself too good to sit at a table with me, or to sleep at the same hotel. . . . I hope yet to have a friend. If not in this world, then in some distant future eon, when men are emancipated from the grossness of the flesh, and mind can seek out mind; then shall I find some kindred spirit, who will sympathize with all that is purest and best in mine, and we will cement a friendship that shall endure throughout the ages. (Journal, March 7, 1882)

At the conclusion of "The Web of Circumstance," Chesnutt postulated this same world of Platonic thought and ideals:

> Some time, we are told, when the cycle of years has rolled around, there is to be another golden age, when all men will dwell together in love and harmony, and when peace and righteousness shall prevail for a thousand years. God speed the day, and let not the shining thread of hope become so enmeshed in the web of circumstance that we lose sight of it; but give us here and there, and now and then, some little foretaste of this golden age, that we may the more patiently and hopefully await its coming!

This detached, intellectual view of the world was to have a major impact on Chesnutt's personal style of thought and writing. It gave him a tone and perspective of balance and moderating re-

straint, which essentially saw the world in philosophical, understanding tones. It is this perspective which marks so clearly Chesnutt's major works, even the conclusion of a bitter novel like *The
Marrow of Tradition.* Indeed, the way he softened his final
novel, *The Colonel's Dream,* is significant here, as he outlined
the process—and analyzed himself—in a June 29, 1904, letter to
Walter Hines Page.

> . . . as a matter of personal taste I shrink from the sor-
> did and brutal, often unconsciously brutal side of Southern
> life—as I should from the shady side of any other life.

As he continued, we can see just how much a sense of detachment
he desired to achieve when he suggested that

> If I can handle some of these things in a broad and sugges-
> tive way, without disgusting detail—if I could follow even
> afar off the Russian novelists of the past generation, who
> made so clear the condition of a debased peasantry in their
> own land, I might write a great book.

Having looked at some of the power and scope of Chesnutt's
intellectual nature, we come now to discuss a less positive result
of it. To a degree, Chesnutt's fundamental concern for ideas
deeply set him off from the rest of the people around him—both
white and Black; this, needless to say, had a profound effect on
him as a youth. Essentially this was why he left the South and
partially why he took to writing as a mode of self-expression, but
we shall discuss these points later. At this point the basic nature
of this separateness—and the loneliness it engendered—are our
major concerns.

The separateness itself was basically the result of the fundamental difference in interests and ways of thinking which often
characterizes the position of a rapid, educated mind in the midst
of a less educated, rural environment. When we realize further
that the South—both white and Black—was experiencing the

"most intellectually impoverished period in the history of the region,"[2] and that, as a Black man, Chesnutt was even more removed from organized intellectual communion because of rigid
segregation patterns, we can understand how isolated he really
was.

Describing his condition in the South of 1878, Chesnut pictured the world that faced all Southern—and especially Southern
Black—intellectuals of the time.

> I love music. I live in a town where there is some musical
> culture; I have studied and practised till I can understand
> and appreciate good music, but I never hear what little there
> is to be heard. I have studied German, and have no one
> to converse with me but a few Jewish merchants who can
> talk nothing but business. As to procuring instruction in
> Latin, French, German, or music, that is entirely out of
> the question. First-class teachers would not teach a "nig-
> ger," and I would have no other sort. (Journal, October 16,
> 1878)

Perhaps even more telling here, however, is the fact that Chesnutt's intellectual perspective and nature separated him just as
much from his fellow Blacks in the South as it did from the local
whites. In the summer of 1875, for example, he found himself
teaching in a rural Black community ten miles from Spartanburg, S.C. His experiences there reveal how very separate and
different from the local Blacks he found himself to be. His Journal of August 13 marks this ultimate recognition:

> Well! uneducated people are the most bigoted, supersti-
> tious, hardest-headed people in the world! These folks
> downstairs believe in ghosts, luck, horse shoes, cloud-signs,
> witches, and all other kinds of nonsense, and all the argu-
> ment in the world couldn't get it out of them.
> These people don't know words enough for a fellow to
> carry on a conversation with them. He must reduce his

phraseology several degrees lower than that of the first reader, and then all the reason and demonstration has no more effect than a drop of water on a field of dry wheat! "Universal Education" is certainly a much-to-be-wished-for, but, at present, little-to-be-hoped-for blessing.

One week later his difference in temperament and outlook was also impressed upon him.

This is the doggondest country I ever saw to teach in. They say they'll pay your board, and don't do it. They accuse you indirectly of lying, almost of stealing, eavesdrop you, retail every word you say. Eavesdrop you when you're talking to yourself, twist up your words into all sorts of ambiguous meanings, refuse to lend you their mules, etc. They are the most suspicious people in the world, good-sized liars, hypocrites, inquisitive little wenches, etc. I wouldn't teach here another year for fifty dollars a month!

This deep differentness, naturally, led to a strong feeling of isolation and loneliness, basically turning Chesnutt in on himself. Not only did he feel estranged from the people in his town and the less-educated rural Blacks, but he also felt cast off from his family as well, and it was at this point that his intellectual and literary interests became a solace for, as well as a cause of, his isolattoe estrangement. Indeed, this is the period that Helen later alluded to when she discussed "the warm rays of friendship for which his lonely heart yearned in the days of his youth in North Carolina." (*CWC*, p. 289)

It was while he was teaching near Spartanburg that his isolation became complete with the realization that even his family was not really close to him. No one wrote to him during the summer, and, as a result, he sought refuge in literature and his Journal. In one entry, in fact, he records lonely disappointment and quotes Robert Burns in what amounts to a lyrical release of his loneliness.

Today will be the last day of the third week of my school. I wish 'twas the last day of the eighth week. Yesterday Louis went to town for me, and didn't get a letter. And I have written Pa one, Lewis one, Mr. Harris, Miss Vic, Mrs. Schenck, etc. and not one has written me.

Well, if nobody writes to me, I guess I can get along without.

> I'll be merry and free,
> I'll be sad for naebody,
> If naebody care for me,
> I'll care for naebody.
>
> —Burns (July 30, 1875)

So great did the gulf grow that by the summer of 1880 Chesnutt was able to see himself as an isolattoe "prophet," especially estranged from his own family.

"A prophet is not without honor save in his own country and among his own people," and I get a great deal more of encouragement from others than from home folks. The reason I suppose is that home folks cannot appreciate my talents, cannot understand my studies, nor enter into my feelings. (Journal, June 25, 1880)

Likewise, six months later, he not only used similar "prophet" terms, but noted also how complete his isolation was.

I occupy here a position similar to that of Mahomet's Coffui. I am neither fish, flesh, nor fowl—neither "nigger," "white," nor "buckrah". Too "stuck-up" for the colored folks, and, of course, not recognized by the white. (Journal, January 3, 1881)

To a great extent, this growing sense of intellectual isolation had two major effects. First, it led him to begin and then continue his Journal and writing as a mode of self-expression and release. Secondly, it led him back once more into the world of books as an escape now, whereas formerly it had been more a source of enjoyment and knowledge.

This security and private warmth of his books in the face of general isolation interestingly supplied the dominant tone of his Journal's brief sketch, "My Books," of October 16, 1878.

> Have you ever been in my library? Have you read any of my books? They are many, and in a large apartment. If you should travel day and night, by the swiftest means of conveyance, for three whole months you could only make the circuit of its floor.
>
> As for the books, you would not have time to look at them. You might see some of their handsome covers of gilt edges as you hurried past, but you could have no idea of their contents.

Though he was describing a place that was still separate from the rest of the world, what is significant here is that the perception of that place was one of warmth and snugness rather than lonely isolation. This, in effect, was what literature and books offered to the early Chesnutt. In fact, he made this point even clearer in a later Journal discussion of books.

> What a blessing is literature, and how grateful we should be to the publishers who have placed its treasures within reach of the poorest. Shut up in my study, without the companionship of one congenial mind, I can enjoy the greatest wits and scholars of England, can revel in the genius of her poets and statesmen, and by a slight effort of imagination, find myself in the company of the greatest men of earth. (March 7, 1882)

Finally, however, his library was not solace enough, so the result of his isolation became his desire to escape the whole Southern milieu altogether.

I get more and more tired of the South. I pine for civilization and companionship. I sometimes hesitate about deciding to go, because I am engaged in good work, and have
been doing, I fondly hope, some little good. But many reasons urge me the other way. . . . And I shudder to think
of exposing my children to the social and intellectual pro-
scription to which I have been a victim. (Journal, March 7,
1882)

Racial Isolattoe

At the same time that Chesnutt was intellectually separated
from those around him in his formative youth, he was racially
isolated as well—from both Blacks and whites. Most obvious
was his separation from Southern whites in the late nineteenth
century, and perhaps we only need mention once again the harsh
and violent discrimination so prevalent in that region at that
time. Equally important, though less predictable, was his separation from his fellow Blacks.

Much of this racial isolation was forced upon the young Chesnutt by his light color and the fact that he did not really fit into
any group in the South—especially with his intellectual interests
and accomplishments; and it is clear that he recognized and
deeply felt this social cleavage which was forced upon him. This
led him to lament directly in his Journal at age twenty-three how
he was "neither fish, flesh, nor fowl"; we can feel the sense of
estrangement which the position placed upon him. We have
already noted several personal experiences in rural South Carolina. A Journal entry from the same period is especially note-
worthy in establishing racial as well as educational grounds for
this estrangement. Upon arriving near Spartanburg, Chesnutt
was impressed by the very strong hostility shown by the dark
Blacks in the area to a little eight-year-old mulatto girl "because
she was yellow." (Journal, June 7, 1875) It is probable that the
light color of Chesnutt's own skin called forth a similar reaction
in the same rural Blacks.

This separation was forced upon Chesnutt as a youth. But it

is clear that he eventually chose and staked out a position of nonracial "isolation" for his mature life, and it is important to examine the reasons for this choice.

One might assume that this choice stemmed from social and economic grounds, as Chesnutt presumably saw that his light skin and literary.talent might aid his chances of success in American society if left free from racial prejudice. Only minimal support can be found for this interpretation, however. On the one hand we have Chesnutt's Journal entry of July 31, 1875, when, at the tender age of seventeen, he first realized the possibilities of escaping racial prejudice altogether through his skin color. As he noted in that entry,

> Twice today, or oftener, I have been taken for "white." At the pond this morning one fellow said he'd "be dammed if there was any nigger blood in me." At Coleman's I passed. On the road an old chap, seeing the trunks, took me for a student coming from school. I believe I'll leave here and pass anyhow, for I am as white as any of them.

But it is important to note that Chesnutt never seriously considered this possibility.

More support can be found for an economic interpretation of Chesnutt's isolattoe position, at least in his early years of writing. His first book, *The Conjure Woman*, was announced and advertised without any mention of Chesnutt's race, a fact which he, himself, discussed in detail several years later. Related to this understanding of Chesnutt's motives is the fact that he was clearly aware of the economic implications which racial identification would have for a Black author during that period. It was for this reason that as far back as 1891, in discussing the possible publication of *Rena Walden and other Stories* and after stipulating his own background as "an American of acknowledged African descent," Chesnutt observed in a September 8, 1891, letter to Houghton, Mifflin Company that

> I should not want this fact to be stated in the book, nor advertised, unless the publisher advised it . . . because I do

not know whether it would affect its reception favorably or unfavorably, or at all.

Equally explicit was a letter he wrote to Mrs. S. Alice Haldeman five years later on February 1, 1896. As he noted,

> Colored people are sometimes sensitive about advertising the fact of their color, and also labor under the impression that it would interfere with their literary success, and may not therefore make the fact known in every instance, even to their publishers.

Whatever weight we place on these letters, it is undeniably clear that Chesnutt's race became widely known to the literary world at large with William Dean Howells' review of "Mr. Charles W. Chesnutt's Stories" in 1900, and at no time did Chesnutt try to obscure or repress this fact, either at the time of the review or thereafter. In fact, as we look back on his earlier correspondence with George Washington Cable and Houghton, Mifflin Company we see further proof that he was completely explicit as to his race in introducing himself to both these major literary connections, alluding directly to his "ties of blood" in his initial (Spring, 1889) letter to Cable and to his "acknowledged African descent" in his first (September 8, 1891) correspondence with the Houghton, Mifflin firm.

Despite these two possible interpretations of Chesnutt's choice, it seems clear that his sense of himself as a unique, non-racial individual was neither a social nor economic decision. It was, ultimately, a philosophical and personal position. There was in him a profound sense of self and a deep desire to become a unique, unstereotyped individual—a desire, in short, to become a man. "I will live down the prejudice," he told his Journal on October 16, 1878; "I will crush it out. I will show to the world that a man may spring from a race of slaves. . . ." As he stated in his Journal even more directly three years later,

> I have the greatest desire to be good—to become a *man* in the highest sense of the word. (July 21, 1881)

Related to this desire for unique, individual fulfillment, also
went the desire to be judged always by the highest and most
demanding standards. This is what he felt he owed himself;
simultaneously, it was how he sought to prove himself to society
as well. In his initial letter to Houghton, Mifflin Company, for
example, he stated two reasons why he thought his race should
not be disclosed at that time should *Rena Walden and other
Stories* be published. His first reason, as we have seen above,
was largely pragmatic. His second reason, however, "because
I would not have the book judged by any standard lower than
that set for other writers," went far deeper into his artistic sense
of himself and shows us just how much he was concerned about
developing a strong, individual artistic integrity. "If some of
these stories have stood the test of admission into *The Atlantic,*"
he continued, "I am willing to submit them all to the public on
their merits."

In a similar vein, it seems quite likely that Chesnutt turned
down a chance to be an associate editor of Albion Tourgee's
fledgling magazine, *The Basis, a Weekly Magazine of Citizenship*, in 1895 simply because it was offered to him on a racial
basis. Earlier Chesnutt had turned down a similar offer from
Tourgee in 1893 on the economic basis that "it could not pay me
for giving up my business."[15] (Letter to Tourgee, November 27,
1893) Now, in this second offer, another note may have crept in.
Chesnutt's declining letter itself is lost to us today, but we do
have Tourgee's letter responding to Chesnutt's negative decision,
and that letter develops a rather patronizing tone and thesis.

> No doubt what you say in explanation of the colored
> peoples' course is entirely correct . . . It seems to me need-
> ful that they should embrace every chance to acquire white
> association—become familiar to white peoples' thought as
> operative, business, literary, and every other sort of associ-
> ates. I think it would have been worth almost everything
> to have had a colored Associate Editor on The Basis, &c, &c,
> for the colored people, I mean. (Letter to Chesnutt, Sep-
> tember 5, 1895)

Though Tourgee obviously meant well, we can imagine Chesnutt's reaction to this view of himself as a token, nametag "colored Associate Editor." Add to this tasteless proposal the fact that "for the colored people, I mean" was a scribbled-in afterthought, its black ink contrasting sharply with the typewriter print which conveyed the rest of the letter, and it is not hard to guess that this sort of feeling towards Chesnutt on Tourgee's part was one of the major factors that kept the individualistic and antiracial Chesnutt from even considering the offer.

At the same time that Chesnutt sought unique nonracial identity and worth on a personal basis, he sought it on a social and philosophical basis as well, seeking to give the concept currency among whites and Blacks alike. He consequently made it a life-long point not only to attack racial segregation by whites (which, of course, lay at the heart of his writing and social involvement) but to discourage as well various sporadic attempts by Blacks to solidify and develop their own sense of "bloc" racial identity.

As he saw it in a social light, "the current doctrine of race integrity, which was then being preached assiduously to the Negro," (*CWC*, p. 210) was just as bad as that racial separation instigated by the whites, for it was working against all that America stood for. In fact, this new Black racialness, as Chesnutt saw it, was often reinforcing the white racism which was so prevalent in the country at that time. "We are told that we must glory in our color and zealously guard it as a priceless heritage," he noted in addressing the Boston Literary and Historical Association in 1905.

> Frankly I take no stock in this doctrine. It seems to be a modern invention of the white people to perpetuate the color line. It is they who preach it, and it is their racial integrity which they wish to preserve—they have never been unduly careful of the purity of the black race. . . .
>
> Most other people who come to this country seek to lose their separate identity as soon as possible and to become Americans with no distinguishing mark. . . . Are we to

help the white people to build up walls between themselves
and us, to fence in a gloomy back yard for our descendents
to play in?[3]

And it was with this same reasoning that he sent the following
letter to Fred Moore, editor of *The New York Age,* on December
15, 1910:

> Replying to your letter under another cover, requesting
> my opinion concerning the proper method of celebrating the
> fiftieth anniversary of the freedom of the Negro in 1913, I
> hope you will not think me indifferent in matters pertaining
> to the welfare of the race, but in this town the Emancipation
> Proclamation is celebrated by the colored people every year,
> and I have sometimes thought that it might be well if they
> could forget that they were slaves, or at least give the white
> people a chance to forget it.

More profoundly, Chesnutt was philosophically convinced that
race was merely a surface aspect of man's character and worth.
As he explained his position in a discussion of the printing of
his first book, *The Conjure Woman*, he noted that

> Indeed, my race was never mentioned by the publishers in
> announcing or advertising the book. From my own view-
> point it was a personal matter. It never occurred to me to
> claim any merit because of it, and I have always resented the
> denial of anything on account of it.[4]

As he ultimately saw it,

> Why should a man be proud any more than he should be
> ashamed of anything for which he is not responsible? Manly
> self-respect based upon one's humanity, a self-respect which
> claims nothing for color and yields nothing to color, every
> man should cherish.[5]

Such was Chesnutt's fundamental understanding of himself and the world he sought around him: no groups, no colors, no artificial categories—only individual men.

CHAPTER IV

Chesnutt's Basic Nature: Social Crusader

General Idealist

As noted above, Chesnutt's major approach to life was individualistic, partially because it was the "American way" of Ben Franklin and Horatio Alger, partially because his education and social advantages set him off from those around him, and partially because the light color of his skin set him off even more, leaving him in his own eyes a racially unique individual. Yet, despite all this, he ultimately chose to be a Black spokesman and forceful representative of the race.

Throughout his life Chesnutt had always been an idealist, moralist, and educator, and so it was not too unexpected when he took up the role of Black spokesman in 1899 after having been an isolattoe for the first forty years of his life. On the one hand, there always was in him a strong sense of justice and an equally strong antipathy to injustice. As he evaluated himself in 1879, his temperament was "a *potpourri* of harmonies and discords," one half of which housed the attributes of the social crusader.

> A large degree of energy, perseverance, and fidelity. A quick conscience, and an instinctive aversion to anything mean or dishonest; a strong sense of justice, and a great susceptibility to wrong or prejudice in any shape. (Journal, Summer, 1879)

There was also a very strong sense of the moralist and educator in him, and these aspects eventually complemented his social conscience, determining in part the tone of his crusading and, to some extent, the didactic, literary medium.

On its least profound level, the moralist-educator approach meant that Chesnutt was concerned with respectability and its appearances, as outward signs of inner moral worth; supporting this are parts of his early Journal and several other parts of his personal writings.

The very first page of his Journal, in fact, shows us the importance of respectability to the sixteen-year-old Chesnutt. "I have been reading, 'A Handbook for Home Improvement,' published by Fowler & Wells, New York," he tells us in the opening sentence of the Journal, and he then proceeds to delve into the subject:

> It comprises "How to Write," "How to Behave," "How to Talk & How to do Business." It is a very good book and I shall proceed to copy a few paragraphs.[2] (July 1, 1879)

The admonitions that follow are interesting for the socially conscious mores that they represent. "The Daily Bath (To keep clean you must bathe frequently)." "The Feet (The feet are particularly liable to become offensively odoriferous, especially when the perspiration is profuse. Frequent washings with cold water with the occasional use of warm water and soap, are absolutely necessary to cleanliness.)" And even "Spitting"—all come in for detailed discussion by Fowler and Wells, and all are copied down with detailed adoration by the young Chesnutt.

Above all, the passages conclude, "Watch yourself carefully, and if you have any such habits break them up at once. These may seem little things, but they have their weight, and go far in determining the character of the impression we make upon those around us."

Of further interest along these lines is Chesnutt's evaluation of William Wells Brown's book, *The Negro in the Rebellion,* where somehow Chesnutt's professional scholarship is elbowed aside by his concern for respectable appearances.

I have skimmed *The Negro in the Rebellion* by Dr. Brown
and it only strengthens me in my opinion that the Negro is
yet to become known who can write a good book. Dr.
Brown's books are mere compilations and if they were not
written by a colored man, they would not sell for enough to
pay for the printing. I read them merely for facts, but I
could appreciate the facts better if they were well presented.
The book reminds me of a gentleman in a dirty shirt. You
are rather apt to doubt his gentility under such circumstances. I am sometimes doubtful of the facts for the same
reason—they make a shabby appearance. (Journal, March
17, 1881)

Significantly enough, it seems that this part of Chesnutt's nature was clearly recognized by his contemporaries—even as it
appeared outside the racial sphere where it obviously expended
most of its energy. Thus he notes in an August 14, 1898, letter to
Walter Hines Page that he received "compliments right and left
from the best people of Cleveland on the ethics . . . of 'The
Wife of His Youth'!" And, if the people of Cleveland saw it,
publishers saw it even more clearly.

In April, 1899, therefore, Chesnutt received a circular from the
"editorial rooms" of *The Youth's Companion.* Of greater interest was the letter that accompanied the circular, which asked
Chesnutt to contribute a story to *The Companion* because he
seemed so suited to that kind of writing.

May I ask whether you have ever thought of *The Youth's
Companion* as a medium for the publication of short
stories? Through the *Atlantic,* I have made the acquaintance
of your work, which must now win a wide recognition in
your volume. It is rather in such a story as "The Wife of His
Youth", however, than as the tales which have a supernatur-
al element that I have felt strongly the presence of many
qualities which would appeal to the Companion's multitude of readers.

Two years later, Chesnutt received a similar letter from Mrs. Belle K. Towne, managing editor of *Young People's Weekly* in Chicago. There is no telling how or where she heard of Chesnutt, but it is clear that she had an insight into the kind of moral and instructional writer he was.

> Mr. Charles W. Chestnut, [sic]
> Dear Sir:
> Will you not try us with a short story of about three thousand words in length. For a story that suits us of that length, we will pay $75.00, without waiting for issue. Young People's Weekly has a circulation of two hundred and thirty thousand. It goes straight into Christian homes and is read from one corner to the other by earnest young people. We want a story that will help a boy make a man of himself. (May 11, 1901)

There is no record that Chesnutt replied to this letter, but it is, of course, revealing that the letter saw Chesnutt's moral interest as the core of his literary personality.

Racial Crusader

We now need to see Chesnutt in the framework in which he was most forceful: moralizing and fighting against racial segregation in this country. Because he had lived in the South and suffered the anguishes and pain of racial hostility for most of his early life, it is not surprising to find that his moralist-educator approach to the world soon channeled itself into terms of racial justice as Chesnutt became a direct spokesman for all Black Americans.

The reasoning here is clear. As he wrote to Cable on May 3, 1889, after turning down the opportunity to work for Cable's crusading Open Letter Club, Chesnutt still hoped

to do what I can in the good cause of human rights, and
am not likely to grow lukewarm in it, for if no nobler motive
inspired me, my own interests and those of many who are
dear to me are at stake.

Chesnutt's own direct statements of his crusading interests are
equally clear. After declaring his desire to "go to the North"
where "I will live down the prejudice, I will crush it out," Chesnutt couched his next sentence in the altruistic tones that we have
come to recognize as the product of his idealistic nature and its
general desires to exalt his race and gain "the approbation of
God." (Journal, October 16, 1878) Six months later he felt once
more this crusading zeal and declared that "I will trust in God
and work," noting that the work "I shall undertake not for myself alone, but for my children, for the people with whom I am
connected, for humanity!" (Journal, April 23, 1879)

Needless to say, a social crusader is what he soon became. The
literary aspect of this crusading, an aspect that runs the spectrum
from letters and lectures to articles and stories, will be discussed
in detail later. In additon to this, Chesnutt's crusading led him
past the notepad and out of his library, into the streets and meetings of various racial, social and political organizations.

On the one hand, there was his interest in political affairs and
the concrete, tangible amelioration they offered the Freedman
after the Civil War. Influenced, perhaps, by the fact that his
father had been "county commissioner and justice of the peace
for Cumberland County" in the late 1860s, (*CWC*, p. 5) one
evening in April, 1880, Chesnutt found himself attending a Republican convention at the Market House in Fayetteville and
actually accepting the Republican nomination for town commissioner. Even though friends soon "spoke of my indiscretion"
and persuaded him to withdraw, (Journal, May 8, 1880) as early
as age twenty-two Chesnutt had thereby made it clear that he
was very much interested in some tangible commitment to redress social wrongs.

Even as a Republican sympathizer, however, Chesnutt was too much the intelligent, independent thinker to commit himself blindly to a party label. Therefore, while men like Frederick Douglass were praising Garfield in 1881 for "his just and generous intentions" towards "the colored people" and for his fundamental position as "a wise and patriotic statesman, and a friend of our race,"[1] Chesnutt was detached and critical enough to note in his Journal Garfield's "scanty recognition of the claims of colored office-seekers" and, from an equally objective perspective, to see himself as "a Republican on principle" but one who believed in remaining uncommitted and supporting the party that offered the most to Blacks. (May 4, 1881) Even though he never went further in physically pursuing a political post, his interest in local and national politics remained strong. As late as 1904 he was in a position to receive a September 17 letter from the editor of *The Boston Colored Citizen*, asking him to "let me have a few lines from you" for a pre-election symposium on "the Negro's duty to the Republican Party in the present campaign." Equally significant is the fact that he quickly replied to Alexander's request and enclosed a statement for the symposium. (October 11, 1904)

Perhaps more imprtant than Chesnutt's sporadic activity with political parties was his involvement with a variety of racial organizations that began to champion the Black man's cause at the turn of the century. This, more than anything else, showed his commitment to the race, as Chesnutt more and more became one of its spokesmen.

In some ways he was a pioneer in these various groups. One of the first organizations established by Negroes to influence the American public in their behalf was the Committee of Twelve for the Advancement of the Interests of the Negro Race. Formed in New York in 1904, with Booker T. Washington chairman and with members such as Hugh M. Browne, Archibald Grimke, T. Thomas Fortune and Kelly Miller, the aim of the Committee was "to turn the attention of the race to the importance of constructive, progressive effort, and the attention of the country to Negro successes" and "to correct the errors and misstatements concerning the progress and activities of the race, as well as to make known the truth regarding the acts of the white race affecting us"—all "with a view of perfecting a larger and more systematic effort in the unification of the race." When the first vacancy occurred in April, 1905, Chesnutt was unanimously elected to the Committee. (*CWC*, p. 197)

Characteristically, however, he spent some time discussing the goals and principles of the group before he accepted, asserting in a June 2, 1905, letter to Hugh M. Browne, the detachment and "individual intellect" perspective which he always sought. Nevertheless, despite some reservations about the group's containing men "whose views vary so widely as do the views of some of those on the committee," the social crusader in him triumphed over the isolattoe, and he merged his individuality with the group's corporate membership.

His participation in this group, however, was marginal; his subsequent correspondence with Chairman Washington shows that he was constantly defining his own position on the various problems on which the Committee took a stand.[2]

Similarly he was an early member of the National Association for the Advancement of Colored People as it developed in 1909 and 1910. When, in May, 1909, "a group of liberal-minded Americans who believed in democracy . . . called a conference at Cooper Union in New York City to discuss the status of the Negro and to formulate a plan to improve his positon," Chesnutt was urged to attend, but, perhaps symbolically, "pressure of business prevented him." (*CWC*, p. 231) The result of this conference was the formation of an organization called the National Negro Committee, which became the NAACP one year later. Chesnutt was immediately attracted to this organization and became an active member. He addressed the group while it was still the National Negro Committee in May, 1910, on "The Effect of Disfranchisement in the Courts"[3] and soon became socially active in organizing the Cleveland branch of the NAACP. In 1912 he further became a Cleveland member of its Advisory Committee. (*CWC*, pp. 239, 240, 271) The same year he was on the National Board of Directors.[4] In 1927 he had an honorarium for talented young writers named after him by W.E.B. DuBois and the NAACP's Magazine, *The Crisis;*[5] in 1928 he received the organization's highest tribute, the Spingarn Medal, in recognition of his pioneering work as a literary artist and his distinguished career as a public-spirited citizen. (*CWC* p. 302)

Even as he willingly belonged to this organization, however, Chesnutt's position during the period—and throughout his life— was always that of an individualistic, self-defining intellectual. Thus, even while he was constantly differing with Booker T. Washington and the Committee of Twelve throughout the early 1900s, he never joined the chorus of Black voices publicly attacking Washington throughout the period.

In 1901 he replied to the suggestion of William Monroe Trotter, editor of the *Boston Guardian,* that he attack Washington's policies and actions. Chesnutt's answering letter was a model reply of the detached, balanced intellectual seeking his own personal middle ground. He even couched his detachment in artistic terms:

> I note your various suggestions to myself, mostly with reference to Mr. Washington. I feel quite as deeply interested as any one can in maintaining the rights of the Negro, North, South and everywhere; but I prefer, personally, to do it directly, rather than by attacking some one else. . . .
>
> I could not have followed his course; neither do I see my way to adopt the extreme positon you have taken. His school has accomplished a great deal of good; I have been there and seen it. I am willing to approve the good, and where I disagree with him, to preach the opposite doctrine strenuously. But I aim to be a literary artist, and acrimonious personalities are the death of art. (Dec., 28, 1901)

The final sentence of the letter perhaps expressed Chesnutt's positon best, as he concluded "With best wishes for the *Guardian*, and with the hope that we may all work together, *each in his own way*, for truth and justice. . . ."

Two years later, Chesnutt faced a similar suggestion, this time to join with Dubois in attacking Washington, and again Chesnutt chose an individualistic middle ground. Referring to a book of essays entitled *The Negro Problem* (published in 1903 by James Pott and Co. of New York and contributed to by such men as Chesnutt, DuBois, Washington, and Fortune), DuBois wrote to Chesnutt while the various articles were still in progress and suggested that Chesnutt directly write against Washington's policies. Said DuBois,

> Speak out in no uncertain tones—we've got to stop Mr. Washington's heresies and we might as well get at the unpleasant task. (May 5, 1903)

Chesnutt, however, dismissed the suggestion and treated his topic of "Disfranchisement" completely on his own terms.

Later in that year, Chesnutt received an October 11, 1903, letter from Trotter's *Boston Guardian,* stating in somewhat inflated terms that "Boston and New England invites Cleveland [sic] first citizen in the person of C. W. Chesnutt to come" and give a notable reception for "Messrs. Trotter and Martin," who were to be "liberated" November 7.[6] The underlying purpose was not only to welcome back these victims of "treason" who "have stepped from their obscurity into their immortality," but also to make a definite "attestation of the fact that educated men of our race like yourself are unitedly opposed to Bookerism in politics." There is no evidence that Chesnutt ever replied or attended.

Of most dramatic interest to us here is Chesnutt's reaction to another proposed attack on Washington in 1910. Already a member of the General Committee of the NAACP, he nevertheless refused to follow the association's lead in signing a protest entitled "Race Relations in the United States," written by Du-Bois and others to "repudiate Washington's utterances," made while Washington was traveling that year in England and Europe. Partially for social, partially for organizational, and basically for personal reasons (i.e. dislike of personal animosity and emotional "violence"), Chesnutt's reply to DuBois again declined to join the attack and sign the protest.

> . . . In view of the very close relations of members of my family with Tuskegee—my son is in Mr. Washington's office, one of my daughters has taught there for several summers, and another was Mrs. Washington's visitor for a number of weeks this year—and in view further of the fact that I am a nominal member of the Committee of Twelve and signed my name to Mr. Washington's latest appeal for an increase of the Tuskegee endowment, I question whether it would be quite in good taste for me to sign what in effect is in the nature of an impugnment of Mr. Washington's veracity, or at least which it would be only human in him to look upon in the light of a personal attack.

In fact, Chesnutt conveyed his position even more fully in the final paragraph of his long letter:

> . . . There are many things yet to be done; some of them, of which Mr. Washington has fought shy, the NAACP seeks to accomplish. There is plenty of room and plenty of work for both. I make no criticism of any of the gentlemen who have signed the appeal, but personally I should not, as I say, like to "pitch into" Mr. Washington. (November 21, 1910)

A member of racial organizations he was; and, in the case of the NAACP, an active, lifetime member he was. Yet, even when he clearly accepted the role of Black spokesman that such membership reinforced, Chesnutt was always himself first, and an official "Black spokesman" second.

For this reason, Chesnutt's greatest societal efforts were achieved as an individual spokesman. This was, of course, most true of his writings; yet, it was also the case with his direct social action. As a private citizen and member of the Cleveland bar, for example, he wrote to Senator Theodore E. Burton of Ohio, protesting the proposed "appointment of Judge Hook to the Supreme Bench" because of "an unfavorable and prejudiced decision of his in a 'jim crow' railroad case," and hoping that Burton would vote against confirmation. (December 10, 1912) One year later he undertook to fight the proposed anti-intermarriage bill before the Ohio House of Representatives. Again as an individual citizen, and as a court reporter who had accompanied and reported Mayor Newton Baker's campaign speeches in 1912, Chesnutt went to the Mayor's office to talk with Newton D. Baker and ask him to use his influence in support of the protest." (*CWC*, pp. 245-46, 257) He further sent a cordial letter to Mayor Baker several days after the interview. (April 3, 1913)

On a more local level, Chesnutt was also active. Also during 1913, Cleveland celebrated the Centennial of Perry's victory over the British in the Battle of Lake Erie. For this occasion, Chesnutt served as chairman of "the Committee of Colored Organizations" and prepared for the publicity department of the Centennial Committee an article discussing the part played by Black sailors and soldiers in the War of 1812. (*CWC*, p. 259) On an even more municipal level, he was instrumental in establishing and continuing a Social Settlement house in the Central Avenue area of Cleveland. As early as 1905, under the auspices of the Negro Board of Trade, he delivered a short address entitled "Does Central Avenue Need a Social Settlement House?" For the next nine years, however, "the colored people were poor and unable to finance such a project, and the wealthy white people were not sufficiently interested; so nothing was done about it." Then, in 1914, under Chesnutt's renewed impetus, the Men's Club of the Second Presbyterian Church took up the idea again, and the final achievement was a modern, philanthropically financed settlement house that later became an agency of the Community Fund in 1919 and ultimately attained national recognition as Karamu House, the name which it adopted some years later. (*CWC*, pp. 260-263)

When *The Birth of a Nation*, Thomas Dixon's filmed glorification of the Ku Klux Klan and vituperative slander of the American Black man, came on the American scene in 1915 and was to be shown to a group of young people under the auspices of Ohio's State Agricultural Department, Chesnutt wrote immediately to Governor Frank B. Willis, protesting its proposed showing "as part of the entertainment." (November 23, 1915) Two years later, when the movie attempted once more to gain the approval of Ohio's board of censors during World War I, Chesnutt wrote more forcefully and dramatically to the Secretary of Cleveland's Chamber of Commerce, Munson R. Havens, "as a member of the Chamber, and as a member of the Executive Committee of the local Branch of the National Association for the Advancement of Colored People." Noting that "The principal villain of the story, the would-be rapist, is portrayed as a colored captain in the Union Army," Chesnutt developed his argument for himself and "those on behalf of whom I speak."

> The colored people are loyal citizens, without perhaps a great deal of encouragement, in some quarters, to loyalty, indeed in spite of serious discouragement; but it seems to me and those on behalf of whom I speak, that such an insult to the national uniform when worn by men of color, as the public exhibition of such a picture as "The Birth of A Nation," which as a work of pictorial art is a superb and impressive thing, and all the more vicious for that reason, should not be permitted at this time, when all citizens should stand together to support the honor of the nation. (April 3, 1917)

As the years moved on, Chesnutt sporadically continued his personal career as individual spokesman for the race. He was

getting older now, and, after a stroke in 1910 and a serious illness in 1920, he had much less energy. Still, his sense of dedication to the racial cause continued.

Throughout the First World War, he and other Black leaders
such as Emmett J. Scott and James Weldon Johnson continually
investigated the harsh and unjust treatment of Negro soldiers in
Southern training camps (*CWC*, p. 275) and sought, as Chesnutt espressed it in a November 24, 1917, letter to Captain William R. Green of Camp Sheridan, Montgomery, Alabama, "to
promote improved conditions among the colored soldiers."
Later, in 1928, "Chesnutt once more took up the cudgels for the
Negro by appearing, on behalf of colored labor, before a Senate
Committee at Washington, against the Shipstead Anti-Injunc-
tion Bill," where, armed "with affidavits telling of the brutal
treatment of Negro workers by many unions," he made a strong
plea for Black labor. (*CWC*, p. 301)

Perhaps the most dramatic example of his continuing concern
about the race problem in America and about his role as spokesman is to be found in 1923, when Chesnutt was sixty-five and
far less active than before, He was deeply upset at Harvard University's attempt at that time to exclude Black students from its
dormitories and dining halls. When a flippant discussion of the
controversy appeared in a Cleveland paper, Chesnutt's letter
to Charles T. Henderson, editor of the *Cleveland Topics*, was
almost massive in its power, showing the same emotional fervor
which marked Chesnutt's most dramatic passages in *The Marrow
of Tradition*. It was restrained and gentlemanly, to be sure, as
his personal writing always was, but within that restraint it was
strong and almost savagely direct: the voice of a spokesman
still passionately at war with racial injustice and insensitivity
even at age sixty-five. After citing some of the more offensive
passages in the article, Chesnutt proceeded:

> If this utterance had emanated from a Florida "cracker"
> or a Georgia "red neck," or even an Alabama senator, I
> should not have been surprised; but from a man brought up
> in Cleveland, educated in the public schools where he went

to school with colored children, and with a mother such as yours, who was widely known as a generous and broad-minded woman, who to my personal knowledge has eaten in public with colored people, it came as a surprise, to say the least.

I really cannot understand the basis of your emotional turmoil, which is apparently so great that you cannot find decent language to express it. I suspected that you did not know what you were writing about, which I have verified by ascertaining that you are not a Harvard man. Colored students have always lived in the dormitories and eaten in the dining halls at Harvard; I have paid the bills of one of them and ought to know. The "living together" and "eating with white folks" involves no more intimacy than life in a hotel, and you know or ought to know that colored men are received as guests at some of the best hotels in Cleveland, that eight or ten of them are members of the City Club and eat in its dining room, and I have seen brown men eating in the sacred precincts of the Union Club, and at the University Club.

I am quite sure that had you had any such feeling against Jews, you would not have expressed it publicly in any such manner, nor, had you had a hundred subscribers whom you knew to be colored, would you have gone out of your way to insult them, if only as a matter of policy, to say nothing of good taste.

I shall not indulge in the childish gesture of saying "Stop my paper," since I have paid for it in advance, but I shall hereafter take it up with suspicion and qualify my admiration with reflection. (April 20, 1923)

It must have provided Chesnutt with some satisfaction to have the return letter from Henderson express his personal apology to Chesnutt for the "unpardonable stupidity of the 'smart' item"; and Chesnutt was assured that the particular columnist who had written the piece would be supervised thereafter (*CWC*, p. 295)

CHAPTER V

Contemporary Recognition
of Chesnutt

As a result of his literary and political involvement for the race, Chesnutt soon became clearly identified in the nation as a major Black spokesman. His willingness to accept and pursue this role is a major tribute to the social crusading which made up a large part of his basic nature; it is significant to note just how extensive this acknowledgement was.

By Literary Figures

To the outside, official world of literary critics, this recognition of Chesnutt as racial spokesman was especially rapid, since they found in him the first artistic Black voice in American prose literature and thus tended to note his social statements because they valued his literary talent. Without our running the gamut of critics and reviewers, perhaps just a brief look at one of the outstanding of this period, William Dean Howells, will suffice.

In May, 1900, Howells' appreciative article, "Mr. Charles W. Chesnutt's Stories," in *The Atlantic Monthly* contained the first and most extensive recognition of Chesnutt's talent as a writer. Referring most specifically to *The Conjure Woman* and "The Wife of His Youth," Howells's praise was generous and sincere, and celebrated in detail both Chesnutt's technical skill and his spontaneous imagination. And while Howells's appreciation was extensively of Chesnutt as an "artist" *per se*, it is important to us here that Howells also clearly recognized Chesnutt's racial identity and source of material. "He sees his people very clearly, very justly," Howells noted, "and he shows them as he sees them."

Almost immediately we must add that Howells deliberately moved to bypass this racial approach to Chesnutt in further extensive statements. Thus, while the second paragraph of his review began by announcing that, despite some prior uncertainty, "Now, however, it is known that the author of this story 'The Wife of His Youth' is of negro blood," the thrust of Howells' appreciation lay in the other direction.

> But the volumes of fiction *are* remarkable above many, above most short stories by people entirely white, and would be worthy of unusual notice if they were not the work of a man not entirely white.

In other words,

> It is not from their racial interest that we could first wish to speak of them, though they must have a very great and very just claim upon the critic. It is much more simply and directly, as works of art, that they make their appeal, and we must allow the force of this quite independently of the other interest.[1]

A year and a half later, Howells again praised Chesnutt's artistry and again made apparent to his readers the racial context from which Chesnutt's artistry had sprung. Thus while concluding his assessment on the same "artist above all" note of his 1900 review, nevertheless the body of Howells' review now stressed Chesnutt's point of view as a racial spokesman.

> The Marrow of Tradition, like everything else he has written, has to do with the relations of the blacks and

whites, and in that republic of letters where all men are free
and equal he stands up for his own people with a courage
which has more justice than mercy in it. The book is, in fact,
bitter, bitter. There is no reason in history why it should not
be so, if wrong is to be repaid with hate, and yet it would be
better if it was not so bitter. I am not saying that he is so
inartistic as to play the advocate; whatever his minor foibles
may be, he is an artist whom his step-brother Americans
may well be proud of. . . .[2]

From this time on, of course, all major readers and critics of
American fiction were aware of Chesnutt's racial identity; and
this made Chesnutt somewhat more aware of it as well.

Along with the critics, a variety of editors and publishers soon
came to see Chesnutt as a major Black spokesman on the American scene and, perhaps, as *the* major Black spokesman on the
twentieth-century literary scene. In their professional way, then,
they acknowledged Chesnutt's preeminence by their requests for
his services as reviewer and writer of socio-literary material.

In July, 1899, while visiting the Boston office of Houghton,
Mifflin Company, Chesnutt was introduced to M.A. DeWolfe
Howe, associate editor of *The Youth's Companion* and editor
also of the *Beacon Biographies of Eminent Americans* series,
both of which were published by Small, Maynard & Co. of
Boston. This happened right after the growing reception and
success of Chesnutt's story, "The Wife of His Youth," which
in turn was being enhanced by the more recent recognition
which *The Conjure Woman* had attracted. In the discussion
that ensued between Chesnutt and Howe, the idea soon sprang
up that a biography of Frederick Douglass ought to be included in the Beacon series, and that Chesnutt was the man to
write it. Planning on ten weeks for completing the manuscript,
Chesnutt promised to have the book ready by October 15.
(*CWC*, pp. 112-113)

This book became his first major piece of literary/sociological
writing. In fact, as he noted to Howe in a September 5, 1899,
letter, "It is a new line for me, but I am not at all appalled by it,

and shall I think do very well with it." Furthermore, it is clear
that it was to be somewhat polemical and crusading, as well as
biographical. As Chesnutt noted in a letter to Lewis H. Douglass,
asking him for a good picture of his father,

> I hope with the material at hand to be able to construct
> in even the limited time at my disposal, a dignified and ap-
> preciative sketch—a birdseye view as it were—of the life of
> our most distinguished citizen of African descent.

And in concluding his letter he reaffirmed this purpose.

> It is my sincere desire to honor the memory, as adequately
> as the scope of this little work will permit, of one whom the
> world delighted to honor for so many years. (August 23,
> 1899)

The invitation to write this biography, and the biography itself,
now formed the first tangible recognition by American publishers of Chesnutt's status as a Black spokesman. This recognition was to spread rapidly.

Before the Douglass biography was off the presses, Small,
Maynard also asked Chesnutt to write some sociological articles,
in the same vein as the biography. In a letter of October 25, 1899,
Herbert Small, the president of the firm, after having seen the
final manuscript of the biography, wrote to Chesnutt and suggested that he now write a "series of essays, discussing from the
point of view of the man of letters" the literature and life of the
Black man. Significantly enough, like the Douglass biography,
this book was intended to be a popular, expository and somewhat polemical work. As Small further developed his idea to
Chesnutt,

> I do not mean a serious, heavy book at all. I mean just
> such a book as will be easy and delightful to read, and by its
> entertaining quality do more to influence the public than a
> whole ton of more serious works.

There is no evidence that Chesnutt ever followed up Small's offer here. What is of greatest importance, however, is the level of literary and racial spokesman to which these offers and work lifted the crusading writer in Chesnutt.

Hard on the heels of his book and correspondence with Small, Maynard came a November 18, 1899, request from the *Saturday Evening Post* that Chesnutt write a review of Booker T. Washington's forthcoming volume "The Future of the American Negro." The result of this offer was Chesnutt's article "On the Future of His People," which appeared in the *Saturday Evening Post* of January 10, 1900.

Before the *Saturday Evening Post* article was released—or even written—Chesnutt's newly acquired stature as spokesman brought him a parallel and warmly casual offer from Jeanette L. Gilder, editor of *The Critic*, "to review Booker T. Washington's latest book—I have forgotten the exact title—for the Critic." When this suggestion brought the reply from Chesnutt that he was already committed to writing a review of Washington's book for the *Saturday Evening Post*, Miss Gilder's return letter noted that this would not interfere with his reviewing it for *The Critic*. In fact, she then went on to give Chesnutt what amounted to a carte blanche offer of her magazine's pages, if he liked, to "take Mr. Washington's book as a text to preach a sermon of your own." (December 1, 1899) Chesnutt's response to this offer was his "A Plea for the American Negro," which appeared in *The Critic* of February, 1900.

Needless to say, having his review of a leading Black spokesman of this time published in a major popular American magazine brought Chesnutt into the higher realm of becoming a leading racial spokesman himself. And from this time on, Chesnutt was to accept and maintain this role, even through the Negro Renaissance of the 1920s, when some of Chesnutt's controlled and gentlemanly tones found little favor with the more vibrant nationalism which was then springing up.[3]

The most immediate gain from this new stature was a request from the *Boston Transcript* for Chesnutt to write a series of three sociological papers on the race question in America. Entitled

"The Future American," which was probably meant to echo the title of Washington's recent book, they were written at the direct suggestion of Joseph Edgar Chamberlin, editor of the *Transcript*. They ultimately appeared in *Boston Transcript* issues of August 18, August 25, and September 1, 1900, and were quite profound and controversial, What created the controversy was Chesnutt's third article with its sociological discussion and prophesy of future amalgamation in American society.

> The only thing that ever succeeded in keeping two races apart when living on the same soil—the only true ground of caste— is religion, and, as has been alluded to in the case of the Jews, this is only superficially successful. The colored people are the same as the whites in religion; they have the same standards and methods of culture, the same ideals, and the presence of the successful white race as a constant incentive to their ambition. The ultimate result is not difficult to foresee. The races will be quite as effectively amalgamated by lightening the Negroes as they would be by darkening the whites.[4]

A few months after Chesnutt's three articles for the *Transcript*, Chamberlin suggested another series of articles, asking Chesnutt to write some letters from the South and to cover the annual conference at Tuskegee in February, Tuskegee having recently become an important item in the *Transcript's* coverage since that publication had just recently "adopted" that institution "as one of the causes that it most consistently presented to the favorable consideration of its readers."[5] What grew from these proposals later in 1901 were Chesnutt's "The White and The Black"[6] and "The Negro's Franchise,"[7] but both were increasingly overshadowed by a more spectacular interest which had been developing for Chesnutt throughout the spring of that year.

Early in 1901, Macmillan Company had published a book entitled *The American Negro* by an unknown Black man named William Hannibal Thomas. The book was viciously defamatory concerning the Black race and was filled with some savage and outrageous fabrications that purported to be historical fact. Essentially, it "documented" from an "inside" perspective all the anti-Black stereotypes current at the time: sexual promiscuity, inherent stupidity, "Sambo" childishness, etc. In short, it was a pseudo-sociological book written by a shrewd Black writer intent on catering to the prejudices and distortions in the minds of his white readers.

Originally Chesnutt had written to Chamberlin to protest a favorable review of Thomas's book which Chamberlin had misguidedly written. Chamberlin now offered the *Transcript's* pages to Chesnutt if he could develop enough facts to discredit Thomas and his material, something which Chesnutt and some friends had already set about doing. Simultaneously, as a further measure of Chesnutt's recognition as a racial spokesman, he received an informal, and hectic, telegram from Jeanette Gilder of *The Critic* asking, in its entirety,

CAN YOU GIVE US FIFTEEN HUNDRED
WORDS SCATHING THOMAS BOOK BY TWELFTH
ANSWER TO NEW YORK. (MARCH 8, 1901)

So incensed was Chesnutt over the Thomas book that he returned his review of it in less than a week, the tone and position of which even surpassed Miss Gilder's concept of "scathing." Her letter of March 15, 1901, acknowledging the receipt of Chesnutt's article,[8] is quite clear on this point.

> Many, many thanks for your promptness and for the article, which is capital. I have trimmed it down a little, as the wicked Thomas might have us up for libel if we printed it just as it stands. I think there is enough left to make him feel ashamed of himself, if he has any feelings left.

The result of this review, plus an extremely long and documented letter by Chesnutt to Macmillan, entirely discredited Thomas's character for authorship of any book on any subject, which had the ultimate effect of forcing the reluctant publisher to withdraw the book from sale and take it out of circulation as much as possible. (*CWC*, pp. 162-163) This, in some ways, was one of the high points of Chesnutt's early career as racial spokesman.

From this time on, however, various time gaps appear between offers to Chesnutt for articles and reviews on racial matters from major magazines and publishers. Partially this was because Chesnutt was now deeply engrossed in his writing of fiction and in the various promotional and publicity aspects which usually accompany the publication of such books. However, it was also partially because Chesnutt was becoming too outspoken and direct in his indictments of America's cruel injustice to Blacks.

This first gap, then, covered between early 1901, when Chamberlin and Miss Gilder had approached Chesnutt, and January 12, 1903, when James Pott & Co. wrote to him about the publication of a volume "presenting the negro problem from the negro's point of view, being a series of papers by representative leaders of the race." Chesnutt clearly was acknowledged as one of the foremost spokesmen of his race, and to some extent the Pott editors indicated that they had learned of Chesnutt's prominence in this field through his literary works. Thus, they suggested that Chesnutt write on the "disfranchisement of the negro in the south" which they supposed "from reading your various stories" would be "most likely to interest you particularly."

Chesnutt responded with a generally favorable answer, but he also wanted to know further who were to be "the other writers with whose contributions mine would be bound up," noting that the names of DuBois, Washington, and Dunbar, whom Pott had mentioned in the first letter, were "all right." (January 31, 1903) The Pott response included Bishop Tanner as part as the list, and, more significantly, it then went on to comment on the American readership of the time and how that readership chose to acknowledge and recognize Black "spokesmen."

> We believe this will satisfy you as to the character of the book, as we believe these names represent, together with yours, the most promising, and at the same time most conservative element among your people.

"Perhaps it is not necessary," the letter continued,

> for us to say anthing in regard to the manner in which you
> should treat the subject which we suggest, but we believe you
> understand the advisability of making as conservative a
> statement of the facts as is possible in presenting this phase
> of the question in the strongest way.

From this we can see just where the Black "spokesmen" stood
in 1903 America, and we can further understand how selectively
the title of "spokesman" was meted out by the white publishers
and readers to those Blacks who said the least unsettling things.
Nevertheless, the Pott letter did add a redeeming clause that ultimately induced Chesnutt to write the article.

> Of course we would have no objection to any statement
> which you might make in the course of the article which you
> would substantiate at the same time by citing incidents, or
> whatsoever, in proof thereof. (February 5, 1903)

In fact, so involved was Chesnutt with the topic and the now
open-ended terms that he proceeded to write twice as long an
article as Pott had asked for. Much of their subsequent correspondence dealt with the problem of the length and the effect it
would have on the financial terms of the contract, which originally called for "$50 for an essay of 2500 words" with "2¢ per
word for anything over that number." So intent was Chesnutt on
the argument and logic of his piece that he concerned himself less
with the money here than with the artistic sense of a complete
job. He, therefore, let himself be paid less than the contract called
for just so that his work could be printed in its entirety. (Letter
to Pott & Co., July 2, 1903)

It was a full two years before Chesnutt again made any sort
of public statement regarding the position of American Blacks.
Then in June of 1905, visiting Boston for the graduation of his
son from Harvard, he was invited to address the Boston Literary

and Historical Association on the subject of "Race Prejudice: Its Causes and Its Cures."

Essentially a shortened version of Chesnutt's earlier articles for the *Boston Transcript*, this speech "brought much bitter criticism upon Chesnutt" and caused him to receive "abusive letters, many of them from illiterate and anonymous writers, and some unpleasant notoriety." As in the third article of the 1900 series five years before, Chesnutt's major point in his address was the sociological value of amalgamation in American society. As he stated it most succinctly, "I not only believe that the mixture of races will in time become an accomplished fact, but that it will be a good thing for all concerned." And, as in the earlier articles, this theme found few who were receptive. (*CWC*, p. 41)

In 1906 Chesnutt received his second-from-the-last invitation to address the American public on the race question in America; and not only was this the last invitation he would receive until 1915, but it was also a rather minor book he was being asked to review. On January 5, 1906, then, Little, Brown & Co. sent Chesnutt a copy of *The Brothers' War* by John C. Reed of Atlanta, and asked "to be favored with your frank opinion, particularly of Mr. Reed's view on the Negro question."

Chesnutt's answer showed both his power in literary and social statement and his growing tone of racial disillusion. Thanking the publishers for their courtesy in sending Reed's book, Chesnutt nevertheless regretted that "it does not commend itself to me, nor could I commend it to others." Then he continued,

> Whatever quality of temperate statement it may possess in some regards, is counterbalanced by its extremely unjust and ungenerous attitude toward the Negro, to the writing down of whom the book is mainly devoted. It is the same old wolf in sheep's clothing. In spite of the legend on the cover, I do not think that 50 years hence, any one will write, and I feel quite sure that no one will publish a book devoted to the justification of slavery, the glorification of the Klu Klux Klan, and a deification of Jefferson Davis and the

gang of traitors who sought to destroy this Republic and perpetuate human slavery. (February 17, 1906)

In a letter of February 18, 1915, Chesnutt was sought by Bobbs-Merrill Co. to read the proof sheets on Paul Leland Haworth's *America in Ferment*, a book dealing with everything from the "standard of living and its cost" to "immigration" and "socialism." In his reply, intended for publication, Chesnutt commented most specifically on the chapter dealing with "The Color Line," which, presumably, is why the proof sheets were sent to him, although the initial letter does not mention this chapter at all. Having favorably appraised the chapter, Chesnutt then spread out and briefly praised "the illuminating discussion of the questions of citizenship and Women's Suffrage, and indeed the whole book." (April 23, 1915)

Thus, Chesnutt was still an acknowledged racial authority in 1915: one who could treat "The Color Line" as it occurred in both the North and the South. Equally important, as we read his review, is the fact that Chesnutt's own tone had softened during the nine-year interlude, and his return comments to Bobbs-Merrill showed much less anger and disillusion than the voice that reviewed *The Brothers' War* in 1906. Also reestablishing itself with this more detached and softened tone was Chesnutt's early philosophical and cosmic perspective that saw the world and its problems from the intellectual isolattoe's standpoint. Chesnutt was returning to his interest in "the question of citizenship" in general.

Finally, in 1916, Chesnutt's reputation as racial spokesman was still strong; and now, perhaps with the gap left by Washington's death in November, 1915, the country seemed more attuned to listen. On March 20, 1916, Chesnutt received a very interesting letter from John J. Spurgeon, executive editor of the Philadelphia *Public Ledger*, stating,

We should welcome from you from time to time information, not necessarily to be published, but which in your judgement might serve as a proper basis for comment on important affairs of which you are especially cognizant.

The reason behind this request is quite revealing and may show a growing desire in 1916 for racial truth.

Before expressing editorial opinions we would know the situation in its true bearings; we wish to be unusually well informed, and therefore more responsible in our utterances than newspapers that are not national in their scope and purposes.

This was Chesnutt's last acknowledgement as a racial leader by the contemporary literary world.

By Fellow Civil Rights Leaders

To his fellow civil rights leaders, Chesnutt's position as spokesman was equally secure and acknowledged. On the more obvious, testimonial level, it included direct honors and words of praise. And on a more literary level, by those leaders who were publishers or editors of racially crusading magazines and newspapers, respect for Chesnutt was measured by the numerous ways and occasions in which they sought him out for help and guidance.

Perhaps of least interest to us is that verbal and testimonial appreciation which Chesnutt received during his lifetime from important figures and groups in the civil rights movement. One part of this consisted of such letters as that from Hampton Institute's *Southern Workman* of December 4, 1899, which commended Chesnutt for "succeeding in greater measure than any other author of your race has done, in welding the new life and the old";[7] or the letter from Charles W. Anderson, one of the original members of the Committee of Twelve for the Advancement of the Interests of the Negro Race, which declared that *The Marrow of Tradition* was a "noble plea for the race"; (December 11, 1901) or the letter from Archibald Grimke, original Treasurer of the Committee of Twelve and later major figure in the NAACP, which asserted, "You have done good service not only to the Negro but to the South and to the North of the nation as well, whether they recognize that service today or not." (September 15, 1905) Likewise, the selection of Chesnutt by W.E.B. DuBois as one of the ten Blacks who formed the "Advance Guard of the Race" in 1903 was a major tribute to Chesnutt's role as a Black figure and spokesman.[8]

There were also more formal testimonials offered to Chesnutt as racial spokesman. He received an honorary doctor of laws degree from Wilberforce University in June, 1913,[9] and was awarded the NAACP's Spingarn Medal in 1928 for his "pioneer work as literary artist depicting the life and struggles of Americans of Negro descent, and for his long and useful career as scholar, worker, and freeman of one of America's greatest cities." (*The Crisis*, June, 1928) And just one year prior to that honor the NAACP had established a special prize fund for the best articles in the 1927 *Crisis* and called that fund the "Charles Waddell Chesnutt Honorarium."[10]

The other major appreciation of Chesnutt as racial spokesman by fellow leaders in civil rights work took a more literary and practical approach.

The first and most dramatic aspect of this literary recognition came in the form of numerous offers and requests for Chesnutt either to join the editorial board of an established racially crusading publication or else to help found and develop a new one. And what is so impressive about these offers is the frequency with which they were made and the caliber of the people making them.

As early as 1889 Chesnutt had become interested in the crusading Open Letter Club: "an association of thoughtful Southern men of broad vision who were seriously trying to find some way to solve the race problem justly." Their method of working towards this end was to provide a completely open forum "for the interchange of information of every sort, and from every direction, valuable to the moral, intellectual, and material interests of the South." (*CWC*, p. 43.)

Among the leading figures in the group was George Washington Cable, and it was through Cable's literary interest in Chesnutt that Chesnutt became interested in the organization. Soon he openly joined the Club and was given letters (from Southern correspondents) to paraphrase and shorten, so that the original writer would accept the shortened version for publication. In addition Chesnutt would then write a parallel letter to the Club, attempting to "Convince, rather than convict" the original writer (and the Club's readership) that the original writer's anti-Black opinion was misguided. Similarly, Cable would send Chesnutt a synopsis of a short paper or letter and ask him to "point out its sophistries, as I know you can."

With Chesnutt's interest and ability proved in this field and the sudden birth of a fear that his business in Cleveland might be hurt by certain legislation in the Ohio legislature, Chesnutt visited Cable at his home in Northampton, Massachusetts to have a personal talk with him. One result was an invitation from Cable for Chesnutt to join him in "this noble work" as his personal secretary in Northampton, an offer Chesnutt did not accept. By the time he was thirty-one, then, Chesnutt's literary ability and social commitment had been both recognized and sought after.[11]

Late in 1889, Chesnutt received a September 13 letter from Charles N. Hunter, editor of *The Progressive Educator* asking Chesnutt to help him "effect an engagement with some reputable newspaper to furnish a weekly letter giving in detail the condition of public sentiment here and the difficulty besetting the Negro."

Three years later Chesnutt entered into correspondence with Albien W. Tourgee, the Ohio lawyer who had settled in North Carolina on what he was later to call "A Fool's Errand." When Tourgee finally understood the sordid conditions in the South and his personal inability to change them significantly, he thereupon wrote his tremendously popular novel with the same title (New York, 1879), detailing his adventures in the South. In fact, it was this book that initially stirred Chesnutt to want to become a writer. (Journal, March 16, 1860)

The result of Chesnutt's correspondence with Tourgee now was the suggestion from Tourgee (November 23, 1893) that Chesnutt help him establish, finance, and sell stock in a new national journal which would promote the Black man's cause across the country. The *National Citizen* was the proposed name, and Chesnutt was to become associate editor. For reason largely economic, Chesnutt declined the offer in a letter of November 27, 1893. Probably for the same reasons the journal, it seems, never got started.

Two years later (September 5, 1895) Tourgee wrote to Chesnutt again with essentially the same crusading magazine proposal. The name of this suggested magazine was *The Basis, a Weekly Magazine of Citizenship*, and this one did become a reality. Again, however, Chesnutt turned the associate editorship down.

Eight years after Tourgee sought Chesnutt for the fledgling *Basis*, DuBois wrote Chesnutt a long letter, lamenting the Black man's helpless position in America with no major vocal champion to fight for him. DuBois proposed in a May 5, 1903, letter that he and Chesnutt begin a journal together that would speak for the Black man. Chesnutt concurred in the need and lamented the anemic "colored" publications on the American scene. Nevertheless, he decided not to accept the opportunity, warning DuBois of the risks and problems involved. (July, 1903)

Chesnutt received his last major recognition in this vein when he was asked on December 19, 1905, by T. Thomas Fortune, editor of *The New York Age*, to "carry out your purpose and come and be one of us here." Once more Chesnutt declined.

The importance of these offers now is not so much that Chesnutt declined them—an aspect of his economic life that we have seen in greater detail above. The significance lies in the fact that Chesnutt was being seen so clearly and so often as almost *the* major racial-literary figure to be appealed to when a new or old crusading publication wished to establish or improve both its literary and social stature. Especially when we consider the prominence of the men who sought him out with these frequent offers, this was major and continuous recognition of Chesnutt's own stature in the eyes of his fellow civil rights crusaders.

Besides these major offers of an editorial board position and guiding influence on a crusading publication, Chesnutt's stature was recognized also by various editors and publishers offering him carte blanche use of their magazines' pages for anything he wished to write. The correspondence on this is voluminous and is highlighted by open-ended offers from the following people: Jean E. Davis, Managing Editor of the *Southern Workman and Hampton School Record*, on October 4, 1899; William S. Braithwaite, proposing a new magazine on November 29, 1902, and calling on Chesnutt as "the very first writer of our race"; J.L. Nichols & Co., proposing on August 22, 1903, a new magazine entitled the *Voice of the South*; J.A. Hopkins, business manager of *The Voice of the Negro*, on December 7, 1903; Robert E. Jones, editor of the *Southwestern Christian Advocate*, on July 7, 1904; Fred R. Moore, editor and publisher of *The Colored American Magazine*, on December 12, 1906; and W.E.B.DuBois, pleading for contributions to the NAACP's *The Crisis*, on February 6, 1915.

Though Chesnutt turned down the offers from Braithwaite (because the magazine never did materialize), Nichols, and Moore, he did send the *Southern Workman* three short stories— "Lonesome Ben" (March, 1900), "Tobe's Tribulations" (November, 1900), and "The Partners" (May, 1901)—and added an article on "The Free Colored People of North Carolina" of May, 1902. Likewise, he allowed Hopkins' *The Voice of the Negro* to publish his article on "Peonage—the New Slaver of the South" (September, 1904) and offered Jones' *Advocate* an article on the "Courtship of Lincoln," which appeared in the February 4, 1909, issue of that magazine. Finally, answering DuBois's plea for contributions, Chesnut had his short story on "Mr. Taylor's Funeral" (April and May, 1915) and his article on "Women's Rights" (August, 1915) published in *The Crisis*.

Needless to say, implicit in all these carte blanche offers from fellow civil rights leaders was the clear recognition of Chesnutt as a major Black spokesman of the period. For this role of concerned racial leader was one of the three major aspects of Chesnutt's life, and it profoundly formed the basis of most of his major writings.

CHAPTER VI

Why Chesnutt Wrote

Basic Ambivalence of Interests

Now that we have examined the three aspects of Chesnutt's basic nature, it becomes clear just how incompatible they were at times and how much ambivalence and conflict raged through some of his major decisions. In like manner, it should be equally clear that many of his major decisions and projects were not the result of merely a single motive, as Chesnutt has often been pictured, but were quite clearly the result of mixed motives, pointing, for that individual moment, in the same direction. For these reasons it is important for us to examine Chesnutt's major literary decisions in light of what we know to be his essential interests, for it is only in this way that we can come to understand the meaning of the man and the nature of his work.

Fundamentally, there were two major decisions in Chesnutt's life: his decision to devote himself strongly and completely to writing in 1899 and his decision to finally cease all major writing in 1905. It is within the scope of these two decisions, then, that we must begin our discussion of Chesnutt as writer. Although an observer can never fully understand the motivation of another, and indeed the subject may not understand himself, we do have Chesnutt's complete journals, much of his correspondence, and his other writings. Working with these materials we can make some evaluation of his writings.

Tradition suggests that we note anew the three main interests in Chesnutt's life: money, intellectualness, and social crusading, and then simply line them up in their purified, concrete solidity. To do so, however, would be quite misleading, especially for our understanding of Chesnutt's motives during his early, Journal-keeping days. Ambivalence and conflicts were extremely visible during his early thoughts about writing, so that almost from entry to entry his motives and interests tended to flow back and forth into each other. For this reason we will treat his earliest comments on writing in the natural order of their appearance: the chronological sequence in which they flickered across his consciousness.

The very first allusions to writing in the Journal approach the subject on essentially artistic grounds. On July 15, 1879, we find Chesnutt quoting whole verses of the religious hymn, "The Old, Old Story," a section of Byron's *Don Juan*, and Burns' lyrical "Green grow the rashes, O!" One month later we find his first attempt at creative writing with his short story "Lost in a Swamp," and this is soon followed by "Frisk's First Rat," "A Storm at Sea," and "Bruno."

With only a touch of mediocre, doggerel verse in the interim, Chesnutt's next mention of writing is also artistic in genesis and intent. Alluding to some poetry which he wrote and submitted to a magazine, his statements about his verse are interestingly tough-minded in his expression of the true artist's concern with nothing less than first rate, rigorous standards for his work and talent. "A few weeks ago," he records,

> I sent a letter and some bits of verse to the Christian Union. I have never heard from them, and as I requested The Editor to consign them to the wastebasket (which he would have done anyway) if they were not worth publishing, I presume he did so; but as they were puerile productions, and sent to a paper of high literary Character, they were not fit for it. The Editor of our Gazette offered to publish them, but my object was not to see them in print, but to find out whether they were worth printing or not. (April 23, 1879)

A little later in that year, with Chesnutt still at age twenty, he discussed writing as a full career for the first time, and at this moment his motives were strictly geared to the acquistion of "Fame." Examining himself objectively and acknowledging his numerous interests even at that point in his life, he noted how

> I have a fatal propensity for building air castles—"Aerial Architecture" you might call it—a fault very common to youth. The different professions I have embraced, the plans I have formed for the future could be counted by thousands —and all, in my brilliant imagination, were but so many different entrances to the Temple of Fame. I have been a lawyer, Physician, Architect, Farmer, Minister, Teacher, Poet, Musician, Reporter, Editor, Author, Politician, etc. . . *ad infinitum*, and in each I have risen to the top of my profession. (Summer, 1879)

In 1880, that hectic period in which Chesnutt was very much concerned with leaving the South and obtaining "my proper standing in the world," the conflicts and ambivalences of motive were furiously bubbling to the surface. At one moment he was a stymied artist:

> I frequently have a bright thought flash, like a meteor through my mind—the plan of a story which I wish to write in the future;—a striking character, which I think would figure well in a novel;—a poetic fancy;—a new invention in mechanics; but most of these disappear like meteors, after flashing across my mind; though I may hope they will reappear at some future time. (March 11, 1880)

Five days later he discussed Judge Albion Tourgee's popular novel, *A Fool's Errand*, with his eye predominantly on the wealth and fame which writing such a popular book could bring.

> Judge Tourgee has sold the Fool's Errand, I understand, for $20,000. I suppose he had already received a large royalty

on the sale of the first few editions. The work has gained an astonishing degree of popularity, and is to be translated into the French.

And as he continued to think about the book and what relevance its success might have for him, Chesnutt once more returned to its "rich and famous" aspects.

> Nearly all his stories are more or less about colored people, and that very feature is one source of their popularity. . . . And if Judge Tourgee, with his necessarily limited intercourse with colored people, and with his limited stay in the South, can write such interesting descriptions, such vivid pictures of southern life and character as to make himself rich and famous, why could not a colored man . . . write as good a book about the South as Judge Tourgee has written.

And suddenly, in the same entry, the realm of art was once more returned to. "I intend to record my impressions of men and things, and such incidents or conversations which take place within my knowledge," Chesnutt declared.

> With a view of future use in literary work I shall not record stale negro minstrel, or worn out newspaper squibs on the "man and brother." I shall leave the realm of fiction, where most of this stuff is manufactured, and come down to hard facts." (March 16, 1880)

Surprisingly enough, missing from every discussion of writing up to May 29, 1880, had been any mention of the racial crusading to which Chesnutt later so strongly dedicated himself. In this oft-quoted entry we find Chesnutt's first manifesto of racial crusading through literature. "I think I must write a book," he declared, noting how "it has been my cherished dream, and I feel an influence that I cannot resist calling me to the task." He then began his social statement.

Besides, if I do write, I shall write for a purpose, a high, holy purpose, and this will inspire me to greater effort. The object of my writings would be not so much the elevation of the colored people as the elevation of the whites—for I consider the unjust spirit of caste which is so insidious as to pervade a whole nation, and so powerful as to subject a whole race and all connected with it to scorn and social ostracism —I consider this a barrier to the moral progress of the American people; and I would be one of the first to head a determined, organized crusade against it.

As he continued, he discussed why he linked this social purpose with the literary medium. This "crusade" must have a special approach:

Not a fierce indiscriminate onset, not an appeal to force, for this is something that force can but slightly affect, but a moral revolution which must be brought about in a different manner. The subtle almost indefinable feeling of repulsion toward the Negro, which is common to most Americans— cannot be stormed and taken by assault; the garrison will not capitulate, so their position must be mined, and we will find ourselves in their midst before they think it.

Indeed, so strong was Chesnutt's belief in this purpose that he concluded by reaffirming once more the strength of his intent. "If I can do anything to further this work, and can see any likelihood of obtaining success in it," he recorded at the time, "I would gladly devote my life to it."

Here it was, as strikingly and explicitly put forth as it ever would be. And even though comments about artistic fame ("my cherished dream") and material "success" flowed fleetingly across the scene, basically the manifesto of social crusading stood intact—with one omission. When the passage is usually quoted, it begins with Chesnutt's famous "I must write a book." statement. However, the actual Journal entry as a whole does not begin there, and it is of importance to us to note just what sort of discussion precedes this declaration. Just prior to the statement, then, Chesnutt had been introspectively evaluating himself and his present surroundings. As he looked at himself and his life as an educator in Fayetteville, he reflected that

> There are just two courses in life open to me. One is the pursuit of pleasure; the other is mental activity, constant employment of the mind and purpose toward some good end, —culture, mental or spiritual. Neither my tastes nor habits incline me to seek mere animal enjoyment. . . . My mind is so constituted that it cannot remain idle. . . .

Following this discussion of his need for constant intellectual activity was his assessment of his intellectual and occupational environment. As he saw it, he was a man with an active mind in a "supernaturally dull and prosaic town," a town that could not offer him the necessary "debate, argument, interchange and criticism of opinion" which is necessary for an active mind to remain incisive. And, as for the challenge of his job, "my profession requires of me about six hours out of the twenty-four."

"But I have almost lost my subject," he concludes. " 'An idle brain is the Devil's workship,' and I was discussing some plan to keep my brain employed. . . . I think I must write a book." This, then—this psychological, environmental, and almost moral discussion of idleness—was the specific spark for Chesnutt's determination to begin major writings. The social crusader was still there to be sure, but the point is that so were allusions to "cherished dreams," "success," and an extremely long discussion of "idleness." The ambivalence and fluctuations are obvious.

Furthermore, this idleness in Chesnutt's life at that time greatly intensified the feelings of isolation and loneliness which were a constant condition of his early days. There is a case to be made in fact for concluding that loneliness was the essential reason that Chesnutt began any writing *per se*. For it was when he was alone in 1874 and teaching for the summer in a rural district near Charlotte that he originally began his Journal, and it is clear that the Journal was meant as an intellectual and personal companion in the absence of any other sympathetic ear. Even as late as June 25, 1880, his loneliness led him to note in his Journal that "I must take my Journal for my confidant."

By March 26, 1881, the fullness of Chesnutt's ambivalent interests had finally reached the surface, and in an extremely insightful piece of self-analysis he described for himself the various forces and interests which were leading him to write.

> Every time I read a good novel, I want to write one. It is the dream of my life—to be an author! It is not so much the *monstrari digits*, though that has something to do with any aspirations. It is not altogether the money. It is a mixture of motives. I want fame; I want money; I want to raise my children in a different rank of life from that which I sprang from.

As he continued, he noted how

> In my present vocation, I would never accumulate a competency, with all the economy and prudence, and parsimony in the world. In law or medicine, I would be compelled to wait half a lifetime to accomplish anything. But literature pays—the successful.

and noted further how

> There is a fascination about this calling that draws a scribbler irresistibly toward its doors. He knows that the chance of success is hardly one out of a hundred; but he is foolish enough to believe, or sanguine enough to hope, that he will be the successful one.

With this "mixture of motives," then, Chesnutt was determined to begin.

I am confident that I can succeed, in some degree, at any
rate. It is the only thing I can do without capital, under my
present circumstances, except teach. My three months vacation is before me after the lapse of another three, and I
shall strike for an entering wedge in the literary world,
which I can drive in further afterwards. "Where there's a
will etc . . ." and there is certainly a will in this case.

The turbulent breadth and richness of the emerging writer's
latent interests were now on the surface, and he now saw in himself the economic, artistic, and social considerations which were
leading him to a literary career, and saw further just how in-
voluted and "mixed" they were. Thus as we pursue these three
major interests within their own realms now, we need to remember that no one of them ever existed separately. For, even as
Chesnutt became more of an artist and social crusader as his
career matured, we cannot allow ourselves to forget that beneath the surface the same turbulent ambivalences were still
at work.

The Importance of Money

As we have seen, money and what it could buy was a major
interest of Chesnutt throughout his life. In his Journal, in personal letters, and in his various business actions it is clear that he was
strongly concerned with amassing wealth for the conveniences
and security which it could buy. This same aspect of his nature
played a major role in his choice of writing as a profession. The
major proclamation of this we have just seen, in his concern with
literature as the fastest way to wealth for him, but there were, of
course, further testaments to this as well.

As early as 1800 Chesnutt began to toy with the idea of writing
as a profession, and from the beginning he weighed the choice in
economic terms.

It is of interest to note in the Journal how he reacted to the
work of an earlier writer, Thomas B. Macaulay, six months after

Chesnutt's own manifesto on how "I must write a book." "Macaulay's Life is very interesting," he began.

> His was a great and glorious career . . . If I could earn
> a tenth of his fame, or make a tenth part of his money, I
> would have good cause to be content. (January 15, 1881)

In fact, just the choice of Macaulay as a literary hero is meaningful here.

Later, while he was still debating literature as a career, many of
Chesnutt's calculations looked at the question in terms of sales
and profits and what sort of markets he would attempt to reach.
Realizing that Northerners would be his potential customers,
he early assessed their interest in his product as he evaluated
Tourgee's success in the field.

> Nearly all his stories are more or less about colored peo-
> ple, and this very feature is one source of their popularity.
> There is something romantic, to the northern mind, about
> the southern Negro. . . . they lend a willing ear to all that
> is spoken or written concerning their character, habits, etc.
> (March 16, 1880)

And he noted four months later that

> the colored man is still in America, and likely to be here
> for some time to come; and he will never cease to be the ob-
> ject of popular interest and sympathy in the North, as long
> as he is the object of oppression and prejudice in the South.
> (July 13, 1880)

Nine years later, when Chesnutt was once more seriously debating his future, he again saw a large market and "demand" for
Black literature, from which a "livelihood" could be obtained.

> It seems to me that there is a growing demand for litera-
> ture dealing with the Negro, and for information concerning

subjects with which he is in any manner connected—his progress in various parts of the world—in the United States, Brazil, in South America, and in other lands. It seems to me that these subjects would open up a vast field and a literary field in which a writer who was connected with these people by ties of blood and stronger ties of sympathy, could be *facile princeps*, other things being equal, or in which such a writer could at least earn a livelihood. (Letter to Cable, March, 1889)

And eleven years after that, as his career was now freshly underway, he again commented on the potentially strong audience for which he would write. Referring to *The House Behind the Cedars* and its theme of "passing" and intermarriage, he wrote to Henry Douglas Robins of Houghton Mifflin and expressed his hopes on the subject.

I hope the book may raise some commotion, I hardly care in what quarter, though whether, from the nature of the theme it will, I don't know. I published recently a series of articles in the *Boston Transcript* on the same general subject, which brought me a number of interesting letters from places as widely separated as Boston and Los Angeles. (September 27, 1900)

Furthermore, he continued,

The question of "miscegenation" was brought up at the recent conference of leading white men of the South who met at Montgomery, Alabama, to discuss the race problem; and one of the solutions put forth involved the future amalgamation with the white race of at least a remnant of the black population. So that the subject I think may be regarded as generally opened up for discussion, and inferentially for literary treatment.

Nor was Chesnutt alone in his optimistic assessment of a purchasing public for his writings. During this same period he received a number of letters from editors and publishers who also discussed this aspect of writing and who confirmed Chesnutt's optimistic feelings about it. Writing to him on October 2, 1897, and praising his stories, "The Dumb Witness" and "The Bouquet," Walter Hines Page, editor of *Atlantic Monthly,* added his own feelings and generally encouraged Chesnutt on the potential market for his kind of material. Two years later Chesnutt received an even greater word of encouragement from Robins. Discussing how *The Wife of His Youth* should be advertised for best sales, and noting the amount of interest white Americans were currently showing in Black material, Robins observed that

> With the recent coming forward of Mr. Washington, the publication of his book, the growing interest in Tuskegee, and the public notice attracted to the general subject of the colored people, we believe it will be well worth while to bring the book forward in a number of places in the way indicated; that is, as a book of stories treating of a subject, which, (as a Southerner I may say it gladly) is at last approaching a possibility of enlightened and civilized treatment. (December 8, 1899)

All of this economic assessment of the literary market is significant to us here because it shows how large financial concerns loomed in Chesnutt's early consciousness as a writer. His very first letter to Houghton Mifflin (September 8, 1891) is dramatic evidence of this. After introducing his "Rena Walden" as "the first contribution by an American of acknowledged African descent to purely imaginative literature," he then went on to announce his major concern at the moment.

> The question of terms is an important one to me. I offer this for publication because I understand that the volume of

short stories is more favorably received by the public now
than ever before. The copyright I would procure and retain
for myself.

Eight years later (December 5, 1899), soon after *The Wife of
His Youth* was published, Chesnutt wrote to his future son-in-
law, Edward C. Williams, and candidly expressed his plural interests in its marketing and reception.

> *The Wife of His Youth* is out. I am afraid it is a little late
> for the best Christmas trade. The bookstores here are going
> to give it a window display—portrait of the author, view
> of his study, original paintings from which illustrations are
> made, etc. It is a very handsome book, I think, and I am
> looking forward with some interest to two things—how it
> will be reviewed, and how it will sell!

One of the best examples of how the interest in money dominated
Chesnutt's interests in art and social crusading early in his career is to be found in his sequel of letters to George Washington
Cable. In this series of three letters, spread over a five year period, we witness two of the four major moments of debate which
Chesnutt went through before he finally cast his lot with a full
time literary career on September 30, 1899. If we omit his initial
decision to write a Journal—a decision which had, in its deep
loneliness, sprung from a very profound sense of art—there were
four major periods in which Chesnutt was attracted to literature
in a professional, occupational way. His desire to "write a book"
was the first, and we have already seen how idleness, fame, and
wealth played the major roles in that thought process. Furthermore, let us note that nothing really came of that because Chesnutt himself felt his lack of experience in the field and thus felt
that he was basically doing little more than building more "air
castles" for himself. His second and third considerations of that
career came in 1889 and 1895 and were manifest in his correspondence with Cable. The fourth and final moment of decision was
that which led him to go into "the author business" in 1899.

His first letter to Cable, in March of 1889, dealt with his first extensively serious look into the field as a professional commitment, and the three opening paragraphs, with their practical planning and citation of income figures, are quite explicit in revealing Chesnutt's motives at the time.

My Dear Sir:

Permit me to trouble you long enough for you to read this letter concerning a purely personal matter. I have been chiefly employed, during the past two years, as a stenographic reporter in the Courts of this county, intending to use this business as something to occupy my leisure time while awaiting the growth of a law practice. But by a very natural process, the thing to which I have given most time has hindered instead of helped the thing it intended to assist. As a consequence, I have built up a business mainly as a stenographer, which brought me in last year an income of two thousand dollars.

But there is a bill pending in the Legislature of this state for the appointment of two official stenographers for this county. There are five or six men now engaged in a free-for-all for this work, and probably all of these will be applicants for the two positions. I have perhaps more than a fighting chance—certainly that, for one of them. If I should secure it, it would pay a salary of $1500.00 a year with fees to the probably amount of $1,000.00 or $1,500.00 more; and it would in all probability occupy all of my time.

In the event of a failure on my part to secure one of these positions, I shall be compelled to turn my attention to other fields of effort. And my object in writing to you is to ask your opinion as to the wisdom, or rashness, of my adopting literature as a means of support.

The discussion here is strictly one of economics, and we can see that Chesnutt's sole interest was in financial security. The subsequent chain of events further emphasized this fact.

Cable's April 13 reply to Chesnutt's letter was an invitation for Chesnutt to come to Northhampton and be Cable's personal secretary, aiding him in "this noble work" of civil rights writing in which Cable's Open Letter Club was engaged and in which Chesnutt himself had already done some work. It was a chance to be both a writer and a social crusader at the same time, but, less than three weeks later, Chesnutt rejected the offer. The reason? Money, and family responsibilities.

> My Dear Mr. Cable:
> I regret to say that after mature deliberation, I have reached the conclusion that I could not afford to come to Northampton for any sum which, judging from the figures you have already mentioned, you would probably feel justified in offering me. The contingency which immediately inspired my first letter to you did not happen—that is, the appointment of official stenographers—so that my business is not affected in that direction. My earnings for the month just ended, as per memorandum lying before me, are just $250.65. I have made a change in my business which will, I hope, enable me to increase the income from it with less work on my part individually. So you will see that even $1200.00 or $1500.00 a year would, in comparison, be a sacrifice of half my income—a sacrifice which I, personally, would not hesitate to make, in view of the compensating advantages, but which my duty to my family, and other considerations which would perhaps not interest you, constrain me not to make. (May 3, 1889)

For another year the correspondence between the two continued. Chesnutt became quite active as a ghost writer-researcher for the Open Letter Club, and he further began to actively write major literary material, especially the first version of *The House Behind the Cedars*, which was at the time a short story entitled "Rena Walden." Cable offered several interesting comments and suggestions on "Rena," and, when it was rejected by *Century*

Magazine, Cable sensitively suggested that Chesnutt "lay 'Rena Walden' carefully aside for the present" until he could make the masterpiece of it which his talent deserved. (October 2, 1890) At this point Chesnutt ceased writing and went back to his stenographic career.

It was to be five years before the artistic flame in Chesnutt began to burn strongly again. Replying to a letter from Cable suggesting that Chesnutt "again enter the literary field," Chesnutt returned to the subject of "Rena" with a new maturity and a stronger, more intense sense of himself as an artist.

> Several days before I received your letter I had taken up the MS of "Rena Walden" with a view to re-writing it. I found myself much better able to realize the force of some criticisms of it that were made four or five years ago, when you were good enough to interest yourself in it. I have re-cast the story, and in its present form it is a compact, well-balanced novelette of 25,000 to 28,000 words. With four or five years of added study of life and literature I was able to see, I think, the defects that existed in it, and I venture now to regard it, not only as an interesting story, but as a work of literary art. I shall offer it for publication in a magazine, and whether successful in that or not, shall publish it in a book form. I hope to write many stories, and would like to make a worthy *debut* with this one (April 11, 1895)

Yet even as Chesnutt had suddenly found the determined artist inside himself, half of his consciousness still remained financial as it would, essentially, throughout his life. "My years of silence have not been unfruitful," he continued in his letter.

> I believe I am much better qualified to write now than I was five years since; and I have not used up a fund of interesting material which I might have expended on 'prentice work. Furthermore, I have saved ten to fifteen thousand dollars since I was with you at Northampton, and have the

feeling of security which even a little of this world's goods gives, so that I can now devote more time, and, if necessary, some money to securing a place in literature.

Finally, in September of 1899 Chesnutt decided to devote himself completely to writing as a full-time career. Characteristically, the final criteria here were also financial. As his daughter recalls the period,

> Chesnutt had spent months trying to decide whether he could afford to give up his business and devote himself to literature. The income from his business was very good, but the Chesnutt standard of living was very good also. His two older daughters were half way through college and his son, still in high school, was preparing for Harvard. The income from his literary productions at that time could not possibly support the family, and this was always his first consideration. But many new openings in the literary world were being offered him and these he could not accept without giving up his business and devoting all his time to literary work. Susan and he talked it over evening after evening. They studied all their expenses, decided where they could reduce them, made a budget for the next two years, and finally decided that the business could go. (*CWC*, p. 118)

On September, 1899, Chesnutt became a full-time writer.

We may wonder what sort of artist Chesnutt might have become if money had not loomed so large in his thoughts, but this is partially what makes him so intriguing a writer and, finally, so great an artist. For he was a man born to economic aspirations: concerned about his responsibilities to support himself and family, and interested, as well, in the creature comforts which his economic goals could provide. All of this made him real and human—especially when we consider the American scene of the late nineteenth century and its Horatio Alger "success" ethos. At the same time, burning somewhere beneath this world of security, responsibility and material indulgence was a major artistic flame struggling to escape into the open air.

This, then, was his greatness: that he was a man sorely and continuously tempted to live for comfort and money alone, yet a man whose deep commitment to art and a social cause led him to transcend the Franklinesque "plan of life which I had heretofore mapped out" and aesthetically live, if only for six years, in that world where "men are emancipated from the grossness of the flesh, and mind can seek out mind."

The Importance of Fame and Art

The second major reason for Chesnutt's choice of a writing career was, on the lowest level, his desire for fame and, on the highest level, his intellectual, artistic nature. We have already discussed above the importance of fame as part of Chesnutt's early ambivalence, and his artistic nature is of such significance that we will devote our final chapter in detail. Hence we are now prepared to discuss Chesnutt's third major internal force at this point in his life: his concern for racial justice.

The Importance of Racial Justice

The third and final reason why Chesnutt wrote was to aid and ameliorate the position of Blacks in this country. On the one hand he saw the critical condition of the Black man in the late 1890s and saw how both physically and literarily he was being attacked. On the other hand, Chesnutt was an optimist by nature and thought that the Black man's position could become—and actually was becoming—better. Relatedly he felt that he as writer could further effect this improvement because he felt that literature had a fundamental moral power and that the American public was now ready to read and understand the Black man's point of view. For these reasons, therefore, he consciously set

out to write artistic and socially effective novels of purpose which
would aid Black people in America.

Chesnutt's Awareness of the Physical Situation

To begin with, Chesnutt clearly saw the critical nature of
Black people's social and political condition at this time. As
early as 1878 his Journal recorded his reaction against the barriers of prejudice raised against him as an individual Black in the
South, and he soon began to see the problem on the larger, social
level as well. By 1889 he was worried about the decline in Black
education in the South and recorded in a March letter to Cable
that "I fear that future political action, of which the Mississippi
Constitutional Convention will serve as a prototype, will still
further curtail the opportunities for education of the colored
people in the South." Writing even more publicly to Cable's
Open Letter Club later in the year, Chesnutt enumerated "the
rest of the whole trouble."

> The white people of the South do not want to be governed
> by the Negro at all, whether well or ill; more than that, they
> do not want the Negroes to share with them the power which
> their numbers justly entitle them to. (November 13, 1889)

Not only did Chesnutt search out and concern himself with
those problems, but the gravity of the Black man's position was
constantly borne to him by letters he would receive from
friends in the South who reinforced his general feelings with
concrete, firsthand experiences of their own. In September,
1889, for example, he had been out of North Carolina for
six years and therefore depended on correspondence from
old friends to keep him abreast of racial conditions in the
state. Such a letter was that which he received from Charles
N. Hunter, editor of *The Progressive Educator,* explaining
in detail the new North Carolina Election Law ("a modifica-
tion of the South Carolina inequity"). Hunter proceeded to
summarize the overall scene:

I am sorry that I cannot say that the relations between the races in this state are improving. I am sorry that I cannot say that they have grown no worse since you were here. The contrary is too true. There has not been such bitterness in N.C. since Emancipation barring the year immediately succeeding Reconstruction—the Ku Klux Era. (September 13, 1889)

A similar letter from William H. H. Hart twelve years later enumerated the social problems of that year in equally bleak terms. "Of course your trip South made you sick at heart," Hart began.

The conditions there are past all description and are growing worse hourly— there is only peonage ahead. We have been betrayed and abandoned by those whom we helped to save the Union. (March 29, 1901)

Having arrived in Cleveland and the North in 1883, Chesnutt began to see the problems of prejudice there as well. In a November 27, 1893, letter to Tourgee he noted negatively how

in my intercourse with the best white people of one of the most advanced communities of the United States, with whom my business brings me in daily contact, I have never, to my recollection, heard the subject of the wrongs of the Negro brought up; and when I bring it up myself, which I have frequently done, it is dismissed as quickly as decency will permit. They admit that the thing is all wrong, but they do not regard it as their concern, and do not see how they can remedy it.

On a more personal note, in two separate letters to Cable in 1897 (April 14 and 19) Chesnutt reflected his feelings about discrimination in the North when he asked Cable about possible discrimination that his daughters might face in housing and education if they attended Smith College. Clearly conditions in the general

North had become quite bad for Chesnutt to be so apprehensive about the generally liberal college town of Northampton, Massachusetts.

Perhaps the closest we can come to ascertaining the direct spark to Chesnutt's growing awareness of the Black man's new precariousness in America is to note his reaction to the suddenly worsening conditions in his beloved home state, North Carolina. He had always considered the state to be quite liberal, and in many ways his basic optimism about racial conditions in this country can be traced to the generally optimistic feelings he held about this state of his early youth. Indeed, in a very interesting letter to the *Christian Union* in April, 1879, Chesnutt revealed just how much faith and complete optimism he felt about North Carolina and its posture regarding its Black citizens. Thus, after mentioning the recent "election frauds, and the intimidation of voters in some of the Southern States," Chesnutt went on to show the racial progress that North Carolina, on the other hand, had made, so that "the colored people have, for several years, had little or no trouble in the exercise of their political rights." Added to this was the fact that a "fair proportion of jurors" in the state were Black and a school fund was "distributed in proportion to the number of scholars in each race." In short, Chesnutt wrote, "I take pleasure in saying that many of the Southern States could well take example from N.C. in her attitude towards the colored people." (Journal, April, 1879)

Here was a very optimistic Chesnutt in the spring of 1879. He then went on to generalize this home state optimism to the country as a whole. Referring to the *Christian Union's* mention of "the Jubilee singers, and their concert in Nashville," he remarked that he was "glad to accept the incident at Nashville as a hopeful sign, and one that 'marks an era in the progress of the colored people toward recognition,' " and that he cherished "a fond hope that in this age of improvements, this country of rapid changes, the time of that recognition is not far off."

It is not difficult to understand the shock which Chesnutt felt in 1895, therefore, when North Carolina began its harsh and determined attempt to disfranchise its Black citizens and remove all their political rights. Most shocking to him was "the Wilmington Massacre" of 1898. As his daughter recalls,

> Chesnutt had been very much affected by the savage race riot that had broken out in Wilmington, North Carolina, in the November elections of 1898. He had friends and relatives in Wilmington and had received many reports of the trouble there. Feeling was very strong . . . and much Negro property was damaged. A number of colored people were killed or died later of their wounds. (*CWC*, p. 158)

Chesnutt described his feelings best in an immediate letter to W. H. Page. "I am deeply concerned and very much depressed at the conditon of affairs in North Carolina during the recent campaign," he began.

> I have been for a long time praising the state for its superior fairness and liberality in the treatment of race questions, but I find myself obliged to revise some of my judgments. There is absolutely no excuse for the state of things there, for the State has a very large white majority. It is an outbreak of pure, malignant and altogether indefensible race prejudice, which makes me feel personally humiliated, and ashamed for the country and the state. (November 10, 1878)

And it is most significant that this riot became the genesis of Chesnutt's most powerful and biting novel, *The Marrow of Tradition.*

In a letter of March 22, 1899—a full six months later—Chesnutt was still upset about the riot and wrote another letter to Page, a fellow ex-North Carolinian. After once more referring to "the troubled waters in North Carolina" and Page's recent trip down there to see if he could help ease the situation, Chesnutt cited a letter he had received the day before from Wilmighton, in which "the writer characterizes the town as a place where no Negro can enjoy the blessed privilege of free speech and free press; and where every organization, whether social, political, or industrial, undertaken by our race, must needs meet with opposition from the whites, incited by jealousy and envy." This, in turn, led Chesnutt to assess the racial scene in general.

> With these sentiments [jealousy and envy] controlling the South and the South trying to force them on the North and with the colored race in spite of them moving steadily though slowly upward, there will grow up a state of feeling between the two classes that is not conducive to good government. Oppressive, discriminating and degrading legislation is the logical outcome of such premises; and from present indications it seems that such is to be the order of the day for some time to come.

Becoming more specific, he noted how

> It is difficult ot conceive of a more outrageously unjust and unconstitutional law than the franchise amendment proposed in North Carolina. But I could write on the subject for a week, and I therefore refrain; . . . I will say, however, that the Supreme Court of the United States is in my opinion a dangerous place for a colored man to seek justice. He may go there with maimed rights; he is apt to come away with none at all, and with an adverse decision shutting out even the hope of any future protection there; for the doctrine of *stare decisis* is as strongly entrenched there as the hopeless superiority of the Anglo-Saxon is in the Southern States. (March 22, 1899)

It is hardly coincidental that only six months after this letter Chesnutt finally decided to put aside stenography and middle class detachment in order to devote his talents to literature and the racial evils of 1899 America. Nor is it coincidental that his humorous, "romantic" folklore tales in *The Conjure Woman* were behind him, and the work he began now was more serious and realistic in its treatment of the very tangible social world around him. The racial realities of 1898 had had their effect.

Chesnutt's Awareness of the Literary Situation

Even as the physical conditions of the Black man's world were harsh and oppressive at this period, the literary world was equally hostile. Chesnutt himself was well aware of this, and this is one of the major reasons that he decided to crusade for racial justice by using a literary medium. To begin with, Chesnutt had always been disturbed by the myths and stereotypes which were being promulgated by such Plantation Tradition writers as Thomas Nelson Page and Henry Stillwell Edwards. Even as early as 1880 he was reacting against them in his Journal as he asserted his intention

> to record my impressions of men and things, and such incidents or conversations which take place within my knowledge, with a view of future use in literary work. I shall not record stale negro minstrel, or worn out newspaper squibs on the "man and brother," I shall leave the realm of fiction, where most of this stuff is manufactured, and come down to hard facts. (March 16, 1880)

Four months later he reacted against the romanticism of such white writers as Tourgee who wrote pro-Black novels like *A Fool's Errand*, but did so only in a sentimental and unrealistic manner. "John Green has written a book," Chesnutt recorded in

his Journal. "The subject is the author's experience in the South
. . . and purports to be by a 'Carpetbagger who was born and
bred there.' " In short, "This is one of those ephemeral produc-
tions which have sprung up in the wake of the 'Fool's Errand'
. . . which has created an appetite for this sort of literature."
(July 13, 1880)

In a June 5, 1890, letter to Cable, Chesnutt was even more de-
clarative in his negative reactions to romantic stereotypes on the
contemporary literary scene: both in the works and in the readership. As for the readers, they were not prepared to see either
real Black characters or the biological and social truth which was
implicit in the existence of mulattoes like Rena Walden.

> There are a great many intelligent people who consider the
> class to which Rena and Wain belong as unnatural. I heard
> a gentleman with whom I had just dined, for whom I had
> been doing some difficult work, a man of high standing in
> his profession, of wide reading and as I had thought of great
> liberality, whom I had heard declaim enthusiastically about
> the doctrine of human equality which characterizes our
> institutions—I say this gentleman remarked to me in sub-
> stance that he considered a mulatto an insult to nature, a
> kind of monster that he looked upon with infinite distaste;
> that a black Negro he looked upon with some respect, but
> any laws which tended in any way to bring the two races
> nearer together, were pernicious and in the highest degree
> reprehensible.

Accordingly, the literature of the period reflected this bias.

> I fear there is too much of the same sentiment for mulat-
> toes to make good magazine characters, and I notice that
> all of the many Negroes (excepting your own) whose virtues
> have been given to the world in the magazine press recently,
> have been blacks, full-blooded, and their chief virtues have
> been their dog-like fidelity to their old master, for whom
> they have been willing to sacrifice almost life itself.

Chesnutt himself was not going to dignify and support such myths and stereotypes, even if they did contain some truth. Referring still to the faithful servant stereotype, he noted how

> Such characters exist; not six months ago a Negro in Raleigh, N.C., addressed a letter to the Governor of the State, offering to serve out a term of seven years imprisonment in the penitentiary, for his old master, and those who are familiar with the convict lease system know what that is better than the Negro did. But I can't write about these people, or rather I won't write about them.

Nor was he going to accept the romantic falsity and prejudiced assumptions which underlay the work of most American writers in the field.

> Take Maurice Thompson, for instance. His characters are generally an old, vulgar master, who is usually, when not drunk or asleep, engaged in beating an old Negro. Thomas Nelson Page and Henry S. Edwards depict the sentimental and devoted Negro, who prefers kicks to halfpence. Judge Tourgee's cultivated white Negroes are always bewailing their fate and cursing the drop of black blood which "taints"—I hate the word, it implies corruption—their otherwise pure race.

As he wrote to Page on March 22, 1899,

> The dialect story is one of the sort of Southern stories that make me feel it my duty to write a different sort . . .

Similarly, he was out to refute the direct polemic and vituperation which also was on the contemporary literary scene. As he recalled many years later,

> Thomas Dixon was writing the Negro down industriously and with marked popular success. Thomas Nelson Page was

disguising the harshness of slavery under the mask of sentiment. The trend of public sentiment at the moment was distinctly away from the Negro.[1]

Nor was this polemic merely literary in its origin. Hence he de-
cried in a February 2, 1906, letter to Rev. Asa Z. Hall:

> The chorus of detraction and defamation which has char-
> acterized the unkind, ungenerous, unchristian crusade
> against the common manhood rights of the Negro, which
> has been conducted so vociferously by a little clique of
> Southern leaders who have been poisoning the minds of the
> American people for the last ten or fifteen years.

And he noted earlier in a May 9, 1902, letter to Edgar D. Crumpacker how "There has always been a great deal of Southern
claptrap about the disastrous results that would follow the
intermingling of blood."

Likewise, the Northern press was also biased in its treatment of
Blacks and its handling of these myths and stereotypes. Just as
Chesnutt had scorned certain "worn out newspaper squibs" in
his March 16, 1880, Journal, so did he find the problem of the
press equally prevalent twenty-eight years later when he noted in
a letter to Mrs. C. W. Clifford how

> Newspapers are looking for two things—something sen-
> sational, no matter how radical it is, or in default of the sen-
> sational, something that will fit in with current public
> opinion and make pleasant reading. It is the fad nowadays
> to ignore the rights of the Negro and emphasize his duties.
> (October 15, 1908)

Later on in his life Chesnutt again came into contact with this
Northern press bias. In replying to a letter from Charles T. Hall-
iman of the *Chicago Evening Post* "about the segregation pattern
that was being imposed upon the colored people in the depart-

ments at Washington by the Wilson administration" and how "the situation in Washington needed publicity, and that it was hard to get it from the newspapers," Chesnutt recounted how

> I have lately had some experience with the "languidness of newspapers in our case." As chairman of one of the committees for the local Perry Centenary Celebration, I prepared and submitted to the publicity department of the Centennial Committee an article setting forth the part played by colored sailors and soldiers in the War of 1812. The article appeared in the *Cleveland Plain Dealer*, but the publicity agent informs me that the *Leader* would not print it. (September 15, 1913)

Indeed, it is notable that Chesnutt depicted a biased, inflammatory newspaper in a Southern town as one of the major forces at work in his incisively biting novel, *The Marrow of Tradition*.

As a result of all the biased literature, the average white American had no idea of what real, individual Black people were like. For even at its best, white fiction about Black characters had failed to understand or even see individuals. Indeed, as one literary historian has noted about the period, "it is white society, white viewpoints, which writing about the Negro has clarified," with the result that "Negro characters have remained, for the most part, lacking necessary elements of unique individuality."[2] This, more than anything else, was what the racial crusader and artist in Chesnutt set out to rectify.

It was to fill this void that Chesnutt became a writer himself— both in essay form and in fiction. In his youth he had realized the scarcity of good Black writers, and he very early decided that he could become the first writer of note for his race. As he recorded in his Journal for March 17, 1881,

> I have skimmed *The Negro in the Rebellion* by Dr. Brown and it only strengthens me in my opinion that the Negro is yet to become known who can write a good book. Dr. Brown's books are mere compilations and if they were

not writen by a colored man, they would not sell for enough
to pay for the printing.

Ten years later he was equally conscious of his opportunity to
be a pioneer Black writer. In a September 8, 1891, letter to the
Houghton Mifflin Company, regarding his proposed collection
of short stories entitled "Rena Walden and other Stories," he
made a significant appraisal of the book and of himself as
author. "There is one fact which would give this volume distinction," he began,

> It is the first contribution by an American of acknowl-
> edged African descent to purely imaginative literature.
>   In this case, the infusion of African blood is very small—
> is not in fact a visible admixture—but it is enough, combined
> with the fact that the writer was practically brought up in
> the South, to give him knowledge of the people whose de-
> scription is attempted. These people have never been treated
> from a closely sympathetic standpoint; they have not had
> their day in court. Their friends have written of them, and
> their enemies; but this is, so far as I know, the first instance
> where a writer with any of their own blood has attempted a
> literary portrayal of them. If these stories have any merit,
> I think it is more owing to this new point of view than to any
> other thing.

And eight years later Chesnutt again noted his qualification as a
"first" novelist dealing with this racial subject matter. Referring
to Page's suggestion that Houghton Mifflin entitle Chesnutt's
second book *The Wife of His Youth, and Other Stories of the
Color Line*, Chesnutt had some comments of his own.

> I have not been able to think of any better title, and all
> the stories deal with that subject directly, except one which
> treats it, I might say, collaterally. So, unless there is some
> good reason to the contrary, I rather think that name would

very aptly characterize the volume; and I should like to hope that the stories depict life as it is, in certain aspects that no one has ever before attempted. (August 23, 1899)

Just as Chesnutt saw himself in this pioneering light, so was he recognized in the same terms by those around him. Regarding his *Conjure* stories, Chesnutt's preeminence was early acknowledged. Suggesting that the stories be collected into book form in 1898, Page assured Chesnutt that "I cannot help feeling that that would succeed." Page continued:

> All the readers who have read your stories agree on this —that "The Goophered Grapevine" and "Po' Sandy," and the one or two others that have the same original quality that these show, are stories that are sure to live—in fact, I know of nothing so good of their kind anywhere. (March 30, 1898)

Likewise with *The Wife of His Youth* and *The House Behind the Cedars*, Chesnutt made further strides into new areas: giving American literature a view of the mulattoes' world for the first time, a perspective which could only be provided by a member of the depicted group. Thus William Dean Howells noted about *Wife of His Youth*:

> We had known the nethermost world of the grotesque and comical Negro and the terrible and tragic Negro through the white observer on the outside . . . but it had remained with Mr. Chesnutt to acquaint us with these regions where the paler shades dwell.[3]

Interestingly enough, R. W. Gilder, editor of *Century Magazine,* noted essentially this same fact when discussing Chesnutt's story "Rena Walden," which Chesnutt later expanded into *The House Behind the Cedars*. As he wrote to Cable on May 28, 1890, "Its subject is new, and the point of view." It was essentially because of this newness, in fact, that Gilder rejected publishing "Rena" since he felt that his traditionally minded white readers would not respond favorably to the mulatto-world subject matter.

In *The Marrow of Tradition* Chesnutt broke new ground again, and this was immediately recognized. "In the Marrow," wrote Charles W. Anderson to Chesnutt, "you have not only made a noble plea for the Race before the great tribunal of public opinion, but you have told the story, better than it has yet been told, of the peculiar relations which subsist between the intelligent Colored people of the South and their white neighbors of all classes." (Dec. 11, 1901) And Chesnutt's biographer supports Anderson's assessment, in her discussion of *Marrow's* reception.

> The great dailies, the weeklies, the foreign language periodicals, the magazines devoted to literary criticism, all reviewed it at great length. The Northern papers expressed unqualified praise for it, stressing the fact that it was the first novel in American literature to depict the collision between the whites and the educated, cultivated colored people of the South (*CWC*, p. 176).

In short,

> His characters were new figures in fiction—and his readers were made aware, for the first time, of the mental agony, the soul-maiming suffering of the intelligent, well-educated, aspiring colored people in the South. (*CWC*, p. 178)

The list of acknowledgements of Chesnutt's uniqueness is endless. Yet perhaps the most significant comment in this vein was that offered by the *New York Mail and Express* of December 9, 1899. For in its review of *The Wife of His Youth* it realized most clearly the ultimate uniqueness and new approach which Chesnutt was so deeply concerned with offering the American readership: the understanding of the Black man as an individual human being, humanly alive to a country which had lived on ignorance and stereotypes for over two hundred years.

In *The Wife of His Youth and Other Stories of the Color Line* by Charles W. Chesnutt, we have a variation of most of the methods employed by American story-writers in handling the characterizations of our colored population, either before or since their emancipation, from a humorous or a pathetic point of view, and one that is so striking and so novel that it may fairly be called a new departure in Afro-American fiction, or a new and wise departure in art, since, instead of trying on the one hand to move our compassion for the Negro, because we have inflicted so much suffering on his race in the past, or on the other hand, to study and enjoy him, because he is such a comical, laughable creature, so childlike and irresponsible—it simply aims to interest us in him as an individual human being, without regard to the straightness or kinkiness of his hair, or the amount of nigritude in the color of his skin.

Yet the point must not be lost here. For while all these kudos and acknowledgements are rightly to be seen as dramatic achievements for Chesnutt as a pioneer crusading writer, they correspondingly represent direct incrimination of the American literary scene prior to Chesnutt for its tremendous lack of honest treatment of Black people in America. It was this void which Chesnutt attempted to fill as a writer, even as he directly attacked the more hostile stereotypes which had earlier filled that void and the vicious social conditons amidst which Black Americans daily lived and suffered.

Chesnutt's Optimism Regarding Racial Progress

Despite the harshness of the social and literary world around him, Chesnutt did believe that conditions could improve, and believed further that he could be instrumental in effecting that improvement. In fact, it was this basic general optimism which led him to the writing of his major works.

In some sense Chesnutt was an optimist all his life, and saw the Black American's situation as favorably as it could be seen. As he assessed himself in his Summer, 1879 Journal, "My temperament, as I comprehend it, . . . is a compound of the sanguine and nervous temperaments. A large degree of energy, perseverence, and fidelity." An optimist in general, Chesnutt was specifically optimistic about America's racial situation, a cast of mind which he probably developed as a small boy and youth. When a child in Oberlin, Ohio, he saw his father become a member of the successful Underground Railroad. At the end of the war, he witnessed the establishment of the Freedmen's Bureau schools, and later, at age fourteen, he became pupil-teacher in the Normal school at Fayetteville. In fact, in 1880, at twenty-two he became the full principal of the school. Significantly enough, such a rise within the system for himself paralleled and even surpassed his father's own rise in postbellum Fayetteville to the official positions of county commissioner and justice of the peace for Cumberland County. (*CWC*, pp. 3-25) In short, his early life led him to believe in the effectiveness and eventual success of the bourgeois aspirations embodied by his family and his readings in the Ben Franklin and Horatio Alger vein.

Throughout these same early years, therefore, he tended to see the silver lining of the Black man's position in the South. We have already noted his optimistic 1879 letter to the *Christian Union* in which he concluded that, despite considerable "election frauds, and the intimidation of voters in some of the Southern States," he took "pleasure in saying that many of the Southern States could well take example from N.C. in her attitude towards the Colored people." In referring to the *Christian Union's* mention of "the Jubilee singers, and their concert in Nashville," he further asserted that

I am glad to accept the indicated incident at Nashville as a hopeful sign and one that "marks an era in the progress of the colored people toward recognition," and cherish a fond hope that, in this age of improvements, this country of rapid changes, the time of that recognition is not far off.

Two years later, Chesnutt was encouraged enough to project in his Journal some of his recent experiences in the Fayetteville area and conclude that "several things have occurred lately which lead me to think that the colored man is moving upward very fast." (May 4, 1881) And, eighteen years later, even in the depths of that despair which gripped him after the Wilmington Massacre and the sweeping Southern surge toward violent disfranchisement, Chesnutt was still able to assert to Page that the Black man was nevertheless "moving steadily though slowly upward."

Perhaps the most amazing aspect of Chesnutt's optimism was its perseverence, even when bitter disappointment struck him personally and directly. Despite his disillusion over the lack of success for *Cedars* in 1900 and *Marrow* in 1901—and his realization that this was a strong testament to America's lack of racial enlightenment and progress—Chesnutt found himself writing to Congressional Representative Edgar D. Crumpacker that Thomas Dixon's vicious novel, *The Leopard's Spots*, "doubtless represents the views of an extreme and I trust a very small proportion of Southern people." Furthermore, he thought, even though Dixon was "a North Carolinian, and for the past two or three years race feeling has been very acute in that State"; and even though Chesnutt himself "was down there about a year ago for several weeks and was surprised at its intensity"; nevertheless "I found a number of thoughtful men who regarded that attitude as merely temporary and growing out of certain conditions which would not be permanent." (May 9, 1902)

It is not surprising, therefore, to find that this optimism persisted in Chesnutt's own work. Even after he had written *The Colonel's Dream*—his last novel, and one in which the Colonel's (i.e. Chesnutt's) dream of progressively reconstructing the South dramatically failed, with the Colonel moving back to the North in acknowledged defeat—Chesnutt could still write to Jerome B. Howard and claim that

> That which for the Colonel was a dream will in the hands of others or a succession of others more patient, become a reality, I trust. I have faith in humanity, and if that faith is justifiable, the problems involved in the Southern situation will in time be worked out in a number for the best happiness of all concerned. (Sept. 18, 1905)

And later, after the novel itself had failed and Chesnutt had given up writing altogether in response to this ultimate defeat, his ability to flush Phoenixes from among life's rubble still had not deserted him. Hence he was still able to see the darkness of the night as proof that the dawn was coming. As he wrote to Booker T. Washington on March 3, 1906,

> I think a little more anti-Negro agitation in the South will very likely result in an effort at the North to see, for the welfare of the whole country, that the Thirteenth, Fourteenth, and Fifteenth Amendments shall become not only the theoretical but the real law of the land.

In short, throughout his life Chesnutt's optimism prevailed, continually rooted in the social faith that he had so strongly developed by the age of twenty-one.

> I believe that the American People will recognize worth, ability, or talent wherever it shows itself, and that as the colored people, as a class, show themselves worthy of respect and recognition, the old prejudice will vanish, or wear away, and the *Colored Man* in America will be considered, not as a separate race, not as a stranger and a pariah, but as a friend and brother, that he may become a strong pillar in the Temple of American Liberty, and be

"bone of one bone, flesh of one flesh" with the New American Nation. (Journal, April, 1879)

This belief in the future was fundamentally why he wrote.

Chesnutt's Choice of Literature as His Medium

Having realized the social and literary predicament of the Black man, and having decided that the situation was improvable, Chesnutt thereupon set out to help effect the necessary changes. We have already seen the basic crusader in him. We now need to understand why writing was the medium chosen for this crusade. Partially Chesnutt used literature because half of the problem itself was literary; partially he chose it because it was his dominant social skill. There were, however, two other considerations. First, Chesnutt saw literature as a strong social and moral force. As early as age twenty-three he was able to note in his Journal how

> I believe that . . . there is no agency so potent for leading the youthful mind to high aspirations as good books . . . . The writer of such a book as "David Copperfield" or "John Halifax" gives to literature a moral force, whose effect upon the young of future generations is simply incalculable. (July 21, 1881)

Furthermore, the literary milieu of the period was governed largely by the moral-oriented precepts of William Dean Howells, of whom Chesnutt was very much aware. Coming under Howells's influence, he saw the subtle, positive changes which literature could effect in a society. As he had noted in one of his first major declarations of purpose, literature was to be his indirect weapon for social change:

> Not a fierce indiscriminate onset, not an appeal to force, for this is something that force can but slightly affect, but a moral revolution which must be brought about in a differ-

ent manner. The subtle almost indefinable feeling of repulsion toward the Negro, which is common to most Americans—cannot be stormed and taken by assault; the garrison will not capitulate, so their position must be mined, and we will find ourselves in their midst before they think it. (Journal, May 29, 1880)

A second major factor here was Chesnutt's belief that, aside from those who were staunchly prejudiced, there were many American people who were morally ready to hear a Black writer's realistic voice on racial matters. He had in fact a constant belief in "the conscience of the white people,"[4] and this, coupled with the early approval of his work by readers and publishers, made him feel that his kind of writing was in demand on the American scene. Such was this feeling that at its peak in 1900 he was able to exclaim to his daughters at Smith that he had just sold a story to *Century Magazine* "and have had requests from two of the biggest publishers in the United States for my next novel. They want a strong race problem novel, and somebody shall have it." (*CWC*, p. 159)

For all these reasons, therefore, Chesnutt chose literature as his medium for social crusading, and the question now is why he personally felt qualified. On the one hand, he was skilled in the art of writing generally. As he described his versatility to Cable in early 1889,

> I can turn my head and hand to several kinds of literary work, can write a story, a funny skit, can turn a verse, and write a serious essay. I have even written a novel, though it has never seen the light, nor been offered to a publisher. I know German pretty well, French passably well, and could translate either into grammatical English, and I trust, for the sake of a long-suffering public, into better English than a great many of the translations that are dumped on the market.

Furthermore, the subject matter was familiar and important to him. After analyzing Tourgee's success with *A Fool's Errand*, Chesnutt found himself looking inward and asking why he shouldn't be even more successful. His answer came most declaratively two months later:

> Fifteen years of life in the South, in one of the most eventful eras of its history, among a people whose life is rich in the elements of romance, under conditions calculated to stir one's soul to the very depths—I think there is a fund of experience, a supply of material, which a skillful pen could work up with tremendous effect. (Journal, May 29, 1880)

And so he decided that he "must write a book" for "a high, holy purpose"—"a moral revolution" based on the "elevation of the whites." Thus while most of his writings dealt with his material in an artistic, indirect manner, it is clear that Chesnutt was also avowedly crusading. In 1891, for example, he noted to Houghton Mifflin that his major purpose in writing "Rena Walden" was to treat the Southern Freedmen "from a closely sympathetic standpoint" because "they have not had *their day in court.*" (Sept. 8, 1891; italics mine) Similarly, in discussing *The Wife of His Youth* on December 12, 1899, he indicated to Houghton Mifflin that

> The book was written with the distinct hope that it might have its influence in directing attention to certain aspects of the race question which are quite familiar to those on the unfortunate side of it; and I should be glad to have that view of it emphasized if in your opinion the book is strong enough to stand it; for a sermon that is labeled a sermon must be a good one to get a hearing.

And two days later he reinforced this concept with equal clarity. As he told Houghton Mifflin again,

I suspect a good many copies of "The Wife of His Youth" will be sold among colored people when they discover, by hearing others speak of it, that it is a book of tracts in their behalf, and written from their side. (Dec. 14, 1879)

Statements like this by Chesnutt are rather numerous, but perhaps the most sweeping and explicit came from a discussion of *The Marrow of Tradition* in a letter to a Mrs. W. E. Henderson in 1905. Referring to the book's message and purpose, Chesnutt noted that

The book was written, *as all my books have been,* with a purpose . . . the hope that it might create sympathy for the colored people of the South in the very difficult position they now occupy. (Nov. 11, 1905; italics mine)

This, ultimately, was the major reason why Chesnutt wrote.

CHAPTER VII

Why Chesnutt Ceased Writing

Because he was almost universally praised as a literary artist—except where political or social prejudice influenced the critic's vision, Chesnutt's decision to stop writing concerned only two aspects of his nature: his economic interests and his commitment to social change. We will now treat them in that order.

Economic Factors

Chesnutt was always concerned about economic security and the importance of money to himself and his family; and this aspect of his nature was always in his consciousness. It had been one of the major criteria considered when he was deciding to go into writing as a full-time profession; similarly it was a major criterion for his decision to quit.

We have seen Chesnutt's general interest in money in great detail above; and we have seen as well that it carried over into and throughout his literary life. As much as he cared that his books be artistically "good" and that they have a significant social effect on this country, he cared equally about their popularity and the sales to which that popularity should lead.

Indeed, having seen how many of Chesnutt's early thoughts on writing were oriented towards financial success, we are prepared to understand how much attention he then devoted to the pragmatic, commerical aspects of authorship once he began to write in earnest.

Almost as soon as he decided to devote himself to a full-time career of writing, therefore, he became aware of the commercial responsibilities a writer was expected to perform in order to help promote his works. As a man of commerce and business affairs himself, Chesnutt eagerly immersed himself in these responsibilities. It was a strong commitment with him, and it took three forms: joining the lecture circuit in order to make himself and his work better known; devising promotional advertising for his books; and even setting up sales consignments in special areas.

As a lecturer, Chesnutt was quite active—especially early in his career. As early as August, 1899—the month prior to his official decision to turn professional—he began to make himself physically known in Eastern literary circles. In that month he accepted an offer from Walter Hines Page "to substitute for him in a lecture course at Greenacres, a summer school in Elliot, Maine." "As Page suggested and Chesnutt knew, "this would be a good piece of advertising and would help him in his work." Chesnutt's own reaction to his appearance was enthusiastic while still characteristically modest, as he described to Page how "I had the close attention of the audience, and made a good impression, receiving quite as much applause as they could find decent excuse for giving me."

Two months later he took to the lecture circuit in earnest and told Houghton Mifflin how he had promoted his work by "a little reading I gave last night" in anticipation of *Wife of His Youth's* coming out "by November 11th." (October 11, 1899) Two weeks later he recorded his intentions to the publishers of his forthcoming biography of Fredrick Douglass: "I am going to give some public readings, one in Washington on November 17," he wrote, and these will pave the way for my books; and after this season, I shall devote a good deal of time to platform work; I am told I read my stories very effectively. (October 26, 1899)

Six days later he returned to the subject in greater detail in a letter to Edward C. Williams.

I gave a reading last night in a country lecture course in the historic town of Kirtland. I am going to read next week for a charitable club here, small gathering. Go to Washington, read there the 17th. Have an idea that I shall keep myself pretty fully occupied. (November 2, 1899)

And, over the next few years, he was kept quite busy, as he used the lecture circuit to professionally promote his early books.

As for devising reviews and advertising displays for his books, Chesnutt was equally active. In his first months of professional life, he was contacted by Small, Maynard & Co. and asked for a "list of names of persons who would be willing to handle the life of Douglass, with suggestions as to terms to be offered them." He was asked, as well, for "a list of special papers to which they [Small, Maynard] might send copies for review—particulary, Afro-American papers—in order to promote the sale of the book among colored people." Significantly enough, an identical request came from Houghton Mifflin six weeks later, and in reply to both letters Chesnutt sent a detailed "representative" list of "Afro-American newspapers."[1] Related to this matter of promoting his work to Black readers through Black reviewers, Chesnutt offered other ideas during this period. On December 12, he noted that he would soon provide Houghton Mifflin with a list of "the half-dozen persons to whom a book might be sent for an opinion," and he then contemplated the pragmatic feasibility of asking Booker T. Washington to fill such a role.

About Booker Washington, I don't know. Anything he might say would doubtless be valuable if he would venture to express himself favorably on a book supposed from the Southern standpoint to preach heretical doctrine. Perhaps one ought not to ask him, however, until the Southern reviews come in.[2]

Two days later he suggested that, in approaching the Afro-American newspapers whose list he was enclosing, Houghton Mifflin should do more than merely send copies of the book. They should, he suggested, stress the racial importance of the books. "If copies are sent to any of these papers for review," he noted,

I imagine it would be worth the trouble to have a few carbon copies of passages from several notices such as the one I shall quote herein, and the one I quoted in my last letter, and send them along with the book, so as to sort of steer the appeal to his racial sympathies.[3]

Becoming even more specific, Chesnutt notified Houghton Mifflin eleven days later that T. Thomas Fortune, editor of the *New York Age*, "has written me that he will with pleasure write an 'appreciation' of the book," and two years later Chesnutt became equally specific in suggesting that advance copies of *Marrow* be sent to "such representative men as Mr. Booker T. Washington, Professor W.E.B. DuBois, and Thomas Nelson Page"—adding Page because he realized the value of controversy and debate in addition to praise. (October 2, 1901)

In addition to ideas for attracting specifically Black readers Chesnutt also had interest in other, more general promotional concerns. Mentions of this in his corrspondence with Houghton Mifflin are numerous, and perhaps just one example will suffice. In reply to the publisher's expression of interest in "undertaking special work on behalf of *The Wife of His Youth*," Chesnutt answered some of the general questions asked by Houghton Mifflin and then began to make some creative suggestions of his own.

It occurs to me that the drawings or oil sketches made for the illustrations to *The Wife of His Youth* would be good stuff for window displays. I have been promised one of the *The Wife of His Youth* scenes, but will cheerfully waive my claim until any possible good use can be made of it.

I have a set of proofs of *The Conjure Woman*, if they would be on any use in a window. Have you ever made up a window display showing a book in the various stages of production— the rough draft, the various revisions, the proof-sheets or revises, the unbound book, the completed book (with various editions), the portrait of the author, view of his study, and so on? I suppose you have, (November 12, 1889)

Perhaps most indicative—and discouraging—of Chesnutt's concern for sales and advertising was an "article" which he wrote for "The Publisher's Page" of the *Cleveland World* of October 30, 1901. "Charles W. Chesnutt's Own View of His New Story 'The Marrow of Tradition' " it was called, and its purpose was to boost sales of the soon-to-be published book in question.

"I have been asked to make for this page a brief summary of the motive and chief points of my forthcoming novel, 'The Marrow of Tradition,' " he began, and then proceeded to outline the book's contents, approach, and importance. "The primary object of this story, " he noted, "as it should be of every work of fiction, is to entertain." And yet, he continued, "It belongs in the category of purpose novels, inasmuch as it seeks to throw light upon the vexed moral and sociological problems which grow out of the presence, in our southern states, of two diverse races, in nearly equal number."

After six succeeding paragraphs of background analysis and plot summary, we find a strange paragraph which seems to be working against everything for which Chesnutt had stood and written. Especially when we remember his contempt for the Plantation Tradition sterotypes of Thomas Nelson Page and others of his school; and remember as well his negative statement to George Washington Cable, regarding those "popular" Black characters of the day, whose "chief virtues have been their dog-like fidelity to their old master;" we can only assume that the following paragraph was included in order to placate and stoop to the interests and emotional biases of Chesnutt's potential readers, both North and South. "Among the characters" in *Marrow*, he then continued,

> are a typical old "Mammy," a faithful servant who is willing to die for his master and an ideal old aristocrat who practically sacrifices his life to save that of his servant.

Myth and degrading stereotype: obviously Chesnutt was beginning to feel a definite economic need to cater to his readership in this uncharacteristic, degrading fashion. The truth, of course, is that he was. Finances had always been important to him, and now, after the minimal returns from *Cedars*, he found such concerns looming larger and larger in his life.

The third aspect of Chesnutt's involvement in these pragmatic matters was his concern with direct book sales. Along with certain offhand suggestions which Chesnutt occasionally made regarding sales of his books—such as his letter to Small, Maynard suggesting that "The *Douglass Biography* might possibly be available for use in some of those Washington, D.C., schools, if size and price can be harmonized,"—(November 19,1900), Chesnutt occasionally became more deeply involved in the commercial market where his book had to complete. Two examples here should suffice.

In a November 19,1900, letter to Houghton Mifflin regarding the potential sales of *Cedars* in Cleveland, for example, he hoped that *Cedars* would be good enough to popularly succeed on its own merits; but he realized also that there was a special problem which the competition offered in the Cleveland market. Such a novel as his, he noted,

> has to contend against an enormous number of books which are not left to that method [i.e., success by merit]. One book-

seller here bought 1,000 copies of "Alice of Old Vincennes" and another 250, before publication, relying on the publishers' advertising. . . . Stone & Co., Small, Maynard & Company, and such houses, have a way of stocking up books around here, especially in one bookstore, which the booksellers get, I suppose at special rates, or on consignment; and it is quite evident that it is these books which they try to work off in all sorts of ways.

As he further noted,

I know that is not your method, and that it is not a good method, and that it seldom makes a poor book go very far.

It does, however, stand in the way, to a certain extent, of even the best books . . .

One month later Chesnutt became even more forcefully involved. Discussing a local bookstore, Burrows Bros., and the sales of *Cedars* in Cleveland, Chesnutt noted that,

I have an idea that they sell most of the books on which they can get the best terms, for they have intelligent and pushing salesmen, who tell people what they want. I spoke to Mr. Cathcart, their buyer, yesterday, about getting them in a good lot of my books stacking them up conspicously, and selling them. He said to me that if you would consign 250 to them, he would do it. (December 27, 1900)

After then noting that "I have an idea that your house seldom if ever consigns books," Chesnutt felt compelled to add that "if you do not care to consign them, you may secure the account by charging it against me."

Somewhat related to this sort of involvement was the program which Chesnutt specifically mapped out for sales of his books in Washington, D.C. As he introduced the arrangement to Houghton Mifflin on November 24, 1899.

During my recent visit to Washington I have been working
up more or less interest in my books, and to a certain extent
among a class of readers who are not ordinarily large buyers
of works of fiction, but who can be very easily reached by a
little personal attention. I have made arrangement for some
books to be sold there . . .

The "agent" for this was to be a relative of his, "Master E.
French Tyson, 212 K. St., N.W." Significantly enough, Chesnutt
repeated this suggestion on August 16, 1905, to Doubleday, Page
& Company in discussing the potential sales of *The Colonel's
Dream.* As he announced to Page,

> Mr. H. French Tyson, a young relative of mine, and a student
> of Harvard, wishes to take some orders among the colored
> people (mainly) of Washington, D.C., where he lives, for
> my forthcoming book, "The Colonel's Dream." . . . I have
> heretofore had an arrangement with Houghton & Company
> to furnish him the books on my account, as the author's rate,
> or as good a rate as they would allow. He has been suc-
> cessful in selling several hundred of my former books, and
> reaches some people whom ordinary advertising would not
> reach.

Such was the importance of financial returns in Chesnutt's
carrying out—and stopping—his writing career. Needless to say,
when *Cedars, Marrow,* and *The Colonel's Dream* did not sell up
to expectations, Chesnutt ceased his writing career altogether
and returned to his business in Cleveland.

Social Conditions

At the same time, it is equally true that Chesnutt's concern
over the American racial scene also prompted his termination of
writing in 1905. By that year it became starkly clear to him that

the position of Black people in this country had not really improved since he had undertaken professional writing in September of 1899. Indeed, if anything, racial conditions had gotten worse; he was constantly being reminded of this by papers and people around him.

After a fairly eventful first year of professional writing in 1900, during which Chesnutt expended most of his energy in the promotion of *The Wife of His Youth* and the writing of *Cedars*, he found that social events in 1901 began to disturb him anew, even as they had in 1898 with the Wilmington Massacre. As his biographer notes,

> Chesnutt started the year of 1901 in a somewhat pessimistic frame of mind, for the condition of the Negro in the South was becoming intolerable. By amending their state constitutions, Mississippi, South Carolina, Louisiana, and North Carolina had already robbed the Negro of his suffrage and consequently of his rights . . . By this disfranchisement the colored people were left utterly defenseless, without any representation in the government or in the courts, and with no voice in electing the people who might be fair and just to them. (*CWC*, p. 158)

Not surprisingly, these conditions revived in Chesnutt his earlier horror at the Wilmington riot of 1898, and he decided after *Cedars* to begin a novel based on that riot in the hopes that this would waken the slumbering American conscience. Racial conditions were becoming worse throughout the South, and the need for positive concern was crucial. For fresh background and knowledge, therefore, in February, 1901, he made a tour of the South, "reading and lecturing at some of the leading schools and colleges for colored people." The results of this trip were not surprising: he "reached home very much depressed about race relations in the South."

This depression was to last throughout the remainder of his major writing period, interspersed with those characteristic flurries of optimism which led to his writing of *Marrow* and *The Colonel's Dream* in the hope that conditions were still literarily salvagable in the country. Writing peripherally to the Macmillan Company on April 26, 1901, about a scurrilous, anti-Black book which they had allowed to go under their imprint, Chesnutt noted most pointedly that "The Negro in the United States stands at present in a critical position: his status as a slave is ended; his position as a freeman has not yet been made secure." Such security was not, however, even on the horizon. Six months later Chesnutt was to see another major anti-Black upheavel in the South.

On October 26, 1901, President Theodore Roosevelt invited Booker T. Washington to dinner at the White House. More dramatic and significant than this "hopeful" sign of racial program was the country's immediate reaction to Roosevelt's gesture. Even such Northern, "liberal" papers as *The New York Times* considered the dinner "unfortunate," and the feverish outbreak of violence in the South was especially depressing. As Francis J. Garrison of Houghton Mifflin analyzed it in a letter to Chesnutt,

> The outburst of the South over Booker Washington's dining at the White House shows how barbarous the whites of that section still are, and the frequent burnings at the stake, which were scarcely known in slavery days, indicate still more how little we have advanced from the dark middle ages. [4] (November 9, 1901)

Despite the carnage which was now so openly rampant, not only "liberal" Northern newspapers, but even "liberal" Northern congressmen, were unconcerned about the Black man's plight. This was made abundantly clear to Chesnutt in a March 31, 1902, letter from the nominally liberal Congressman. E. D. Crumpacker. As Crumpacker noted in mincing, qualified terms, the race question "is exceedingly involved, and I hope that before many years an intelligent public sentiment will direct judicious action upon correct lines." At the same time, however, he added, "Whatever legislation there may be, the Colored man must in large measure work out his own destiny. We can only surround him with helpful conditions. He must not be taught to depend too much upon legislation."

Chesnutt's reply stressed that the "race question is doubtless destined to receive a great deal of attention on the part of the public for a long time to come" and that "it is a matter in which the North is under obligation to intervene . . . to see that justice is done to all concerned, and that the spirit of our institutions is not sacrificed merely to promote the selfish interests of any one faction of the people." (May 9, 1902) But there was little more that he could do. The mood of the country was not one concerned with the Black American's civil rights.

Nor was it going to get better. A full year after his correspondence with Crumpacker—midway between his disappointment over *Marrow* and his final dejection over the *The Colonel's Dream*—Chesnutt saw this quite clearly. As he noted in his article on "The Disfranchisement of the Negro," the rights of Blacks, especially in the South, "are at a lower ebb than at any time during the thirty-five years of their freedom, and the race prejudice more intense and uncompromising."[2]

Even so, Chesnutt would write one more major work, *The Colonel's Dream*; and only with its failure would he cease writing altogether. By then it would be apparent to him that the South was starkly intent on re-enslaving the freedmen and that the North was basically unconcerned. With social conditions deteriorating in this fashion and with Chesnutt's own writing having no visible effect upon them, he found himself with no alternative but to leave the literary field and repair to his stenography and the world of local civil rights work to which he devoted the rest of his life. A great career had ended prematurely; the American public had made its racial prejudices known, and felt.

CHAPTER VIII

The Full Spectrum of Chesnutt's Writing

To this point, our concern has been with Chesnutt as a man within a sociological and literary environment. In our final two chapters, however, we will focus our discussion directly on his writings and a study of him as a literary artist. This immediate chapter will quantitatively explore the full range of Chesnutt's work, allowing us to devote the final chapter to a qualitative analysis of Chesnutt's artistry and genius in selected major works.

Chesnutt's Direct Prose

Most of Chesnutt's prose dealt with racial material in sociological and historical terms. His May, 1902, article for the *Southern Workman* on "The Free Colored People of North Carolina," for example, was based very clearly on Chesnutt's personal and historical understanding of the state in which he had been reared. In a similarly personal and sociological vein was his article in the May,1901, issue of *Modern Culture* on "Superstitions and Folk Lore of the South."

More political and didactic was the majority of Chesnutt's articles and essays during his major writing period. "What is a White Man?" in *The Independent* of May 30, 1899; "A Plea for the American Negro" in *The Critic* of February, 1900; "The White and the Black" in the *Boston Transcript* of March 20, 1901: all represent this dominant phase of his prose concern. Its importance grew in the middle of his mature period with a three-part series of articles for the *Boston Transcript* in 1900, entitled generally "The Future American" and subtitled, respectively, "What the Race Is Likely to Become in the Process of Time" (August 18), "A Steam of Dark Blood in the Veins of Southern Whites" (August 25, and "A Complete Race Amalgamation Likely to Occur" (September 1). The climax of this vein of Chesnutt's direct prose was his essay on "The Disfranchisement of the Negro," which appeared as part of a book entitled *The Negro Problem,* whose subtitle announced that it was "A Series of Articles by Representative American Negroes of Today" and whose list of contributors included such men as Booker T. Washington, W. E. B. Dubois, T. Thomas Fortune, and Paul Laurence Dunbar.

Ocassionally, prose statements by Chesnutt on this subject appeared as book reviews, as was the case with "On the Future of His People" in the January 1900, *Saturday Evening Post* (a review of Booker T. Washington's *The Future of the American Negro*) and with "A Defamer of His Race" in *The Critic* of April 1901, Chesnutt's scathing reaction to William Hannibal Thomas's scurrilous defamation of the race in *The American Negro*. Occasionally, also, a trip to the South would stir up personal feelings in Chesnutt which would result in an article such as the one he wrote for *The Cleveland Leader* of March 31, 1901: "A Visit to Tuskegee." Indeed, one of Chesnutt's most powerful presentations of his social feelings came through his biography of *Fredrick Douglass* in 1899.

Though political considerations were Chesnutt's major interest in his direct prose, he was also motivated as an artist interested in his field and a man who enjoyed writing about subjects which simply interested him. In the former, most of his statements on art came later in his life, after his reputation had been established. Indeed the prime purpose of his three articles on art, coming in the 1920s for such magazines as *The Crisis,* was to be a spur and guide to the dynamic "Harlem Renaissance" which was beginning to develop. Thus, "The Mission of the Drama" in *Cygnet* of January, 1920; "The Negro in Art" in *The Crisis* of November, 1926; and "Post-Bellum—Pre-Harlem" in *The Crisis* of June, 1931; all expressed Chesnutt's theoretical as well as practicing interest in literature and art for a generation of Black writers just beginning to come into its own.

In those writings which were simply for enjoyment or personal involvement, Chesnutt showed great variety of styles and interests. On the one hand there was nonracial whimsy in his tongue-in-cheek "Advice to Young Men" of November, 1886, in *The Social Circle Journal*; this tone, with perhaps a greater attention to racial matters, also appeared in "'A Multitude of Counselors" in *Independent* of April 2, 1891. Nor was he limited to this form and tone. It was as a purely raceless historian that he wrote an article on "Lincoln's Courtship" for the *Southwestern Christian Advocate* of February 4, 1901; and one year later he was a political didacticist again—this time on the subject of "Women's Rights" in *The Crisis* of August, 1910.

Chesnutt's direct prose interests were obviously wide and deep. Our concern here, however, deals with the manner in which he turned his thoughts and feelings into artistic media.

As we come to discuss Chesnutt's fictional work more directly, we become immediately conscious of the value of seeing his fiction in terms of chronological periods. With some writers this approach is often forced and essentially invalid as a meaningful entrance into their most significant writings. With Chesnutt, however, it is an important first step towards understanding most of what he stood for as a writer, especially since much of his work was sociological in nature and thus mirrored actual events and feelings in the contemporary world around him.

For our purpose we can separate his fictional writings into four major periods. First were his early Journal stories. Then came his "apprentice" period, extending from the date of his first published story in 1886 to his first published book, *The Conjure Woman*, and his desire to devote himself to writing as a career on September 30, 1899. (*CWC*, p. 118) Next came his "mature" period of major works from 1899 through 1905, beginning with his optimistic dedication of himself to a full time writing career, the first result of which was *The Wife of His Youth* in 1899, and ending with the despair and disappointment which he felt with the popular rejection of *The Marrow of Tradition* in 1901 and *The Colonel's Dream* in 1905—a despair which led directly to his renunciation of writing as a career in that latter year. Finally we have the rest of his life, devoted less to literature than to business and tangible social concerns like NAACP work in Cleveland.

Prelude: The Journal Stories

The earliest stories in the Journal are "literary" in the worst sense of the word. Most of them take their characters, their situations, and often even their dialogue from books which Chesnutt had presumably read, rather than from experiences which he had actually undergone or feelings which he had personally felt. In Howellsian terms, Chesnutt had had his ear less to "nature's lips" than to voices and situations which he had met solely through books.

In the Journal entry of August 14, 1874, therefore, we have Chesnutt's first attempt at original writing: "Lost in a Swamp, an Adventure by C.W.C." The story begins nicely with dialogue and a first person narrator, achieving an immediate dramatic effect; but otherwise it is a rather uninspired story of a boy on an errand who becomes lost in a swamp as darkness starts to close in. It is complete with the traditional "furniture" of such a suspense story: frogs croaking, wolves howling, and "gloomy reflections;" and it ends just as predictably with the narrator, aided by the moon, finding an inhabited house and staying safely through the night. Chesnutt's comment is of some interest here, as he tells us that "The above is my first real attempt at literature" and that "The reader will please pardon all faults and errors."

Nine days later Chesnutt's second story is entered. "Beneath you will find another attempt at a story," he records with characteristic modesty, and we find ourselves introduced to "Frisk's First Rat," the story of a young kitten's triumph in seeking out and killing a rat almost as large as he. The writing here is still immature and heavily "literary" in its search for dramatic effect. For example, in the heroic mold, Frisk's "breast heaved . . . his eyes flashed fire. . . . while in his bosom burned a desire to distinguish himself." Subsequently, Frisk achieves a "glorious victory" over his "fallen foe."

A partial extenuation of this pasteboard melodrama lies perhaps in the story's final paragraph. For if the concluding sentence "And now my dear children, don't you think Frisk was a pretty smart hunter?" indicates that the story was written for Chesnutt's own younger brothers and sisters, the melodramatic quality of the language may be more easily accepted.

A scant two days later found Chesnutt reading *Quackenbos' Composition and Rhetoric,* a book which suggested to him that he should write some essay or anecdote himself. "One is here given," he adds, and we are then presented his third story, "A Storm at Sea." More a short sketch than a complete story, the writing is still encumbered with artificial dialect meant to capture how "old Tars" are supposed to speak:

> "Jim," said he to the helmsman, "do you think we will have fine weather all day?"
> "Dunno, Cap'n," said the old tar.

On the other hand, there is a greater force and vibrancy in Chesnutt's own narrative descriptions here. The writing itself is still not unique or notable as prose expression, but it has become more crisply imaginative and has begun to gather a more assured sense of itself. When Chesnutt describes an ocean storm, for example, he seems to pour a greater intensity of feeling into that description when he sees how the "waves welled mountains high," how "the lightenings darted their forked tongues across the sky in wild confusion," and how, ultimately, "In this wild turmoil of waters, the ship seemed as a child's toy in the hands of a giant." This is still not deathless prose, perhaps, but it is far more dramatic and lyrical than anything Chesnutt had written so far.

His fourth story, "Bruno" is an extremely interesting one for what it shows us of the inner, deeper Chesnutt. Entered under the same August 25, 1874, date as "A Storm at Sea," the story is far more self-revealing in its choice of narrator, plot, and general situation. "Bruno," then, is a semi-anecdotal sketch about how our first person narrator becomes owner of Bruno, a large Newfoundland dog. Of major interest here is the narrative position which the sixteen-year-old author assumes, for it is clear that this is a role with which he readily identifies. He is a doctor of importance and stature in a small town who, upon discovering Bruno's original owner lying in the street, becomes concerned about the man's condition. Instead of struggling to lift the man himself however, the narrator's social position allows a far greater sense of control. Hence "I ordered him moved into a drugstore nearby . . .I then had him removed to bed in a boarding house."

This seems a small point, perhaps; but within the scope of Chesnutt's own daily life and sense of middle class, professional purpose we can see just now clearly he has channeled his concern for people into a professional, prestigious, socially respected role. As we have noted extensively above, this concern of Chesnutt's was something he carried with him throughout his life. Correspondingly, it is a concern which will find its way into a good many of his later writings.

One other aspect of "Bruno" is important here, and that is the growth of realism which it shows over the earlier, fairy tale stories. What strikes us is the incisive nature of some of the narrator's perceptions about people around him. Far from the world of romantic anecdotes and children's tales, such comments now see men clearly and with a strong sense of realistic honesty. Such a comment is Chesnutt's insightful assessment of the average crowd.

> As it is a noticeable fact that crowds are always willing to witness an accident, it is equally as noticeable that they are very slow to render any assistance in such cases, (except in cases of a fire or something of the kind, where they manage to do as much harm as good).

This is not to claim, of course, that Chesnutt developed into a realistic writer over the course of these early stories, especially since there was a period of only eleven days between the first one and the last. Yet this was to be a major part of his later significant writing.

We have no record of any other writing which Chesnutt may have done over the next eleven years. In an entry dated September 13, 1885, however, we find his fifth and essentially last Journal story. "Yesterday afternoon two clerks went the round of the auditor's office of the Nickel Plate Ry. to bid the clerks goodby," it begins, and the story itself is merely a pair of anecdotal character sketches based on Chesnutt's own experiences at the Nickel Plate Railway in Cleveland in the early 1880s where he worked for several years in the accounting department. As his daughter describes his interests during this period.

> At night, after his day's work was over, he would write down all the interesting incidents of the day, and thus stored up material for some of the humorous writings which were later published in *Puck* and *Tid-Bits*. (*C.W.C.*, p. 35)

Miss Chesnutt does not discuss this particular story, but her comment here is relevant, for it represents the anecdotal genesis and light, humorous quality of many of Chesnutt's early stories. Indeed, not only was this interest in the everyday world of common, raceless people and humorous situation important to him as an early writer, but it was of interest to him throughout his life. For his continual goal was to live his life as a man, on his own terms, without pigeonholing himself into racial categories. Thus we will note that even after he became established as a writer of conjure stories and "color line" material in 1899, he still was nonracial enough to write three full-length raceless novels and one major short story in his later, mature period of creativity.

However, Chesnutt's first published story *was* a story rooted in racial material and was a narrative of far greater merit and depth than one would expect by looking at his Journal work. "Uncle Peter's House" was his first published story and his first major entrance into the depiction of a racial situation.

The Apprentice Period (1886-1898)

By and large, Chesnutt's early stories can be placed into two distinct categories: those written in a light, popular vein and those concerned with racial characters and racial themes. Most of the former stories are satirical and witty, often featuring white (i.e., raceless) characters in an urban, professional business world; and generally they were written for Chesnutt's own witty enjoyment and for his desire to establish a literary reputation on the national magazine scene. The latter, racial group itself rather clearly divided into two parts. Several stories are "racial" only in the sense that the characters are Black, i.e., they are less social-concern stories than they are universal, "human foible" stories that use Black characters as the specific situation from which the general foible is to be drawn (in the same way that Sarah Orne Jewett used New Hampshirites, Mary Noilles Murfree used Appalachian figures, and all the "local color" followers of William Dean Howells used specific situations from their own personal experiences from which to draw general morals on general human conduct). On the other hand, several of these racial stories were very clearly written around Black characters because the social comment in them is one that deals specifically with the Black man's position in America.

It is significant that Chesnutt's first published story was one of the social comment, racial stories. "Uncle Peter's House," appearing in *The Cleveland News and Herald* in 1885, is a racial tragedy concerned with the bitter hardships and prejudice which the newly freed Black man faced in the South during Reconstruction; and, as such, the story has a great deal of social realism about it.

Having eventually overcome most of his social and economic obstacles, Peter was finally on the threshold of success and the construction of a new home. However, just as he was completing the chimmey, he accidentally fell from the roof, suffering fatal internal injuries . In his last moments, surrounded by his wife and son, he laments not having finished the house for them, is comforted with the real vision and song of "A mansion in hebben I see," and dies.

The story itself concludes on an optimistic note, as Peter's wife and son carry on towards the completion of the house. As the last paragraph tells us, the grove of elm trees which Peter planted before his death also "is thriving and will probably shade the yard nicely by the time the house is painted and the green blinds hung." Despite this optimistic, "romantic" note, however, the story achieves most of its power from the harshly realistic, historical elements in it.

There is, first of all, the fact that nobody in the area will sell Peter any land to build on, and the only one who finally does is a Northern turpentine man, who does so only because his trees have exhausted the soil and rendered it useless for any further commercial timber. Secondly, Chesnutt realistically depicts the average freedman's economic plight right after the war when Peter, because he has no capital, falls "an easy prey to the plausible eloquence of a big land owner, who persuaded him to buy a mule on time and rent a farm on shares." The net result of contract is that Peter ends his first season deeply in debt.
this run-down mule, poor land, exorbitant credit rates and share contract is that Peter ends his first season deeply in debt.

Two other realistic elements are presented now. The first of these concerns Peter's oldest son and Southern justice. The son becomes involved in a brawl and is convicted, and Peter's sacrificing for a good lawyer may have been the only thing that kept the son from being hanged. Or, Chesnutt explains, there may have been other reasons here as well:

> . . . possibly, too, the jury were influenced by the consideration that to hang him would be an expense to the county while the ten years' penal term could be utilized for the public good in building the railroads which were at this time beginning to stretch across the State and bring it into closer communication with the rest of the world.

It will be no coincidence that Chesnutt will return to indict this convict lease system in far greater detail in his final two novels.

The final and most dramatic element deals with the local KKK group, whose violent night rides for "amusement" (the traditional rationalization for the KKK's postwar genesis in Tennessee) result in the burning down of Peter's house. Pointedly accompanying the "entertaining" bonfire is an incisive comment which Chesnutt puts in the mouth of one of the sheet wearers. As he sees it, "The idee of a nigger livin' in a two-story house is jes' ridic'lous," and this, of course, is the real reasoning behind the Klan's harassment and ultimate use of violence to maintain the Southern *status quo*. Significantly, Chesnutt goes into further detail as he extends the dramatic moment here to include all individuals in the South—white and Black —who would run afoul of the Klan's politics." "The bell tolls for thee too," he seems to be implying when he notes that a typical Klan "prank" was to attach "to the gate of a prominent citizen of opposite political opinions"

> a placard ornamented with what was intended as the picture of a coffin, and containing a notice to leave the country in thirty days, on pain of the consequence.

Again it will be no coincidence that such a note will form the grisly climax of Chesnutt's dramatic final novel, *The Colonel's Dream*, nineteen years later.

Other early stories in this vein were "Aunt Lucy's Search, " appearing in *Family Fiction* of April 16, 1887, and "The Sheriff's Children," appearing in *The Independent* of November 7, 1889. The former is a tender and heroic tale of an old Black woman who spends her postbellum freedom searching for and touchingly finding all her children who were sold away from her during slavery. The latter is one of Chesnutt's most bitter stories, dealing with a white sheriff in a Southern town who sires a mulatto son, characteristically refuses to acknowledge him, and then is haunted by guilt and reproach when this son returns to the sheriff's town and ultimately chooses to bleed to death in his "father's" jail as his ultimate rejection of a world and father who could treat a human being in such an inhuman way.

Then there were those racial stories which were rooted in Black experience but whose meaning and tone tended towards understanding and often satirizing universal human experience. One of the earliest of these was the story of "How Dasdy Came Through," appearing in *Family Fiction* of February 12, 1887. A warm, genial narrative of young love, it is also a satire of revivalist religions which feature the active, thrashing "passing through" of the repentant sinner "caught up" in the emotional ecstasy of religious salvation. The plot of the story revolves around the young girl Dasdy and her successful attempt to capture the heart of a young man in her church. Though they had been fond of each other initially, when another girl in the congregation seeks to lure him away from Dasdy, she in turn presses to win him back. The appeal of this new rival is the fine clothing which she wears each Sunday to church, so one Sunday Dasdy very calculatingly attaches herself to the same group of penitents as her rival and dramatically manages to tear to pieces her rival's Sunday finery in the middle of her "ecstatic" moment of sanctification. The irony, of course, is that Dasdy really did "come through" on the human level, as she managed to win her man back through the destruction of her rival's competitive appeal.

An earlier and somewhat perplexing story in this vein was Chesnutt's second published story, "A Tight Boot," appearing in the January 30, 1886, issue of *The Cleveland News and Herald*. The story itself seems innocuous enough as a satire of people who falsely seek to appear greater than they are, yet one wonders how it was read by Cleveland readers of the period.

Subtitled "A Humorous Southern Story," it is about—and strongly satirizes—an antebellum slave who tries to act bigger than he is by wearing his master's boots to a fancy ball and then being caught and chastened when he can't get the tight boot off in the crucial moment of detection. On one level this merely looks like—and was probably intended to be—a reverse Cinderella story, with the moral being a Socratic "Know thyself and act with the honest perception of who you are." Thus, after his chastening experience, the protagonist, Bob, "was not known to indulge again in the luxury of wearing other men's boots."

For the 1886 Cleveland audience, however, this story must have seemed an example of the negative minstrel stereotype which Chesnutt had so consciously set himself to fight. Thus Bob is portrayed as a typically ignorant, buffoonish and "uppity" adjunct to the "comic Negro" stereotype which so delighted the minds of the condescending, patronizing whites of the period. Whatever the story's intended moral, we can only guess the actual effect which it had on its Cleveland readers. This is what makes it so perplexing.

Perhaps the best story in this racial-yet-universal vein is "Po' Sandy," which appeared in *Atlantic Monthly* in May, 1888. It subsequently appeared as the second story in *The Conjure Woman*, and since its method and meaning are integrally part of that work, we will leave our discussion of it until our analysis of *The Conjure Woman* and the sort of artistry and perspective which it represents.

The second major type of story by Chesnutt during this apprentice period was that dealing with white characters; these also appeared in two related, yet different, veins.

First and less important were local color stories, usually in rural settings, which humorously satirized universal foilbles. The best example is "Tom's Warm Welcome," Chesnutt's fifth published story, which appeared in the November 27, 1886, issue of *Family Fiction*. "An Idyll of North Carolina Sand-Hill Life" is its subtitle, and it is essentially a tall tale and local color story told to our unnamed, first person narrator by Dugald McDugald about "ole Tom Macdonal'."

The story is humorous and well told. It deals with how "pore an no 'count" Tom is smitten by Jinnie Campbell; how he schemes to be present at a dance at her house to which he is decidedly not invited; and how he is completely put to rout by Jinnie's father, who keeps cheering Tom to partake in everything with "Don't be back'ard. You wa'nt invited to the dancin', but Lord bless me, you're jest as welcome as ef you had a ' been." The satire concludes with Tom suddenly inheriting a plantation "down in Sampson County," at which point his stock in the community immediately soars, he is allowed to marry Jinnie, and every family in the area makes it a point to "tuk 'im up then."

The second group of Chesnutt's "raceless" stories of this period were even more universal than the local color stories like "Tom's Warm Welcome." These were the satires written for magazines like *Puck,* usually dealing with urban business and professional situations.

The earliest story in this vein, ostensibly an article which appeared in *The Social Circle Journal* of November, 1886, under the pseudonym "Uncle Solomon," was a piece devoted to giving whimsical "Advice to Young Men." "Marriages are getting to be such common, every-year affairs in Cleveland," the writer begins,

> that I think it might be well to lay down a few rules for the guidance of young men who may be contemplating matrimony. The rules are based on experience—the experience of other people. I made up my mind to get married some years ago, but haven't had time yet.

Such is its tone and such are its gems of wisdom. Listed in a numerical hierarchy, number three is a fair sample:

> 3. Always marry for money. . . . Some men find music teachers a good investment; others have been successful with milliners and dressmakers; but perhaps the safest thing for a

prudent man is a good laundress . . . .In fact I am now hesitating between a Euclid Avenue heiress and a washerwoman with a large business.

More sophisticated than this were the stories which Chesnutt began to write specificially for such magazines as *Tid-Bits* and *Puck*. The first of these was "A Busy Day in a Lawyer's Office," appearing in *Tid-Bits* of January 15, 1887. Basically it is a general social satire of the contemporary scene, lawyers, women, and so on.

> "Ah! good-morning, madam," said the lawyer with a smile of recognition, placing a chair for his client. "How are you getting along with your last husband Mrs._____ I forget your present name?"
>
> "Mrs. Rogg. Oh, we've quarrelled already, and I want a divorce."
>
> "Let me see," said the attorney reflectively, "this is the _____"
>
> "The fifth," replied the young woman. "You promised to make a reduction of ten per cent each time."

Of significant interest in this story is its echoing of literature which we earlier saw Chesnutt reading in his youth. As his Journal entry of August 25, 1874, notes "I have reread *Pickwick Papers* by Dickens, and, it was not at all old to me. I enjoyed it very much". It comes as no surprise, then, to find that much of Chesnutt's social satire here is quite Dickensian in tone and technique:

> "Why, certainly," said Dr. Vaseline, rubbing his oily hands together.

Two months after this piece, *Tid-Bits* carried another in the same vein in its April 16, 1887, issue. "A Soulless Corportion" is the brief anecdotal account of a staid, imposing-looking woman who tries to collect two hundred dollars for an expensive, jewelry filled suitcase lost in a collision. When the suitcase is subsequently found in a creek and its value doesn't exceed five dollars, the woman accepts fifteen dollars for water damage and says haughtily (undercut by dialect) as she leaves,

> "I wouldn't a thought a rich comp'ny like this would insult a lady that way. But all men ain't gentlemen; an' corporations ain't got no souls nohow."

The first *Puck* story, "How a Good Man Went Wrong," appeared a year later in the November 28, 1888, issue. It was in this same "satire of the times" vein, its gentle humor all revolving around a note sent within a small town by District Messenger Service which inefficiently doesn't arrive until eighteen years later. The best of the *Puck* stories, however, didn't appear until April 24, 1889. Greatly transcending the other satires, it is an early example of Chesnutt's artistic, subtle complexity of structure and meaning, even as it seems to be merely a surface satire.

"The Orgin of the Hatchet Story" is the whimsical yet pointed account of how an American archeologist grows up at first greatly impressed by George Washington's hatchet experience. Progressively he becomes more and more annoyed at it, until he actually comes to dislike George himself.

In later life an archeological trip takes him to Egypt, where he accidentally discovers a scroll which tells the 19th Dynasty story of Rameses III and his son, Rameses IV. Needless to say, Rameses IV is given a scimitar by his father and, in the latter's absence, begins "trying the temper of his new blade." The parallel of George Washington's story is almost exact, and our narrator's veneration for the name of Washington is ironically restored when he realizes that "The hated Hatchet Story was merely one of those myths which, floating down the stream of tradition, become attached in successive generations to popular heroes. . . . This is the basis of the ironic satire of fablized patriotism.

What is perhaps more interesting to us here is the exact nature of "Rammy's mischievous activities" and the final, "touching" scene between father and son.

"First he neatly sliced off the ear of the Nubian eunuch who waited at the door of the royal presence chamber. Then, toddling to the apartments of his mama, he deftly sliced off the headdress of one of the ladies in waiting, taking quite a slice of the scalp along with it; and, proceeding to the palace kitchen, skillfully amputated the little finger of one of the cooks, whose hand happened to be in a position convenient for the experiment.

"Passing thence out into the courtyard, he came up, unperceived, behind a servant who was kneeling before a wooden bench, polishing the royal crown with a soft brick. His head was bent forward, exposing the back of his neck in such a manner that Rammy could not resist the temptation, and playfully raising his puny right arm, he severed the head from the servant's body with one stroke,—such was the keenness of his blade. Such was his embarrassment, however, to discover that he had slain his father's favorite Hebrew slave, Abednego.

"The situation was a painful one, and he did not have time to reflect upon it before he heard the footsteps of his royal father approaching. Yielding to the impulse of the moment, the royal infant hastily concealed himself in a large earthen water-jar which stood close by.

"When Rameses III saw the dead body of his favorite slave, his rage at first knew no bounds: "Who slew my Hebrew slave?" he cried.

"In a moment all the members of the household had gathered in the courtyard. They, one and all, had disclaimed any responsibility for the unfortunate death, when the head of young Rammy appeared above the rim of the water-jar, from which he lightly sprang and prostrated himself at his father's feet.

" 'Sire,' he said, 'I can not tell a lie. I did it with my little scimitar.'

"For a moment Rameses III was speechless with conflicting emotions. Then the trembling bystanders saw the great monarch's face soften, and heard him exclaim, in feeling tones:

" 'Come to my arms, my son! I would rather you had killed a thousand Hebrew slaves than to have told a lie. I thank Isis that she has given me such a son.' "

Needless to say, there is an obvious social moral beneath this "Hatchet Story"; yet it is made so deftly and the satire's irony-within-irony structure is so delicately pointed that the moral never seems obtrusive at all. Thus, as well as a charmingly told, gentle satire, "The Origin of the Hatchet Story" is also an example of how the bastion of prejudice can be undermined through deeply felt yet delicately controlled art.

The Mature Period (1889-1905)

In his mature period, Chesnutt's writings seemed less diversified than in his earlier period, a situation which is understandable when we remember that he undertook writing as a profession in direct response to progressively worsening social conditions in America. In any case, all of his published work during this period, with the exception of his sophisticated bagatelle "Baxter's Procrustes," is racial in subject matter and essentially serious and realistic in approach.

Having said this, however, we must immediately interject an important note of caution suggested by Arna Bontemps in a July 7, 1967 interview with this author at Fisk University. One of the great dangers of judging a Black writer's work during this period, Mr. Bontemps reminds us, is that generally we are dealing only with the published work of that writer. This, he asserts, can be a very misleading approach since the publishers of Black writers of the early 1900s often rejected a great deal of material which the writer thought important but which the publisher feared no one would buy.

Such is the case with Chesnutt. Interestingly enough, with the exception of his very first novel, *Mandy Oxendine,* an intriguing socially concerned novel which was completed in 1897, all of Chesnutt's rejected novels during this period were not racial novels at all, but were various kinds of "white" novels. *A Business Career* in 1898, *The Rainbow Chasers* in 1900, *Evelyn's Husband* in 1903: all were completely raceless novels that reflected Chesnutt's interest in the Howellsian, Jamesian novels of the period. With this said, however, we must now return to the various racially oriented, published works during the period, for these are Chesnutt's major works of this period.

As we have noted, Chesnutt's work of this period are all generally serious and realistic, and there are several reasons for this dominant tone. On the one hand, Chesnutt was no longer a fledging writer so eager to obtain recognition and the pleasure of being "published" that he would write the kind of frothy, light material which *Tid-Bits, Puck,* and *The Cleveland News* and *Herald* desired. And a mature artist now, he felt free to turn his attention to serious subjects which he felt mattered deeply to the world around him. He still retained his own unique interests and literary enjoyments, as his three unpublished "white" novels so dramatically attest; yet his social sense of commitment was more important in his life during this period. We have already noted that he consciously dedicated himself to a writing career in 1889 and that this commitment was made in direct response to his shock over the violence and brutality shown in the Wilmington Massacre of 1898, which heightened and intensified those social fears he had been feeling over the violent wave of disfranchisement sweeping the South since the early 1890s.

Even so, his first work of this period was one of great variety. His collection of short stories, entitled *The Wife of His Youth,* concerned itself with material and stories of "the Color Line." The major point for us, however, is not so much what kind of material was presented here, but how and in what ways that material was presented. Setting, characters, themes and tones: variety and range were found in all these areas.

The first and title story of the collection, "The Wife of His Youth, " is a sensitive, powerful drama of racial identity and the Socratic commitment to honest self-awareness and self-acceptance. It is the story of how a light-skinned, well-to-do, socially aspiring Black man in Groveland, a Mr. Ryder, is faced with the sudden choice between admitting or simply ignoring his past, slavery marriage to a dark, ignorant slave girl who had shriveled into a quaint, "amusing" figure: a woman whose past relationship to Ryder would hardly be an asset to him with his present "Blue Vein" social set.

Somehow, however, after "gazing thoughtfully at the reflection of his own face" in his bedroom mirror, Ryder finds the deep courage to announce to all the gathered members of his set that this woman is "the wife of his youth." Both tender and compelling, it is a beautifully and significantly conceived story which is structured and developed with great artistic effect.

The second story in the collection, "Her Virginia Mammy," is equally brilliant in its fusion of suspense and deep tenderness. Directly following "The Wife of His Youth," it is essentially the former story's basic plot as seem from a different point of view and resolved with the completely opposite theme. For where the former story stressed the need for deep, painful honesty, the later story stresses the importance of sensitive—yet still painful and courageous—dissemblance.

The plot of this story is one in which an old slave mother searches after the war for her lost mulatto daughter and finally finds her doing well as a dance teacher in a Northern city. The girl does not know that she is a mulatto; knows only that she is an orphan; and is engaged to marry a handsome, successful boy whom she deeply loves. All that has kept her from agreeing to his persistent proposals of marriage is her desire to discover her background; for she wants to be sure that she comes from the same "quality" family that he represents as the descendent of a Mayflower arrivee, Connecticut governor, and so on.

When Mrs. Harper, the old slave woman, eventually finds her daughter Clara, she is about to exclaim with joy and "reclaim" her daughter with the truth of her parentage when she, Mrs. Harper, suddenly realizes with great sensitivity that her daughter does not want to know that her mother is Black—that her daughter's whole concept of who she wants to be will be shattered. Half way through her story about the past, therefore, Mrs. Harper sacrifices all her future happiness for her daughter's, and without directly lying, tells Clara of the high family breeding of her father, without mentioning the fact that she is her mother: at which point Clara assumes that Mrs. Harper was simply a family servant—her "Virginia Mammy." Irony, pathos, suspense, pain and love: all are here and all are beautifully fused together.

The third story in the collection, "The Sheriff's Children," we have discussed above in terms of its incisive, striking sense of realistic bitterness about the South; it goes without saying that this story is different radically from the first two in all aspects of setting, characters, theme and tone. It is, in fact, a very sobering experience.

The fourth story, in turn, differs from all three of its predecessors in tone, if not completely in theme and setting. "A Matter of Principle" is a satire of the sort of "Blue Vein" socialites whom we saw as background in "The Wife of His Youth." These are cultured, educated mulattoes in Northern cities like Groveland (i.e., Cleveland) who develop for themselves a whole social clique which stresses as its first and greatest virtue the lightness of each member's skin. As Chesnutt allows one of its members in "The Wife of His Youth" to explain,

> "I have no race prejudice . . . but we people of mixed blood are ground between the upper and nether millstone. Our fate lies between absorption by the white race and extinction in the black. The one doesn't want us yet, but may

take us in time. The other would welcome us, but it would
be for us a backward step."

The plot here is close to slapstick in its satire, all hinging on a
case of similar names and mistaken identity. But the ironic moral
is very clear: those who lead artificial lives based on absurd criteria for basic values will find themselves disappointed and
empty (handed) in the end.

Each of the other stories in the collection adds its own unique
quality to the book's overall dimension. "The Passing of Grandison" is another farcical satire, this time undermining the antebellum stereotype of the "contented slave," as Grandison
seemingly is a man who simply doesn't want to escape from his
masters, no matter how many opportunities they give—and
eventually thrust on—him. In fact, he even drags himself back
South after being forcibly abducted into free Canada, which
brings joy and cheer to the hearts of his white owners, who "knew"
all along that this was the contented nature of all slaves—until
the next day dawns and they discover that Grandison has returned only to lead his whole family to the freedom that lies
North.

Another "enjoyably meaningful" story is "Uncle Wellington's
Wives." This is the saga of a middle-aged Southern Black man
who, once the war ends, finds himself free and his ears full of
exotic reports about the kind of money and freedom which the
North now offers. Furthermore, though he is married to an industrious, loving woman (whose work actually supports both of
them, since Uncle Wellington finds leisure more congenial to his
nature), he is told by a local lawyer friend that he is free of this
slavery marriage also if he wishes.

So off he goes North to a new town, a new situation, and eventually a new wife. She is Irish, and her color represents the
epitome of "social freedom" to Uncle Wellington, until his job
and eventually his marriage begin to bump over rocky terrain:
at which point his new wife leaves him (unwilling to support
him in the leisurely manner to which he had been accustomed),

and he finds the North suddenly too hostile and cold to his taste. At this point he returns home, penitent and prodigal, and is taken back by his old wife on their original easy terms. "The grass," Chesnutt fabliau-ishly suggests, "is not always greener."

After the fragile, tender story of "The Bouquet," Chesnutt's most powerful story concludes the collection. This is "The Web of Circumstance," and it shows Chesnutt at his best.

The story deals with a hard-working blacksmith in a small Southern town. Ben Davis is a conscientious and industrious worker—the epitome of the American success figure—and his future looks very bright. However, he has two things against him; one obvious, the other more deceptively lethal. On the one hand, he is Black and living in the South, which means that should he ever get into trouble with the law, even his industriousness would be of no aid, for Southern "justice" of the period brings with it a predilection towards Black guilt and overly long prison sentences. The second albatross in Ben's future is his young mulatto helper, who secretly envies Ben's success and wishes to undercut it in any way possible.

The "way" that presents itself in the story comes in the form of a handsome buggy whip which a certain Colonel Thornton has and which Ben openly admires one day as he is shoeing Thornton's horse. Soon afterwards, the whip is missed by Thornton, and a subsequent search locates it hidden in Ben's shop. Enter Southern justice.

Needless to say, everyone in the all-white court considers Ben guilty almost by definition, including his lawyer, who thereupon conducts a very medicore defense. Furthermore, Ben is convicted on the circumstantial evidence alone and is sentenced to five years in the penitentiary at hard labor largely because, as the judge declares in his presentence oratorio, Ben is being punished as a racial example. Indeed, as the judge notes with a typical quantity of prejudging,

> "Your conduct is wholly without excuse, and I can only regard your crime as the result of a tendency to offenses of

this nature, a tendency which is only too common among
your people."

Significantly, Chesnutt as structural artist has two other
prisoners sentenced by the judge just prior to Ben that day, and
Chesnutt pointedly compares the sentences involved. The first
case involves a young white man convicted of manslaughter,
who is "admonished of the sanctity of human life" and then
given a one-year sentence. The second is a young white clerk
convicted of forgery. Having "connections" and a white skin,
he receives a sentence of six months in the county jail and a fine
of one hundred dollars. Ben then gets five years for the circumstantial "theft" of a riding whip.

Five years later Ben comes home to find the complete dissolu-
tion of his house, his family, his whole life. His wife has recently
drowned, probably while drunk say the neighbors; and his son
has just been lynched for shooting a white man. Even the ru-
mors which the neighbors remember about Ben's "crime" are
painful to him—ranging from horse stealing to murder; and he
finds that all he once had is gone. The five years have produced
a total tragedy.

Brooding over all this, with nascent plans for exacting revenge from Thornton via a huge bludgeon which he has just cut,
Ben falls asleep in a field near Thornton's and is later awakened
by a "sweet little child" solicitously murmuring over him. It is
Thornton's daughter; and though for a brief instant Ben sees
her as the potential object of his revenge, the tender innocence
of the girl and her childlike concern for him immediately dispel
this feeling. After all of the harsh voices and sounds of prison
life, Chesnutt tells us, the girl's innocent concern for him is
deeply soothing. As a result, "he lay there with half-closed eyes
while the child brought leaves and flowers and laid them on his
face and on his breast, and arranged them with little caressing
taps."

Time passes, the girl is off at a distance picking more flowers
for him, when Ben hears a horse coming along the path behind

him. Realizing that it is probably Thornton, he springs to his feet, club in hand, momentarily undecided as to his course of action. "But either the instinct of the convict, beaten, driven, and debased, or the influence of the child, which was still strong upon him, impelled him, after the first momentary pause, to flee as though seeking safety." Unfortunately, however, his path away from Thornton leads him towards the little girl, and as Thornton "turned the corner of the path, what he saw was a desperate-looking negro, clad in filthy rags, and carrying in his hand a murderous bludgeon, running toward the child." Accordingly, "A sickening fear came over the father's heart, and drawing the ever-ready revolver, which according to Southern custom he carried always upon his person, he fired with unerring aim. Ben Davis ran a few yards farther, faltered, threw out his hands, and fell dead at the child's feet."

The poignancy, the anguish, the drama all end here. There is a space on the page and a hushed stillness in the reader's feelings before Chesnutt returns with a final paragraph—his final plea. As an artist, a sensitive man, and almost a prophet in some sense, he says his own requiem—and prayer—over Ben's crumpled form:

> Some time, we are told, when the cycle of years has rolled around, there is to be another golden age, when all men will dwell together in love and harmony, and when peace and righteousness shall prevail for a thousand years. God speed the day, and let not the shining thread of hope become so enmeshed in the web of circumstance that we lose sight of it; but give us here and there, and now and then, some little foretaste of this golden age, that we may the more patiently and hopefully await its coming!

It is, magnificently, the finest moment in the book—and is, as well, the natural culmination of the cosmic artist.

Chesnutt's three major novels of this period remain to be discussed. *The House Behind the Cedars* was published in 1900,

The Marrow of Tradition in 1901, and *The Colonel's Dream* in 1905. All three are racial and based on social protest. All three are also major works of art in themselves. As such, we will discuss them in our final chapter on Chesnutt's literary artistry.

The Decline Period (1906-1932)

Because of his disappointment over the poor receptions accorded *Marrow* and *The Colonel's Dream,* Chesnutt, entering his period of decline, never finished another realistic racial novel. Indeed he never published another novel at all; and the one which he did write and finish somewhere near 1906 was uncharacteristically mellow and nostalgic. Romantically placed in ante-bellum New Orleans, *Paul Marchand, F.M.C.* shows just how dispirited Chesnutt was when he realized that the American people were not ready to face realistic, contemporary racial material. Instead, they hungered for the safe world of the romantic past, and this is where Chesnutt let *Paul Marchand* lead him. The novel is well made and dramatically effective in spots, but it is a far cry from the strength and power which he exhibited in *Cedars, Marrow,* and *The Colonel's Dream.*

Besides *Paul Marchand,* Chesnutt published only three short stories over the final twenty-seven years of his life. In April, 1906, "The Prophet Peter", in *Hathaway-Brown Magazine,* showed Chesnutt still at his artistic prime. Like several of Chesnutt's other stories, the story satirically deals with a Black character who hypocritically utilizes his religious position for personal gain. Peter is a revivalist minister who predicts the Day of Doom and then surreptitiously buys up his followers' land as they abandon all their possessions and await the Final Judgment.

Unlike several of Chesnutt's stories in this vein, the satire here is softened at the end by a very delicate, almost tender tone. After Prophet Peter returns, completely crazed, to the poor house where he had started, one of his followers rather touchingly speaks his epitaph, which ends the story.

"Pete alluz were a fool," she would say, placidly,—"I lived with him long enough to know,—an' now he ain't got no sense at all." And then she would add, with a certain naive pride, "But he were a big prophet an' a healer one time, he shore were."

Six and nine years later, Chesnutt wrote his final two stories for *The Crisis* at the behest of W. E. B. DuBois, who was struggling to get the magazine on its feet. Both stories are rather interesting.

"The Doll," written for the April, 1912 issue, is a dramatic, powerful story of inner conflict between revenge and a certain moral-social responsibility to one's people. The protagonist is a Black barber with a thriving business in the city (a success symbol for his race to aspire to) who is one day suddenly tempted to slit the throat of a white Southern colonel whom he is shaving and whom he recognizes as the man who shot the barber's father back in the South. The debate rages back and forth in the barber's mind, until he finally decides that the upward movement of his race is more important than his own personal satisfaction through vengeance.

There are, at this point, two interrelated ironies which we learn. On the one hand we learn that the colonel *knew* who this barber was, and he sees the barber's decision as just another proof that Blacks "are born to serve and to submit . . . . They have no proper self-respect; they will neither resent an insult, nor defend a right, nor avenge a wrong." Immediately after this, however, as we are reevaluating the story with this first irony in mind, that reevaluation is itself reevaluated for us by the objective bystander Northern judge who has accompanied the colonel to the barber shop, knows all the circumstances, and comes deeply to admire the strength and determination which the barber's powerful self-control represents.

"Mr. Taylor's Funeral," three years later, shows Chesnutt reverting to the kind of genial satire of human foibles which he had written twenty-eight years earlier. A satire on the hypocritical abuses of religion, the plot deals with the way Mr. Taylor's funeral is used by both his wife and the good-looking pastor of her old church in order to strike up a budding romance of their own. It is fair, if undistinguished, satire.

With "Mr. Taylor's Funeral" completed, Chesnutt's portfolio of published works was also completed. He was fifty-seven at the time, involved in various business and social concerns such as the Cleveland branch of the NAACP, and perhaps this was reason enough to stop writing. It is to his great credit as an artist, however, that the strong fire for literary self-expression still blazed within him, so that we find him working on still another novel as late as 1928, when he was seventy years old. The *Quarry* is not one of his better works as it stands; yet once more it shows him concerned with realistic social matters in the world immediately around him, based as it is on an actual experience which occurred to the Chesnutts in their 1920 Cleveland home. More important, it shows just how strong the artist and social crusader were in him throughout the full length of his life. On November 15, 1932, Chesnutt died.

CHAPTER IX

The Greatness of Chesnutt's Art:
Techniques, Themes and Purposes

A great literary artist is one who possesses deep, significant ideas and feelings and who commands, as well, the technical ability to present those ideas and feelings effectively within an artistic medium. Such a man was Charles W. Chesnutt.

Technical Skill and Craftsmanship

The second aspect of Chesnutt's greatness—his technical skill and craftsman's concern with structure and technique—had become dramatically evident as early as his first published book. Indeed, *The Conjure Woman*[1] offers us a significant and representative insight into Chesnutt's technical artistry, especially since the book seems so ingenuously simple on its surface.

The Conjure Woman is a collection of stories which all take place on the same postbellum plantation in North Carolina. No longer a real plantation, it is an estate just moved into after the war by a Northern couple partially interested in growing grapes, but actually more concerned with bracing the wife's poor health by retiring to the leisurely pace and healthy climate of that Southern state. The stories themselves all contain a folk tale spun to our narrator and his wife by the old, Black caretaker, Uncle Julius. On one level the book seems simply a delightful collection of folk tales about conjuration, witchcraft, and rural superstition—much in the vein of Joel Chandler Harris' Uncle Remus tales.

However, each story—and the book as a whole—is far deeper and more complex than that. Each story usually is a play within a play. For in each story Uncle Julius tells his own tale with an ulterior, personal motive in mind. As Chesnutt himself noted in his 1931 article "Post-Bellum—Pre-Harlem,"

> In every instance Julius had an axe to grind, for himself or his church, or some member of his family, or a white friend. The introductions to the stories, which were written in the best English I could command, developed the characters of Julius' employers and his own, and the wind-up of each story reveals the old man's ulterior purpose, which, as a general thing, is accomplished.[2]

In the first story, "The Goophered Grapevine," for example, Julius tells the tale of how the plantation's grapevines were and still are hexed and "goophered" by an old conjure woman. The purpose of the tale is to discourage the narrator from going into the grape business as he had planned, which will then leave all the grapes which grow there for Julius himself to pick. The result of the first story, however, is that our Northern, analytic narrator sees through Julius and successfully goes about his plans for grape growing. End of Round One: Northern, scientific sophistication triumphs over Southern, romantic, superstition (manipulated by an equally alert sophistication).

In the next story, "Po' Sandy," the result is somewhat different. Here the narrator's wife wants a new kitchen, and the narrator thereupon decides to use the well-preserved wood of an old schoolhouse on the property for this purpose. At this point

Julius tells the couple a tale of how the wood that made the schoolhouse came from a tree that was actually not a tree at all. It was a slave who had been transformed into that tree by his sweetheart, in order to save him from being sold from the plantation. This accounts for the moaning and groaning, Julius notes, which can occasionally be heard from the place.

As it turns out, Julius' emotional, Southern superstition story does not affect our Northern, rational narrator; but it does affect his wife (i.e., we have a battle of the sexes throughout the book as well as a battle of cultures: male vs. female; practical vs. leisurely; rational vs. emotional; Northern vs. Southern: a duality which Julius essentially transcends; believing in the Southern world enough to know its stories and sense of leisure, but being enough of a pragmatist as well to know how to manipulate and use those tales). Our narrator, therefore, decides to build the new kitchen with some other wood. Not coincidentally, a week or two thereafter, our narrator returns from a business trip to learn from his wife that "there has been a split in the Sandy Run Colored Baptist Church, on the temperance question" and Julius, being one of the seceders, "came to me yesterday and asked if they might not hold meetings in the old schoolhouse for the present." Julius, then, has won Round Two, through his tale's persuasion of the narrator's wife. And while the narrator himself is not taken in, he does accede to his wife's feelings.

Contests like this occur in every story—and are the spinal structure which links the individual stories together into what finally becomes a novelistic whole. Further variety and depth of encounter and characterization develop throughout the "novel". In a story like "The Conjurer's Revenge," Julius actually does dupe the narrator to Julius's own advantage. However, just when it looks as if we are dealing with allegorical figures here: i.e., trickster vs. Northern male rationalist vs. female sentimentalist, Julius' own deep humanity is revealed. In story III, in order to save his young, ignorant grandson's job on the plantation, he spins his yarn about how much like a horrible nightmare slavery was for the slave. In story V he uses his tale for the benefit of the narrator's wife, who is stricken with a severe illness but who pulls out of it through her faith in a rabbit's foot about which Julius has told her a tale. And then, in story VIII, Julius tells a tale that saves the future marriage of a pretty, headstrong girl who has just had a fight with her boy friend and is on the brink of bitterly destroying the whole relationship. The young girl is the ward of our narrator, and Julius's tale indirectly convinces the narrator, his wife and the girl to change their plans and take their Sunday ride along the Lumberton Plank Road—where, as "luck" would have it, the boyfriend happens along and the two lovers fondly make up.

The scope, depth, intricacy and feeling of these stories, both in themselves and as a whole "novel," are impressive, and are a testament both to Chesnutt's technical skill as a structural craftsman and also to his depth and feeling as a deeper, universal artist. Indeed, technical skill and universal breadth are the two major hallmarks of Chesnutt's art.

Perhaps the most impressive embodiment of Chesnutt's technical artistry was his last novel, *The Colonel's Dream.*[3] The book's financial and popular failure at the hands of a biased, prejudiced readership should not blind us to its obvious artistic success when viewed by readers no longer caught up in the political and social narrowness of the early 1900s. It is this artistry, then, that we shall examine here.

Before we consider the artistry of *The Colonel's Dream,* perhaps a brief summary of the novel is in order. It is a simple plot: Colonel French is a successful New York businessman who, after completing a last successful deal, returns to the Clarendon, N.C., pine country of his childhood. While there, he becomes interested in the economic and moral backwardness of the South and decides to introduce Northern methods and attitudes into the Southern milieu through the establishment of an industrial cotton mill, higher wages for both white and Black workers, and a subsequent rising standard of living. When the mill fails because of Snopes-like local pressure, and French's attempt to bury his old Black playmate in the French family plot also fails, the Colonel returns to New York and the novel is over.

The skeletal structure of *The Colonel's Dream* is a kind of missionary travel novel, which operates on the framework of a national allegory, as Colonel French travels South with Northern ideas and attempts an economic conversion. French himself is a national American hero "type": a figure of military bearing who is also a successful businessman. He is also a man who represents the "whole country," coupling a Southern past with a Northern present and attempting to unite the two under the banner of his industrial Northern way of life. The geographic movement and semiallegorical characterization are essential elements of the plot structure: both are important, not only for the traditional elements contained, but also for the innovations which Chesnutt added.

The Colonel's Dream uses a "visiting narrator," travel novel technique, the sort that was so widely in use at the end of the nineteenth century in this country. Because of its value for bringing two sets of cultural ideas and ways of life together, almost all of America's novelists of the period employed it. Henry James, Mark Twain, William Dean Howells all worked extensively within its framework. It was likewise used as the format for the local color writers of the period, both North and South. Where Sarah Orne Jewett and Mary Wilkins Freeman used it to explore the rural areas of Vermont and Massachusetts, the writers of the South used it for everything from the savage class satire of Augustus Baldwin Longstreet to the delicate local etchings of the little Tennessee spinster, Mary Noailles Murfree. The format, then, was already effectively established.

What is of equal importance to us is the fact that most of the novels in this subgenre were barefacedly unrealistic in their basic structure. They were "vacation" novels in which the narrator had little real motivation for the trip and just seemed to appear somehow on the scene with only the barest of structural mechanics to assist our belief in him. In one way *The Colonel's Dream* shares some of this artificiality in order to establish its national allegory. For French is really too young, handsome, rich, and free from entanglements to be realistically believable. Moreover, his son Phil is also overdrawn in fairytale fashion, having a perpetual "sweet temper" and "loving disposition." Yet we need only look at the characterization of French to see how hard Chesnutt has worked to break the stereotype feeling which often accompanies a symbolic national allegory. We note first how French faints at the end of the tense opening chapter, thereby destroying the rugged, successful, nonchalant American hero who everyone from Cooper to James had symbolically delineated before Chesnutt. In fact, not only does he faint, but he then loses his allegorical aura by sheepishly trying to joke his way out of it. Finally, even more realism creeps in when French's partner, in an explanatory aside, tells us how hard the latter has worked and how little sleep he has had. Clearly this hero is a real man.

Equally significant is the fact that French is a man with a tragic flaw stemming from his personality, and not just an allegorical hero who is defeated by a hostile, looming society. While he is partially the storybook hero of wealth, charm, money, ideals, and leisure, he is also the realistic product of his own past. Thus he brings to his crusade to the heathen South the same traits that made him successful in New York, and for that reason he is defeated. In the South he is pushing against an ingrown society that values prejudice and petty revenge even more than it does money, whereas in New York's business world French has been accustomed to hand-to-hand combat among single individuals or corporations who all shared the same monetary values. Therefore the persistence and drive which have made French successful in the North now greatly harm him in Clarendon; and he is too insensitive to realize this fact. As Chesnutt realistically portrays him, the Colonel is not only too weak to be victorious everywhere, but he is even blind at times.

This same realism is very deftly carried over into the overall structure of the novel as well: making it seem more realistic than the demands of its epic subject would seem to allow it.

Accordingly, French does not just take off for the South on a good will reconstruction mission; nor is his trip merely a matter of personal whim now that his business concerns in New York are completed. Instead, the little irrelevancies of plot which we almost skipped over as we read the early chapters now come to show their significance. That faint of French's was not just realistic characterization and an attempt to deflate a major figure. As explained by French's partner, it came as the result of overwork, and this is important, for the central plot is now initiated by French's doctor *ordering* him to take a vacation to some mild climate. It is not a crusade, nor is it to last more than a month or so. In fact, the South is not even considered at first as the place for this vacation. Instead, we overhear the physician logically eliminate many other places first: the Riviera, southern California, Palm Beach and Jekyll Island, until he suggests the pine country of French's youth. Equally significant about the early exposition is the way in which the dramatic opening moment of French's successful last business deal has very nicely provided him with both the money and the freedom from business which this trip structure requires.

The next structural problem with which Chesnutt must wrestle is that of freeing French from all past emotional ties so that he can become romantically involved with Laura Treadwell in Clarendon. This offers definite problems, since French has a son; but Chesnutt develops a solution by merely mentioning French's "loss" of his wife sometime earlier: a loss which leaves no sentimental traces on the man because of the great difference in age between the two.

Of course, the novelistic purpose of this marriage in the first place is to provide French with a son and a relaxed way with women, but Phil now creates further structural problems. For while he is an implicit symbol of the new generation's hope in the South (when he dies, all French's hope dies with him), he is also a little boy with no mother and a working father. This creates problems of its own as Chesnutt must somehow explain who has been taking care of Phil in New York and how that person will affect the French family in the South. Chesnutt's answer to this is technically brilliant—and necessary, since a nondescript, traveling babysitter would ruin the allegory of the novel and further complicate the necessary isolation of protagonists which the travel novel demands. The answer is that the trip is only to be a month's vacation and that Jordan, Phil's guardian, "is in love and does not wish to leave New York." It all seems so simple, and yet it is actually quite intricate as it hinges on the shortness of the vacation, which in turn has been realistically supported by doctor's orders, French's health, his freedom from business affairs, and his financial ability to travel in the first place.

The planning behind the realism here is impressive, for we are witnessing the art of making the structure of the artificial travel novel seem natural. A difficult effect to achieve, it is the art of creating a plot structure with what Tolstoy calls a sense of "inevitability," while, at the same time, making that structure seem organically, not artificially, inevitable. This is a difficult feat at all times, but Chesnutt manages it effectively.

Now let us look at Chesnutt's deft use of characters as indirect spokesmen for his own intellectual position. Essentially a technique to keep the novelist from having to make pointed or poetic statements that would appear didactic or mawkish in his own mouth, this device approaches T. S. Eliot's conception of the "objective correlative" and is especially valid in an allegorical novel where the symbols occasionally need to be explained or commented upon. Clearly the novelist can't very well comment on his own symbols, so he lets his characters amplify his meanings for him.

For example, Chesnutt has the Colonel mentally comment on the symbolic meaning inherent in one of Clarendon's sturdy weatherboard houses:

> Heart-pine and live-oak, mused the colonel, like other things Southern, live long and die hard.

Later a larger symbolic moment is created and commented on by a mere local onlooker:

> While they were talking upon this latter theme . . . looking up they saw that a horse, attached to a loaded wagon, had fallen in the roadway. . . . Five or six Negroes were trying to quiet the animal, and release him from the shafts, while a dozen white men looked on and made suggestions.
>
> "An illustration," said the major, pointing through the window toward the scene without, "of what we've got to contend with. Six niggers can't get one horse up without twice as many white men to tell them how. That's why the South is behind the No'th."

This device allows Chesnutt to put the harsh philosophic summation of the novel into a single epigram without turning himself into an epigrammatic novelist. We can almost hear the novel's denouement in French's statement near the end that "The best people . . . are an abstraction," yet we do not feel that the novelist has turned editorialist and explained his novel to us at the end. In Chesnutt's mouth it would be didactic polemicism; in French's mouth, however, it becomes merely a suggestion of meaning. It is clear that we are dealing with an artist here and not a pamphleteer.

Chestnutt uses this device also to open the novel to large, "wondering" questions of cosmic significance. We note, for example, the delicacy of feeling and statement in little Phil's question to his father about the family cemetery plot ("eternity," in a sense, even as it is also a piece of Southern sod) and the faithful ex-slave, Peter.

> "Papa," he said, upon one of those peaceful afternoons, "there's room enough for all of us, isn't there—you, and me, and Uncle Peter?"

And we note the same wistful, cosmic naiveté when Phil asks Peter,

> "Tombstones always tell the truth, don't they, Uncle Peter?"

What is happening here is that Chesnutt is asking these large, eternal, and therefore often cumbersome questions through the mouth of a pretty and poignantly naive child—in whose mouth they lose their overbearing complexity and become somehow charming, even as they retain their deadly significance.

Even more interesting in *The Colonel's Dream* is Chesnutt's development of background symbols for the narrative—a tonal and structural device revealed in his use of Viney and her paralysis. Within the framework of the plot itself, Viney is a peripheral character. She is the mulatto slave woman who has been housekeeper and mistress to old Malcolm Dudley at the period when his uncle supposedly hid a million dollars somewhere on the Dudley estate. Since that time, the estate—as all Southern wealth—has declined, and the hidden money now looms extremely important. Since Malcolm is now "plumb 'stracted" and completely out of his doddering mind, Viney is the only key that can open the economic door to a modern Southern commercial rise. This is operative on both the human and the allegorical level of the novel.

There is, however, an accompanying string attached to this key. For if Malcolm is mad, Viney's tongue is correspondingly paralyzed, and she is therefore unable to tell where the money is. The paralysis itself, symbolically enough, is the result of a beating which Malcolm let another white man inflict on her at that time; and since that beating she has remained paralyzed—as the Southern Black in general has been paralyzed by the violence inflicted upon him.

Related to this is the question of handwriting. For Viney knows where the money is; and if she could only write, she could explain all. However, the Southern white man has never willingly taught the Black man to "write", so once more—on both levels—we have the problem of interracial noncommunication.

The symbolism so far is clear and powerful. Sociologically truthful and correct, it forms a very substantial background subplot. Then, all of a sudden, we receive an ironic jolt in this relationship between white master and mulatto mistress. One hundred pages after we thought we had the symbolic progression solved and subsumed into the recesses of the novel, we suddenly learn that Viney could speak—can speak in fact. For twenty-five years she has feigned paralysis, keeping her master vainly searching for a pot of gold which she knew had never been left there. It has been revenge and the justified spite of a woman scorned, and it is the major moment of the novel. Not only is it still psychologically and symbolically as true as the earlier assessment of the paralysis, but the moment of revelation also leads us to an explosive power and pathos so searing and turbulent that, in this fourth from the last chapter, we suddenly see a fiercer and more psychologically incisive Chesnutt than we would have ever guessed could develop from a travel novel structure.

> "You had me whipped," she said . . . whipped—whipped—whipped—whipped—by a poor white dog. . . . But I have had my revenge!"

> His [Malcolm's] voice failed, and his eyes closed for the last time. When she saw that he was dead, by a strange revulsion of feeling the wall of outraged pride and hatred and revenge, built upon one brutal and bitterly repented mistake, and labouriously maintained for half a lifetime in her woman's heart that even slavery could not crush, crumbled and fell and let pass over it in one great final flood the pent-up passions of the past. Bursting into tears—strange tears from eyes that had long forgot to weep—old Viney threw herself down upon her knees by the bed-

side, and seizing old Malcolm's emaciated hand in both her own, covered it with kisses, fervent kisses, the ghosts of the passionate kisses of their distant youth.

The turbulent passion and pain of the Dostoevski-like moment is soon over, but its power is not easily forgotten, for it has marked a tremendous new level to which Chesnutt has brought the symbolic travel novel.

Major Themes and Purposes

Having discussed Chesnutt's technical skill and craftsmanship, we come now to the more important analysis of his themes. Basically, the ideas in, and purposes behind, his greatest writings were three. First, there was his concern for attacking and changing racial evils in this country, especially in the South. More subconscious, but equally pervasive, was his felt need to work out his own personal identity within the framework of some of his stories. And finally, overarching these two purposes was Chesnutt's deep desire to present to the world his philosophy of man's universal relation to the cosmos and to his fellow man.

Racial Justice

As we noted earlier, Chesnutt's mature period was the one in which he crusaded most openly. Significantly enough, it was that same period which found him devoted to the novel as artistic medium: as if the added length and depth which that genre offered him were crucially needed for the social task to which he was dedicated. Thus *The House Behind the Cedars, The Marrow of Tradition,* and *The Colonel's Dream* are not only Chesnutt's major works of this period, but they are his major crusading works as well. As such, they delineate best the literary role of Chesnutt as social crusader, and *The Marrow of Tradition*[4] is clearly the best example of this, especially in its comprehensive treatment of the physical, literary and overall scenes against which Chesnutt found himself pitted.

The Physical Scene. The story takes place in Wellington, a small Southern seaport town concerned most with tobacco and turpentine; and the situation comes very close to duplicating Chesnutt's own remembrances of Wilmington. The time in question is clearly that of the 1890s when whatever social and political progress Reconstruction had made was being rapidly eroded and destroyed by white reactionaries in the South. The very first political allusion in the novel mentions the "Fusion" groups and the rise of Populism which tried to make meaningful the social and political order which Reconstruction had ostensibly set out to create. Through the eyes of a "White-Supremacy" spouting newspaper editor, then, we learn just how galling this Populistic democracy was to the unreconstructed Southerner. "Public affairs in the state," Major Carteret notes to himself,

> were not going to his satisfaction. At the last state election his own party, after an almost unbroken rule of twenty years, had been defeated by the so-called "Fusion" ticket, a combination of Republicans and Populists. A clean sweep had been made of the offices in the state, which were now filled by new men. Many of the smaller places had gone to colored men, their people having voted almost solidly for the Fusion ticket. In spite of the fact that the population of Wellington was two-thirds colored, this state of things was gall and wormwood to the defeated party, of which the Morning Chronicle was the acknowledged organ. Major Carteret shared this feeling. (30)

In further detailing this situation, Chesnutt presents us with a historical spectrum of those unreconstructed Southerners who formed the basis of the chicanery and violence which led to this period's being called the "nadir" of Reconstruction in the South. Indeed, Wellington's "Big Three," as they saw themselves, are spelled out for us in detail through direct moments of character exposition.

Carteret himself is introduced to us as something close to the New South's middle class aristocrat. A man with "an old name" in the State, Carteret finds, with the birth of a son, that "all the old pride of race, class, and family welled up anew" in him. With the birth of this only heir, he begins to plan his son's future in his mind, for, "Quite obviously the career of a Carteret must not be left to chance,—it must be planned and worked out with a due sense of the value of good blood." In detail, thereupon, Chesnutt presents us with Carteret's economic holdings and interests:

> There lay upon his desk a letter from a well-known promoter, offering the major an investment which promised large returns, though several years must elapse before the enterprise could be put upon a paying basis. The element of time, however, was not immediately important. The Morning Chronicle provided him an ample income. The money available for this investment was part of his wife's patrimony. It was invested in a local cotton mill, which was paying ten per cent, but this was a beggarly return compared with the immense profits promised by the offered investment,—profits which would enable his son, upon reaching manhood, to take a place in the world commensurate with the dignity of his ancestors, one of whom, only a few generations removed, had owned an estate of ninety thousand acres of land and six thousand slaves. (29-30)

The other two members of the triumvirate enter Carteret's office almost immediately after this discussion of the Major, and they form the two extremes of the spectrum: General Belmont, the shrewd but courtly old aristocrat and Captain McBane, the sadistic "poor-white" who is graspingly fighting his way up in the New South's economy and social strata. As Belmont enters Carteret's office, he is described in warm, not unpleasant detail: a "dapper little gentlemen" with "crow's-feet about his eyes, which twinkled with a hard and, at times, humorous shrewdness." Carteret immediately "gave his hand cordially to the gentlemen thus describing." (31) McBane, on the other hand, "was strikingly different in appearance from his companion" and is symbolically introduced in terms of his "broad shoulders, burly form, square jaw, and heavy chin" which "betokened strength, energy, and unscrupulousness." Significantly, Carteret greets McBane with a "quite perceptible diminution of warmth" compared to that which he had bestowed upon Belmont. (32)

After these emotive, suggestive descriptions of the two men, Chesnutt goes into even greater expository detail in order to bring these characters to us in their allegorical, sociological importance. Once more they are placed side by side, and once more they represent the upper and lower ends of the active anti-Reconstruction Southern spectrum.

> General Belmont, the smaller of the two, was a man of good family, a lawyer by profession, and took an active part in state and local politics. Aristocratic by birth and instinct, and a former owner of slaves, . . .

and this sociological description continues for seventeen more lines. (33-34) Captain George McBane, on the other hand,

> had sprung from the poor-white class, to which, even more than to slaves, the abolition of slavery had opened the door of opportunity. No longer overshadowed by a slaveholding caste, some of this class had rapidly pushed themselves forward.

Once again Chesnutt continues to describe his character as a historical class figure, this time devoting twenty-seven additional lines to the process. (34-35) Such are the thoroughness and length of Chesnutt's expository introductions.

With these important introductions out of the way, Chesnutt immediately links his characters to the plot and the novel's future. "At sight, therefore, of these two men, with whose careers and characters he was entirely familiar," Chesnutt informs us,

Carteret felt sweep over his mind the conviction that now was the time and these the instruments with which to undertake the redemption of the state from the evil fate which had befallen it. (35)

Whatever else it may also include, then, *Marrow* is clearly going to be a historical novel.

And it is. One of the points which history records and Chesnutt pointedly discusses is that the white reaction to Reconstruction in several parts of the South was not initially or inherently antagonistic. Indeed, despite various continuing campaigns attacking Reconstruction in most parts of the South, this antagonism was not a widespread phenomenon. Indeed, "Until Carteret and his committee began their baleful campaign the people of the state were living in peace and harmony." (80)

As a result of their first formal meeting, now, the "Big Three" divide up their roles in fomenting their White Supremacy "revolution" and riot, and once more Chesnutt is historical in his assigning of roles to these allegorical characters of his.

This political conference was fruitful in results. Acting upon the plans there laid out, McBane traveled extensively through the state, working up sentiment in favor of the new movement. He possessed a certain forceful eloquence; and white supremacy was so obviously the divine intention that he had merely to affirm the doctrine in order to secure adherents.

General Belmont, whose business required him to spend much of the winter in Washington and New York, lost no opportunity to get the ear of lawmakers, editors, and other leaders of national opinion, and to impress upon them, with persuasive eloquence, the impossibility of maintaining existing conditions, and the tremendous blunder which had been made in conferring the franchise upon the emancipated race.

Carteret conducted the press campaign, and held out to the Republicans of the North the glittering hope that, with the elimination of the negro vote, and a proper deference to Southern feeling, a strong white Republican party might be built up in the New South. (91)

This sort of material, then, forms the groundwork for the historical, protest part of our drama. Many peripheral, yet significant historical aspects of racial life in the South are also included. One aspect treated in this manner is that of racial discrimination on railways. Thus as the white Dr. Burns and his young Black protege, Dr. Miller, are journeying South from Philadelphia, they suddenly reach the Virginia state line, at which point Dr. Miller is made to go sit in the dusty, dilapidated "Colored" car. As Dr. Burns attempts to protest this and argumentatively asks the conductor how he, the conductor, can prevent Dr. Miller's staying in the "White" car if Dr. Miller were to insist, Chesnutt categorically explains the harsh truth of this law through the mouth of the conductor himself:

"This law gives me the right to remove him by force. I can call on the train crew to assist me, or on the other passengers. If I should choose to put him off the train entirely, in the middle of a swamp, he would have no redress—the law so provides. If I did not wish to use force, I could simply switch this car off at the next siding, transfer the white passengers to another, and leave you and your friend in possession until you are arrested and fined or imprisoned." (54-55)

Another aspect of Southern racial life which Chesnutt touches upon is that of the Ku Klux Klan and its infamous night rides. Indeed it was a KKK ride which killed Josh Green's father and drove his mother frenetically mad, so that Josh, one of the two major Black protagonists in *Marrow,* owes to this his whole design in life: to revenge his family and kill the man who headed that ride. Ironically enough, it is the brutal violence of the KKK ride which gives the Blacks of Wellington their most heroic and determined figure. As Chesnutt muses about Josh—in part wistfully assessing his own role of passivity and aestheticism in contrast to Josh's role of action unto death, he notes that

> Here was a negro who could remember an injury, who could shape his life to a definite purpose, if not a high or holy one. When his race reached the point where they would resent a wrong, there was hope that they might soon attain the stage where, they would try, and, if need be, die, to defend a right. (112)

Perhaps the most bitterly treated aspect of racial discrimination in the novel is that of "Southern justice." On its least emotional level, there are several allusions to the South's brutal system of hiring out convict labor to men like McBane, whose methods, as we have seen above, "had not commended themselves to humane people," with the result that "charges of cruelty and worse had been preferred against him." (34) The indictment, of course, is of the whole system and not merely McBane; and Chesnutt was to return to this issue in greater detail in his next and final published novel, *The Colonel's Dream.*

Far more upsetting to Chesnutt was the basic Southern sense of justice that conceived of solving crimes by immediately pinning the guilt on any available Black man who happened along. On the one hand, Chesnutt as lawyer and man of balanced perspective saw that part of the Southern myth of the "criminal Negro" was partially valid, based on several crucial, extenuating circumstances. Thus he begins his discussion of the investigation of Mrs. Ochiltree's murder with this sense of balanced viewpoint in mind. "Suspicion was at once directed toward the negroes," he notes, dropping almost immediately into the present tense that makes his moral indictment all the more immediate and directly relevant.

as it always is when an unexplained crime is committed in a Southern community. The suspicion was not entirely an illogical one. Having been, for generations, trained up to thriftlessness, theft, and immorality, against which only thirty years of very limited opportunity can be offset, during which brief period they have been denied in large measure the healthful social stimulus and sympathy which holds men in the path of rectitude, colored people might reasonably be expected to commit at least a share of crime proportionate to their numbers. The population of the town was at least two thirds colored. The chances were, therefore, in the absence of evidence, at least two to one that a man of color had committed the crime. The Southern tendency to charge the negroes with all the crime and immorality of that region, unjust and exaggerated as the claim may be, was therefore not without a logical basis to the extent above indicated. (178-79)

However, Chesnutt continues,

It must not be imagined that any logic was needed, or any reasoning consciously worked out. The mere suggestion that the crime had been committed by a negro was equivalent to proof against any negro that might be suspected and could not prove his innocence. A committee of white men was hastily formed. Acting independently of the police force, which was practically ignored as likely to favor the negroes, this committee set to work to discover the murderer. (179)

This is Southern injustice in general, he tells us, and then proceeds to go into specific detail as Mr. Delamer's old and faithful servant, Sandy, is mistakenly accused of Mrs. Ochiltree's murder. Sandy does not seem to be type for the crime, but there is some circumstantial evidence. More importantly, the crime seems to have been perpetrated by a Black man on that sacred cow, the Southern white woman, so the town is all the more aroused and desirous of the first Black they catch. Indeed, as Chesnut has McBane note, the crowd doesn't really care whether it has caught the right Black man at all.

> "Burn the nigger," reiterated McBane, "We seem to have the right nigger, but whether we have or not, burn *a* nigger. It is an assault upon the white race, in the person of old Mrs. Ochiltree, committed by the black race, in the person of some nigger. It would justify the white people in burning *any* nigger. The example would be all the more powerful if we got the wrong one. It would serve notice on the niggers that we shall hold the whole race responsible for the misdeeds of each individual." (182)

At this point Belmont puts in a classical, historical note, which then allows Chesnutt to explain historically through McBane why Reconstruction was perhaps even more brutal to the freedman than was slavery.

> "In ancient Rome," said the general, "when a master was killed by a slave, all his slaves were put to the sword."
> "We couldn't afford that before the war," said McBane, "but the niggers don't belong to anybody now, and there's nothing to prevent our doing as we please with them. A dead nigger is no loss to any white man. I say, burn the nigger." (183)

With the arrest of Sandy, the town's mind turns immediately and traditionally to lynching, and here Chestnutt extends his indictment to the traditional Southern sheriff who often let his Black prisoners be taken from him and hanged by a white mob before any sort of trial had been held. Chesnutt had attacked this practice most extensively in his first, unpublished, novel, *Mandy Oxendine;* and here he notes again the traditional ruse which the sheriff would hide behind when the mob advanced to his jail's door and demanded his prisoner.

"Take good care of your prisoner, sheriff," he said sternly, as he was conducted to the door. "He will not be long in your custody, and I shall see that you are held strictly accountable for his safety." (209)

The sheriff's reply is historically typical.

"I'll do what I can, sir," replied the sheriff in an even tone and seemingly not greatly impressed by this warning. "If the prisoner is taken from me, it will be because the force that comes for him is too strong for resistance." (209)

A full history of Southern lynching could be written under the euphemistic subtitle of "Force . . . Too Strong for Resistance," and this is Chesnutt's explicit point here.

What finally galls Chesnutt the most is the incredible air of sadism and violence which pervades the whole Southern system of justice when relating to the Black man. We saw this extensively in our first chapters above, and Chesnutt also cites its existence in bitter and incisive detail.

With Sandy in jail under the sheriff's phlegmatic "guard," the town has already started making plans for its traditional pretrial lynching. It is to be a social affair for sadists, and Chesnutt describes the preparations and mood for us in caustic, incisive precision.

Already the preparations were under way for the impending execution. A T-rail from the railroad yard had been procured, and men were burying it in the square before the jail. Others were bringing chains, and a load of pine wood was piled in convenient proximity. Some enterprising individual had begun the erection of seats from which, for a pecuniary consideration, the spectacle might be the more easily and comfortably viewed.

Ellis was stopped once or twice by persons of his acquaintance. From one he learned that the railroads would

run excursions from the neighboring towns in order to bring
spectators to the scene; from another that the burning was
to take place early in the evening, so that the children might
not be kept up beyond their usual bedtime. In one group
that he passed he heard several young men discussing the
question of which portions of the negro's body they would
prefer for souvenirs. Ellis shuddered and hastened forward.
(219-20)

And lest we think that Chesnutt's tone here is merely an accidental occurrence in the novel, we need merely move to the
conclusion of the novel to see that it isn't. For there he describes
the indiscriminate, wholesale murder of Blacks during the riot
with a similarly bitter, caustic metaphor when, after passing a
corner in town at which "lay the body of another man, with the
red blood oozing from a ghastly wound in the forehead," he
notes how,

The negroes seemed to have been killed, as the band plays
in circus parades, at the street intersections, where the
example would be most effective. (287)

With this discussion of Chesnutt's bitter tone, now, we are
ready to return to a major discussion of the ultimate riot itself
and how he describes it. Through the middle part of the novel,
of course, he has unraveled in greater depth his historical
understanding and concern over the impending riots. Citations
of this understanding are rather numerous; and when they occur,
Chesnutt often goes into them in great depth and at great length.
Such a case is his discussion in Chapter XXVIII of how the "Big
Three" campaign for white supremacy was progressing: a chapter almost wholly devoted to historical material.

Starting with Wellington and North Carolina, he expands
and discusses the rest of the nation as well, bringing in many
of the aspects of the period which we have noted in our earlier

chapters. After noting that the conspiracy seemed to be only gradually advancing in Wellington, he notes that this was really not the case—either in Wellington or in the United States as a whole. As Chesnutt the historian saw it in its complexity and length,

> The lull, however, was only temporary, and more apparent than real, for the forces adverse to the negro were merely gathering strength for a more vigorous assault. While little was said in Wellington, public sentiment all over the country became every day more favorable to the views of the conspirators. The nation was rushing forward with giant strides toward colossal wealth and world-dominion, before the exigencies of which mere abstract ethical theories must not be permitted to stand. The same argument that justified the conquest of an inferior nation could not be denied to those who sought the suppression of an inferior race. (238)

On the more local level,

> In the South, an obscure jealousy of the negro's progress, an obscure fear of the very equality so contemptuously denied, furnished a rich soil for successful agitation. Statistics of crime, ingeniously manipulated, were made to present a fearful showing against the negro. Vital statistics were made to prove that he had degenerated from an imaginary standard of physical excellence which had existed under the benign influence of slavery. Constant lynchings emphasized his impotence, and bred everywhere a growing contempt for his rights. (238).

Moreover,

> At the North, a new Pharaoh had risen, who knew not Israel—a new generation, who knew little of the fierce

epoch, and derived their opinions of him from the "coon song" and the police reports. Those of his old friends who survived were disappointed that he had not flown with clipped wings; that he had not in one generation of limited opportunity attained the level of the whites. The whole race question seemed to have reached a sort of *impasse,* a blind alley, of which no one could see the outlet. The negro had become a target at which any one might try a shot. Schoolboys gravely debated the question as to whether or not the negro should exercise the franchise. The pessimist gave him up in despair; while the optimist, smilingly confident that everything would come out all right in the end, also turned aside and went his bouyant way to more pleasing themes. (238-39)

These, then, were the dominant moods and thoughts throughout the country. With the nation ironically almost united in its willingness to forego Reconstruction and willing, thereby, to disfranchise and re-enslave the freedman, it was only a matter of time before it found the mechanism towards this end. On this point Chesnutt is especially specific and historically expository.

The device finally hit upon for disfranchising the colored people in this particular state was the notorious "grandfather clause." After providing various restrictions of the suffrage, based upon education, character, and property, which it was deemed would in effect disfranchise the colored race, an exception was made in favor of all citizens whose fathers or grandfathers had been entitled to vote prior to 1867. Since none but white men could vote prior to 1867, this exception obviously took in the poor and ignorant whites, while the same class of negroes were excluded. (240)

And he continues the discussion by analyzing the motives and effects in greater detail.

It was ingenious, but it was not fair. In due time a consti-tutional convention was called, in which the above scheme was adopted and submitted to a vote of the people for ra-tification. The campaign was fought on the color line. Many white Republicans, deluded with the hope that by the elimi-nation of the negro vote their party might receive accessions from the Democratic ranks, went over to the white party. By fraud in one place, by terrorism in another, and every-where by the resistless moral force of the united whites, the negroes were reduced to the apathy of despair, their few white allies demoralized, and the amendment adopted by a large majority. The negroes were taught that this is a white man's country, and that the sooner they make up their minds to this fact, the better for all concerned. The white people would be good to them so long as they be-haved themselves and kept their place. (240-41)

As he goes on even further, it becomes clear that the historian in Chesnutt is also a moral philosopher, for on occasion the time tense of his verbs changes and moves into the present tense—and ultimately into the future, with a sense of fearful moral prophesy presaging Malcolm X's "chickens coming home to roost" meta-phor by fifty years. "The great steal was made," he tells us.

but the thieves did not turn honest—the scheme still shows the mark of the burglar's tools'. Sins, like chickens, come home to roost. The South paid a fearful price for the wrong of negro slavery; in some form or other it will doubt-less reap the fruits of this later inquity. *(241)*

With this growing white desire to re-enslave the freedman, it is only natural that he would seek to defend his freedom and his rights. Indeed that conflict lies at the heart of the historical plot in the novel. Yet even before the courageous Josh Green gathers his men for their desperate defiance of the rampaging whites, Chesnutt presages for us the probable result of such defiance

when he historically yet specifically describes the physical helplessness of the Black man in the rural, small town South of the
period. Thus he notes in his characteristically precise and cate-
gorical manner just how this futility was to be recognized.

> The colored people became alarmed at the murmurings
> of the whites, which seemed to presage a coming storm. A
> number of them sought to arm themselves, but ascertained,
> upon inquiring at the stores, that no white merchant would
> sell a negro firearms. Since all the dealers in this sort of
> merchandise were white men, the negroes had to be satis-
> fied with oiling up old army muskets which some of them
> possessed, and a few revolvers with which a small rowdy
> element generally managed to keep themselves supplied.
> Upon an effort being made to purchase firearms from a
> Northern city, the express company, controlled by local
> men, refused to accept the consignment. The white people,
> on the other hand, procured both arms and ammunition in
> large quantities, and the Wellington Grays drilled with great
> assiduity at their armory. (*248-49*)

Indeed when Josh comes on stage with his men and tries to
persuade Dr. Miller to lead them, Miller, as Chesnutt's dramatic
personification, adds to the sense of physical helplessness as he
declines the heroic position which Josh offers him:

> "Listen, men," he said. "We would only be throwing our
> lives away. Suppose we made a determined stand and won
> a temporary victory. By morning every train, every boat,
> every road leading into Wellington, would be crowded with
> white men,—as they probably will be any way,—with arms
> in their hands, curses on their lips, and vengeance in their
> hearts. In the minds of those who make and administer the
> laws, we have no standing in the court of conscience. They
> would kill us in the fight, or they would hang us afterwards,
> —one way or another, we should be doomed." (*282*)

With all this as prelude now, the riot finally comes in Chapter XXXV. There, in the opening two paragraphs, Chesnutt describes in general, crystallized detail the physical world which he has been fighting throughout the novel—and throughout his life. It is the violent, brutal, warped world of the post-Reconstruction white South.

> The proceedings of the day—planned originally as a "demonstration," dignified subsequently as a "revolution," under any name the culmination of the conspiracy formed by Carteret and his colleagues—had by seven o'clock in the afternoon developed into a murderous riot. Crowds of white men and half-grown boys, drunk with whiskey or with license, raged through the streets, beating, chasing, or killing any negro so unfortunate as to fall into their hands. Why any particular negro was assailed, no one stopped to inquire, it was merely a white mob thirsting for black blood, with no more conscience or discrimination than would be exercised by a wolf in a sheepfold. It was race against race, the whites against the negroes; and it was a one-sided affair, for until Josh Green got together his body of armed men, no effective resistance had been made by any colored person, and the individuals who had been killed had so far left no marks upon the enemy by which they might be remembered.
>
> "Kill the niggers!" rang out now and then through the dusk, and far down the street and along intersecting thoroughfares distant voices took up the ominous refrain,— "Kill the niggers! Kill the damned niggers!" (*298*)

This distorted, brutal world, then, was the basis of Chesnutt's constant protest and social crusading, and *The Marrow of Tradition* was where he made his strongest, most direct case. Significantly enough, *Marrow* was the novel that was most strongly denounced for its subject matter and tone by Southern and Northern reviewers alike; in fact, the blind and narrow reception

of this book was one of the major reasons why Chesnutt ultimately drew his writing career to a close in 1905.

The Literary Scene. At the same time that Chesnutt was obviously fighting the above physical conditions which the freedman
faced during the period, he was also, as we have noted already,
fighting the psychological and literary distortions which the
Black man faced throughout the country. Stereotypes and myths,
romances and rhetoric; all were barriers to the Black man's attaining his rightful place in American society and ascertaining
his identity in his own mind as well. Chesnutt's role in fighting
this literary-psychological battle was twofold. On the one hand
he wanted to call attention to the amount of myths and stereotypes being propagated throughout the country; on the other,
in their places he meant to supply the truth about real Black characters—their feelings and their thoughts.

In attacking the stereotypes, Chesnutt's major target was
the white press, North and South, which propagated these stereotypes. Thus, in *Marrow*, it was Major Carteret, the editor of the
Morning Chronicle, who fomented the beginning of the White
Supremacy movement in Wellington.

> Taking for his theme the unfitness of the negro to partici-
> pate in government,—an unfitness due to his limited edu-
> cation, his lack of experience, his criminal tendencies, and
> more especially to his hopeless mental and physical inferior-
> ity to the white race—the major had demonstrated, it seemed
> to him clearly enough, that the ballot in the hands of the
> negro was a menace to the commonwealth. (31)

And at the conclusion of the first major White Supremacy meeting of Carteret, Belmont and McBane, Chesnutt explains to us
through the mouth of Belmont just how powerful the press can
be in influencing local and national thought on such a crucial
issue. "We must be armed at all points," Cateret states near the
conclusion of the meeting, "—we must make our campaign a
national one."

"For instance," resumed the general, "you, Carteret, represent the Associated Press. Through your hands passes all the news of the state. What more powerful medium for the propagation of the idea? The man who would govern a nation by writing its songs was a blethering idiot beside the fellow who can edit its news dispatches." (82-83)

Accordingly, at the first opportunity, Sandy's supposed attack on Mrs. Ochiltree, the *Morning Chronicle* pours forth a whole range of Southern stereotypes: from the myth of the white woman's sacred purity to that of the "debased" Black man's brute nature. Indeed, though nobody knows anything definite about the supposed "murder" (it was later discovered to be an accident) or the "murderer" (the man in question was finally found to be white), Carteret's inflammatory, bombastic prose is rapidly on the scene. As soon as the rumor is out, therefore,

Carteret immediately put into press an extra edition of the Morning Chronicle, which was soon upon the streets, giving details of the crime, which was characterized as an atrocious assault upon a defenseless old lady, whose age and sex would have protected her from harm at the hands of any one but a brute in the lowest human form. This event, the Chronicle suggestion, had only confirmed the opinion, which had been of late growing upon the white people, that drastic efforts were necessary to protect the white women of the South against brutal, lascivious, and murderous assaults at the hands of negro men. (185)

Indeed, as Carteret continued, in an effort to incite action as well as feeling,

It was only another significant example of the results which might have been foreseen from the application of a false and pernicious political theory, by which ignorance, clothed in a little brief authority, was sought to be exalted over knowledge, vice over virtue, an inferior and degraded

race above the heaven-crowned Anglo-Saxon. If an out-
raged people, justly infuriated, and impatient of the slow
processes of the courts, should assert their inherent sov-
ereignty, which the law all was merely intended to embody,
and should choose, in obedience to the higher law, to set
aside, temporarily, the ordinary judicial procedure, it
would serve as a warning and an example to the vicious
elements of the community, of the swift and terrible punishment which would fall, like the judgment of God, upon any
one who laid sacrilegious hands upon white womanhood.
(185-86)

Furthermore, even after Sandy is definitely cleared and white
Tom Delamere is known to have committed the crime of robbing
Mrs. Ochiltree and accidentally causing her death, the *Morning
Chronicle* does not make known who the real criminal is and
likewise does nothing to dispel the fierce racial stereotype which
it has set aglow in its townsmen's hearts. Indeed, as the whites
seek to cover up the case and save themselves the embarrassment of admitting that a white man had committed a "black,
brutal" crime,

Nothing further was ever done about the case; but though
the crime went unpunished, it carried evil in its train. As we
have seen, the charge against [Sandy] Campbell had been
made against the whole colored race. All over the United
States the Associated Press had flashed the report of another dastardly outrage by a burly black brute,—all black
brutes it seems are burly,—and of the impending lynching
with its prospective horrors. This news, being highly sensational in its character, had been displayed in large black type
on the front pages of the daily papers. The dispatch that
followed to the effect that the accused had been found innocent and the lynching frustrated, received slight attention, if
any, in a fine-print paragraph on an inside page. The facts
of the case never came out at all. The family honor of the

Delameres was preserved, and the prestige of the white race
in Wellington was not seriously impaired. (233-34)

This, then, was the world of stereotype and rhetoric which
Chesnutt was clearly fighting in *Marrow*. Indeed, in a profound
passage of almost pure, incisive bitterness, Chesnutt discusses
just how pervasive and warping this sort of prejudging through
stereotype can be. It is towards the end of the novel and Dr.
Miller is musing on the heroic courage of Josh, when it suddenly
occurs to him that, to people with distorted vision, even Josh's
heroism will become debased. As he notes,

> The colored men might win a momentary victory, though
> it was extremely doubtful; and they would as surely reap the
> harvest later on. The qualities which in a white man would
> win the applause of the world would in a negro be taken as
> the marks of savagery. So thoroughly diseased was public
> opinion in matters of race that the negro who died for the
> common rights of humanity might look for no meed of
> miration or glory. At such a time, in the white man's eyes,
> a negro's courage would be mere desperation; his love of
> liberty, a mere animal dislike of restraint. Every finer hu-
> man instinct would be interpreted in terms of savagery. Or,
> if forced to admire, they would none the less repress. They
> would applaud his courage while they stretched his neck, or
> carried off the fragments of his mangled body as souvenirs,
> in much the same way that savages preserve the scalps or
> eat the hearts of their enemies. (296)

At the same time that Chesnutt was fighting the promulgation
by whites of false stereotypes about the Black man, he was also
concerned with presenting honest, real Black characters to
white and Black readers alike. This accounts for the wide spectrum of Black characters which the novel offers: ranging from
the subservient, shuffling character of Jerry to the strong, courageous and militant figure of Josh.

The obvious use of contrasts and spectra here is significant, since it represents Chesnutt's attempt to create a historical-allegorical novel as well as a personal, romantic one. Just as we saw various characters like McBane, Carteret, and Belmont arrayed together in order to represent whole segments of white Southern society, so do Chesnutt's realistic Black characters play equally large roles, in addition to their unique personalities. Indeed, so important is this spectrum of characters that we can see Chesnutt's own ambivalent position towards some of them as he implicitly assesses his own role in fighting racial injustice in this country, a point which we will examine in greater detail later. It is obvious that this spectrum and contrast of Black characters is as much meant to be read by Black readers searching for a positive, identifiable role in the movement towards freedom as it is meant for the detachedly or marginally interested whites who might be interested in the story as a piece of contemporary history.

Naturally, Chesnutt was very much aware of the problems a Black man faced in defining his life's role in the South. The premium was placed on being a servile nonentity, and any deviation from this constrictive norm was often fatal. As Dr. Miller sharply notes in assessing his own professional ambitions.

> It was a veritable bed of Procrustes, this standard which the whites had set for the negroes. Those who grew above it must have their heads cut off, figuratively speaking,—must be forced back to the level assigned to their race; those who fell beneath the standard set had their necks stretched, literally enough, as the ghastly record in the daily papers gave conclusive evidence. (61)

Indeed, as we have seen above, the question of identity with the common people was always a major one for the isolattoe, intellectual in Chesnutt; and it was partially this inner conflict which was externalized in his spectrum of Black characters in *Marrow*, as he was deeply torn between the moderate, practical,

professional Dr. Miller and the more heroic, but less sophisticated and analytic, Josh Green.

There are, then, three different kinds of Black characters in
the novel: embodied by the subservient Jerry, the progressive
professional Dr. Miller, and the courageously heroic, essentially
"reckless" Josh Green. At one extreme of the spectrum, Jerry
is Major Carteret's porter and is content—and almost intent
—on retaining this "august" position in the Southern white
man's world no matter how much humbleness it entails. Indeed
the very first moment we meet him he responds to Gen. Belmont's
nod "with a bow and a scrape" and doesn't care what sort of
verbal abuse anyone gives him as long as they let him keep the
change from whatever errand he is sent on. Indeed most of his
conscious thought as recorded by Chesnutt concerns just how
to go about scheming for such small change.

Jerry's grandmother, significantly, is also from this mold and
tells us of her and Jerry's ambitions in the Southern white man's
world. In discussing the modern generation of young Blacks
whom Mrs. Cateret thinks are "too self-assertive," Mammy
Jane agrees whole heartedly and explains her limited aspirations
in life. In contrast to the new generation, Mammy Jane tells her
mistress how,

> I's fetch' my gran'son' Jerry up ter be 'umble, an' keep in
> 'is place. An' I tells dese other niggers dat ef dey'd do de
> same, an' not crowd de white folks, dey'd git' ernuff ter
> eat, an' live out dcir days in peace an' comfo't. But dey don'
> min' me—dey don' min' me!" (44)

In a similar manner, when the White Supremacy movement
gets under way, Jerry aligns himself as much with the whites as
possible. As Chesnutt himself directly explains immediately thereafter, "to please the white folks was Jerry's consistent aim in
life."

The choice of values by Mammy Jane and Jerry—to sacrifice
all freedom and self-identity—is done with the ultimate desire

of being on the safe side if any racial trouble should spring up. Thus Mammy Jane is rewarded in her above discussion with Mrs. Carteret by the latter's assertion that "you shall never want so long as we have anything. We would share our last crust with you." Jerry also gets similar periodic assurances from Major Carteret. And the ultimate irony is, of course, that, when the riot finally does break out, both Jerry and Mammy Jane are killed in the day's brutality: shot randomly as common "niggers," far from the thoughts—and protection—of their supposed benefactors.

On the far other end of the spectrum we have Josh, who knows he is going to die avenging the KKK ride which killed his father and drove his mother mad. Captain McBane was the leader of that ride, and it is inevitable to Josh that he will die killing McBane. This knowledge of inevitable death—a "reckless' position in its deepest sense—is a tremendous librating force in Josh's life. Having already recognized and accepted an early death, he no longer has to bow and scrape to anyone in life. He can, in essence, live like man.

Early in the novel, Dr. Miller learns of Josh's ultimate desire to kill McBane, and he attempts to dissuade Josh from the act. Josh's answer is almost classic in its honest realism, and the reader cannot help but feel that seventy-five percent of Chesnutt's own nature at this moment is aligned with Josh, in preference to the alter ego Miller with whom Chesnutt usually identifies.

> "You had better put away those murderous fancies, Josh" he said seriously. "The Bible says that we should 'forgive our enemies, bless them that curse us, and do good to them that despitefully use us.'"
>
> "Yas, suh, I've l'arnt all dat in Sunday school, an' I've heared de preachers say it time an' time ag'in. But it 'pears ter me dat dis fergitfulnss an' forgiveniss is mighty one-sided. De w'ite folks don' fergive nothin' de niggers does. Dey got up de Ku-Klux, dey said, on 'count er de kyarpit-baggers. Dey be'n talkin' 'bout de kyarpit-baggers ever sence, an' dey 'pears ter fergot all 'bout de Ku-Klux. But I ain'

fergot. De niggers is be'n train' ter fergiveniss; an' fer fear
dey might fergit how ter fergive, de w'ite folks gives 'em
somethin' new ev'y now an' den, ter practice on. A w'ite
man kin do w'at he wants ter a nigger, but de minute de
nigger gits back at 'im, up goes de nigger, an' don' come
down tell somebody cuts 'im down. If a nigger gits a' office,
er de race 'pears ter be prosperin' too much, de w'ite folks up
an' kills a few, so dat de res' kin keep on fergivin' an' bein'
thankful dat dey're lef' alive. Don' talk ter me 'bout dese
w'ite folks,—I knows 'em, I does! Ef a nigger wants ter git
down on his marrow-bones, an' eat dirt, an' call 'em
'marster,' *he's* a good nigger, dere's room for *him*. But I
ain' no w'ite folks' nigger, I ain'. I don' call no man 'marster.'
I don' wan' nothin' but w'at I wo' for, but I wants all er dat.
I never moles's no w'ite man, 'less'n he moles's me fust'. But
w'en de ole 'oman [Josh's invalid, half-crazed mother] dies,
doctah, an' I gits a good chance at dat w'ite man,—dere ain'
no use talkin' suh!—dere's gwine ter be a mix-up, an' a
fune'al, er two fune'als—er may be mo', ef anybody is keer-
liss enough to git in de way." (*113-14*)

With this sense of fatalism and realistic insight into the South
as it is , Josh becomes the most heroic and magnificent figure
in the novel. When the riot begins, therefore, it is he who attempts
to organize the Blacks for physical self-defense. Significantly, he
is again juxtaposed against Dr. Miller's position in this effort as
he and a group of other Blacks come to Miller and the Black
lawyer Watson for leadership. Both Watson and Miller pragmati-
cally decline, claiming the duty which they owe to their families
and citing, as well, the pessimistic physical realities for such a
physical confrontation with the whites in a small, rural Southern
town surrounded by similar towns. Out of the ashes of their
pragmatic, moderate refusal to fight, Josh draws forth his own
inner heroic strength. "Now we're gwine out ter de cotton com-
press, an' git a lot er colored men tergether," he tells Miller and
Watson,

"an' ef de w'ite folks 'sturbs me, I shouldn't be s'prise' ef
dere'd be a mix-up;—an'ef dere is, me an one w'ite man'll
stan' befo' de jedgment th'one er God dis day; an' it won't
be me w'at'll be 'feared er de jedgment. Come along, boys!
Dese gentlemen may have somethin' ter live fer; but ez fer
my pa't, I'd ruther be a dead nigger any day dan a live dog!"
(284)

Indeed our ultimate realization of Chesnutt's ambivalence
towards—perhaps "envy of" is the real truth—Josh comes from
his final, epitaph-like discussion of Josh's last moments. Josh and
his men take their defensive positions in the new Black hospital
[a symbolic embodiment of Miller's aspirations for moderate
progress in the South], until the hospital is set afire by the white
mob [a direct symbolic comment, obviously, on Miller's posi-
tion]. At this point Josh and his men are forced to come out:
either to surrender or to die fighting. This is how Chesnutt treats
Josh's final moments.

Josh Green, the tallest and biggest of them all, had not
apparently been touched. Some of the crowd paused in in-
voluntary admiration of this black giant, famed on the
wharves for his strength, sweeping down upon them, a smile
upon his face, his eyes lit up with a rapt expression which
seemed to take him out of mortal ken. This impression was
heightened by his apparent immunity from the shower of
lead which less susceptible persons had continued to pour
at him.
Armed with a hugh bowie-knife, a relic of the civil war,
which he had carried on his person for many years for a
definite purpose, and which he had kept sharpened to a
razor edge, he reached the line of the crowd. All but the
bravest shrank back. Like a wedge he dashed through the
mob, which parted instinctively before him, and all oblivious
of the rain of lead which fell around him, reached a point
where Captain McBane, the bravest man in the party, stood

waiting to meet him. A pistol-flame flashed in his face, but he went on, and raising his powerful right arm, buried his knife to the hilt in the heart of the enemy. When the crowd dashed forward to wreak vengeance on his dead body, they found him with a smile still upon his face. (309)

The majesty, courage and almost mystical power of Josh here are clearly visible. Eons away from Jerry on the human spectrum and several levels above Miller as well, Josh dies like a man and Chesnutt applauds his transcendent courage even as he doubts and debates the pragmatic wisdom of his action. This, then, is the range of Black characters in *Marrow*, and they are meant to dispel the world of stereotypes and offer a world of realistic and even heroic Black men.

The Overall Scene. The ultimate basis of Chesnutt's protest in *Marrow*—spanning both the brutal physical and distorted literary conditions of the South—was his bitter realization of just how little the Southern white man's friendship could be counted on when the chips were down. If there is an underlying theme in the novel, this is clearly it.

On a most artistic, indirect level, Chesnutt makes this point in a softly delicate, if caustic, manner. Three times in the novel a basically "good" but weak white figure fails to stand up for his principles of justice, and each time his semiacknowledgment of failure is delicately couched by Chesnutt in a Pontius Pilate allusion. As early as Chapter VII, we witness the famous Dr. Burns, noted white surgeon from the North, come to Wellington to perform a crucial operation on Major Carteret's son. Having ridden down from Philadelphia on the train with Dr. Miller, and having been Dr. Miller's teacher in medical school and an admirer of the skill and international reputation which Miller had accrued since then, Burns invites Miller to assist in the operation. What he doesn't realize is the adamant prejudice which Carteret and the whole Southern town in general hold towards Black doctors, and soon the pressure is put on Burns to proceed with the operation before Miller can arrive, even though Burns had promised to wait.

At first Burns is enraged at the unfairness of the prejudice, but soon it is all "explained" to him in its "local custom" way. Equally soon, Burns agrees to proceed without Miller, haunted faintly by a Pilate-like twinge of conscience.

> "I shall nevertheless feel humiliated when I meet Miller again," he said, "but of course if there is a personal question involved, that alters the situation. Had it been merely a matter of color, I should have maintained my position. As things stand, I wash my hands of the whole affair, so far as Miller is concerned, like Pontius Pilate—yes, indeed, sir, I feel very much like that individual." (73-74)

Twenty chapters later we find the old Southern gentleman Mr. Delamere, the last of the truly gentle and honorable men of the antebellum South, in a somewhat similar position. His servant Sandy has been accused of killing Mrs. Ochiltree, and Mr. Delamere comes to Sandy's defense, since he knows that Sandy's equally aristocratic, gentlemanly nature could not have committed such an act. The town, meanwhile, is up in arms, and the trappings for a lynching are being rapidly gathered. The pervasive lust for blood is less a matter of seeing justice done that it is a matter of expressing deep-seated racial hatred, and Mr. Delamere has all he can do to help Sandy get any kind of hearing at all.

What hearing he does receive takes place in Carteret's newspaper office, and there Delamere learns that Sandy is indeed innocent, but that Delamere's own grandson, Tom, is the guilty party. Justice now calls upon Delamere and Carteret to reveal the truth and explode the myth of the vicious "black brute" which has fed the inflamed minds of the townspeople. When faced with the need for such a hard truth, however, the basically good man Delamere falters; and, as he and Carteret agree not to reveal the real truth, Delamere intones the Pontius Pilate refrain himself:

"Carteret," said the old man, in a voice eloquent of the struggle through which he had passed, "I would not perjure myself to prolong my own miserable existence another day, but God will forgive a sin committed to save another's life. Upon your head be it, Carteret, and not on mine!" (229)

Eight chapters later the Wellington riot is underway on its full-scale vicious course. Carteret's newspaper has created and fanned the racist passions afoot, and essentially the riot is his creation. However, Carteret is basically a "good" man in some sense, and never really realized the kind of carnage he was instigating. When faced with the horror he has loosed and when stymied in his first feeble efforts to restrain it, Carteret also seeks the original Pilate's peace-of-mind-through-rationalization.

"Let us leave this inferno, Ellis," said Carteret, sick with anger and disgust. He had just become aware that a negro was being killed, though he did not know whom. [Ironically it is Jerry.] "We can do nothing. The negroes have themselves to blame,—they tempted us beyond endurance. I counseled firmness, and firm measures were taken, and our purpose was accomplished. I am not responsible for these subsequent horrors,—I wash my hands of them. Let us go!" (307)

In such a way does Chesnutt powerfully, yet artistically, establish this underlying theme. Yet should we have missed the theme through its indirect sense of placement and allusion, he has two of his responsible, moderate Negro characters blast the truth to us directly—in a way that is all the more forceful because the characters involved are so essentially moderate.

The first statement of this comes midway through the novel and is spoken by Dr. Miller as he assesses the fact that none of the whites to whom he had spoken (before Mr. Delamere) would come out and defend Sandy, even though they all felt him to be innocent.

"That is the situation," added Miller, summing up. "Their friendship for us, a slender stream at the best, dries up entirely when it strikes their prejudices. There is seemingly not one white man in Wellington who will speak a word for law, order, decency, or humanity. Those who do not participate will stand idly by and see an untried man deliberately and brutally murdered. Race prejudice is the devil unchained." (194)

As the far more violent riot itself sweeps on twenty chapters later, the Black lawyer Watson accidentally meets Miller outside the town limits, as Watson himself is fleeing for his life. Caught unprepared and almost killed before he could escape, Watson scathingly denounces his nominal white "friends" who could have warned and easily saved him.

"Yesterday I had a hundred white friends in the town, or thought I had,—men who spoke pleasantly to me on the street, and sometimes gave me their hands to shake. Not one of them said to me today: 'Watson, stay at home this afternoon.' I might have been killed, like any one of half a dozen others who have bit the dust, for any word that one of my 'friends' had said to warn me. When the race cry is started in this neck of the woods, friendship, religion, humanity, reason, all shrivel up like dry leaves in a raging furnace." (280)

This, then, is the bitter underlying theme of the novel; and it marks the strongest cry of outrage and protest which Chesnutt will ever utter as a writer—which is why *Marrow* is his strongest and most savagely honest novel dealing with the racial situation in America. This is why it struck his white readers so forcefully and seared their collective guilt so fiercely that they were afraid to acknowledge any truth in the novel at all. This is why they frenetically attacked it in any and every way they could. It was that good.

Self-Scrutiny

The next highest level of Chesnutt's art was that which he attained as a concerned and sensitively searching man. Not only was this the sort of sensitivity which all great artists have towards the various characters and situations which they portray, but it had a quality of deep personal honesty and involvement as well. In short, if one of the prime functions of art is to seek out and express the deeper, inner man, then Chesnutt's writing attained this level throughout his life.

The chief question of Chesnutt's deepest life concerned his racial position in this country. His position in the universe he knew well, and this is what gave him the universal scope which we will discuss next. Regarding his position on the American social scene, however, he was never quite sure.

We have already examined the conflict between isolattoe and racial spokesman in Chesnutt's personal life, and it is now important to note it in his writings. The conflict is most directly expressed in two works: his Journal of 1879 and *The Marrow of Tradition* of 1901. As a twenty-one-year-old, Chesnutt took a train ride North to explore professional opportunities there, and on the return trip found himself in a coach with an educated white man and a group of loud, frolicsome Black farmhands. The vision became forever etched in his mind.

In his "summer" entry of that 1879 Journal, he recounts the trip.

> It was pleasant enough till we took on about fifty darkies who were going to Norfolk to work on a truck farm. . . . As the day was warm and the people rather dirty, the odor may better be imagined than described. Although it was nothing to me, I could sympathize with my fellow traveler, who stuck his head out of the window, and swore he would never be caught in such a scrape again.

Significantly enough, the cultured, educated and middle class aspiring man that he was, Chesnutt's feelings here were closer to those of "my fellow traveler."

Even at the same moment, however, he did reach out and feel
a certain affinity with the fifty workers, in and for themselves.

It was a merry crowd, however, especially one young
fellow who would gravely line out a hymn and then sing it
himself, with all the intonations of a camp meeting. His sister, he said, sat in his lap, though the affectionate way in which
he embraced her seemed to our unsophisticated eyes, to
render the relationship doubtful, at the least.

"Who am I closest to?" is, of course, the question plaguing him
here.

Twenty-two years later—in the midst of his major novel of
racial commitment and crusading, *The Marrow of Tradition*—the
very same scene asserts itself. Dr. Miller, the young professional
Black doctor who is Chesnutt's dramatic personification in the
story, is riding from New York to North Carolina. He is alone
and in a strictly "Colored" coach this time, but the discussion is
basically the same despite these differences. Indeed, it goes into
greater philosophical depth as well.

Toward evening the train drew up at a station where quite
a swarm of farm laborers, fresh from their daily toil,
swarmed out from the conspicuously labeled colored waiting-
room, and got into the car with Miller. They were a jolly,
goodnatured crowd, and, free from the embarrassing presence of white people, proceeded to enjoy themselves after
their own fashion. Here an amorous fellow sat with his
arm around a buxom girl's waist. A musically inclined individual—his talents did not go far beyond inclination—produced a mouth-organ and struck up a tune, to which a limber-
legged boy danced in the aisle. They were noisy, loquacious,
happy, dirty, and malodorous. They were his people, and he
felt a certain expansive warmth toward them in spite of their
obvious shortcomings. By and by, however, the air became

too close, and he went out upon the platform. For the sake of the democratic ideal, which meant so much to his race, he might have endured the affliction. He could easily imagine that people of refinement, with the power in their hands, might be tempted to strain the democratic ideal in order to avoid such contact; but personally, and apart from the mere matter of racial sympathy, these people were just as offensive to him as to the whites in the other end of the train. Surely, if a classification of passengers on trains was at all desirable, it might be made upon some more logical and considerate basis than a mere arbitrary, tactless, and, by the very nature of things, brutal drawing of a color line. (60-61)

Without expending too much time on the works involved here, it should be noted that Chesnutt was, throughout his artistic life, torn by this problem of personal (and artistic) identification. As early as his fourth story in the Journal, we find the first person narrator in "Bruno" portraying a professional, socially respected doctor—far above the crowd of regular townspeople with whom he dwells.

In his second short story, "A Tight Boot," we find him satirizing the slave Bob almost in "comic Negro" stereotype terms. In his later stories for *Puck* and *Tid-Bits*, moreover, we find that his settings and all his first person narrators are cultured, educated, professional white businessmen; and in "Gratitude," as a matter of fact, we find that the first person narrator is a white businessman while the story satirizes a Black book salesman who tries to "con" the businessman with what the story sees as a "sympathy-for-the-race" pitch. Further related to all of this, of course, are the many unpublished all-white novels of Chesnutt's own mature period, and we should note again that the first-person narrator in *The Conjure Woman* is a white Northern businessman come South for the climate.

Even Chesnutt's final published novel, significantly, is the story—in third-person narrative form to be sure—of a Northern white businessman, Colonel French, whose dream to convert the South fails and who thereupon leaves the South and goes back North forever. It is no coincidence here that Chesnutt directly aligns himself with the crusading, altruistic, educated Colonel, and the failure of the Colonel's dream in the novel closely parallels Chesnutt's own failure with his dream of success concerning *The Marrow of Tradition,* the novel written just before *The Colonel's Dream.* Equally relevant here is that when *The Colonel's Dream* as a novel fails, both economically and socially, both the Colonel and Chesnutt fold their crusading tents and steal silently away forever.

One further aspect of this question should be mentioned here, and that is a discussion of the very many "passing" stories which Chesnutt wrote and thereby unveiled his own inner feelings: stories dealing with Blacks who were light enough to pass for white and stories which then recounted the result of such "passing" attempts. Essentially, as we might expect, the attitudes which Chesnutt reveals here are basically ambivalent.

As we saw above, Chesnutt himself had thought of passing early in his life, but had rejected the idea, though we can feel the fascination it temporarily held for him.

In his works, therefore, we find the same tearing ambivalence present. In his first, but unpublished novel, *Mandy Oxendine,* the heroine of the title decides to pass for white; but this attempt ultimately leads to her tragic end when love and marriage complicate the issue. Even so, it is clear from Chesnutt's underlying tender and sympathetic tone toward Mandy that he deeply sympathizes with her attempt and somehow wishes her well. Such, exactly, is the tragic case with Rena in *The House Behind the Cedars* of 1900. Her brother, John, however, does successfully pass, and Chesnutt clearly wishes him well. In both of these full novels, then, the theme for the heroine is "Thou shalt not pass," but the tone beneath the theme clearly sympathizes—almost empathizes—with them.

Coming between *Mandy* and *Cedars* was *The Wife of His Youth,* and there the first two stories show the ultimate ambivalence in Chesnutt. The theme of the first story, "The Wife of His Youth," is that a man must be honest and admit his racial past. Thus Mr. Ryder's conscience will not let him "pass" from dark slave fieldhand background to lightskinned "Blue Vein" mulatto society. He must courageously introduce to the world the dark-skinned, shriveled "wife of his youth." On the other hand, in the very next story in the collection, "Her Virginia Mammy," the whole point is that Mrs. Harper, the ex-slave mother, deliberately allows her daughter to "pass" in order to lead a fuller life with the white man that she loves. The daughter is ignorant of who or what her mother is (and this ignorance may be the reason why Chesnutt feels that passing will work in this one exception to his thematic canon on the female issue); but the point is that, no matter what the themes of these several stories, the tones and feelings were clearly ambivalent: wishing the passing women well, though realizing their inevitable failure, and allowing the passing of John Warwick and the ignorant Clara to be an actual success. As for Chesnutt's own life, of course, racial conscience and pride of integrity never allowed him to disown his basic self.

Such were the avenues in which the inner artist sought to find and express itself in Chesnutt's work—with perhaps one of the most obvious moments of self-debate coming in *Marrow*, as we have seen in detail above, where Chesnutt quite consciously is fighting between his rational identification with the professional moderate Dr. Miller and his emotional admiration for the for the uneducated but courageously heroic Josh Green. The inner man—and the inner artist—were clearly never at rest through Chesnutt's life and writings; and this is what formed the second level of his artistic sensitivity.

Cosmic Harmony

On the third and ultimately highest level of his art, Chesnutt was no longer a man intent on ambivalently exploring and working out his social and political position here in American; instead he was an artist who deeply understood his position in the universe and his relationship to his fellow men as they all fit into the same cosmos.

On its most tangible level, Chesnutt was deeply sure of the Black man's just and inevitable place in American society. As he has Colonel French proclaim in *The Colonel's Dream*, the success and progress of any society like America's depends on the interwoven, combined success of all the groups in that society. "I am rather inclined to think," the Colonel begins with obvious understatement,

> that these people have a future; that there is a place for them here; that they have made fair progress under discouraging circumstances; that they will not disappear from our midst for many generations, if ever; and that in the meantime, as we make or mar them, we shall make or mar our civilization. No society can be greater or wiser or better than the average of all its elements.[5]

Indeed this was a point which Chesnutt was to make throughout his life, both in his fiction and in his more personal writings. As he concluded a September 18, 1904, letter to Robert Anderson of Lansdowne, Pennsylvania, for example, Chesnutt's position was equally clear: "There can be but one citizenship in a free country," he summarized, "if the laws make or recognize any distinctions, then that country is not free."

Examples of statements like this, of course, are legion in Chesnutt's correspondence, and we are actually more concerned with his published writings than with his personal letters. As we return to *The Colonel's Dream*, which was his last and most prophetic novel, we are further struck by the fact that French, the Northern businessman who comes South to set up industries, is concerned with helping the total South: both Black and white. Couched in messianic terms, French inwardly muses on his purpose.

> He would like to do something for humanity, something to offset Fetters and his kind, who were preying upon the weaknesses of the people, enslaving white and black alike

. . . . It required no great stretch of imagination to see the town, a few years hence, a busy hive of industry, where no man, and no woman obliged to work, need be without employment at fair wages; where the trinity of peace, prosperity and progress would reign supreme; where men like Fetters and methods like his would no longer be tolerated. The forces of enlightenment, set in motion by his aid, and supported by just laws, should engage the retrograde forces represented by Fetters. (117-118)

In Chesnutt's "Dedication" to this novel, these same concepts of enlightment and total humanity are central.

To the great number of those who are seeking, in whatever manner or degree, from near at hand or far away, to bring the forces of enlightenment to bear upon the vexed problems which harass the South, this volume is inscribed, with the hope that it may contribute to the same good end.

If there be nothing new between its cover, neither is love new, nor faith, nor hope, nor disappointment, nor sorrow. Yet life is not the less worth living because of these, nor has any man truly lived until he has tasted of them all. (4)

It is not surprising that Chesnutt saw the overcoming of racial problems and the establishment of humanity and social cohesion in this nation not merely as a specific national goal but as the essential goal and future of all human endeavors. As he noted in a September 29, 1903, letter to Dr. Charles F. Thwing, this was essentially a personal, individual problem, but its implications were universal. "The key of the whole problem is stated in your proposition that it is to be treated as a problem of the individual and not one of races," Chesnutt concurs, and then he set forth the universal implications of this struggle.

If the American people can fuse out of the diverse races which now inhabit this continent a really free people among whom every individual, regardless of anything but his talents and his citizenship, shall find open to him every worthy career for which he may demonstrate his fitness, it will in my opinion have achieved very nearly the ultimate problem of civilization.

In his treatment of individual, human characters outside of this national-allegorical aspect, Chesnutt showed great sensitivity for an extremely large range of individuals.   In fact this is where his sense of universalism first shows itself.   Through his professional life in Cleveland and other Northern cities   he knew and felt a definite affinity for white businessmen,   lawyers, stock brokers, and others like them. These, therefore, form a large segment of his characters; from the early apprentice period stories to those three unpublished novels of his major period. Likewise his early days in the North Carolina sand hills gave him a certain insight into and knowledge of poor whites of that rural region, characters who then found their way into several early stories like "Tom's Warm Welcome" and who also become major background figures in some of his Southern novels like *Mandy Oxendine.*

Black characters, of course, are the ones with whom Chesnutt is basically identified; "the Laureate of the Color Line" was, of course, a deserved title. Yet what is most important here is the range of Black characters portrayed. Poor farmers and laborers like Uncle Peter in "Uncle Peter's House" and Frank in *The House Behind the Cedars;* rough wharf workers and "convicts" like Josh in *The Marrow of Tradition* and Bud Johnson in *The Colonel's Dream*; professionals like the lawyer Watson and Dr. Miller in *Marrow*; and, on its most sublime level, "folk bards" like Uncle Julius in the *Conjure* stories and, in some sense, similar "folk bard" tricksters like the religious revival preacher in "The Prophet Peter" or equally "trickster" laymen like Dasdy as she "came through." The range, then, reaches all strata of rural and urban society at the turn of the century.

In terms of racial attitudes, Chesnutt also covered the full spectrum of character positions. In *Marrow* alone he gave a fairly detailed account of contemporary Southern white feelings on the subject, with the "Big Three" on the bottom, the mass of ordinary people in the middle, and such a lonely "concerned" figure as Ellis anemically at the top. As for Northern white attitudes, his next novel, *The Colonel's Dream*, gave us the concerned industrialist who deeply cares about this country's social problems; and throughout so many of his works Chesnutt constantly introduced committed Northern white teachers who came south in the early days of Reconstruction in order to help educate freedmen ("The March of Progress") and poor white (*Evelyn's Husband*) alike.

Furthermore, there was an equally full spectrum of Black character positions in his works. In the South this ranged from the sychophantic, subservient characters like Jerry and Mammy Jane; to the moderate, professional Dr. Miller; to the courageous, heroic Josh Green. And, in the North, Chesnutt added a full extra dimension to this in his treatment of the mulatto "Blue Vein" societies which saw themselves in their own racially "elite" category: not quite white enough to be accepted by the Caucasian "divinities," but certainly less "tainted" than Blacks of the darker shades.

Throughout all this we should further note the great range of tones which Chesnutt brought to all these characters: from satire to bitterness to compassion, all with sensitivity and feeling. Most significant, perhaps, is the fact that he was able to feel a close sympathy for, or understanding of, the essence of all his characters—even those whom he basically despised, like Captain McBane in *Marrow*, or those whom he satirized, like the "Blue Vein socialites. Thus it is crucial to note that at the climax of the historical portion of *Marrow*, where Josh rushes forth to kill and be killed by McBane, Chesnutt gives the despised McBane his one due. He is, despite his basic bigotry and brutality, and despite all the contempt which Chesnutt has for him on these grounds, still described as "the bravest man in the party" of whites taking part in the riot, a testament to that one admirable quality which he does possess. Likewise, despite all Chesnutt's

satiric scorn for the "Blue Veins," his tender sympathy towards
Clara in "Her Virginia Mammy" and the courage he shows Mr.
Ryder to possess in "The Wife of His Youth" display Chesnutt's
own deep and wide range of sensitivity towards all people as individual entities on the face of the earth—individuals who, if
nothing else, deserve at least a fair understanding of why they
are what they are.

Of crucial significance here is a review which followed the publication of *The Wife of His Youth:* a review which Chesnutt liked
so much that he included it verbatim, in his December 14, 1899,
letter to Houghton Mifflin, in case they might have missed it.
Though the review limits itself to a discussion of Chesnutt's depiction of Black characters (simply because that is what *Wife
of Youth* specifically concerned itself with), its point is applicable
to all of his character depictions throughout his career.

"In *The Wife of His Youth, and Other Stories of the Color
Line*, by Charles W. Chesnutt," the review in the December 9
issue of the *New York Mail and Express* begins,

> we have a variation of most of the methods employed by
> American story-writers in handling the characterizations of
> our colored population . . . and one that is so striking
> and so novel that it may fairly be called a new departure in
> Afro-American fiction, or a fine and wise departure in art,
> since, instead of trying on the one hand to move our com-
> passion for the negro, because we have inflicted so much
> suffering on his race in the past, or, on the other hand, to
> study and enjoy him, because he is such a comical, laughable
> creature, so childlike and irresponsible—it simply aims to
> interest us in him as an individual human being, without re-
> gard to the straightness or kinkiness of his hair, or the
> amount of nigritude in the color of his skin.

With this ability to see and appreciate, in its deepest sense, all
men as individuals, Chesnutt also understood the truth that this
individualness was a corollary to, not a conflict with, the fact

that all men were the same in a human and cosmic sense. This was the theme that lay at the core of most of his work, from some of his lesser known stories to most of his more widely read novels. Most interesting of these stories is "The March of Progress," the story of a young white woman from New England who came South after the war to teach in the Freedmen's Bureau schools. Miss Henrietta Noble is her semiallegorical name, and she "has libbed mong' an' made herse'f one of us, an' endyoed havin' her own people look down on her" for fifteen years now. Indeed, through her dedication, she has "growed ole an' gray wukkin' fer us an' our child'n."

Just recently, however, the Blacks of Patesville have been given the appointment of a committee of themselves to manage the colored schools of the town. Immediately, two thirds of the three man committee decide to hire a Black man for the position, because, as they put it, "The time has come in the history of our people when we should stand together. In this age of organization the march of progress requires that we help ourselves or be left behind." The two spokesmen for this position represent the middle class and "substantial citizen" part of the Black population, and they conclude on a noticeably Darwinian note.

> "Now, gentlemen, that's the situation. Shall we keep Miss Noble, or shall we stand by our own people? It seems to me there can hardly be but one answer. Self-preservation is the first law of nature."

"Ole Abe" Johnson, representing the still-poor Black man in the South, a man who "drove a dray, and did odd jobs of hauling," is the third member of the committee, and he now makes a simple yet touching speech for Miss Noble and all that the concerned North has done for his people, and she is elected through the homely truth of his position. When given this news, Miss Noble is extremely grateful and is suddenly seized by a heart attack from which she never regains consciousness.

The story is in some ways an overly sentimental and allegorically appreciative tale, yet it is of major significance in assessing Chesnutt's overall position. For even though Chesnutt clearly sees and gives great direct attention to the Black people's need to stand together, especially in the realm of economics where, as Mr. Gillispie, the middle class barber, notes, "there's just two things they [Blacks] can find to do—to preach in our own pulpits, an' teach in our own schools . . ."; and even though Chesnutt almost always in his work identifies with the rising middle class position; his final position here is one which stresses "Ole Abe's" grass-roots appreciation of the concerned white Northern woman who has committed her life to living in and for the Black community. Equally important, as his final summation of Miss Noble shows, is the fact that Miss Noble's work also served the white community even though this was never really recognized, so that in the final analysis she was both a racial and a universal force.

More dramatic is the climax of *Marrow,* where, even in the midst of Chesnutt's strongest novel of historical bitterness, the brotherhood of men—and, most especially, the sisterhood of women—is the final theme of the novel. This major assertion is what allows Julia Miller (who has been disinherited all her life by Mrs. Ochiltree and Olivia Carteret, even though she is Olivia's legitimate half-sister) to tell her husband to perform the operation that will save the Carteret's son and only child. Most dramatically, this decision by Julia comes immediately after the Millers have just seen their own son and only child killed in the Wellington riot which Major Carteret ignited. Thus, somehow, the shared brotherhood and sisterhood of all peoples here on earth transcends for Julia and Chesnutt whatever differences and conflicts may lie between individuals: and this then becomes his final dramatic assertion in this novel, which in so many other ways has stressed a real pessimism and bitterness in its historical discussions. In a sense it is almost as if Chesnutt's universal faith has somehow overcome his more specific historical analysis.

From this understanding of all man's humanity, Chesnutt essentially rose to a cosmic, almost prophetic understanding of the question of human relationships. As early as age twenty-four he had been searching for this kind of human union and communion, when he had noted in his March, 7, 1882, Journal how "I hope yet to have a friend. If not in this world, then in some distant future eon, when men are emancipated from the grossness of flesh, and mind can seek out mind." And we have seen his prayer-prophesy of this union and communion in the final paragraph of his final story in *The Wife of His Youth:*

> Some time, we are told, when the cycle of years has rolled around, there is to be another golden age, when all men will dwell together in love and harmony, and when peace and righteousness shall prevail for a thousand years. God speed the day, and let not the shining thread of hope become so enmeshed in the web of circumstance that we lose sight of it; but give us here and there, and now and then, some little foretaste of this golden age, that we may the more patiently and hopefully await its coming! (222-223)

In time this became a definite premise in his mind, so that by 1905—even with the harsh social injustices he could see growing around him, and with the bitter disappointment which he personally suffered in the popular rejection of *Marrow*—he could prophesy the end of the racial problem in American society. Addressing the Boston Literary and Historical Association on "Race Prejudice: Its Causes and Its Cures," Chesnutt chose to conclude with this sense of definite cosmic direction:

> And now to close, may I venture a prophecy? . . . Looking down through the vista of time I see an epoch in our nation's history, not in my time nor in yours, but in the not too distant future, when there shall be in the United States but one people, moulded by the same culture, swayed by the same patriotic ideals, holding their citizenship in such

high esteem, that for another to share it is of itself to entitle
him to fraternal regard; when men will be esteemed and
honored for their character and their talents; when hand
in hand, and heart with heart, all the people of this nation
will join to preserve to all and to each of them for all future
time that ideal of human liberty which the fathers of the
republic set out in the Declaration of Independence, the
ideal for which Lincoln died, the ideal embodied in the
words of the Book—the Book that declares that God is no
respecter of persons, and that of one blood hath He made
all the nations of the earth.[6]

Not only was this universal mandate to be manifest in the
realm of human history, but of greatest importance to us was
the fact that Chesnutt also saw it as the principal basis of art
and of his own personal life. Discussing the role of art in a 1926
interview for *The Crisis,*[7] he addressed his remarks directly to
this point. "The prevailing weakness of Negro writings, from
the viewpoint of art," he suggested,

is that they are too subjective. The colored writer, generally speaking, has not yet passed the point of thinking of
himself first as a Negro, burdened with the responsibility
of defending and uplifting his race. Such a frame of mind,
however praiseworthy from a moral standpoint, is bad for
art. Tell your story, and if it is on a vital subject, well told,
with an outcome that commends itself to right-thinking
people, it will, if interesting, be an effective brief for whatever cause it incidentally may postulate.

Even more commanding was his overall statement of the realm
of art and its relation to human reality as he saw it. In answer to
the question "Can any author be criticized for painting the
worst or the best characters of a group?" Chesnutt once more
stressed the universal nature of human existence and stressed
again the range and individuality which he saw the world com-

posed of and which, therefore, he saw the world of art dedicated to portraying. "It depends on how and what he writes about them," he began.

> A true picture of life would include the good, the bad, and the indifferent. Most people, of whatever group, belong to the third class, and are therefore not interesting subjects of fiction. A writer who made all Negroes bad and all white people good, or 'vice versa,' would not be a true artist, and could justly be criticized.

In short, he essentially proclaimed, art is the cosmic, universal world which allows the artist complete freedom to perceive and express the cosmic, universal truths which are around him:

> The realm of art is almost the only territory in which the mind is free, and of all the arts that of creative fiction is the freest. Painting, sculpture, music, poetry, the stage, are all more or less hampered by convention—even jazz has been tamed and harnessed, and there are rules for writing free verse. The man with the pen in the field of fiction is the only free lance, with the whole world to tilt at. Within the very wide limits of the present day conception of decency, he can write what he pleases. I see no possible reason why a colored writer should not have the same freedom. We want no color line in literature.

And perhaps the ultimate proof of Chesnutt's belief in the universal world of all men as individuals and brothers was the fact that he lived the concept as well as wrote about it.

Final Assessment

As we come to see Chesnutt in perspective now, it becomes clear that his literary greatness lies on several different levels. He was, of course, the first Black author of profound and diversified short stories: from Southern conjure tales to Northern "Blue Vein" satire. He was also the first Black writer of significantly artistic novels, and was the first to be nationally acclaimed for his artistic craftsmanship. On his highest level, moreover, he partook of the eternal, cosmic artist: the Platonic searcher after Truth and Beauty and individual human dignity. More than a mere protester, more than a literary technician, Chesnutt was a craftsman and prophet combined. It is on this level that his artistic greatness ultimately lies.

At the same time, Chesnutt was no Greek god of flawless marble, as he is often portrayed; no literary Christ-figure of complete altruism and dedication to a social cause, who was finally crucified by the boorish rabble. Rather, he was a very human man, as well as a great social crusader and literary artist. Indeed, we have seen how he originally aspired to be an author largely because it was the easiest and quickest pathway in 1880 for fame and wealth in this country. For Chesnutt was human and American, and he early aspired to all the comfort, leisure, and independence that this country has symbolized to its people ever since Ben Franklin cradled those two clumsy loaves of bread under his arms and marched into Philadelphia on his way to London, Paris, and the hundred dollar bill

Furthermore, not only were Chesnutt's early motives mixed in regard to his literary career, but his early feelings were equally mixed when it came to defining his "self" in social terms. Basically, Chesnutt did not think of himself as a Black man or Black writer. Instead, he dwelt in a double no-man's land: first, that of light skin color and "free issue" parentage, which made him too "uppity" for most local Blacks and too "dark" for the local whites; and second, that of a sensitive, intellectual nature, which set him off from every one in the nineteenth-century South, both Black and white. Hence he saw himself originally as a lonely isolattoe with no allegiance to any group or anything other than the strongly divergent artist-materialist drives within him and the higher Truths he saw around—and above—him.

What marks Chesnutt's greatness and interest then—in addition to his tremendous abilities as a writer and his profound, sensitive feeling for people—is the fact that he became a major artist, and saw the greatness in himself most clearly, when he found a cause far larger than himself to believe in and work for; and this ultimate sense of commitment in a man is, of course, crucial. His realization of himself as a committed social spokesman and crusader was not, somehow, what we would call a basically "racial" commitment. Rather, the "cosmic" Chesnutt saw the problems of discrimination, insensitivity, hatred, and violence on a higher, moral, universally human level—which is, ultimately, where the power of all great writers finally lies.

Notes

Notes to Chapter I

1. John Hope Franklin, *Reconstruction After the Civil War* (Chicago, 1951), pp. 23-24.

2. See Charles W. Chesnutt's unpublished novel, *Paul Marchand, F.M.C.*, for a picture of just how intelligent and well-educated many of Louisiana's Blacks were. (Manuscript, Charles Waddell Chesnutt Collection, Erastus Milo Cravath Memorial Library, Fisk University, Nashville, Tennessee. Cited hereafter as CC.)

3. Abraham Lincoln, "Proclamation on the Wade-Davis Bill," July 8, 1864; reprinted in Richard Hofstadter, *Great Issues in American History,* Vol. II (New York, 1958), pp. 9-10.

4. Richard N. Current, *Reconstruction (1865-1877)* (Englewood Cliffs, N.J.), p. 4.

5. Franklin, p. 36.

6. Cited in Franklin, p. 36.

7. See Chesnutt's article on "Peonage—the New Slaver of the South," intended for the September, 1904 issue of *The Voice of the Negro* (referred to in a letter to Chesnutt from J. Max Barber, August 6, 1904, Correspondence with Individuals, CC).

8. Note Chesnutt's indictment of the Southern prison "hiring system" in his 1905 novel, *The Colonel's Dream.*

9. "The Mississippi Black Code, 1865; "reprinted in Current, p. 42.

10. Letter from C.W. Chesnutt to Robert Anderson, September 18, 1904, Correspondence with Individuals, CC.

11. W.E.B. DuBois, "The Souls of Black Folk," *Three Negro Classics* (New York, 1965), p. 236.

12. Thaddeus Stevens, Speech in Lancaster, Pa., September 6, 1865; reprinted in Current, p. 14.

13. DuBois, p. 234.

14. Rayford W. Logan, The Betrayal of the Negro (New York, 1965), pp. 77-78.

15. Ibid., p. 199.

16. Significantly enough, it was the starkness of the North Carolina disfranchisement and its 1898 Wilmington massacre which finally convinced Chesnutt that Reconstruction had been a failure. At this moment, therefore, he finally dedicated his life and writings to the role of social crusader.

17. Frederick Douglass, *Life and Times of Frederick Douglass* (New York, 1962), pp. 503-504.

18. For an idea of how it even formed the basis of the South's entertainment, see William Wells Brown's citations of Southern newspapers as cited in J. Noel Heermance, *William Wells Brown and Clotelle* (Hamden, Conn., 1969) pp. 139-140.

19. W.J. Cash, *The Mind of the South* (Garden City, N.Y., 1956), p. 85.

20. Blanche K. Bruce, Speech in the Senate, March 31, 1876; reprinted in Hofstadter, pp. 44-45.

21. Douglass, p. 524.

22. Helen M. Chesnutt, *Charles Waddell Chesnutt* (Chapel Hill, N.C., 1952), p. 104. It is interesting to further note that Chesnutt's very first novel, *Mandy Oxendine* (ca. 1897), has its dramatic climax hinge on the attempted lynching of a Black man—a lynching which was set off because a "political contest was impending" and "there was a kind of feeling in the air that danger threatened the supremacy of the party in power," (*Mandy Oxendine*, p. 158, manuscript, CC.)

23. Franklin, p. 157. See also the numerous first-hand accounts of violence cited by and published in such Congressional reports of the period as the *Report of the Joint Select Committee to Inquire into the Condition of Affairs in the Late Insurrectionary States*, 13 vols. (Washington, 1872) and the earlier, 1866, report of the Joint Committee of Fifteen, which collected "more than seven hundred pages" of testimony that Franklin calls a "dreary recital of inhumanity." (Franklin, pp. 57-58.)

24. Cited in Logan, p. 25.

25. Cited in Logan, p. 100.

26. Franklin, p. 96.

27. Reprinted in Hofstadter, p. 43.

28. Gunnar Myrdal, *An American Dilemma* (New York, 1962), p. 738. To realize how pervasive this loss of morality was, note such divergent "authorities" as Tammany Hall's George Washington Plunkitt (William L. Riordan, *Plunkitt of Tammany Hall* (New York, 1963) and *McClure's* syndicated "muckraker," Lincoln Steffens (Lincoln Steffens, *The Shame of the Cities*, (New York, 1948)).

29. Charles W. Chesnutt, "Post-Bellum—Pre-Harlem," *The Colophon: A Book Collector's Quarterly*, Part Five (New York, 1931). third page.

30. C.W. Chesnutt, Journal, May 29, 1880, Charles Waddell Chesnutt Collection, Erastus Milo Cravath Memorial Library, Fisk University, Nashville, Tennessee. Cited hereafter as CC.

31. C.W. Chesnutt, "Post-Bellum—Pre-Harlem," third page.

32. Ibid.

33. W.J. Cash, *The Mind of the South* (Garden City, N.Y., 1956), p. 73.

34. Cash, p. 94-95.

35. See Sterling A. Brown, *The Negro in American Fiction*, Washington, D.C., 1937.

36. Ralph McGill, "The South Has Many Faces." *The Atlantic Monthly*, November, 1963. p. 63.

37. Cash, pp. 63-64.

38. Ibid. pp. 64-65.

39. Rayford W. Logan, *The Betrayal of the Negro* (New York, 1965), p. 181.

40. C. Vann Woodward, *The Strange Career of Jim Crow* (New York, 1955) p. 78.

41. Logan, p. 19.

42. Ibid., p. 267-268.

43. Ibid., p. 298. See Chesnutt's indictment of these "burly black brute" terms and this kind of inflammatory journalism in his depiction of the Morning Chronicle in *The Marrow of Tradition*. See especially pages 185 and 233.

44. Sterling A. Brown, "Negro Character as Seen by White Authors," *The Journal of Negro Education*, Vol. II (April, 1933), 180.

Notes to Chapter II

1. Charles Waddell Chesnutt, Journal, July 16, 1875, Charles Waddell Chesnutt Collection, Erastus Milo Cravath Memorial Library, Fisk University. Cited hereafter as CC.

2. Andrew Carnegie, "Wealth," *North American Review*, 148 (June, 1889), 664.

3. Cotton Mather, *Two Brief Discourses, one Directing a Christian in his General Calling another Directing him in his Personal Calling* (Boston, 1701), p. 37.

4. Ibid., p. 48.

5. Ibid., p. 38.

6. Ralph Henry Gabriel, *The Course of American Democratic Thought* (New York, 1940), p. 156.

7. H.L. Reade, *Success in Business, of Money and How to Make It* (Hartford, Conn., 1875), p. xii.

8. Daniel Seely Gregory, *Christian Ethics* (Philadelphia, 1875), p. 224.

9. Russell H. Conwell, *Acres of Diamonds* (Philadelphia, 1890) p. 19.

10. The Right Reverend William Lawrence, "The Relation of Wealth to Morals," World's Work, 1 (January, 1901), 290.

11. Ibid., 287.

12. Ibid.

13. Gabriel, p. 164.

14. L.U. Reavis, *Thoughts for the Young Men of America, or a Few Practical Words of Advice to those Born in Poverty and Destined to be Reared in Orphanage* (New York, 1873, pp. 11-12)

15. William Makepeace Thayer, *Tact, Push and Principle* (New York 1889), p. 354.

16. Gabriel, p. 164.

17. Robert E. Spiller, *Literary History of the United States* (New York, 1948), p. 226.

18. E. Franklin Frazier, *Black Bourgeoisie*, (New York, 1965), pp. 31-35.

19. William E.B. DuBois, "The Souls of Black Folk," *Three Negro Classics* (New York, 1965), p. 237.

20. Frazier, p. 38.

21. Frederick Douglass, Life and Times of *Frederick Douglass* (New York, 1902, pp. 504-506.

22. Frazier, p. 56.

23. Helen M. Chesnutt, *Charles Waddell Chesnutt* (Chapel Hill, N.C., 1952), pp. 1-8. Cited hereafter as *CWC*.

24. Note, for example, her letter to Charles in 1884, discussing her desire to buy a black silk dress. As she explained it, "I am wearing the same dress I wore all last winter, and 'twill never do for me to look worse than other folks, it might cause people to make unpleasant remarks, etc." (January 22, 1884; reprinted in H.M. Chesnutt, p. 36)

25. C. W. Chesnutt, "The Web of Circumstance, *The Wife of His Youth* (Boston, 1899), p. 294.

26. "The History of Shorthand Writing in North Carolina," *State Normal* and Industrial College, Greensboro, N.C. *Magazine*, V (October, 1900), 1-10.

27. DuBois, "Possibilities of the Negro," *The Booklovers Magazine*, Vol. II, No. 1 (July, 1903), 3-13.

Notes to Chapter III

1. C.W. Chesnutt, *The Quarry*, manuscript, CC.

2. C. Vann Woodward, "Man from Chapel Hill," *The New York Times Book Review*, September 27, 1964, p. 48.

3. C. W. Chesnutt, "Race Prejudice: Its Causes and Its Cure," Alexander's Magazine (July, 1905), 25.

4. C.W. Chesnutt, "Post-Bellum—Pre-Harlem," *Colophon: A Book Collector's Quarterly*, Part Five (New York, 1931), fifth page.

5. C.W. Chesnutt, "Race Prejudice," 25.

Notes to Chapter IV

1. Frederick Douglass, *Life and Times of Frederick Douglass* (New York, 1962), pp. 476-477.

2. See, for examples, letters from C.W. Chesnutt to Booker T. Washington; October 9, 1906; November 3, 1906; December 1, 1908; Correspondence with Washington, CC.

3. Letter from C.W. Chesnutt to William E. Walling, Esq., April 18, 1910, Correspondence with Individuals, CC.

4. Letter to C. W. Chesnutt from W. E. Burghardt DuBois, April 1, 1912, Correspondence with Publishers, CC.

5. Ibid., January 4, 1927.

6. "Liberated" from a short sentence in prison, incurred that summer when Trotter, his sister, and others had heckled Washington so vigorously in the Columbus Avenue A.M.E. Zion Church, Boston, that their activities resulted in the prison sentence. (Rayford. W. Logan, *The Negro in the United States* (Princeton, N.J., 1957), p. 63.)

Notes to Chapter V

1. William Dean Howells, "Mr. Charles W. Chesnutt's Stories," *Atlantic Monthly*, LXXXV (May, 1900, pp. 699-700.

2. W.D. Howells, "A Psychological Counter-Current in Recent Fiction". *The North American Review* (December, 1901), pg. 881.

3. See V.F. Calverton, ed., "Introduction," *Anthology of American Negro Literature* (New York, 1929).

4. C.W. Chesnutt, "The Future American: A Complete Race Amalgamation Likely to Occur," *Boston Transcript*, September 1, 1900.

5. Logan, p. 215.

6. C. W. Chesnutt, "The White and The Black," *Boston Transcript*, March 20, 1901.

7. Ibid., "The Negro's Franchise," *Boston Transcript*, May 11, 1901.

8. DuBois, "Possibilities of the Negro", *The Booklovers Magazine*, Vol. II, No. 1, (July, 1903), pg. 2.

9. Letter to C.W. Chesnutt from A.J. White, Secretary, Faculty Committee, Wilberforce University, June 2, 1913, Correspondence with Individuals, CC.

10. Letter to C.W. Chesnutt from DuBois, January 4, 1927. Correspondence with Publishers, CC.

11. See letters from Cable to Chesnutt of April 13; May 30; and September 26, 1889.

Notes to Chapter VI

1. C. W. Chesnutt, "Post-Bellum"—Pre-Harlem," *The Colophon* (New York, 1931); (pages unnumbered).

2. Robert A. Lively, *Fiction Fights the Civil War* (Chapel Hill, 1957), p. 49.

3. William D. Howells, "Mr. Charles W. Chesnutt's Stories," *The Atlantic Monthly* (May 1900), p. 701.

4. Letter from C. W. Chesnutt to Dr. R. M. Hall, November 6, 1909, Correspondence with Individuals, CC.

Notes to Chapter VII

1.. Letters from C. W. Chesnutt to Small, Maynard & Co., October 26, 1899, and to Houghton, Mifflin & Co., December 14, 1899, Correspondence with Publishers, CC.

2. C. W. Chesnutt, "The Disfranchisment of the Negro," *The Negro Problem: A Series of Articles by Representative American Negroes of To-Day* (New York, 1903, p. 104).

Notes to Chapter IX

1. Charles W. Chesnutt, *The Conjure Woman* (Boston, 1898).

2. C. W. Chesnutt, "Post-Bellum—Pre-Harlem," *The Crisis,* June, 1931., pp. 193-194. *The Colophon,* Pg. 5, 1931.

3. C. W. Chesnutt, *The Colonel's Dream* (New York, 1905).

4. C. W. Chesnutt, *The Marrow of Tradition* (Boston, 1901). All subsequent citations of *Marrow* page numbers in the body of this chapter will refer to this edition of that novel, the only hardcover edition ever published. A paperback edition has recently been published by the University of Michigan Press, but even that edition's format and pagination are exact facsimiles of the original.

5. C. W. Chesnutt, *The Colonel's Dream* (New York, 1905), p. 165.

6. C. W. Chesnutt, "Race Prejudice: Its Causes and Its Cure," *Alexander's Magazine* (July, 1905), p. 26.

7. C. W. Chesnutt, "The Negro in Art," *The Crisis,* (November, 1926), p. 28.

Bibliography

Works by Charles W. Chesnutt

"Advice to Young Men," *The Social Circle Journal* (November, 1886). Clipping, Charles Waddell Chesnutt Collection, Erastus Milo Cravath Memorial Library, Fisk University, Nashville, Tennessee. Cited hereafter as CC.
"Aunt Lucy's Search," *Family Fiction,* April 16, 1887. Clipping, CC.
"Aunt Mimy's Son," *The Youth's Companion,* March 1, 1900. Clipping, CC.
"Baxter's Procrustes," *Atlantic Monthly,* XCIII (June, 1904), 823-830.
"A Busy Day in a Lawyer's Office," *Tid-Bits,* January 15, 1887. Clipping, CC.
A Business Affair. Manuscript, CC.
"A Cause Celebre," *Puck,* January 14, 1891. Clipping, CC.
The Colonel's Dream. New York, 1905.
The Conjure Woman. Boston and New York, 1899. Composed of the following short stories:
> "The Conjurer's Revenge" (pp. 103-131)
> "The Gray Wolf's Ha'nt" (pp. 162-194)
> "The Gray Wolf's Ha'nt (pp. 162-194)
> "Hot-Foot Hannibal" (pp. 195-229)
> "Mars Jeem's Nightmare" (pp. 64-102)

"Po' Sandy" (pp. 36-63)
"Sis Becky's Pickaninny" (pp. 132-161)
"Dave's Neckliss," *Atlantic Monthly,* LXIV (October, 1899), 500-508.
"A Defamer of His Race," *The Critic,* XXXVIII (April, 1901), 350-351.
"The Disfranchisement of the Negro," *The Negro Problem: A Series of Articles by Representative American Negroes of To-Day.* New York, 1903, pp. 77-124.
"The Doll," *The Crisis,* III (April, 1912), 248-252.
"The Dumb Witness," Manuscript, CC.
Etiquette (Good Manners). Manuscript, CC.
Evelyn's Husband. Manuscript, CC.
Frederick Douglass. Boston, 1899.
"The Free Colored People of North Carolina," *Southern Workman,* XXX (May, 1901). Clipping, CC.
"The Future American: A Complete Race Amalgamation Likely to Occur," *Boston Transcript,* September 1, 1900. Clipping, CC.
"The Future American: A Stream of Dark Blood in the Veins of Southern Whites," *Boston Transcript,* August 25, 1900. Clipping, CC.
"The Future American: What the Race is Likely to Become in the Process of Time," *Boston Transcript,* August 18, 1900. Clipping, CC.
"Gratitude," *Puck,* December, 1888. Clipping, CC.
The House Behind the Cedars. Boston, 1900.
"How a Good Man Went Wrong," *Puck,* November 28, 1888. Clipping, CC.
"How Dasdy Came Through," *Family Fiction,* February 17, 1887. Clipping, CC.
"Lincoln's Courtship," *Southwestern Christian Advocate,* February 4, 1909. Clipping, CC.
"Lonesome Ben," *Southern Workman,* XXIX (March, 1900). Clipping, CC.
Mandy Oxendine. Manuscript, CC.

"The March of Progress," *The Century Illustrated Monthly Magazine,* LXI (January, 1901). Clipping, CC.
The Marrow of Tradition. Boston and New York, 1901.
"The Mission of the Drama," *Cygnet* (January, 1920). Clipping, CC.
"Mr. Taylor's Funeral," *The Crisis,* IX (April, 1915), 313-316; and *The Crisis,* X (May, 1915), 34-37.
"The Negro's Franchise," *Boston Transcript,* May 11, 1901. Clipping, CC.
"The Origin of the Hatchet Story," *Puck,* April 24, 1889. Clipping, CC.
Paul Marchand, FMC. Manuscript, CC.
"Peonage, or the New Slavery," *Voice of the Negro,* I (September, 1904). Clipping, CC.
"A Plea for the American Negro," *The Critic* (February, 1900). Clipping, CC.
"Po' Sandy," *Atlantic Monthly,* May, 1888. Clipping, CC.
"Post-Bellum—Pre-Harlem," *The Colophon: A Book Collector's Quarterly,* Part Five. New York, 1931.
"The Prophet Peter," *Hathaway-Brown Magazine* (April, 1906), 51-56.
The Quarry. Manuscript, CC.
"Race Prejudice: Its Cause and Its Cure," *Alexander's Magazine,* I (July, 1905), 21-26.
The Rainbow Chasers. Manuscript, CC.
Rena Walden and other Stories. Manuscript submitted to Houghton Mifflin in 1891. Rejected at that time, the title story was later expanded into novel length and ultimately published as *The House Behind the Cedars* in 1900.
"The Sheriff's Children," *The Independent,* November 7, 1889.
"A Soulless Corporation," *Tid-Bits,* April 16, 1887. Clipping, CC.
"Superstitions and Folk Lore of the South," *Modern Culture* (May, 1901). Clipping, CC.
"The Sway-Backed House," *The Outlook,* LXVI (November, 1900), 588-593.

"A Tight Boot," *The Cleveland News and Herald,* January 30, 1886. Clipping, CC.

"Tobe's Tribulations," *Southern Workman,* XXIX (November, 1900), 656-664.

"Tom's Warm Welcome," *Family Fiction,* November 27, 1886. Clipping, CC.

"Uncle Peter's House," *The Cleveland News and Herald,* 1885. Clipping, CC.

"A Visit to Tuskegee," *The Cleveland Leader,* March 31, 1901. Clipping, CC.

"What Is a White Man?" *The Independent,* May 30, 1889. Clipping, CC.

"The White and The Black," *Boston Transcript,* March 20, 1901. Clipping, CC.

The Wife of His Youth and Other Stories of the Color Line. Boston and New York, 1899. Composed of the following short stories:

       "The Bouquet" (pp. 269-290)
       "Cicely's Dream" (pp. 132-167)
       "Her Virginia Mammy" (pp. 25-59)
       "A Matter of Principle" (pp. 94-131)
       "The Passing of Grandison" (pp. 168-202)
       "The Sheriff's Children" (pp. 60-93)
       "Uncle Wellington's Wives" (pp. 203-268)
       "The Web of Circumstance" (pp. 291-323)
       "The Wife of His Youth" (pp. 1-24)

"Women's Rights," *The Crisis* (August, 1910), 182-183.

Works by Other Writers

Bloom, Sol. *The Story of the Constitution.* Washington, 1937.

Brodie, Fawn M. "Who Won the Civil War, Anyway?" *The New York Times Book Review,* August 5, 1962, p. 1.

Brown, Sterling A. "Negro Character as Seen by White Authors," *The Journal of Negro Education,* Vol. II (April, 1933), 179-203.

Calverton, V. F., ed. "Introduction," *Anthology of American Negro Literature.* New York, 1929.

Carnegie, Andrew. "Wealth," *North American Review,* 148 (June, 1889), 653-664.

Cash, W. J. *The Mind of the South.* Garden City, N.Y., 1957.

Chesnutt, Helen M. *Charles Waddell Chesnutt.* Chapel Hill, N. C., 1952.

Conwell, Russell H. *Acres of Diamonds.* Philadelphia, 1890.

Current, Richard N. Reconstruction [1865-1877]. Englewood Cliffs, N. J., 1965.

Dollard, John. *Caste and Class in a Southern Town.* Garden City, N.Y., 1957.

Douglass, Frederick. *Life and Times of Frederick Douglass.* New York, 1962.

DuBois, W. E. B. "Possibilities of the Negro," *The Booklovers Magazine,* Vol. II, No. 1 (July, 1903), 3-9.

_____. "Postscript: Chesnutt," *The Crisis,* XL (January, 1933), 20.

_____. "The Souls of Black Folk," *Three Negro Classics.* New York, 1965.

Elkins, Stanley M. *Slavery.* Chicago, 1954.

Franklin, John Hope. *Reconstruction After the Civil War.* Chicago, 1951.

Frazier, E. Franklin. *Black Bourgeoisie.* New York, 1965.

Freeney, Mildred and Mary T. Henry (comps.). *A List of Manuscripts, Published Works and Related Items in the Charles Waddell Chesnutt Collection of the Erastus Milo Cravath Memorial Library, Fisk University.* Nashville, Tennessee, 1954.

Gabriel, Ralph Henry. *The Course of American Democratic Thought.* New York, 1940.

Gregory, Daniel Seeley. *Christian Ethics.* Philadelphia, 1875.

Heermance, J. Noel. *William Wells Brown and Clotelle.* Hamden, Connecticut, 1969.

"The History of Shorthand Writing in North Carolina," *State Normal* [and Industrial College, Greensboro, N.C.]

Magazine, V (October, 1900), 1-9.

Hofstadter, Richard. *Great Issues in American History,* Vol. II. New York, 1958.

Howells, William Dean. "Mr. Charles W. Chesnutt's Stories," *Atlantic Monthly,* LXXXV (May, 1900), 699-701.

_____. "A Psychological Counter-Current in Recent Fiction," *The North American Review* (December, 1901), 872-888.

Krout, John A. *United States Since 1865.* New York, 1955.

Lawrence, The Right Reverend William. "The Relation of Wealth to Morals," *World's Work,* 1 (January, 1901), 286-292.

Logan, Dr. Rayford W. *The Betrayal of the Negro.* New York, 1965.

_____. *The Negro in the United States.* Princeton, N. J., 1957.

Mather, Cotton, *Two Brief Discourses, one Directing a Christian in his General Calling, another Directing him in his Personal Calling.* Boston, 1701.

McGill, Ralph. "The South Has Many Faces," *Atlantic Monthly* (November, 1963), 63-72.

Myrdal, Gunnar. *An American Dilemma.* New York, 1962.

Reade, H. L. *Success in Business, of Money and How to Make It.* Hartford, Connecticut, 1875.

Reavis, L. U. *Thoughts for the Young Men of America, or a Few Practical Words of Advice to those Born in Poverty and Destined to be Reared in Orphanage.* New York, 1873.

Report of the Joint Select Committee to Inquire into the Condition of Affairs in the Late Insurrectionary States, 13 vols. Washington, 1872.

Riordan, William L. *Plunkitt of Tammany Hall.* New York, 1963.

Spiller, Robert E. *Literary History of the United States.* New York, 1948.

Steffens, Lincoln. *The Shame of the Cities.* New York, 1948.

Thayer, William Makepeace. *Tact, Push and Principle.* New York, 1889.

Thomas, William Hannibal. *The American Negro.* New York, 1901.

Tourgee, Albion W. *A Fool's Errand.* New York, 1879.

United States Bureau of Census. *Negro Population, 1790-1915.* Washington, 1918.

Washington, Booker T. and others. *The Negro Problem.* New York, 1903.

Woodward, C. Vann. "Man from Chapel Hill," *The New York Times Book Review,* September 27, 1964, p. 48.

——————. *The Strange Career of Jim Crow.* New York, 1955.

Other Sources

Chesnutt, Charles Waddell, Collection. Correspondence with George Washington Cable. Erastus Milo Cravath Memorial Library, Fisk University, Nashville, Tennessee. Cited hereafter as CC.

——————. Correspondence with Individuals. CC.

——————. Correspondence with Publishers. CC.

——————. Journals and Notebooks of Charles W. Chesnutt. CC.

Index